Train Hoppe

SWITCHING TRACKS

OUT OF THE TRASH

LENA GIBSON

Black Rose Writing | Texas

First printing

This is a work of fiction. Names, characters, businesses, places, events, and incidents are either the products of the author's imagination or used in a fictitious manner. Any resemblance to actual persons, living or dead, or actual events is purely coincidental.

ISBN: 978-1-68513-364-1
PUBLISHED BY BLACK ROSE WRITING
www.blackrosewriting.com

Printed in the United States of America
Suggested Retail Price (SRP) US $24.95 / CA $27.95

Switching Tracks is printed in Minion Pro

*As a planet-friendly publisher, Black Rose Writing does its best to eliminate unnecessary waste to reduce paper usage and energy costs, while never compromising the reading experience. As a result, the final word count vs. page count may not meet common expectations.

For my grandparents, who shared their love of stories.

PRAISE FOR
SWITCHING TRACKS

"Gibson lays the tracks into an exciting new post-apocalyptic world where corporate greed controls the necessities of life, one ancient society's trash is today's salvation, and the heart of one heroine can save a country's soul."
–D. Lambert, author of *Son of No Man* series

"Gibson's writing is one of the tightest and best I've read in some years; her imaginative setting and characters are exactly what one might expect of our human race in 2195."
–J. Ivanel Johnson, award-winning author of the *JUST (e)STATE* mysteries

"*Switching Tracks* had me enthralled from the beginning. The story is well-structured, revelatory, and beautifully written. The character descriptions are almost visual. There is enough mystery and clues to keep the pages turning beyond your bedtime."
–Robert Allen Stowe, author of *The Third Pitch* and the soon-to-be-released *The Fires of Rubicon*

"Lena Gibson creates another thought-provoking series that will keep you up at night."
–A.J. McCarthy, award-winning mystery author

"The future (2195) looks to be a lifetime of slavery and misery, but with a map and a key Elsa can change her, her friends', and her family's future. They struggle to protect what will change their future, is the struggle and loss worth the prize?"
–Stephen W. Briggs, author of *Beside Us*

"An engrossing story of nascent love, adventure and intrigue, set in 2195. It's an adroitly crafted story that transports the reader into future landscapes via Gibson's masterful world-crafting. If you are a fan of dystopian stories, with romance in your heart, you will love this book—don't miss it!"
–Bill Schweitzer, author of *Doves in a Tempest*

"Once you crack open the pages on this futuristic neo-western, be prepared to be seduced by adventure. *Switching Tracks* is a train-hopping, romance-blooming, treasure-seeking, full-throttle experience. Lena Gibson once again proves that she's the master of the genre mash-up."
–David Buzan, author of *In the Lair of Legends*

"A page turning climate dystopian packed with romance, unforgettable characters, and tension that kept me reading right until the very end."
–Eileen Cook, author of *You Owe Me A Murder*

"Lena Gibson's *Switching Tracks* is a stunning series opener filled with majestic world-building, heart-grabbing characters, and a quest to redeem a fallen humanity. In Elsa, readers have an unlikely hero they can't help but fall in love with."
–Cam Torrens, award-winning author of *Stable* and *False Summit*

"Although science fiction, *Switching Tracks* reads like an adventure romance embedded in a background of catastrophic climate change and dystopian politics. It is this background that enriches the plot and makes it timely as well as entertaining."
–Carolyn Geduld, author of *Who Shall Die*

"Fast-paced, compelling, and brilliantly written, *Switching Tracks* is an epic tale of loss, sacrifice, and redemption, providing an unexpected but satisfying resolution and the promise of more tales to come."
–KJ Fieler, author of *Shadow Runner*

"With an ensemble of fresh, relatable characters and a well-written plot with a satisfying ending, *Switching Tracks* is sure to please fans of fast-paced, edge-of-your-seat dystopian fiction."
–Michele Amitrani, author of the *Rebels of Olympus* and the *Omnilogos Singularity* series

OUT OF THE TRASH

CHAPTER 1: ELSA

SoCal-2195

Garbage heaps are treasure troves if you have the eye to recognize true value. Elsa's great-grandmother had been telling her that since she was knee-high to a cockroach. They scavenged to survive. That's why Elsa had worked with painstaking care to fashion the new tunnel into the mountain of compacted refuse, where she'd reached the correct depth to hit late-twentieth and early twenty-first-century trash. This was where the paydirt was located, but scavenging was never a sure thing.

She braced and supported her excavation so she wouldn't be trapped in an avalanche of filth. Her heart rate quickened in anticipation. What would she find today?

While Elsa worked the tunnel, her great-grandmother, Granny Lee, guarded the entrance of their licensed recovery sector within the largest landfill in SoCal—referred to as the Heap. Interlopers and thieves often interfered with the sites, so Granny carried a loaded shotgun—which she wasn't shy about using. They'd worked this shaft for days and the current tunnel should be worth excavating for another week, though it was always a gamble and Elsa had been disappointed before.

Old newspapers that had been buried and never exposed to the elements were interesting and still legible at times, but GreenCorps only paid plastic tokens for pots and pans, solid plastic, and metal objects. Some metals rusted, their coating worn away, or pitted and corroded, but stainless steel was like solid gold. Not that she'd ever found much precious metal, except what could be recovered in minute quantities from extinct electronics.

Hard to believe that her finds had been considered junk a couple of centuries ago. People today couldn't be so wasteful. After almost two hundred years in this landfill, most things still intact had value as scavenger currency. Her most valuable find had been a jar of assorted coin from before 2008. That had fed them for over a year. A set of chipped cookware might yield a week's food and water for herself and Granny.

Elsa advanced her cross-brace, moved her battered lantern forward, and dug with a trowel to separate one layer of garbage from another. She stacked treasures, old clothes and shoes, and items that might have value at resale to GreenCorps. Some were worth keeping for personal use.

She reached an area with rocks and dirt—backfill—that separated it from the level below. Filling her bucket, she hauled it part-way up the tunnel before attaching it to the pulley and rope system with a tug. Granny yanked it outside, then returned the empty bucket. Elsa rotated her neck and hips, easing cramped muscles.

Elsa refilled the bucket and sent it to the surface, keeping wads of filthy plastic bags and plastic sheeting on the side to clean and separate later on the surface. They would twist and weave the flexible strips of old bags into clothing, bedding, and useful day-to-day items, even some footwear.

Returning to the face of the excavation site, Elsa's heart pounded as she uncovered a rounded chunk of smooth black plastic with a metal ring at the end. It looked like a pot handle. Heap gold.

She reined in her excitement, slowing her extraction to avoid collapsing the tunnel, and removed her bulky work gloves. Wadded-up clumps of mushy paper, broken bits of plastic, disposable diaper balloons, and chunks of rotten wood surrounded what she was trying to extract. Scattered throughout this layer were the white chunks of Styrofoam packing that Granny said resembled popcorn. It had its uses too, but she didn't need to collect it today as she had a sufficient stash at home.

She freed the stainless pot with a gleam of satisfaction. The twenty-first century had the richest garbage, and she studied it with a keen eye. The pot had a shallow dent and a couple of spots of rust that she poked. She smiled. They weren't deep and should buff out. A little more effort rewarded her with the lid as well. The pot and its lid were nicer than anything they used at home, though they seldom cooked beyond boiling water and oatmeal. At the market, this alone should earn days' worth of food and water tokens.

Underground, it was easy to lose track of time, but her tired muscles informed her it was quitting time. She looked anew at the gaping hole. She'd try for one more item.

She groped inside, her arm encased in warm guck to the shoulder, and she fumbled for easy-to-grab, solid items. Often, she'd find treasure in patches. Today, her hand closed on a cylindrical tube—too thick around to be a pot handle.

The wall made a sucking sound as it released, and she moved it into the light of her lantern. What was it? The tube was made of metal. Her fingers tingled when she ran them over the smooth surface, the way they did when she found something spectacular.

Her back twinged, grounding her in reality. She needed to get out and stand straight. She'd take the tube home to clean and examine.

Elsa carried both the bucket and her finds up the tunnel, her back spasming as she crouched to half crawl through the low tunnel near the entrance. It was tight, even for someone of her petite stature. The constricted section made it more difficult for thieves to snoop during the night. Even if it reduced her escape options and was prone to collapse, it also made the upper portion of the passage easier to barricade. Casual, lazy robbers would be kept from poaching the exposed trash.

She set down the bucket with the rest of the day's haul about ten feet in from Granny's position and left the lantern beside the entrance for tomorrow. Though inside the Heap, there was light from outside now. Elsa consolidated her finds at day's end, shoving the metal tube into her satchel instead of the bucket. You couldn't be too careful with items of value.

She wiped the sweat from her dirty face on her sleeve and took a swig of her rationed water from her canteen. It was hot at the surface, even in March, and even hotter in the tunnel. The garbage generated its own heat with chemical reactions. It steamed all day, all year. One reason she wore gloves was to protect herself from chemical and steam burns within the trash.

The warm rot seeped into her pores, so Elsa never felt clean. Sludge ground into all exposed cracks and crevices in her skin and under her nails. No scrub brush removed it all. She wished she earned enough to pay for a daily shower or a bath. She compromised by scrubbing with sand and rinsing with previously used gray water. SoCal didn't have water for luxuries unless you were wealthy. Perhaps one day, it would be different.

She donned the standard-issue GreenCorps Uvee goggles that hung around her neck, shuffled closer to the surface, and squinted at the sky, trying to gauge the time. The sun was invisible through the perpetual dust and smog, and the light was dimming. It must be later than she'd thought. Time to go. She hoped she hadn't left leaving too late. Granny seldom questioned Elsa on the job site, but she must be getting concerned.

Working wasn't as fast as when they'd been a three-person operation. Her older sister, Avery, had quit when she'd married a GreenCorps man. Her new family had coins, not just plastic tokens, and ate without sifting through junk.

It was a fine line to walk, staying late enough for a full day's scavenge, but not so late they had to return home after dark with the day's haul. They didn't have passes to be out after curfew. At night, they risked losing their finds to roving patrols of GreenCorps recruits. The local youths who joined were bullies, eager to change sides and work for the oppressor for coin instead of plastic tokens. SoCal was a political prison disguised as a work camp, and Elsa had been born here. Talk about bad luck.

Elsa collected her loot. Besides the pot and tube, she'd found a muffin tin, two bent spoons, and a matching fork. She also bundled her soft plastic, her back aching from hours in a stooped position.

She stepped out of the tunnel and stretched, wincing at the muscles that screamed in protest. Unhooking the pail from the system of ropes and pulleys; she was freed for the day. She dropped the bulk of her treasures in the bucket, making them easier to carry and harder for others to see.

"Hey, Granny. I'm ready to go home."

Granny Lee smiled, showing the two teeth missing in the front while her wispy snow-white hair stuck out from under her sun hat and goggles. Like Elsa, her pants and poncho were handmade, woven from strips of found plastic to protect her skin from the harsh Uvee rays. Her long-sleeved shirt was fabric, scavenged from the Heap. The garment was protective and durable, even though it might feel hot.

The corner of Elsa's mouth twitched. The words used to describe their clothing also applied to Granny—especially durable. Despite her advanced age, she did a full day's work. Her great-grandmother was at least a hundred years old, and Elsa worried what she'd do when Granny became too frail to guard their site. She endeavored not to consider a future without Granny, lest darkness swallow her. Better to focus on the now. Besides, she didn't want to borrow trouble. Perhaps someday she would find a partner or hire help. Most of the women her age and older already belonged to a team. It wouldn't be easy.

Twenty minutes later, they trudged onto the packed earth and crumbled asphalt street where their home was located.

"Long day Elsa," called her friend from the doorway of the neighboring shack.

Janna worked at the beach, sifting out plastic nurdles and rounded bits of glass to sell to GreenCorps for a pittance. GreenCorps reclaimed the beaches, not for environmental reasons, but to reap incredible profits. Each storm and wind brought additional drifts of never-ending junk to shore.

"Maybe we can catch up in a few days. I'm job hunting. Working the closer beaches isn't profitable anymore. I heard they're going to try fish farming. Buy fish stocks from somewhere up north. I'd like to try that."

"Catching up sounds good." It would be nice to speak with someone her own age, though Janna was dreaming if she thought she might get one of the coveted fish farming jobs. They would hire GreenCorps favorites. Elsa nodded to Janna's father sitting on his rickety steps made of broken cinder blocks, where he was gluing the bottom of his shoe together.

"There might be perks, like the odd fish to eat," he said with a return nod.

He grinned, showing his broken and gray front teeth, leftover from his previous job working trainyard security. With people trying to leave SoCal in tough times, it was a rough job. He'd never said why he quit; between steady wages and bribes, it was one of the most profitable ways to make a living. Now his family scraped along as best they could, just like the others. The only better jobs were GreenCorps recruits and suits who traveled for the Corporation.

Elsa sighed. Her stairs needed to be repaired—the loose bricks rolled when stepped on. Their home might resemble a one-story shack more than a house, but it kept a roof over their heads, most of the time. Granny had lived here since she was first widowed and sent here to work. GreenCorps forces had killed her rebel husband and daughter during a skirmish. She didn't talk about those days. Granny had raised her granddaughter, and now her great-granddaughters, here.

The house might be a hundred years old, or at least it looked like it. The glass was long gone from the windows. Most had been boarded up from the inside, but Granny had covered two with translucent sheets of plexiglass to let in sunlight. Not that anyone stayed home during the day, except on the mandatory rest day. Elsa always looked forward to

Sunday, even if Granny said it was just a day to placate the masses and keep them complacent.

This Sunday, Elsa would work on the house. She and Granny waged a constant battle with the roof to keep the elements out. It'd been fixed so many times that the patches had patches. When it rained, which was rare, they used every bucket and dish in the house to collect water. It was too polluted to drink, but they used it for washing. The walls, too, needed attention, to keep out the hot wind, ever-present dust, and vermin.

Scavenging paid for processed food and potable water but seldom stretched beyond necessities, such as clothing and shoes. Elsa glanced down at her scuffed black boots, where her toes stuck out, and scowled—she'd need footwear soon. They fashioned sandals and clothes from plastic, but boots came from the Heap or were purchased—an over-priced luxury from the outside world beyond SoCal, brought in and paid for at GreenCorps prices.

Granny unlocked the door, then relocked it upon entering—this wasn't a neighborhood where anyone left doors open. Whatever wasn't hidden or attached could be stolen from the flimsy homes. They would visit the trading post at the market on the way to work in the morning. All the stores belonged to GreenCorps, but she and Granny frequented one with pleasant staff, though she'd been taught to trust no one. Tonight, they'd sort and wipe clean the metal and plastic items so they'd get the best price.

The house remained dark inside until Elsa turned on the solar-powered lantern. SoCal might not have much rain, but it had ample sun, even through the ever-present smoke and smog. The hard-packed dirt floor was cool compared to outside. Heat radiated from the stone, brick, and cement repurposed to build this section of housing.

When they finished their work, Granny opened the safe, and they threw the day's collection inside. Elsa kept the metal tube separate to clean it and take a better look. It was a mystery. She would put it in the safe later when Granny slept. Elsa was reluctant to show her great-grandmother, who would encourage her to sell it. The only valuables in the house consisted of a spare set of clothing, their bedding, and the battered pot for boiling water. And the shotgun, but that was never far from Granny, who slept with it in arm's reach. It came from her rebel days and was irreplaceable.

Elsa sat on the raised platform that made up her bed at the far end of the main room. The thin mattress was made of woven plastic sheets and filled with Styrofoam packing. The blankets were repurposed from old pieces of fabric. Granny always said living this way would make them tough—make them survivors. Elsa munched on her dinner ration and finished the day's water in her canteen while Granny did the same. They shared a secret smile; they'd lived another day.

An hour later, Granny's soft snores filled the room. While the woven curtain they'd hung between the two rooms provided privacy, it didn't block sound.

Outside the house, whispered voices and the odd laugh carried on the evening breeze. The young men and women who wandered the street at night were seldom loud, but Elsa sensed their presence as they wandered the dark, searching for opportunities and those unfortunate enough to be caught out late. Some of their neighbors were involved with the illicit behavior, but she'd never been tempted to join. She couldn't afford to get in trouble or risk the blighted GreenCorps patrols. She and Granny depended on each other to survive.

She didn't know how the gangs made enough to live on, but the ranks of jobless seemed to grow instead of diminishing. Some had been sentenced here by GreenCorps, others hopped inbound trains, or migrated from other SoCal slums.

Why would anyone choose to be here? What was the world like beyond SoCal? She'd been nowhere else.

Though Elsa wearied of living in the trash with no other options, she wouldn't leave Granny, and the only life she knew. They made enough to get by, but never seemed to get ahead—probably part of the GreenCorps plan. For those sentenced to live in SoCal, they couldn't leave. For those born here, there wasn't a law against leaving, but it was discouraged.

Elsa's eyes grew bleary, though she hadn't read more than a chapter of her current black-market book. She would finish soon and trade it for another. She also planned to get ammunition. Then the boots. Busy thoughts spun in her mind, making it impossible to unwind enough to sleep. Jumping up, she grabbed the metal tube and a rag with which to wipe it clean. She found it easier to clear her mind with something in her hands.

After polishing, the cylinder shone. Made from a lighter silver metal than she was used to finding, it was shiny and, surprisingly, free of scratches. When she shook it, a faint tapping, metallic sound clinked inside with no clear way to open it. On one end, a leaf symbol had been engraved beside the words *'Dept. of Agr.'*

She traced her fingertips over the emblem and its dirt-encrusted grooves. Currents of excitement coursed through her; her hand once more tingling. She'd ask Vic at the market if he knew anything about her mystery item, but she was reluctant to sell. The feeling in her gut told her of its significance. She'd had feelings about things before, but never this strong.

CHAPTER 2: WALKER

Walker closed his travel log and tucked his journal and stubby pencil into his backpack. He crouched between the slowing train cars near the end of the train, preparing to hop off. It wasn't long before they would arrive at the next station. Hayden lounged beneath the overhang of the covered hopper, his laces undone. His brother's pinched features looked more animated than usual and his dark eyes shone. Walker wasn't sure why they'd come here now, but Hayden had pushed for the location. Something Hayden had learned in Reno had made him want to travel to SoCal's Long Beach.

Hayden jumped to his feet, his green coat flapping, but he wouldn't meet Walker's eyes. Was Hayden's agenda different than stated?

Long Beach was a train terminus, and they hadn't hopped here before, though in the last eight years they'd traveled most places the trains ran. This was somewhere they'd avoided.

The dry air tasted smoky and left a sharp taste in Walker's mouth, like breathing greasy smoke. Shit air quality and the smog-filled skies blocked the view of what was supposed to be mountains and ocean. Everything was gray and dismal. Coming into town, the infamous Heap's pungent rotting smell added to the stench. He wasn't even off the train and he wanted to leave.

The past few hours had been dark. There'd been no lights near the train tracks, no villages, no farmhouses, nothing. Nothing out this way seemed enticing. He hoped they would poke around and he could convince Hayden to hop back on the next train.

What had gotten into Hayden? What made him want to come to this forsaken shithole? He'd heard Long Beach, hell, most of SoCal, was a garbage heap, but he hadn't been prepared for the reality. The people who lived here couldn't be healthy. Most were rebels, sent here to scavenge in the GreenCorps work camps, or the rebel's families.

The Corporation thought that if people worked hard to survive, they'd stay out of trouble. SoCal wasn't as unhealthy as Texas—whose burning oil fields were responsible for the smoke overhead—but SoCal was only a step up from the lowest rung of humanity that he'd witnessed.

Walker sighed. They'd made good coin mining near Denver over the winter, so they could have gone anywhere. On the journey here, they'd stopped a couple of times, and each time he'd slipped away from Hayden for a quick detour. Walker had converted his wages to silver coins, then hidden his stash. Hayden might be like his brother, but that didn't mean he could be trusted with coin, which had gone missing on several occasions when nobody else was around. Walker wouldn't give Hayden another chance to steal, especially from him.

At least Hayden had been clean all winter.

It wasn't far from dawn, but Walker didn't know if the haze was smoke or cloud. Either way—a blessing in disguise. The lack of visibility meant they should have time to race out of the trainyard without being seen. He cracked his knuckles and stretched, warming up muscles that had seized up during the ten-hour train ride. Butterflies churned in his stomach. He hated getting off the train somewhere new. Security was sometimes lax in small places like this, but sometimes it was tight. You couldn't predict what you'd get.

He stood by the metal ladder at the rear of the covered train car, his backpack tightened and his boot laces secure. Taking a deep breath, he grimaced. How long would it take to get used to the taste of rotting garbage and smoke? Maybe this would be a brief stay.

The roar of the train kept them from talking as it slowed, so he glanced to make sure Hayden was ready. Hayden braced against the jolting train cars as they braked, waiting for the train to come to a complete halt. When the squealing and clanking stopped, they were off, quick as a flash, running for the makeshift fence that separated the trainyard from the other buildings in town. They didn't have to talk; they'd dashed like this hundreds of times over the years. Best way to deal with the security bulls was not to get caught.

In the pale morning sprint, Walker's first impression of Long Beach was that the buildings were covered in the GreenCorps logo, big letters painted two feet high. This was a corporation town. All food and all water were brought in by GreenCorps, making the people dependent on the corporation. He'd been to others besides his hometown in Santa Fe. They'd have to trade or buy tokens for their stay so they wouldn't waste coin. It was the conversion that ate your savings.

His feet crunched in the gravel until they left the station yard, ducking down a side street into town. Hayden followed. Both young men listened for footsteps or shouts behind them, but there was nothing. They dropped to a slower pace.

"See. Easy as pie," said Hayden, his walk becoming a swagger.

Hayden sounded cocky now, but running to and from the trains still made Walker twitchy.

He grabbed Hayden's arm, forcing him to stop. What was going on? "You going to tell me what made you want to come all the way out here?" Walker clenched his jaw, due an explanation, though he might not get one.

"It's an adventure, somewhere new," said Hayden, shrugging. "Plus, I heard it's warm here almost year-round."

His brother's eyes slid to the side like they did when he was dishonest. Walker had seen it before. But, if he called Hayden on it, he'd just lie.

"Let's find somewhere to sleep for a few hours. I didn't get a lot of rest on the train. I swear they're louder every time we ride." Hayden yawned.

"How about here?" Walker wasn't particular. The alley looked fine for now. It was clean enough. For a town built on and surrounded by garbage, he'd expected more debris in the alley, but it was relatively empty. A few lidded plastic garbage cans stood behind the buildings, but the ground wasn't littered with refuse. They could do worse.

They hunkered down by the fence in a dead-end behind a bar, their backpacks propped behind them. They just needed a couple of hours rest to get them through until they had more light to search for a proper place.

Though Walker had fallen asleep in more uncomfortable positions, this morning, he was unable to settle. Hayden dropped off almost as soon as they stopped moving. His head slumped to the side, a line of drool forming from the corner of his mouth. Walker grinned to himself, though he still couldn't relax. He grabbed his travel log and wrote an entry for their current stop. He used his creased, much-folded paper with sunrise/sunset charts to start the entry. With as much traveling as they did, it was nice to have something consistent.

* * *

March 20th, 2195, Sacramento to Long Beach: ten hours
Sunrise 6:55 a.m. Sunset: 7:50 p.m. Spring Equinox tomorrow.

Travel Notes:
Sacramento: Security medium, trainyard outside town quiet. Used usual campsite.

Long Beach: Security light before dawn. No pursuit, no sign of security forces as we left. Ran to an alley two blocks behind the station. Camp in dead-end behind bar.

Investigate fences and bushes on the far side of the trainyard before departure. Hidden campsite?

Two tracks: One northbound, one south. Terminus of southern track.

Sunrise a glowing ball behind thick smoke. Hurts my eyes. Will need Uvee goggles if we stay more than a couple of days.

Hopped a covered freight car, rode at the back. Standard.

Corporation town. Will need tokens.

Junkyards and scrap yards surround the station. Small business area nearby. Will investigate in the morning. Everything stinks like rotting garbage and smoke.

Walker had nothing else of import to note, so he stowed his book and tried once more to rest. He dozed for a short time, but woke as his head nodded to his chest and he startled himself awake. His eyelids felt full of grit, scratching and irritating his tired eyes.

He gave up on sleep. He hated corporation towns. Maybe that was the source of his tension. Hayden had slumped over by the fence, his head now on his pack. He looked peaceful. No point in waiting for him to wake up. It might be ten minutes or it might be five hours.

Walker stood, heaved his backpack on, and fastened the straps. Without a proper stash or hideaway, he was stuck carrying everything with him for now. He tightened his scruffy hiking shoes and headed out of the alley, away from the train station and into town. Hayden could either find him if he woke soon or they'd meet back here later. They'd been together a long time and knew each other's habits.

Walker wandered the dusty town, noting that the pale light of dawn had turned to daylight. There were about a dozen businesses, all with the GreenCorps logo painted on the window. The shops faced a market square in the center, quiet this early in the morning. He was used to the sound of birds—spring was a time for songbirds—and he found the silence eerie.

There wasn't much to Long Beach, besides the Heap dominating the skyline, obscuring his view of the ocean. Bars and brothels stretched for several blocks behind the shops up to the slope of the hill. Not unexpected, as those with coin worked near the railroad station and could afford the offered wares. A road wound back and forth across the face of the hill, to where half a dozen grand houses overlooked the town. He strolled in that direction, hoping to get high enough for a view of the area.

He walked for about half an hour before deciding visibility was too poor. He'd gotten higher than a lot of the smoke, but he couldn't see through it. In the distance, he caught the faint outline of the shoreline. Garbage littered the entire beach. So much for the clean up efforts GreenCorps advertised. He headed back into town to see if Hayden was awake. He was almost back to the alley when he noticed two women striding across the square.

They were covered almost head to toe in gray clothes that seemed like they were made from woven scraps of fabric and plastic. Ponchos draped across their shoulders and hung down past their waist. They'd cinched loose pants on with tight belts and wore tall boots that looked like they were falling apart at the seams and had been duct-taped until the boots were more tape than boot.

Their strange attire wasn't what drew his eye. It was the two women who dressed the same, walked the same, and had almost the same features. One was old, with wisps of snow-white hair peeking out from under her knit cap. The other was smooth-cheeked and dark-haired. She looked like a "before" version of the old lady. Both women were thin, not quite to the point of emaciation, but their features were angular and sharp. They had an aura of strength or toughness about them. He wouldn't want to get in their way.

The old woman walked as fast as the younger—who couldn't be more than nineteen or twenty. Her cheeks still held a hint of youth. The women didn't pay any attention to him as they marched past, but not only did they have to be related, they matched intensity. They passed his position in the doorway of one of the GreenCorps shops and he noticed their eyes. Perfect clear topaz eyes that sent a jolt to his stomach. He'd only gotten a glimpse, but the old lady, in particular, reminded him of a hawk. They entered a shop at the corner on the distant side of the square. Two fierce hawks.

CHAPTER 3: ELSA PLUS WALKER

Elsa and Granny ate their standard breakfast of oatmeal with a sprinkle of dried berries, then plugged the house's water meter with tokens for both their daily allotted ration of drinking water and household water. Once they turned the meter on, they could use it for the day. They finished getting ready for work and headed to the market to sell yesterday's finds.

The sun had just risen, and the streets were quiet. Granny always said, "The early bird catches the worm." Not that Elsa had seen a lot of birds. Few birds lived here with the foul air and pollution. Perhaps only the resident seagulls and canny crows were tough enough for the harsh conditions.

This was the time of day that Elsa liked best, even if there was nothing beautiful about living in SoCal. She liked the silence. The streets were dirty and everything was coated with a thick layer of gray, oily dust that was impossible to clean. Soap was expensive and gray water wasn't wasted on washing buildings. They saved it for watering food-producing plants like tomatoes or cucumbers that helped keep diseases like scurvy away. Not that anyone could afford more than a pot or two as a garden. Seeds were expensive and hoarded like treasure.

In the market square, she and Granny headed for the GreenCorps trading post near the corner, run by Vic and his wife Martha. GreenCorps had built the store with repurposed multi-colored brick. It shared the building with the GreenCorps security contingent, near the train station where the security force lived and patrolled. It was also where the station yard workers ate their meals with real cooked food. Sometimes after a day on the Heap, the smell of the food was excruciating and made her mouth water. Their dinner was nothing like that; processed food bars were all she and Granny could afford.

"Morning Aki, morning Elsa," Vic said, looking up at their entrance.

Granny nodded in response, and Elsa waved as she looked around.

Inside the trading post was a cluttered hodgepodge of strange items that had been unearthed in the Heap. Woven plastic sheets, reconditioned shoes, and bolts of cotton and wool fabric brought in for the wealthy lined the shelves. Having clothes in anything except a shade of bright yellow or gray was a sign of prosperity. Most of the plastics pulled from the Heap were a faded, mottled gray, the exception were heavy bright yellow bags that littered the refuse and didn't fade.

The post also stocked and sold GreenCorps packaged dried food rations, including the protein and nutrient bars that Elsa and Granny favored because they were nutritious but cheap. Jars of dried berries, oatmeal, and barrels of flour lined the walls. Dried meat, dehydrated fruit, and pasta were available for those with sufficient tokens.

Bottles of beer and moonshine filled the higher shelves behind the counter. Vic's wife made the alcohol, their best seller. Behind the counter was a cooler for items that needed to be refrigerated. Elsa had never afforded anything from inside its chilly interior. Her mouth watering, she stared at the bricks of cheese, baskets of brightly colored fruit, and crisp vegetables. *Maybe one day.*

Elsa placed the items she'd excavated yesterday on the counter and scanned the posters tacked to the wall for news while Granny sat on a chair by the door, scanning a worn newspaper.

The news was courtesy of GreenCorps or their reclamation companies that contracted people to work the Heap, clean the beaches, and load and unload their train cars. It focused on the positive things the Corporation did and their efforts to clean up the environment, rather than their oppressive policies. Elsa was thankful Granny had taught her to read. Many of the born-and-raised SoCal residents couldn't read or write beyond their name. Workers who came from afar liked the news that linked them to the outside world, even when they couldn't leave.

Hesitating, she set the tube on the counter apart from the rest, her body blocking Granny's view. Elsa's fingers lingered, tracing the smooth metal.

"Vic, you ever see something like this?" She spoke in a hushed tone.

The gray-haired proprietor picked it up in his calloused hands. After a slow examination, turning it over and rubbing the surface, he shook his head. Elsa picked up the tube as soon as he was done, feeling possessive.

"Dept of Agr. What does that mean?" Vic looked around and leaned closer to speak. "You should ask your Granny about that logo."

Why did he think Granny would know about it? They didn't have many secrets, but Granny didn't talk about her past. Why might she know about the tube's origin? But Elsa was afraid Granny would make her sell it. Her gut told her she should keep it.

"No idea what it means." She slipped the tube back inside her satchel.

The bell over the door jangled as another customer entered. She glanced back, but it wasn't anyone she recognized. Her stomach clenched, and she turned to look again.

"Excuse me," said the stranger behind her. "Could somebody tell me where I might find work in this town?"

His tone was polite, though he'd interrupted her transaction. He wore patched jeans with holes in both knees, and he had broad shoulders that filled out his dusty jacket. He had an air of contained strength about him that made her keep looking. It shouldn't be a problem for him to find work with a build like that. That wasn't what held her attention.

His clothing wasn't plastic and his skin looked cleaner than the residents, less gray. He must be new to SoCal. At first, she guessed he was young because he was clean-shaven, but a second glance proved he was old enough to shave. With water scarce, a lot of the men in town wore beards. She was jolted by a sense of recognition, though she'd never seen this man before.

The young man looked at her with gray eyes that twinkled with humor, and her cheeks flamed as he moved closer.

"There's a licensing office across the square for the Heap if you have a team," Elsa said, her voice gruff from covering up the nervous tremor. She wracked her brain for a reason for her powerful reaction to him. "And an outfit next to it that needs workers for beach clean-up. GreenCorps is probably hiring at the scrapyard and the railroad for someone your size. Depends what you're looking for."

"Not interested in working for GreenCorps," he said, his eyes darkening.

His mouth twisted on the name. Despite his fabric clothes and well-traveled, confident manner, she placed his age as only a couple of years older than her twenty years.

"Without GreenCorps? You're going to have a hard time finding a job. A bar maybe. Everything else is corporation."

She flushed under his gaze, suddenly self-conscious. He was staring, and she wasn't used to that kind of attention. Her fine dark hair was hacked off to jaw-length and stuffed under her cap. She looked ragged and her figure wasn't much to look at. Living on the edge of starvation made you tough, but left her looking like skin and bones. Or like a fifteen-year-old boy. She'd seen women at the pleasure houses who were well-fed and lived soft lives. Their life expectancy was short due to who they dealt with, but they seldom starved. Those women had rounded hips and breasts. Men liked that soft look and she was all angles.

She returned his intense stare to make a point, then sniffed and turned away. From the corner of her eye, she caught his smirk, as if he'd won somehow. She wasn't a child to get into a staring contest. She didn't need to let him know she found him attractive. He knew. It looked like he had the ego to go with his looks. Attraction meant nothing; she wasn't in the market for a partner.

"Hey, no offense," he said. "My brother and I need to make some coin. Find a place to crash for a week or two. Warmer here than where we came from. Even if it's just March."

The bell over the door jingled again and another young man entered the store, shorter and wirier than the first, but dressed the same way, with torn pants and a long green coat. She didn't recognize him and her stomach didn't react. The first man half-turned with a smile for the newcomer.

"Hayden. You're up. Wondered if you might sleep all day." He turned to Elsa and lowered his voice. "We didn't sleep on the train."

His brother stood in the background. They looked nothing alike. Slight instead of muscular, the newcomer had pinched weasley features. His dark eyes darted from place to place like a nervous tic. With no family resemblance, they might not be brothers by blood.

"I woke up, looked around, and saw you come this way. I'm going to check out the town, somewhere new for a change. I'm glad we hopped our way southbound. Meet you back where we slept in an hour or two?" He waited for a response.

The first man nodded and turned back toward Elsa. Vic was occupied with tabulating the value of her take.

"You're hoppers?" Elsa said, double-checking that Vic wasn't paying attention. If the men weren't staying at a hotel or bar, they could be wanderers.

The newcomer winked and held a finger to his mouth. "Name's Walker."

That was more interesting. She'd seldom had an opportunity to talk to someone who rode the trains, but often wondered what life was like on the road, seeing something new every day instead of the same dreary thing day after day.

"Three day's food and two for water, double portions," said Vic as he pushed his glasses up his nose. He'd finished examining the cleaned-up pot, the handful of cutlery, and assorted small bits. "Best I can do."

Elsa returned her attention to the shopkeeper. His offer wasn't enough. "Three and three."

"Might have been worth that last week," Vic said with a shake of his head. "Water's harder to get. GreenCorps reduced the supply. Again. Only three tankers came in this morning. I checked. Cost goes up. This isn't a negotiation." He dropped his voice as his eyes flicked toward Granny. "If you throw in that tube, I can increase the price to three and three."

Elsa shook her head. "It's unusual. I'm going to hang onto it for now."

"Remember to talk to your Granny about it," said Vic under his breath.

"Reverse it," said Granny from her chair by the door. "And stop whispering." She didn't always speak up, but when she did, people listened. "Three water and two food."

Elsa grit her teeth at her grandmother's interference. It implied that Elsa couldn't make a transaction herself, but she understood negotiation.

"Best I can do is three water and one day's food for both of you," said Vic. "If they don't send more water tankers, next week it probably won't be worth that."

"We'll take it," said the old lady, staring at him with her bright yellow eyes. "Elsa, let's go. We've got work. Scrap metal won't find itself. Stop your flirting."

She stomped from the store without waiting.

Elsa flushed, her cheeks flaming, and her eyebrows shot up. She wasn't a child, and Granny hadn't treated her like one since she was ten and had worked full days at the Heap. She clamped her lips shut, determined not to react.

What had upset Granny? The handsome young man covered his amused laugh with a cough. Elsa shrugged at Vic behind the counter who passed her the water tokens, the protein and nutrient bars, and a bag with oatmeal for tomorrow's breakfast.

Elsa shoved everything into her satchel and hustled out to the street. Her grandmother was already past the station and headed out to the Heap, walking fast. Granny was a block ahead, so Elsa jogged, her stomach tied in knots. It had been a strange morning and something about the encounter in the store had left her unsettled. She didn't like when things happened that she didn't understand.

"We need to work a full day. Cash in each morning before the price goes up again," said Granny without slowing her pace as Elsa caught up. The old woman moved like someone half her age. "I've had this feeling twice before. The cost of water is going to keep shooting up. GreenCorps has done this before. Means rebellion. They're trying to keep us too desperate to care. Too hungry to join. You watch. More troops and martial law."

"You got all that from just one day and one price hike for water?" Elsa's chest was tight after running to catch up. The air quality was worse than usual today.

The older woman shook her head. "I feel it in my bones and my gut. Something bad is coming. Trust me."

They strode at a brisk pace toward their site and the huge landfill that extended for miles past the ruined city and the rebuilt section of houses they lived in. Other small groups and teams of women and children streamed toward the Heap. Most of the men headed toward the scrap yards and a lucky few to the railroad.

"What happened those other times?" Elsa prodded, not wanting to let the subject drop. She hated when Granny acted mysterious. The older woman claimed she'd had premonitions and survived by living by her gut instinct or tingling in her bones. If Granny's bones were telling her it was serious, it was probably true.

Elsa wanted to know more, though Granny wouldn't often talk about her past. Once she'd been part of a rebellion, that much Elsa had learned. The emblem on the tube flashed through her mind. She'd seen that leaf somewhere before; she just couldn't place it. Maybe something from Granny's past? Vic's hint suggested it might be related to the rebels, though how would a tube from twenty-first-century trash relate to modern rebels?

Elsa jumped when Granny spoke.

"Earthquake in 2110 when I was younger than you are now and lived somewhere else. We lost half the town. The survivors rioted for food and water. GreenCorps held back supplies and charged too much for what they brought in. The second time happened here in my first year, after a fire burnt most of the new city up near Reno. We got blamed. GreenCorps raised the price of our water and increased security. That was over forty years ago. We're due for trouble. Good times can't last forever."

These were good times? Elsa shuddered to think about the worse times Granny had lived through. She hoped those times didn't come again.

* * *

Walker
March 21st, 2195, Long Beach
Sunrise 6:54 a.m. Sunset: 7:05 p.m.

Travel Notes:
Investigated the trainyard. Best area to get back on the train is past the station heading north. Level and smooth.

Good hiding places in the bushes.

Heavy security patrol for outbound trains.

Needs to be a nighttime departure.

Saw the beautiful girl from the store again this morning. She's a heapster and the old lady is her grandmother, or maybe her great-grandmother. Calls her Granny. I admire their fierceness. They're independent and don't rely on others to get their tokens. They work for themselves, even if they sell to GreenCorps. Store owner said for a two-person team, they bring in high volumes to sell. Hard workers. He hinted the grandmother was once someone important in the rebellion. Sent here as punishment after her family died. She's so old I wonder which rebellion she took part in. Probably a helluva long time ago. Convenient for me, he's a talker, but I wouldn't tell him secrets.

Can't help but imagine what the younger hawk would look like all cleaned up. Her features were sharp, with prominent cheekbones and eyes that drew me in. Kept thinking about her and how her kind of beauty can't be hidden.

Hayden found a brothel called Ginny's. Said someone told him about it in Reno. Don't have a good feeling about it. He isn't interested in the women, at least not much. He has another motive. Hope we don't have a repeat of what happened two years ago in Vegas. That binge lasted all summer, and he used every cent he'd saved getting wasted. We were lucky to escape town without being pressed into a mining gang or a GreenCorps fire-fighting crew bound for Texas. Hoped those days were over, but I can't be his bloody keeper. Think he already scored a hit. Can't find him anywhere. I'd bet money he's kiting.

The boards and metal sheeting were loose in the alley where we slept yesterday. Pried one up and made an opening in the fence. Built a makeshift shelter between a big rock next to the hill and the back of the fence. When the boards are back in place, you can't tell we're here. It'll do as a place to sleep for a couple of weeks.

Took the only coin I brought to buy food and water tokens. If we stay longer than a week, we'll need temporary work. Maybe somewhere that provides food and water. A bar isn't a bad idea. I've been a bouncer before. Just stand and act tough. This place is dirty, smelly, and expensive. The price of water tokens is the worst I've encountered. Guess when it doesn't rain much, and the groundwater is gone, GreenCorps can charge whatever they want to bring in water.

CHAPTER 4: ELSA PLUS WALKER

At the landfill two days later, an altercation on the surface brought Elsa scuttling upward, the faint raised voices of conflict interrupting her excavation and set her heart racing. Granny's voice became clear as she got closer.

"Piss off, ya hear? I'm not tellin' you again. Fucking hopper."

A shotgun blast and a yelp followed her words. Hopper? One of the two they'd met in the market? The smaller one had shifty eyes and the slick smile of a liar. Her grandmother always aimed her first shot to the side, sometimes wounding an extremity, like an arm or leg. Shoot to wound, not kill. The second shot, she'd do damage. Elsa waited to hear if there was an additional shot, but the disturbance was over. Granny had it covered.

"You're a tough old bird, Granny," she called from the entrance of the tunnel with a shake of her head. She popped out with her canteen. "Has he harassed you before?"

"Nothing I can't handle," the older woman said, staring in the direction the poacher had run. "Just the scrawny one. He's been poking around all day. He stole something from the sector next door. Kid with the gun wasn't fast enough, but I winged 'em. That ought to teach him a lesson."

Elsa drank another sip of water, savoring its wetness, despite its warmth, and turned to head back to work. "Let me know if you need help."

Granny snorted. "I got it." She stared down the Heap, watching the way the hopper had run.

* * *

Three weeks rolled by as Elsa and Granny worked harder than ever before. Elsa took fewer breaks, and they struggled awake before dawn each day. Despite the success in the tunnels and another rich shaft, they got less for their effort. The cost of water rose each week. At Granny's suggestion, they stockpiled the stamped water tokens and locked them in the safe, only getting enough food for a day or two at a time. They stretched the food rations to two-thirds portions each day. Elsa's stomach hollowed out as she lived with a persistent and distracting knot of hunger. They'd never had excess food, but now they got by on less.

They weren't the only ones dealing with these new circumstances. The number of people in town by the shops reduced as everyone scrambled to make ends meet. Water was essential. Everyone hurried and friendly banter between neighbors disappeared, with everyone focused on survival. She and Granny weren't the only ones who were hungry. Elsa slipped Janna a protein bar when Granny wasn't looking, but her friend refused the next time, knowing Elsa would go without.

By the close of the second week, walking anywhere was tense. Elsa looked over her shoulder every few meters and Granny's head was on a swivel, even during daylight. Rumors of daytime robberies increased, but they hadn't had any more trouble on the Heap. It paid for Granny to be known as cantankerous and an excellent marksman. Locals left them alone, at least during daylight, but she and Granny didn't press their luck after dark. Elsa kept her hand on her knife on the trip home each evening. GreenCorps forces roamed in force at night and near the train station.

Toward the end of the third tension-filled week, the stressful situation came to a head. The bucket of trash was full and Elsa trudged up her tunnel with the pile of muck to send it outside. She filled her lungs with fresh air and paused for a quick stretch. She attached the bucket and tugged on the rope, expecting Granny to haul it out, but nothing happened. She yanked again, but still nothing. Her feeling of dread grew. Granny wouldn't ignore her and she wouldn't have left her post. Something was wrong. Elsa crept forward and, as she did, her grandmother's raspy voice carried down the shaft.

"You two get the hell out of here. I told you last time that I have the license for this sector. I pointed out the markers. My warning shot a couple of weeks ago should have been clear. If you're here again, then you're trespassers and thieves. No poaching on my land. Get lost or I'll shoot."

"Listen, lady, we aren't doing any harm."

Elsa recognized the whiney voice of the handsome train hopper's brother. It surprised her the men were still in town, though it might be hard to leave with all the security.

She watched from the shadows, doubting that they could see her inside the garbage shaft. She waited to see if Granny needed help. Emerging now might cause a distraction. Her grandmother didn't back down. The young men looked at each other. The smaller one nodded and rushed Granny, followed by Walker a fraction of a second later. Granny aimed for the larger of the two men. It happened so fast that Elsa and Granny were taken off guard.

The shot missed, going wild. The smaller hopper's momentum continued, and he tackled Granny to the ground. He grabbed her and rolled her over, shoving his grubby hands into her pockets. Elsa rushed forward, her heart in her throat and boiling mad. She was too late to stop the attack.

"Hayden, what're you doing?" said Walker.

Elsa burst from hiding and grabbed fistfuls of garbage and threw it at both men. Chunks of half-decayed wood and muck hit them. Walker moved back with an expression that was hard to read, perhaps regret. She pulled her knife and lunged forward. She didn't want to get too close, so she kicked the smaller one in the ribs and jumped back. He yelped and backed away, his hands empty. It didn't look like he'd taken anything. She narrowed her eyes, keeping the knife raised. Her rage shook her inside, hot and fierce, but her hand was steady.

"What the hell? Get away from my Gran. Step back. NOW."

"The crazy bitch shot me a couple weeks ago. Pellet in my arm got infected," Hayden spat.

Elsa feinted with the knife, the motion drawing his eyes. She kicked the side of his knee and he crumpled to the ground.

She glanced at Walker, who held his hands up in surrender.

"Look, I'm sorry. I didn't realize…"

She wasn't interested in his explanation. He was interrupted by his brother who jumped to his feet and back several paces. He had a slight limp.

"Bitch. You're crazy too." Hayden stepped back again.

She grabbed the shotgun off the ground from beside Granny and stepped forward. She pumped another round into the chamber. "She shot you because you're a dirty thief. Picking on an old lady? What the fuck is wrong with you?" With her peripheral vision, she watched his companion, waiting for him to make a move. She planned to shoot whoever moved first and use the gun like a club on the second.

Hayden took a step forward. His eyes widened as she swung the shotgun to point at his middle. She wasn't aiming for an arm or leg. She wouldn't miss—not at this range. She dared him to take another step. Walker flashed a lopsided smile and gave an almost imperceptible nod. She ignored him.

"Shit, we're just thirsty," the small man said. "We're not interested in dying. We've seen you trading for water tokens for weeks. Not like you can't spare a few."

"Hayden, you need to stop." Walker shifted his gaze to Elsa and flushed. "We're leaving and won't bother you again." The big man's jaw clenched. He glared at his brother and took a couple of steps backward.

"We work hard for the little we have," Elsa said. "Get the hell outta here. Or I'll shoot." Her heart raced, the shotgun heavy in her hands, but she didn't take her eyes off the hoppers. Granny hadn't gotten up yet. She must have had the wind knocked out of her.

Hayden's eyes cut to her grandmother where she lay behind Elsa, but Elsa didn't fall for that trick. She kept her eyes locked on his face. Her trigger finger itched and her lips clamped together in a flat line. She ground her teeth so hard she worried her molars would crack. With her eyes, she dared either of them to make a move.

"Hayden, enough. We gotta go. Now." Walker's face was hard to read, but from the expression of disgust in his eyes, he wouldn't fight.

"Walker, these two are easy marks. We need something to show for the time I've spent staking out their operation. Rush her on three?"

The younger man's whine grated down her spine. He was the lesser threat, so her gaze remained on Walker, who was strong enough to hurt her if he got too close.

Walker's stormy gray eyes turned on his companion. She had the impression he was angry with his brother.

"You lied to me," Walker said. "Give it up, bro."

Hayden glared at him but stepped back.

"I'm sorry." Walker shook his head and backed away. He turned and ran down the garbage heap, followed by his weasley partner.

Her shoulders released and her hands shook so hard it was difficult to hold the gun. She rested the butt on the ground as she turned with a sigh. Her heart almost stopped. Granny lay sprawled on the ground, her forehead dripping with blood from a cut by her hairline. Elsa broke into a cold sweat. Granny looked so small and helpless.

"Granny, are you okay?" Her voice shook.

There was no answer.

Elsa knelt and checked for a pulse with trembling hands. Her breath whooshed out in relief when she found a heartbeat. Elsa lifted her grandmother's canteen from her side and held the water to Granny's mouth. Her grandmother sputtered but drank. Elsa helped her to a sitting position while Granny cradled her right arm, the bones at a funny angle near her wrist.

Elsa shook with rage. She couldn't believe those two. They'd broken her grandmother's arm over water tokens.

She clutched the tokens in her pocket from this morning. They had been safer in the tunnel with her than on the surface. She'd been right, but that wouldn't fix Granny's arm. Now a more serious problem loomed. Elsa couldn't work the shaft alone, and she also needed to pay a medical bill.

"Elsa," Granny looked up, "I can wait for you to close up." Her voice lacked its usual fire. "But we should go soon. Everything is spinning. I'll just sit and catch my breath."

The cut on her grandmother's forehead was shallow. The bleeding had stopped, but the tightness around Granny's eyes showed her pain. Her pale lips looked parched. With the dried blood on the side of her face, she looked rough.

Elsa was torn. Granny needed her arm set, and she needed water. But if they left now, the shaft would remain open. Anyone could enter and take what they found. Elsa lifted Granny's canteen, and it sloshed back and forth. Almost empty. Her grandmother must have given her extra water again. Twice this week, Elsa had thought her canteen was fuller than she'd left it after lunch. Granny had snuck some of her water into Elsa's canteen and had gone without. She'd probably done it every day. No wonder she was dehydrated and dizzy.

Elsa looked around again, searching for watchers. She squinted to determine the time. They needed to leave. The sun was going down, the haze lessening on the western horizon with a hint of sunset glow. On the other hand, Elsa needed to close up and collect their take from today. She'd found a double boiler this morning, though without a lid, and a brass stovetop kettle. It was their best take in days. The plastic bundle was standard size. She rolled it and shoved it into the bucket.

Securing the site took longer than usual, as she worked alone. Elsa didn't know if they'd be back for a few days. How was Granny going to work? She removed her cross-bracers to carry home and took extra time to plug the hole with layers of guck from the emptied buckets. The tunnel inside might collapse, but it should keep other scavengers out. For a while anyway. If they weren't working the site, they'd lose their current yearly contract in two weeks. The license was due for renewal— not that they had the coin.

When Elsa finished, Granny was pale and chalky behind her wrinkles. Even her pressed-together lips were colorless. Elsa carried the heavy bucket and made a bundle of the shotgun and her bracers. Her grandmother wrapped her uninjured arm around Elsa's shoulder and they hobbled down the Heap. Though they walked as fast as possible, Granny limped and progress was slow. She held her arm against her body and moaned if it was unsupported. It took twice as long as usual to return to the row of shacks where they lived.

They were two blocks from home when several shadowy figures emerged from an alley. Elsa couldn't see their faces which made her uneasy. It was almost dark. Her heart raced and her palms became damp. There was nowhere to run or hide.

"Well. Look what we found," a voice said. "Filthy trash pickers. Wonder what loot they've got for us today."

"Heapsters, they reek. We smelled you two coming," said a second male voice.

Ignoring the insult, Elsa said, "My grandmother's hurt. We just want to get home. I need the medic so he can set her arm." She maintained an even tone despite her worry. No good showing weakness.

"You have a pass to be out after dark, Elsa?" The first voice asked as the man came closer.

Her heart sank. It was Janna's older brother. He was four years older than she and Janna were, a burly man with thick muscles, a wild black beard, and hard eyes. They'd recruited him as GreenCorps muscle and he liked to throw around his newfound power. He was the number one person she tried to avoid.

"Wade, please." It wouldn't do any good.

"It's not Wade anymore. I'm Private First-Class Razor now. Do you have a pass or not? Curfew was fifteen minutes ago."

"Pay up, then you can go home," said another voice.

Several others chimed in from the shadows. Elsa and Granny were surrounded. She couldn't fight against these odds and she couldn't reach her gun with all she carried. She also couldn't afford to escalate the violence. She chewed the inside of her cheek, trying to buy time and think of a solution. If she drew attention to the gun, the creeps would take it, too. Perhaps in the near dark, it would be mistaken for another of her garbage braces. They would leave tools so she could work another day, giving them more opportunities to steal in the name of GreenCorps law.

Wade tossed his head toward them and two of the other figures jumped forward. His patrol members grabbed Elsa's bucket.

"Not bad," said one, as he passed the rolled plastic to the girl beside him. "Metal trinkets, some pots. A decent batch of plastic. We can trade those."

He dropped the bucket on the ground, taking everything from inside with a nasty smile. The bucket fell on its side. She hoped it wasn't broken. She kept her eyes on Wade. He jerked his head and his people drifted away.

"I'll take that shotgun too. That's a pretty piece." He stepped forward. "Unless you want to leave the old lady and come with me to work off your debt."

Bile rose in her throat. Elsa couldn't afford to fight this time. Not with Granny injured. She took the gun and tossed it to him without a word. Its value was a lot higher than the price of a curfew violation, but it was worth it to avoid being raped. There'd been a near-miss last fall, too. Janna had intervened and saved Elsa.

Wade and his patrol melted back into the shadows and out of sight while she held her breath. She let them walk away, wishing she could tell them what she thought of their actions. GreenCorps might be there to keep the peace, but more often than not, they were the problem. After Wade and his fellow recruits had gone, she picked up the discarded bucket.

There was nothing Elsa could do. This day had gone from bad to worse. Their profits were gone, and she had nothing to trade. The oatmeal in her bag and a dinner bar were the last of their rations. If the food had been with Granny, it would have been stolen by the hoppers. She had no way to buy more unless she traded water tokens back to Vic, and they needed those for water and the upcoming license fee. Granny was injured and they couldn't pay for medical. The gun was gone, and they'd be vulnerable on the Heap. Worse, Granny wouldn't be able to work. How would Elsa get the coin to take care of their needs?

* * *

Walker
April 13th, 2195, Long Beach
Sunrise: 6:24 a.m. Sunset 7:22 p.m.

Could fucking kill Hayden. He misled me. Lied.

Couple of weeks ago he stormed back here holding his elbow, said some crazy lady shot him for no reason. A piece of steel shot was lodged in his arm. Needed to get it extracted by the medic so it didn't get infected. Turns out the crazy lady was the old hawk. He was on the Heap and tried to steal from her and her granddaughter. The old hawk shot him. I don't blame her. She likely suspects that he's robbed others on the Heap. Hoped he had found a part-time job to pay for his habit, but that isn't how he's been paying for his drugs. It's clear now.

This morning Hayden asked for my help. Said we were just going to scare the hell out of the crazy lady, payback for the gunshot wound. Should have known better. He can be a vindictive asshole. Took me out to the Heap. Convinced me to charge when he did so she wouldn't know where to shoot. That part worked fine, but he kept going. Bowled her over and rummaged in her pockets. Rolled her for water tokens. It was disgusting.

She was old. Older than I thought. At first, I thought he'd knocked the wind out of her, but by the time the young hawk flew out of her tunnel, the old lady's arm was broken. Her head was bleeding. Never would have taken a run at her had I realized who she was. Didn't recognize her sitting there with a hat and Uvee goggles. We're total shit.

The young one is something else. Faced us down with a dull blade, then her grandmother's shotgun. Never seen anyone so beautiful or fierce. She hates me and I don't blame her. I admire her grit. Those blazing yellow eyes are gorgeous, but the look in them today will keep me awake nights.

Hayden didn't seem sorry. Just upset we came away empty-handed. What's wrong with him? Hope he doesn't go after them again, but I fear he might. He's got it in his head that they did him wrong.

How did we become these people?

CHAPTER 5: ELSA

Relieved of their day's take, Elsa and Granny struggled home empty-handed. Granny hadn't said a word throughout the altercation. That worried Elsa more than anything. Granny was a spitfire. Most of the time, she said what she wanted with her acidic tongue. For her to be silent, she must be in a lot of pain. Elsa bit her lower lip and monitored her grandmother's condition, trying to take more of her weight as she trudged the last couple of blocks home.

"Elsa, what happened?"

Janna's father jumped off his front steps from his customary seat. He supported Granny on the other side to the top of the stairs to their house, being careful of her broken arm. Elsa was grateful for his kindness. Tears threatened, but she swallowed them to answer.

"A couple of hoppers rushed her and knocked her over on the Heap. She cut her head, twisted her ankle, and broke her arm. She might be tough, but at her age, her bones are brittle. It was dark by the time I closed up and headed home. We should have come home sooner."

She paused, wondering if she should share the rest, but continued. Her voice shook with pent-up fury and she clenched a fist. "Wade and his new friends took my haul."

Janna's dad shook his head. "That boy should know better. I'm sorry. Can I do anything?"

"Could you get the medic for Granny?"

Her neighbor hesitated and looked at the ground. His voice emerged as no more than a mumble. "I can't pay for it. Times are tough."

Elsa shook her head. "I've got a little. Wade's not your responsibility." She swallowed her disappointment. "I don't want to leave her, but we need Marcus."

"You're a good girl, Elsa." He squeezed her shoulder and yelled into his house, "Going for the medic for Granny Lee next door, back soon."

"Is Janna here?" she said before he'd taken more than a couple of steps.

He turned back into the darkness. "Wade took her somewhere this afternoon for a new job. He didn't say much. Just that she won't be back for a while."

Elsa nodded. What kind of job might Wade have arranged? She kept her face neutral and pushed back her worry. Janna wasn't her focus right now. Granny was family and her priority. She unlocked the door and helped Granny inside as her neighbor disappeared up the street. He whistled as he walked and she pictured his progress up the street, wishing he would hurry.

She lay Granny on her bed and heated some of their precious water for tea. With gentle hands, she used a little hot water to dab the dried blood from Granny's face and cleaned her wound. Her grandmother took the damp cloth and pressed it against her head.

"My bones won't heal anytime soon," the old woman said.

Granny's yellow eyes looked paler than usual. Her voice trembled and sounded defeated. It was the first she'd spoken since they'd left the Heap.

"Let's wait and see what the medic says." The crease between Elsa's brows deepened and her forehead became tight. "I'd rather not borrow trouble."

"I'm done on the site. I'll sign my license over to you, but you're going to need help. Maybe your friend next door when she gets back. You can't go out there alone. It's too rough."

Elsa nodded. "I'll figure it out." Her words sounded confident, but she didn't know what she was going to do. She couldn't afford to pay for help and by the time she paid the medic, there wouldn't be much left. Maybe not enough for the license. Her empty stomach rolled as she hadn't eaten since lunch. The last of the food lay in her bag. Already the bills were daunting.

It didn't take long before the knock sounded at the door. She released a sigh of relief that the medic was so swift. He had a permanent pass to be out after curfew.

"What happened?" the dark-haired young man said. "Something with Granny Lee?"

She beckoned Marcus inside and closed the door. She didn't need every word known throughout the neighborhood tonight. It wouldn't be safe to appear too weak.

Elsa pointed to Granny, who sat on Elsa's bed eating her protein bar. "Thieves pushed her over on the Heap. Twisted ankle, cut on her forehead, and her arm looks broken."

"Don't make no fuss about me," Granny said. "Just need you to set the bone. At my age, I don't need stitches. I'm not going to win any beauty contests anymore."

"I hear you could've won them when you were younger," said the medic with an easy laugh as he knelt down beside her. "My grandfather said you were stunning. Like Elsa here."

He examined her head injury first.

"Keep your eyes off my granddaughter," Granny said, narrowing her eyes. "Unless you want to make an offer of marriage."

"Granny," said Elsa with reproach in her voice. She wasn't a child to need that level of defense. "Marcus came here to help, not get harassed." He was engaged to someone else and his charming comments weren't serious. He rolled his eyes at Elsa when her grandmother's attention was elsewhere and inspected Granny's ankle. He wrapped her twisted ankle in a tensor bandage.

He saved her arm for last.

Marcus set the arm. Granny sat stoically, but hissed in pain when he maneuvered the injured arm. Both bones were broken near her wrist. He left four pills for Granny on the counter. She refused to accept more. This was enough for tonight and tomorrow.

"You're going to need to stay off that foot for a few weeks and you're going to ache all over. I don't think you lost too much blood. But you need to drink more water."

"I'll be fine after tomorrow," Granny said.

Her jaw clenched in a stubborn line. Sometimes watching Granny was like looking in a mirror of the future. Elsa recognized Granny's expression; she'd worn it herself on more than one occasion. They could both be stubborn fools.

"Well, you won't have the strength to work the Heap anytime soon," said Marcus. "You need to stay where people can take care of you while Elsa works."

He looked over his shoulder at Elsa as he spoke. His words were as much for her benefit as Granny's. He was only stating what Elsa had already known. She felt numb.

After he'd gathered his things and accepted one of her precious water tokens as payment, she walked outside with Marcus.

Once alone outside, she handed him a second token without speaking.

He counted out another eight painkillers and passed them to her with a smile.

"If she won't take them, crush them, and mix them in the stubborn old goat's water. She won't get better if she's in agony." He hesitated, perhaps wondering how blunt he could be.

"What else?" She tried to keep her voice steady.

"At her age, it will be a miracle if she recovers enough to work the Heap. Her muscles will atrophy during her time off. Regaining her current level of strength is unlikely."

"How long will it take her to heal?" This time, she heard the dismay in her voice.

"Her ankle needs a few weeks, maybe a month. Her arm, six months. Maybe more. She's over a hundred. It's unreal she's worked this long. I'm sorry I can't do more to help and don't have better news."

Elsa's hope for a quick recovery plummeted. Six months? This was worse than she'd guessed. A catastrophe. Her chest constricted, and she swallowed again. She wouldn't cry.

The medic walked up the dark street until he faded out of sight. She helped Granny hobble to her own bed and lowered the curtain. It wasn't long before Granny's snores filled their shack. Elsa lay awake, tossing and turning, unable to settle. She needed a plan. After several hours, only one idea sprang to mind. She didn't have other options. It was a last resort and she couldn't believe she was considering it. She covered her face and muffled her scream into her pillow. She made no audible sound as her world crumbled.

* * *

Elsa sat with her head propped on their makeshift table, listening to Granny's snores across the room. The last five days had been hell. Granny's painkillers had lasted until the fourth day, and she refused to let Elsa trade for more. While the old woman didn't complain, she was irritable, like a raccoon with a sore tooth, snapping at every comment directed her way. She found fault with everything.

While Granny slept, she muttered, talking about a rebellion that had been put down a lifetime ago. She called out to her late husband. Elsa hadn't realized that her Granny's involvement in the rebellion had run so deep. Her great-grandmother's pained ravings sounded like she'd been a leader and felt responsible when things had gone wrong. No wonder she didn't like to talk about the past. The rebels might still exist, but there'd been no contact for fifty years.

Without work, Elsa didn't have enough to occupy her time. She'd finished the projects around the house that she didn't always have time for, including fixing the roof and the stairs. She used most of her stock of woven plastic on repairs and scavenged nearby for additional brick and two sheets of discarded and rusted metal.

She and Granny couldn't continue like this for much longer. Elsa needed work. She took the afternoons while her grandmother napped, to check with everyone she could think of. There was nothing. They turned her away for heavier menial jobs, like the scrap yards and nobody needed help in the shops. Though she was strong and qualified, she couldn't compete with men for those jobs. She was almost desperate enough to work alone at the Heap.

The stockpile of water tokens shrank as they used their allotted water ration each day and traded another for a week's worth of food. Elsa kept the metal cylinder but decided to ask Vic to inquire with his suppliers from GreenCorps if they'd seen anything like it. Maybe someone would know what it was. Asking Granny about the leaf meant getting the old lady to talk about painful times she tried to forget.

The thought of selling the tube made Elsa sick. It was worth more than what Vic had offered, for the metal alone, even if she'd never been able to open it. Running her hands over it, she still believed that it was valuable, special. With time on her hands, she tried again, feeling compelled to discover what it contained.

With Granny asleep, Elsa removed the tube from the safe for a more thorough examination. The light reflected off a metal box tucked away in the safe, reminding her of Granny's rambled mutterings. Elsa shouldn't look without asking, but she removed it from the back. The box had the leaf emblem on the top. She cursed her stupidity. She should have realized, even if she'd never been allowed to touch the box. It contained mementos of Granny's former life, when she'd been young and part of the rebellion. Elsa peeked at the sleeping form in the other room. There was no indication of movement.

The small wooden box was light. There wasn't much inside. Easing the lid off, she found three photos. One of a group of people she didn't recognize with her grandmother. Granny had been young and beautiful. Not beautiful in a classic sense, but strong and carefree. She was laughing and surrounded by half a dozen adults and four children, one of whom had a distinctive birthmark on his forehead shaped like an ax.

In another photo, a tall man stood at her grandmother's side with his arm around her. Her late husband. The last photo was the couple, older now but still strong and in their prime. They stood with a young woman who must be their daughter. Granny's daughter that she never spoke of. Elsa's grandma. Her name had been Avery, like Elsa's sister.

The box also contained a list of numbers, a map of the train routes, and a pocket knife with a rusted blade. The meager possessions in the box made Elsa's heart ache. This was all that was left of the first forty-five or fifty years of her grandmother's life. At one time, the box had housed a stash of coins, but they'd been used to pay off debts in order to take the girls.

Elsa didn't feel like snooping anymore and returned the box to its usual location. She'd learned what she wanted to know. The leaf emblem was a symbol of the rebellion. She'd better stop asking; it could lead to trouble.

She dribbled a few drops of precious water near the leaf and the lettering on the tube, hoping to find a clue or something she'd missed. She tried twisting, squeezing, then yanking to open it, but nothing worked. There must be a trick or puzzle. She scraped the tip of her knife along the etching of the emblem.

At last, she found an irregularity in the metal. A dot that wasn't the same depth as the lettering or the picture. Hidden within the leaf was a tiny indentation the size of a pinpoint. She located a matching depression on the other end. She grabbed two safety pins and placed the tip of a pin in each hole and pressed. Nothing. She tried again with more pressure. This time, the leaf end released, popping upward. Heart racing, Elsa unscrewed the new section that appeared at the top.

When she dumped the contents into her hand, a silver key dropped into her palm. It felt cool. Surrounding the key in the tube was a thick paper scroll. When she slid it out and unrolled it, she discovered several sheets of paper. A series of maps—six in total. One each for places called: Corvallis, OREGON; Pullman, WASHINGTON; Aberdeen,

IDAHO; Fort Collins, COLORADO; and one each for Davis and Riverside, CALIFORNIA. Adrenaline shot through her and her hands shook.

It wasn't until Elsa examined the latter more closely that she noticed the words Southern and California together and made a connection: SoCal. One map was for this area; they looked old, their paper aged to a dull yellow. Roads were marked that no longer existed, or at least had fallen into disuse. Trains were the way to travel from one place to another now. She'd learned that cars on roads had once been the most common method of personal transportation, but they were long gone.

Her heart sped up. Maybe there was treasure at the locations on the maps. Though she'd never heard of the other places—and they looked distant—not everywhere was unknown. Riverside wasn't far from Long Beach. Stamped at the bottom of each sheet of paper was the date: 2025. She checked the tube again and extracted a smaller sheet of paper that had curved around and stuck to the inside.

When it was unrolled, it was a letter.

'To Whom It May Concern,

Enclosed within are a key and the maps for six bunkers filled with food, water, survival gear, which we incorporated into the federal seed reserve. There are a variety of plants and trees of edible species within (different species at each location). We've allocated these tubes to people who work at the seed reserves, but with the new wave of pandemic gaining strength in the wake of the asteroid collision, it has been challenging to know who or what will survive.

We hope the bunkers will be found and accessed when the population is in a recovery phase. The bunkers are at the locations on the map accessed through stone entry buildings. A metal post with the leaf symbol will mark them.

As chaos rages in our country and the government agencies collapse, we wanted to ensure that our life's work was not in vain. We hope the contents will improve the lives of many and bring back crops and plant species that may have been lost. We worry about the future of people who will have no access to seeds to grow their own food. While the agency may disappear and not exist in the future, I do not trust the Board of Directors of GreenCorps to help anyone except themselves and their investors. Already they have a monopoly on farming and have been claiming huge tracts of land. Without the seeds and diversity they could provide, GreenCorps will take a stranglehold on the economy.

If the worst should come to pass, those able to invest in the future should share and plant the seeds in the bunker. The key can access all six western locations. A different key and series of maps is in the south and a third in the east. The seeds contained are duplicates of the seed varieties placed in the Svalbard Global Seed Vault in the glacier near Norway.

Good luck,

Joshua Muller, Director of the Department of Agriculture'

Each map had a red triangle near the middle. Elsa wasn't sure she understood all the words in the letter, but she got the general idea. The Department of Agriculture had stashed seeds and perhaps other useful supplies that could be worth millions in silver or gold coins, not plastic tokens that were only good as GreenCorps credit. Perhaps people didn't have to live on the edge of starvation. The feeling became stronger. This was what she was meant to do. Find the seeds. She needed to search.

Her mind raced. If she could sell to the right people or, better yet, prove the existence of the bunkers, then sell the knowledge, she could change her life. She didn't want to excavate garbage for the rest of her life and until a week ago, that's what she expected her life to be. She could travel and search for the bunker in SoCal. Riverside didn't look too far away, perhaps two days on foot or a couple of hours by train. She would need to work in order to buy supplies, but it was possible. A thrill shot through her at the idea of an adventure and about a life with hope.

Granny's loud snore brought her back to reality. It was okay to dream, but there was no guarantee that anything of value was still out there. The maps were dated more than a hundred and seventy years ago. Perhaps someone had found the seeds long ago. She took a deep breath. She could plan for a trip to the nearest bunker, but she didn't have the resources right now. She had responsibilities to her great-grandmother and her care. What she needed was to find a solution to their immediate problem. Starvation loomed, and she needed a job.

Tomorrow was Sunday. Regardless of whether she liked the plan she'd developed, it was time for action. She needed to visit her sister. Maybe Avery's husband would help. He was an executive for the railroad and was the ranking GreenCorps officer in town. He might not be home because he sometimes traveled for work, but she'd take a chance. Elsa couldn't ask her sister to return to the Heap—Avery had sworn never to return.

CHAPTER 6: ELSA PLUS WALKER

Elsa didn't go to Avery's house often. Her sister just lived on the hill, but it seemed like a different world. Her feet dragged as she hiked. Jaxon McCoy owned railroad shares and was wealthy. His family was involved with GreenCorps leadership. As much as they loved her sister, she and Granny didn't know why a man like that had become interested in a heapster.

Admittedly, Avery had always cared how she looked and sacrificed precious water each day to wash her face and hands more than most. She'd changed out of her work clothes and had kept a separate outfit for Sundays and shopping. She didn't consider herself a heapster and had always wanted more. Avery had found it when she married the wealthiest man in town.

Even though Elsa hated groveling, Jaxon was a connected man who might have other work. She refused to beg for coin and was willing to work hard, but she needed help.

The streets in this neighborhood, while empty and dusty, weren't filled with trash and worthless, abandoned items like her neighborhood. The air smelled fresher here. It was above the worst of the pollution, far from the landfill, and high enough on the hill to catch errant breezes of fresh air. The old, durable stone buildings looked maintained. All the houses had doors and window shutters that were painted shades of red, blue, and green, unlike the brown and gray that dominated the area below. Rows of solar panels lined their roofs, glinting in the sun. Tall metal lamp posts stood on the street corners that lit the streets at night. Those that used the shadows to cloak their theft wouldn't come here; too much visibility and permanent GreenCorps guards.

Elsa stood on the front stairs and fidgeted with her hat, picking at a hole in the stitching while she waited next to the clean, pale blue front door. She didn't belong here and longed to turn around.

She inhaled deeply, suppressed her pride, and knocked. As footsteps approached inside, she yanked off her cap and shoved it into her pocket. She fluffed her short, dark curls.

Avery answered the door and stepped back, her clean hand pressing against her top lip. For the first second, there was no indication of recognition in her eyes.

She blinked and said, "Elsa?" After she checked up and down the street, she grabbed Elsa's wrist and tugged her inside.

"Who do you think is watching?" Elsa's tone came out sharper than intended. She looked at her sister's clean cotton skirt, snowy white shirt, and polished home. Coming had been a mistake. Her hope sank farther.

"No one," said her sister. "It's good to see you. I don't want Jaxon to hear that I let vagrants in the house."

"I'm not a vagrant." Elsa looked down and winced. She looked like one, dressed in bland gray plastic, a long-sleeved shirt of indeterminate color, with a worn-out poncho and holes in her boots. It was all she had. Her cheeks burned.

"I know that, but the neighbors won't know."

"I need to talk to you about Granny," said Elsa, deciding to get to the point. She didn't want to stay here longer than necessary. Her feet shifted back and forth on the clean tiled floor and she took a deep breath.

"Is she okay?" Avery's brow furrowed and her kind brown eyes showed concern.

"Yes, but she broke her arm and can't work. I came to speak with you about that."

Avery's eyes grew more guarded. "Why don't you go upstairs and clean up? I'll make lunch and you can tell us about it."

Elsa grimaced. "I smell that bad?"

Avery shrugged. "A shower wouldn't hurt."

Elsa smiled. "I was hoping you'd let me wash. Granny counts the water tokens."

Avery laughed, suddenly seeming more like her sister and less like a rich stranger. "Of course she does." Her expression grew more guarded as she glanced over her shoulder. "I'll let Jaxon know you're here, then I'll take you up."

Elsa waited a few minutes, expecting to hear raised voices. She didn't come here often, as she and Jaxon had never gotten along. He was rich, but in her opinion, he wasn't good enough for her sister. Jaxon knew her low opinion of him. She stayed away, so she didn't cause trouble for her sister.

When Avery returned, she wore a red mark on her cheek and wouldn't meet Elsa's eyes. Elsa suspected Jaxon liked his heapster wife because he could dominate her and push her around. She wouldn't be surprised if he had wives or girlfriends in other towns where he traveled. She'd never shared this theory with her sister. There was no point.

"C'mon." Avery headed for the stairs.

"Did he do that?" Elsa's voice was louder than usual. "Just because I'm here? I shouldn't have come."

Avery didn't answer the question. "Don't go," she said, her tone even. "Please. You came for a reason. Plus, I haven't seen you in a long time."

Elsa fumed. This was why she'd waited so long to talk about Granny. It wasn't that Avery wouldn't care. She loved Granny. They both did. Elsa and Avery also believed they owed their grandmother.

They'd promised not to be a burden. Avery had a grand house, beautiful clothes, and enough food and water. She never had to worry about starving, but her husband was one of Elsa's least favorite people. She would hate anyone who laid a hand on her sister. The hoppers who'd hurt Granny were next on her list.

"Lunch in half an hour," Avery said, passing her a towel. "Take your time."

Elsa bit her lip and said nothing else. Speaking to her sister about Jaxon's behavior wouldn't do any good. Avery had chosen this life and seemed happy enough otherwise. Elsa ran her hand across the luxurious cotton towel, a pale green like sagebrush. It was thick, soft, and new. At home, she and Granny shared a couple of patched hand towels that were somewhere between dingy yellow and faded brown. Nothing like this.

The tiled bathroom had both a bathtub and a separate shower with clear glass around it. Elsa opted for the shower. She'd had a bath here once, but felt almost as dirty when she was finished, sitting in a pool of filthy water. She'd been horrified by the dark, greasy ring she'd left in the tub. At least in the shower, the grime disappeared down the drain.

She stripped off her clothes and stacked them on the counter by the sink. Turning on the water, she stuck her hand in to gauge the temperature. Hot water poured from one tap and cold from the other, and she adjusted them until it seemed perfect. At home, the bathroom just had cold and was metered by GreenCorps. The daily water only came on if you'd plugged water tokens into the meter. No exceptions.

Elsa stepped into the spray of hot water with a sigh. She used the shampoo, soap, and conditioner like she'd been shown when Avery first moved here. They smelled like flowers. The water hitting the floor of the shower was almost black at first as she worked the lather through her hair and over her skin. She didn't want to waste water, even if it belonged to Jaxon. She hurried, though she washed her hair twice. Stepping out, she grabbed the soft towel and dried herself. She rubbed lotion on her dried skin that soaked in and smelled sweet.

A knock sounded at the door.

"I have something you can wear," said her sister. "I'll wash yours while we eat."

Elsa's cheeks flushed with embarrassment, but she passed her worn clothes through the door and took her sister's offering. Avery knew how to clean the plastic-based garments without melting them.

The clothes from Avery were well worn, but clean cloth instead of woven plastic strips. The light blue pants were loose on Elsa's thin frame, and she threaded her belt through the loops to make them fit. She added the long-sleeved shirt of cream with red and blue flowers embroidered around the rounded collar and cuffs. It was almost too beautiful to wear. It looked expensive. It hung too long on her, but she imagined how nice it would look if she had a body like her sister's. A regular diet of healthy food had only made Avery more beautiful. She wasn't built like the pleasure house girls, but she had a figure and her skin glowed.

Elsa looked in the mirror. Her skin was creamy white without the usual layer of grime and her yellow-gold eyes looked huge in her angular face. She touched her collar bones, wishing they weren't so prominent. Shaking her head at her silly thoughts, she toweled her hair dry, combed it, and parted it in the middle—more effort than she usually made. Its silky texture was shiny and although it had uneven ends, it looked elegant framing her face. She tucked the front behind her ears.

Clean and dressed up, she didn't feel like herself, but rich and glamorous. How would it feel to be like this every day? Would she take it for granted? Not likely, after so many years of ingrained dirt and rotting garbage. She collected the pair of clean socks and her boots, leaving her feet bare, and went downstairs, following the sound of voices. She set her boots by the door and went toward the kitchen. It was bright and clean, with overhead lights and a refrigerator in the house. Another sign that the McCoys were rich.

Jaxon looked up and whistled when she entered. She clenched her teeth and her steps faltered.

"Who knew your sister was pretty under all that dirt and garbage stink?" he said from where he lounged at the table. His long legs stretched out in front of him.

It sounded like a compliment, but Elsa recognized it as an insult and flushed hot under his gaze. His dark eyes met hers and she jolted with surprise. Real lust filled his glance. The look in his eyes made her feel unclean, though she'd just showered. He was married to her sister.

Avery finished the sandwiches and transferred them to plates with a smile. She didn't notice anything negative about Jaxon's words or anything wrong with how he stared at Elsa.

"Those look great on you. Keep them. You ready to eat?"

Elsa swallowed and nodded. Her sister's cast-off clothing was nicer than anything she'd worn before. She didn't enjoy living on charity, but for once she would have something nice.

Tears stung the back of her throat as she looked at her lunch. The slices of bread looked fresh and had both slabs of meat and thick slices of white cheese. Her mouth watered in anticipation. Her sister looked up with a smile and added a sprig of green grapes with eight or nine grapes to each plate before serving them.

Elsa swallowed. She recognized the fruit from the market, but she'd only eaten them once before, years ago. This was an unheard-of luxury for an everyday meal and she wondered if they ate this way every day. She had a suspicion they did.

"Where are the girls?" Elsa said as she sauntered toward the table. She pretended not to see the look in Jaxon's eyes. The smooth tile floor felt chilly under her bare feet. Despite the heat outside, the house was cool. They must use power to keep it from getting hot in the heat of the day.

"Playing with the kids next door." Avery lowered her eyes and glanced at Jaxon.

They didn't want the girls to see her. They were ashamed that Elsa worked the Heap and was dirt poor. She didn't blame them, though it stung. Her nieces would have a better life away from the Heap.

"Give them a hug from me." She sat at the end of the table, farthest from Jaxon.

Avery smiled and seemed oblivious to the smoldering look Jaxon still directed at Elsa.

"What happened with Granny? You said she's okay."

Avery sat at the table between Elsa and Jaxon. She rested her hand on her husband's arm and smiled her gentle smile. She drew his eye to her. Perhaps she wasn't as naïve or oblivious as she seemed.

"A pair of hoppers took us as easy marks. One bothered her a few times while I was working in the shaft. I didn't know, and she didn't tell me. I only knew about the one time when she shot and winged one of them."

Elsa bit into her sandwich and almost cried at the soft texture and the rampant flavors of food that wasn't a processed bar or gruel. She savored it before continuing, taking small bites to make it last.

"The hoppers came back and rushed her together. Her shot went wild, and they knocked her down. Cut her forehead, twisted her ankle. The real problem is her broken arm. They didn't steal anything, but she's out of commission for six months. I can't afford to be off work that long without a partner."

"So, you came here for money?" Jaxon's eyes lingered on her chest.

Elsa didn't have spare underclothes, and her sister had taken her own to launder. She wore only the embroidered shirt, and she resisted the urge to cross her arms over her chest. She flushed hot at his words, anger rising through her hot and wild, but she willed it into submission, clenching her fists under the table where they'd be invisible.

"Not money, and Avery would never come back to the Heap."

Jaxon shook his head, his mouth pressed flat. "No woman of mine is working the Heap."

This was common knowledge. However, Elsa suppressed her irritation that he spoke for his wife. Avery used to be capable of expressing her own opinions.

"I'm not here with my hand out. I'm just asking for a favor."

"A favor. Like a job?" Jaxon tapped his lip as he thought. It was difficult not to fidget under his predatory gaze.

Elsa took a couple more bites of food. The grapes exploded in her mouth, juicy and sweet, despite his stare. She wouldn't like any job he suggested, but she needed to set aside her personal dislike and hear him out. This was why she'd come.

"Have you got something in mind?" she said at last. "I asked around the market, the junkyard, the scrapyards. Nobody's hiring. Especially not women. Things are tight."

"What's wrong with working the Heap by yourself?" said Jaxon, his eyes narrowed.

The look in his eyes accused her of laziness.

"I could dig it fine," she said, fighting to keep the resentment from her voice. "I do all the excavating now." She lowered her eyes as she played with the stem from the grapes. "But I can't work and protect myself at the same time." She hated to admit weakness, especially to this asshole. "If I don't have help on the pulleys, I would spend most of my time toting garbage, instead of excavating. It will cut my finds in half at least, and that's without considering the increased risk of theft."

"Why don't you find a temporary partner?" said Avery. "Someone who needs work?"

"I don't have anyone I can trust not to steal, make bad side deals, or who won't hurt me." It was too bad Janna had taken a different job and was elsewhere. They would have been a good team.

"If you can't work the Heap," said Jaxon. "You need something different."

He wasn't saying anything she didn't know, but from the gleam in his eye, he had a solution and was stringing her along for his amusement. His top teeth scraped over his bottom lip and he sucked in a breath. He liked his idea. A lot. Elsa got a dreadful feeling in the bottom of her stomach. Her instinct was to turn the job down without giving it a chance. Was this what Granny meant by living by your gut? Her gut might be a warning, but she was going to go against it.

"Ginny could use a server at her place."

"I'm not working in a pleasure house. Life expectancy is ten years max. Most of her girls spend all day kiting on drugs. I'm not like that. I won't touch that stuff. I'm not that desperate." Not yet.

"Just serving drinks." Jaxon held his hands up. "Hear me out. She'll feed you good and make sure you're clean and have water tokens. If you make tips, you might put enough coin away to take a partner on the Heap or buy into a partnership later if your Granny doesn't heal."

She hesitated, picturing working in the bar, but not upstairs. That might not be so bad.

"You'll have to fend off some hands, but nothing a tough girl like you can't handle."

His hands would be on her? A bottomless pit opened in her stomach. He wanted her somewhere he had access. His eyes held a dare. Taking the job would have strings that would be hard to avoid.

"Can I think about it?" said Elsa, trying not to show her distaste.

"You can. You've got a week to decide. After that, Ginny will find someone else."

Asking him had been a horrible idea. There had to be some other way to make coin.

"Thanks for lunch. I should get back to Granny," she said as she stood. "She didn't know I was coming here and must wonder where I am."

Avery got up and gave her a hug. "I'm so glad you came." Her arms clasped around Elsa and her clean floral smell enveloped her. "I'd help more if I could, but I can't go back to the Heap. I'm needed at home with my girls. Charlotte and Rose need me. You understand?"

Elsa nodded.

"You're great. I know you would. Thanks for the shower and for listening. That helps too." She turned to Jaxon. "I appreciate your suggestion. It isn't anything I'd considered. I'll let you know by week's end."

He nodded and picked up his sandwich and took an enormous bite.

"I'll get your other clothes," said Avery as she walked her to the door.

Elsa slid the clean pair of socks onto her feet, then her boots, while she waited for Avery to collect her laundered clothing. She wished she'd gotten to see her nieces, who were one and three. They didn't know her and she barely knew them. She hadn't seen the youngest since she was a newborn. They changed so much between visits.

Avery handed her a cloth bag with the folded clothes inside. There'd be food inside under the clean clothes. A sandwich for Granny, another for herself, or perhaps some fruit.

"See you next week," said Jaxon as he leaned on the doorframe of his home office.

Elsa's blood ran cold at the expression in his dark eyes. She wasn't that desperate, or was she? She had a week to decide. He might not force himself on her, but he'd make it difficult to refuse his advances. His behavior might depend on what Ginny owed him. Setting aside her personal distaste, she didn't want to do that to her sister.

* * *

Walker
April 19th, 2195, Long Beach
Sunrise: 6:16 a.m. Sunset: 7:27 p.m.

Keep seeing the yellow-eyed girl around town this week. I'm embarrassed and try to stay out of her way. Taken a full-time job as a bouncer at Ginny's. Pay is decent, and she has better food than anywhere in town. Picked up a few shifts before this, but need something regular for food and water. Hayden isn't working and won't leave. The formula he's found is strong. He kites all day, hardly comes down. Worse since the attack on the Heap.

Some girls at Ginny's have been real friendly. If I didn't know how much trouble they could get in for kissing me free of charge, I might consider their offers. Been a long time since I was with a woman. Not since the ladies in Santa Fe taught me how to please them before I left home. Hadn't cared until I saw my hawk. Can't get her out of my head.

The boss lady is a sharp old chick, tough as shoe leather, even if she dresses up fancy. Reminds me of mom's old boss, from before we were burnt out in Santa Fe and Hayden and I hit the road. She's an opportunist and would sell anything to make coin. Ginny wouldn't have hired me if I'd been kiting like Hayden or shown any inclination. Gave me a good once over, up and down. Felt like she learned everything about me in one glance. Disconcerting, to say the least. Had someone patch my clothes and lets me shower upstairs.

The yellow-eyed girl didn't look so fierce today. Instead, it looked like her wings were clipped. I'm feeling guilty. If possible, she looks thinner than before. Hungry.

We may have made her life worse. She hasn't been on the Heap, though it's a workday. Wasn't wearing work clothes either. She and her Granny were always the first ones out in the mornings. Haven't seen them on the way back from work all week. Hope the old lady's injuries aren't too serious. Can't afford to be idle in a place like this.

CHAPTER 7: ELSA PLUS WALKER

For the next two mornings, Elsa woke early and made the rounds again to ask about work. She went farther afield, to places she was unaccustomed and hadn't considered, including the railroad. The men laughed at the ridiculous idea of a woman working there. She took along a drawing she'd made of the leaf from the metal cylinder. Would anyone talk to her about the rebellion? One man at the scrapyard recognized the leaf's meaning. She read it in his eyes. But he shook his head without speaking. No information and no job.

Twice in her systematic wander through town, she spotted the hoppers who'd hurt Granny. They had a system. Walker, the good-looking one, would distract people and talk, while Hayden stole insignificant items that fit in his bag or pocket. Walker saw her notice the second time when they were at Vic's. He grinned, perhaps daring her to say something, so she called his bluff.

"Vic, didn't you used to have six cans of peaches by the window?" she said, turning to the kindly proprietor. "I only see four now."

Hayden shot her a look of pure hatred. "They're here on the floor," he said, bending down. He came up with the cans of peaches in his hand. "Someone must have bumped them."

"If you two aren't buying today, why don't you wait outside?" said Vic.

He watched them with narrowed eyes as they went out the door.

Walker winked at her as he left. She couldn't believe they were so bold. Didn't they understand what GreenCorps might do if they were caught? Steep penalties existed for stealing from a corporation store, including deportation to Texas. His amused reaction was unexpected, and she tried to justify their casual theft, to think about why it mattered to her. It didn't harm her, unlike stealing from the Heap. She and Granny were hungry and poor; she didn't dare risk being caught, but it was more than that. Perhaps the young men were more desperate than she imagined or had a unique sense of right and wrong.

"Good catch," Martha said. "They've taken more than half a dozen things the last few weeks, but we haven't caught them in the act." Her mouth pressed flat as she stared out the doorway. "GreenCorps insists we make up the difference."

Vic added a can of peaches to Elsa's order with a wink. "Free of charge."

Her mouth watered in anticipation of the sweet golden fruit.

"Thanks for the peaches. They'll be a special treat."

It was all they had for dinner.

Early the next morning, Elsa left Granny sleeping. She didn't say where she was going, but collected her gear and headed to the Heap. It had been more than a week since she'd been to work. The tunnel had caved in without the sturdy scrap wood and plastic stabilizers she'd taken, although the site didn't appear like it had been raided. So far, other scavengers had respected the boundaries, but it seemed inevitable that someone would poach on a vacant sector.

Rather than start over, she moved the entrance eight feet over, hoping the new shaft would intersect the old once she dug deeper. The work was slow because of constant shoulder checks for intruders or watchers, but she didn't see anyone.

By day's end, all she had for her considerable efforts were a wad of crumpled foil from inside a plastic bag, some game pieces, including a set of five matched dice, and a slotted serving spoon. The new shaft wasn't deep enough yet. She'd found enough for food, not enough for water. She closed the new shaft for the night and took her bracers again, unsure if she'd return tomorrow. Though it wasn't quite the usual quitting time, she headed for the market early.

Vic's eyebrows shot up his forehead when she arrived. "You worked the Heap today." A crease developed between his eyes. "You found a new partner?"

"Just a temporary situation," she said, flipping her sweaty hair back from her face. She'd have to either hack it off or tie it back. Her answer avoided his question.

She left with food for one day. If they could eke out the water tokens for a few weeks while she bought food, maybe she would have time to find a temporary partner, allowing her to decline Jaxon's offer.

The next two days were carbon copies of the first, sparse findings, jangling nerves, and an early quitting time. This was no way to survive.

When Elsa arrived home, Granny wasn't up. Elsa hadn't seen her grandmother anywhere except in bed all week. Elsa had been too busy. A rush of guilt at her neglect washed over her.

"You here, Granny?" The interior of the house was dim as the lights were off. Usually, when someone was home, the main room was lit. Elsa was uneasy about the change.

"Where you been, girl?" Her grandmother's voice was weak but cranky.

"Working. I've got dinner."

"I'm not hungry."

That couldn't be good. Elsa flicked on the overhead light and marched into Granny's tiny room, shoving the curtain aside. Her grandmother was sweaty and flushed. Her eyes were over-bright and glassy. The room had a sickly-sweet odor.

"What's wrong?" said Elsa, trying not to panic.

"My arm hurts. Nothing new. Leave me alone," said her grandmother.

Elsa rested the back of her hand on Granny's forehead. "You're burning up. Show me your arm."

"Nothing to concern you," said her grandmother through clenched teeth.

Elsa ripped the blanket away and exposed her grandmother's arm. It had swollen on one side and flamed an angry red color.

"Why didn't you tell me?" Elsa's voice became strident in her worry. This was the last thing they needed, but hiding it had made it worse. Her heart sank. They couldn't afford another medical bill. The smell might mean the arm was infected inside by the bone. They needed Marcus right away or her grandmother might lose her arm or even her life.

"Leave me be," said Granny. "I'm too old to fuss over. Let me die in peace."

Elsa slammed the door and ran up the street. She wouldn't let Granny die without a fight. Marcus didn't have a clinic and worked out of his house; she hoped he was home. She pounded on his door and was relieved when he answered. He didn't look surprised to see her. In quick tones, she summarized what she'd found.

"I'll get my medicine." He hesitated. "Will you be able to pay for antibiotics? I hate to ask, but I have to know what I'm working with." He rubbed the dark stubble on his jaw.

Elsa swallowed. She could pay, but it would be dear. The stock of water tokens would be next to depleted, leaving only a few. She'd have to go back to Jaxon. Her heart plummeted lower than ever before. She'd once heard an expression about rock bottom. How much farther was it? It must be close.

She nodded. "Do what you need to keep her arm. I want her living and breathing. I've got water tokens, or I can trade them for GreenCorps credit."

"Water tokens are preferred," he said with a nod. "I'm sorry I have to ask, but medicine is expensive and times are tough. They ship antibiotics all the way from Western Canada. If you couldn't pay, my options would be limited. I wouldn't like it, but I could at least make her more comfortable."

"I understand." She didn't have a choice. Granny had taken her and her sister in and looked after them. Her grandmother had saved them, cared for them. Buying medicine was the least Elsa could do, though Granny had never asked for anything in return.

Elsa took a few deep breaths as they returned to Granny. After an injection of strong antibiotics to fight the infection and another thorough examination, Marcus provided antibiotics for a week and a half, accompanied by a stern lecture for his patient. After he left, it was too late in the day to venture to Avery's. After dinner, when Granny had gone back to sleep, Elsa lay in bed running through her options.

She refused to sell the tube, but she also hadn't found any more information about the rebels. Nobody was willing to talk. Deep down, she believed the tube was special, an opportunity if she was brave enough to grab it. She hated the idea of working at Ginny's, but it was her only viable option.

She would try it for a few weeks. She had values and didn't want to compromise them, but survival came first. She might have to bend. The meager take of her solo efforts on the Heap had proven that. Alone, she was too vulnerable to theft, and the take wasn't reliable. She would ignore the premonition that told her to leave town now, to look for the seed bunker.

It was time to talk to Jaxon.

* * *

Saturday morning, she cleaned up the best she could without a mirror and dressed in the clothes from Avery, this time tucking the shirt into her new jeans. There were four remaining water tokens in the safe. She'd decided to ask Avery to take Granny into her home for a few months. She'd give them three water tokens, so they'd know she was contributing. Granny wouldn't be a burden. The cylinder was her insurance policy. If everything went to shit at Ginny's, she could hop a train to Riverside and search for the site on the map.

Granny was in no shape to walk to Avery's and Elsa hoped Jaxon would arrange for transport, maybe one of the pedal cabs from the train station. With her pride tamped down as far as it would go and a lump blocking her throat, Elsa knocked on the door at Avery and Jaxon's. This time, when Avery answered the door, she recognized her sister right away.

"I didn't know if you'd be back," said Avery, biting her lip and glancing inside.

"Granny's arm got infected. I used most of the savings for medicine," Elsa said as she stepped in. "Can Granny stay here to recuperate?" She hated asking for yet another favor. "If I'm working at Ginny's, I can't care for her. I shouldn't leave her at home alone for long. She didn't tell me she was worse. I found out yesterday, and it was almost too late." Her voice cracked on the last words.

"We should check with Jaxon." Avery's eyes darted to the open door of her husband's office.

"Of course. I can contribute the last of the water tokens for her upkeep," said Elsa. "It isn't much, but it's all I have." Three tokens wouldn't matter to a household like this, but Avery knew their value, even if Jaxon might sneer. "This would just be for a couple of months until the infection is healed, and she's back on her feet." She hoped she was telling the truth. Life without Granny would be bleak.

Avery's eyes glistened, and a tear escaped. Maybe she didn't think Jaxon would agree.

A chair in the office scraped as it was pushed back on the hard floor. Jaxon's heavy tread neared as he joined them in the entryway.

"Elsa, come to take me up on my offer?"

"I have. But I have one concern. If I'm not home, I can't look after Granny."

"I'm sure Avery wouldn't mind having her grandmother here for a while." Jaxon licked his lips.

Avery and Elsa exchanged a quick glance of surprise. That was easier than expected, as it wasn't like him to do something that wasn't for personal gain.

He scrutinized Elsa from head to toe and said, "We should go to Ginny's right away and make arrangements. I'll take you myself and introduce the two of you. Ease your way."

"Thank you." Elsa stood tall, but she was shaking inside and her stomach fluttered. She and Granny had always looked after themselves and set their own terms. They'd been their own bosses and in charge of their fate, though it had been an illusion. One accident and their entire way of life had vanished. This was foreign territory. They'd never had much, but she'd kept her pride. Until now.

"I'll arrange for your grandmother to be brought here this afternoon. Avery can fix up a room on the main floor today, can't you?" he said, turning to his wife.

Avery nodded. "Thank you, Jaxon. You take such good care of us."

The gaze he sent Avery was filled with warmth. Elsa was glad he wasn't looking to replace his wife. Maybe he was helping because he truly cared about Avery. Maybe he wasn't all bad.

He collected his hat, put on his boots, and they left. It was about a fifteen-minute walk down the hill into town. They marched in silence, keeping their thoughts to themselves. They were across from the sturdy two-story brick building around the corner from the train station where Ginny operated her business when he spoke.

"Ginny can outfit you with more real clothes. You clean up nice."

"Thank you," she said, staring at the scarlet doors as her unease grew. Loud music spilled outside into the street from the bars beyond. She swallowed, steeling her nerves for the upcoming interview.

"You might wonder why I'm arranging this." He watched her from the side as they walked.

"Yes," she said, wondering what he'd say. It wasn't out of the goodness of his heart or even for Avery. There was something in it for him.

Jaxon cocked his head to the side. "My brother asked me to keep an eye out for someone pretty, someone clean. He comes to town off and on and says it's lonely and too quiet. He could use companionship and conversation. I thought of you."

She doubted his brother wanted conversation. Her skin crawled as she shifted her feet, moving further from Jaxon without being obvious. She took a deep breath. Maybe she wouldn't work here long enough to spend time with his brother.

"When is he due?"

"Jace is coming later this month, maybe next. Is that a problem? You look young and innocent, but you're old enough to know what I'm getting at."

"I don't have experience providing companionship." Her mouth twisted on the last word.

"You won't get any other experience. You're not here to service the others. You'll serve drinks and are off-limits otherwise. Show a little gratitude."

She bit her tongue. At least he wasn't expecting her to be a full-time whore—just part-time—for his brother.

He held her gaze. "You want the job or not?"

She felt desperate and small. She didn't want the job, and she didn't like Jaxon. She didn't like his brother, Jace, even if she knew little about him. None of that was the issue. What would she do to stay alive? She and Granny were days from being without food or water, with no other way to get more.

Jaxon took two steps toward her. His hard eyes drilled into her.

"Can you show him a good time when he's in town? This is the only chance you have to back out. Once your Granny's under my roof and Ginny's given you food, clothes, and a job, you're committed. Say, for six months, or until your grandmother is mobile enough to work the Heap, whichever comes first."

Elsa remembered Marcus' words. Granny might never work the Heap again. She swallowed. She couldn't dwell on that prospect.

"What's Jace like?" The question was to stall, delay the job interview. The answer didn't matter, much.

"Hard-working GreenCorps man. Like me. Handsome enough. It's not relevant though, is it? A tasty piece like you might help him settle down a little. I could use his help with a business venture and want him happy. He has the right contacts to make my idea successful."

Elsa bit her lip. She'd known this wouldn't be easy. Feeling her virtue spiraling down a drain, she didn't trust herself to speak, so she gave a single curt nod.

"Smart choice. Let's go."

Ginny's was one of the pleasure houses that sat together on a block near the railroad station and behind the more traditional businesses and pubs. It seemed busy every time she'd walked past. The business wasn't technically open yet as it was before noon, but the doors stood wide open. It would be jumping by dinnertime and stay that way until close, well after midnight. They gave patrons a pass to get home after curfew. Granny had warned Elsa to stay away from the pleasure houses, but this one in particular. Ginny ran gambling tables and catered to a rough clientele.

Of course, that had made Elsa more curious. She'd snuck in the back once when she'd been fourteen and had been scandalized by the half-dressed women lounging on the couches. Many of them had vacant expressions, clearly kiting. The drugs Ginny supplied were said to be potent. It looked much the same as Elsa remembered, though the women sat at a table eating breakfast. Most of them looked alert, and the food smelled amazing. Beneath the scent of cooked meat and fried potatoes, the air smelled of smoke and the pervasive scent of stale beer and wine.

Elsa avoided drinking because it was expensive, but also because she'd seen how consuming it could be for some, like her father. Others, like Jaxon, had a few drinks from time to time but didn't seem possessed by it. He was unpredictable enough without an addiction.

The walls inside the main bar room were painted deep red and reminded her of blood. The room held fifteen round tables, each spacious enough for five or six men to sit in comfort. At the front was a raised bar counter with ten additional stools. Behind the bar, shelves of alcohol rose toward the ceiling in labeled bottles of clear, brown, green, and pale blue.

"Jaxon," said Ginny, coming across the room from behind the bar.

She was nearing sixty with faded strawberry locks, but had the look of a former beauty with sharp eagle eyes. She saw everything. Her tight skirt and low-cut shirt left little to the imagination. The appreciation of Ginny's figure gleamed in Jaxon's eyes.

The older woman sashayed over and kissed Jaxon on the mouth, leaving a crimson smudge of lipstick.

"Have you brought me a new pet, Love?" The older woman stepped back to examine Elsa from a couple of angles.

"My sister-in-law needs a serving job," he said. "Just on the main floor unless my brother and I come for business. Only then can she serve upstairs. I'll pay for those nights so you don't feel like I've left you short-handed."

"She's pretty scrawny," said Ginny, pursing her lips. "Nice eyes, though."

They spoke about her as though she wasn't there.

"You'd be thin too if you worked the Heap from dawn till dusk for subsistence rations," Elsa snapped.

"Ooh, and a sharp tongue too," Ginny said, clicking her tongue and shaking her head, but a spark of interest entered her look.

Her pale rose-gold locks swayed back and forth, and her generous breasts jiggled as she rocked on her toes. It was hard for Elsa to look away.

"She'll behave. She needs the job. For three squares and tips, she can learn. Besides," he said with a wink, "Some of your regulars like'em sassy. She can warm them up and your girls can bring it home. She won't be competition."

Ginny pursed her lips. "What if someone wants you to go down on him in the back?"

Elsa shook her head. She wasn't sure what that entailed, but she recognized a test. "Stab them with my knife. Tell them to talk to one of your girls instead."

Ginny roared with laughter, a harsh, grating sound. "Jaxon, Honey, I like her." She nodded in approval. "She's green, but I like your bait and switch idea." She turned to Elsa. "You don't poach from my girls and we'll do okay. No kissing, no freebies. It'll give my place a bad name."

"I've never kissed anyone," said Elsa. "It sure as hell won't be for coin."

"I'm liking you better and better," said Ginny. "We'll get you some short skirts, some tall boots, and put a little meat on your bones and you're going to be popular."

Elsa hated how that sounded. Like she was an object, not a person. She didn't like the idea of parading around to turn men on, but appreciated that the expectations were clear. She wouldn't have to do more than serve drinks and let them ogle.

"When would you like me to start?" she said, lifting her chin to appear brave. Inside, she quaked.

"We'll get you set up and start you tonight," said Ginny. "Nothing like fresh blood working the floor on a busy weekend. I'll have one of the girls find you more suitable clothes."

"Thanks, Ginny. Knew I could count on you." Jaxon shook the older woman's hand and kissed her cheek.

"I appreciate your business," said Ginny. "This sounds mutually beneficial."

"What do you have to say to me?" Jaxon said, turning to Elsa.

"Thank you. I appreciate the chance to work."

"I'll leave you two to say your goodbyes," said Ginny. "I'll send Annie over in a minute. She should be done with breakfast."

While Ginny and Jaxon had spoken, several of the girls had watched the breakfast entertainment. Now they faced in different directions. Jaxon grabbed Elsa's arm and hauled her outside onto the porch, where they were alone.

"You catch the part about where my brother and I come for business?"

She nodded and broke out in a cold sweat. She glanced down the street, but there was no one to overhear. The rest of the job sounded okay, but Jaxon's condition was going to be the problem. She would deal with it when the time came. With luck, Jace wouldn't come to town often. Lost in thought, it took her off-guard when Jaxon shoved her against the outside wall. She couldn't see the others inside and doubted they could see her, either.

He ground his hips against her. "How 'bout a kiss for finding you a job?"

She shook her head. Up close, his breath reeked of garlic. Her stomach lurched, repulsed by him. Not by his looks or what he'd eaten, but by his character. "That's not part of the deal."

"Wait and see." He sucked on the side of her neck and squeezed her breast through her shirt. It hurt, but she held still. She wouldn't give him the satisfaction of seeing how scared she was.

"I can't wait to come to Ginny's one night when you've got one of those short skirts on," he said. "You'll have a fun time with my brother."

Bile rose in her throat.

He grabbed her hand and pressed it to his crotch. "Feel how hard I am. That's a compliment. I can be patient, but you owe me for this job. You're going to give it up to me, eventually. I don't mind a little game of chase, as long as I win." He licked her neck and sucked. When she leaned away, her mouth tasted of rot.

"I'll be back soon to check on your progress. Listen to Ginny and be a good girl. Stay away from her special formula. It'll kill you quick."

Elsa tried not to flinch as he stepped away. She was in over her head.

She would work a few shifts. Tonight, tomorrow, the next couple of days. The southbound train came through Tuesdays. By then, Granny would be settled and Elsa could run. She didn't know how to hop a train, but how tough could it be? The thought was fleeting. She couldn't leave Granny or even Avery—they were the only family she had.

Smothering the idea of leaving, she took a deep breath. She would have to figure out how to make it work.

Jaxon was already off the porch and striding back toward his house when she noticed Walker standing in the shadows between this building and the next. Her cheeks burned. Had the hopper heard Jaxon's threats? Would she have trouble with him, too? She clenched her jaw and refused to cry. She looked back, but he was gone.

"Are you the new server?" said a buxom blonde, appearing in the doorway. "Ginny sent me to get you cleaned up and dressed. Show you the ropes."

Elsa nodded and squared her shoulders. "I'm Elsa."

"Annie," said the other woman with a gentle smile. "Come on in."

* * *

Walker
April 23rd, 2195, Long Beach
Sunrise: 6:12 a.m. Sunset: 7:30 p.m.

The young hawk took a job at Ginny's today. Don't like the idea of her working here. Nothing good will come of it. Some railroad bigshot set it up. Wonder how she got mixed up with him. Doesn't seem like he'd be her type. He struts around town like he owns it. He's one of the GreenCorps men who lives up the hill in the old stone houses, the ones big enough for several families.

He had my hawk pinned against the wall. She looked desperate to fight to get away. Wondered if I should have stepped in, but he's friends with Ginny. I can't jeopardize my job. The girl glared at me when he'd gone, those yellow eyes boring into my soul. Should I have stopped him?

Chapter 8: Elsa plus Walker

Annie took Elsa upstairs. Behind the first door on the left, a long closet stretched, filled with real fabric garments on both sides. Some looked almost new. The clash of riotous pastel colors assaulted her eyes.

"Who do these belong to?" Elsa struggled to get her bearings.

"Ginny. Some were left behind, some she bought. We all borrow whatever fits. Our favorites we keep with our stuff for a while. Not a lot will fit you right now. You're pretty thin."

Annie opened drawers and removed a handful of lace scraps and two bras.

"This underwear might fit." She tossed them at Elsa, who caught them.

Underwear? There was nothing to these. She blushed at the thought of wearing skirts with backless underwear. She'd be indecent. Practically naked underneath.

"Ginny suggested tall boots and short skirts." Annie slid several articles from hangers into a bundle over her arm. "You can start with these. What size boots do you wear?"

Elsa shrugged as Annie scooped up two pairs to try. She wore what went on her feet and she could afford. Both pairs had heels. One set looked familiar. She'd found them on the Heap last year and traded them at Vic's. She took another look at the hanging clothes. A couple of dresses also looked like things she'd found, just washed and pressed. Thinking about their origin made them less overwhelming. Not everything from the Heap was trash.

She and Annie left the closet. At the end of the hallway, Annie showed her to the spacious bathroom, which contained three bathtubs, three sinks, and a shower stall. Nothing matched, but everything appeared to be in decent condition, without rust or missing paint. The moist smell of damp towels and floral soap filled the steamy air, but the bathroom was unoccupied. Ginny's girls had either used it already or wouldn't for a while. Annie turned the taps on in the white tub in the corner.

"You know about baths, right?" said Annie.

At Elsa's pointed look, she said, "Some girls don't when they get here. Rule is a bath or shower every day. Only two inches of water in the tub or four minutes in the shower."

"Every day?" Elsa's eyes widened.

"That's why our house is the best," said Annie. "Ginny feeds us and ensures everyone is clean and disease-free. The customers count on it. Costs them more." She shrugged. "Ginny gets the extra unless it's an actual tip."

When the water reached the prescribed level, Annie shut off the flow. She started the water in a second tub.

"I'm just serving drinks," said Elsa.

"For now." Annie's answer was matter of fact. "Maybe you'll want to move up to the second floor at some point. Better coin by far. I started out just serving too. For the first year."

Elsa couldn't imagine working here for a year. This was temporary.

"Put your stuff in here. Your bag too," said Annie, showing her a cupboard with a lock. She handed her a key. "Lock it when you're not here. Keep the key in your bra or your boot. Some of the girls are dirty thieves. Once they're on the junk, they'll steal anything to buy more."

Elsa tossed her bag with her metal tube into the locker. She carried the tube with her wherever she went.

"When you've chosen what fits, keep the work clothes in the locker."

Annie handed Elsa a metal device with short parallel blades above a handle.

"What's this?"

"A razor. I'll show you how to shave. Legs and everywhere else, too."

Annie laughed at Elsa's widened eyes and shucked her clothes, unconcerned about modesty. She turned off the water in the second tub and fastened her hair into a knot on top of her head with an elastic.

Elsa had never seen another woman's body, other than her wrinkled great-grandmother's. Nothing like Annie, who had high full breasts, wide hips, and creamy soft skin. Her body was hairless, as advertised. Annie didn't seem bothered by Elsa's regard. She stepped into the tub and sat. She lathered a bar of homemade soap that smelled like lavender and rubbed it onto her legs. Placing her foot on the edge of the tub, she demonstrated how to shave, chattering while she instructed.

Elsa shrugged out of her clothes, feeling conspicuous and shy. Next to Annie, she felt more boyish than ever, but her new friend didn't seem to notice her lack of figure.

Elsa slipped into the hot water and emulated what Annie had done, being careful not to put too much pressure on the blade. Annie taught her how to shave the rest of herself and she did as instructed, all the while hoping nobody would see her naked. It felt sexy to be so clean, even if strange. It could be her secret, a confidence booster. Elsa finished washing and dried off. She tried the selected clothes to see what would fit. Annie had a sharp eye and had chosen well. Two skirts, three tops, and the boots with the lower heels were the right size. The clothes seemed scandalous and tight, but Annie approved.

"You'll get great tips."

Elsa felt like one of her niece's dolls being dressed to play with.

"Let's trim your hair," Annie said.

She sat Elsa on a chair and combed Elsa's dark hair and evened out the ends in a couple of layers. The shorter lengths flipped up in curls at the bottom, making her face look softer, her chin less angular.

"Why are you being so kind to me?"

"I was new once, too." Annie's pale blue eyes were wistful as they met Elsa's topaz ones in the mirror. "It would have been nice to have someone to guide me back then." She shook her head. "I'm silly, getting all sentimental. Now the finishing touch."

She used a tiny brush on a roller to apply a thin layer of black paste to Elsa's eyelashes and painted her mouth redder with something from a different jar. She showed her how to spread it with her lips and to wipe off any excess.

"You look smoking hot," she said in approval. "Don't be scared to say you're new if you miss an order or get it wrong. The regulars will know, they'll be happy to see someone fresh, and the others will just drool."

The girl in the mirror with the huge golden eyes and the red mouth was a stranger; with the help of tight clothes, there was the illusion of a figure. Elsa couldn't believe she was the same girl who'd been intimidated out of a day's work. She looked sexy but badass, probably tough enough to make thieves beware.

Annie waited at the foot of the stairs as Elsa descended, learning to navigate the treads while wearing heeled boots. It didn't take long to figure out the knack; it was like traversing the uneven Heap. The heels weren't much higher than her regular scruffy boots, even if they were narrower. She caught sight of Walker lounging in a wooden chair near the door; he stood when he saw her. Her stomach fluttered. He was still here. Why was he hanging around? She couldn't read his expression, but he watched her every step, making her cheeks flame.

"This is Walker," Annie said. "One of the bouncers."

"We've met." Elsa clenched her jaw. He worked here, which might be awkward. She hadn't forgiven him.

"Oh good. If you have trouble with someone who won't take no for an answer, call Walker. Not like a pinch or a little grab, but if someone gets rough or pushy or wants a freebie, he'll come running."

His gray eyes stayed on her face, which she appreciated, though her blood still boiled. She had no desire to be dependent on him for anything.

"Didn't expect to see you here," he said.

"The feeling is mutual," she said, trying to tug her skirt lower without being obvious. "My brother-in-law got me the job since I can't work the Heap without my partner. Some assholes put us out of business for a season or two."

"Look," said Walker, "I…"

"Holy shit," said Ginny, coming out of the back room. "They're going to love you, Honey." She turned to Annie. "Tell Lana and Daisy to get ready to be busy. Brunettes are about to be the thing. You're all legs and eyes, girl."

Elsa seethed about being on display, though she was glad that Ginny approved of her appearance. For all the woman seemed friendly, there were lines by the sides of her mouth that indicated she could also be hard. Elsa wanted to avoid her boss's disapproval. She suspected Ginny had to be tough in this business, especially to have survived and risen to the top. She was the owner, not the entertainment.

Annie waved. "I've got to get myself ready, too. See you later. You'll do great."

"Come with me. I'll show you the job." Ginny led Elsa behind the bar. "First rule. No drinking on the job unless a customer pays. Too many girls think I won't find out, but I always do. The first time, I'll dock your pay, the second time you're fired for stealing. No plea will change my mind."

Elsa nodded. She wasn't planning to drink.

"Second rule. Wait for the bartender to make the drinks. You aren't qualified. Third rule. Smile and hustle. Walk fast, they'll think you're hurrying, even if you're slow at the table. Everyone wants the server to move, especially if they like watching your ass."

"How will I keep the drinks straight?" Elsa looked at the wall of alcohol-laden shelves. The bottles held different colors of alcohol, but she couldn't identify any.

"We'll start simple. Beer is easy. We'll fill mugs and it foams." Ginny lifted a mug. "Wine is easy too, with wide glasses. I only serve red." She held up a short glass with a rounded bottom. "Other drinks the bartender will make, but there's only one fancy one a day, the special. Depends if we have juice or something to mix. Otherwise, it's shots. If they ask for a double, tell the bartender. Got that?"

"I think so." Elsa bit her lip, caught herself, and stopped.

"It's about noon and the first patrons should be here soon. Someone sits at a table, then they're yours. Ask what you can get them. If they sit at the bar, I got it."

The first few men straggled in and greeted Ginny by name. They sat at the bar. The boss talked to them and served them drinks before they asked. They must be regulars. Ginny used a bottle marked "Whiskey" for one and poured frothy mugs of beer for the others.

Once all the men had drinks, she introduced Elsa with a casual wave. Ginny held a glass of whiskey in one hand which she sipped from time to time.

"This is Elsa, Jaxon McCoy's sister-in-law. Here to serve drinks for a bit."

The woman half-winked at Elsa.

She'd dropped Jaxon's name to make it clear Elsa was off-limits.

"Just drinks?" said the tall man with a glass of whiskey. He gave Elsa the up-and-down look that she'd better get used to. Speculative and lustful. She stared until he met her eyes and flinched.

"Just drinks," said Ginny with a bolder wink. "But Daisy's free this afternoon."

"Maybe, maybe," said the man, returning his attention to Ginny and the conversation at the bar. Elsa stood straighter and lifted her chin.

A group of four men with the thick plastic covering of laborers entered and sat together at a table. Elsa took their orders. She repeated the list to check it and smiled, her stomach fluttering with nerves, but she had the order correct. She hurried to the bar.

Ginny put the drinks on a tray and said, "Don't spill."

Annie and a dark-haired girl came downstairs and sat at a table with a deck of cards and were joined by another pair of men in GreenCorps uniforms. Elsa took their orders.

The man from the bar who'd ordered whiskey turned to the girls at the table and crooked his finger. "Daisy, I hear you're free this afternoon."

She tittered. "I'm never free, but I'm available."

He smiled. She took his hand and led him upstairs. Her hips swayed with each step. Other eyes from the bar followed until the couple were out of sight.

Elsa supplied the men at the original table with their second round, relaying their order to Ginny at the bar. As it got busier, a surly man with black curly hair and dark skin who didn't speak, replaced Ginny, and poured the drinks Elsa requested. She made a point of remembering who ordered what and was pleased that she didn't get confused, even when it got busy.

Twice, Annie gave her a slight nod or a smile when she passed by her table. By four o'clock it was hectic, and Elsa hurried from table to table. She couldn't keep up with all the customers, but noticed that Ginny's girls handled the bulk of the work after the first round. Often, they sat with the men or were pulled onto someone's lap with a giggle. Ginny had a dozen girls besides Elsa working the crowd.

As Elsa hustled around the room and to the bar and back, they pinched her several times. Three times men grabbed her ass, but she kept moving and ignored them. If she could, she caught someone's eye with a glare. They dropped their eyes first. It was degrading, but she'd expected it. It was part of the job.

Before she realized, it was well after midnight and the occupied tables were taken care of by the other girls, most of whom had been upstairs and back several times. Elsa was dropping from fatigue after a thirteen-hour shift. Other than a short afternoon break for a sandwich, she'd been on her feet all day. The bartender, whose name she discovered was Wes, finally spoke.

"You did good, Kid. Hot food in the back. You should eat." He picked up a small jar, half-full of plastic tokens, several pennies, and a nickel. He shook it. The hard plastic chips and vintage coins clinked inside.

She looked at him, her eyebrows raised. "What's this?"

"Your tips. There's extra for being new. You worked your ass off. Real good for a new girl. You're off the clock. Do you want a drink? You earned one."

She declined with a shake of her head. "Food sounds good, though." She examined the stack of tokens in the jar with wonder. There was more there than she made in two weeks on the Heap. She'd be able to save a bunch if she worked for a few weeks.

"You go eat. I'll keep the jar until you leave."

Refusing to drink, she may have passed a test. Wes no longer seemed surly.

She smiled. "Thanks."

The table at the back had stacks of plates at one end and chairs down both sides. Cooked food sat on enormous platters and deep dishes, steaming hot from the oven. It lined the sideboard. There was meat, potatoes, bread, some kind of roasted orange vegetable, and stew. She hadn't been to a meal with so much food before. She was unsure what to eat first, but decided to try everything. She poured herself a glass of water and filled a plate. She didn't know the names of the other girls at the table, most of whom were polite but not friendly. A few stared vacantly without touching the food on their plates. Others, like her, were hungry and quick to eat.

"Walker, come here," said Ginny.

Elsa kept eating, but she listened as the owner's voice carried. She angled her head to watch with her peripheral vision. She usually minded her own business, but despite her dislike of the man, she was interested in what was going on with Walker. He joined Ginny near the bar.

"Your brother's into me for another measure. He hasn't quite paid off the last one, but he said he needed it now. I know you'll work it off for him. You have an additional duty from now on. You're going to walk Elsa home after her shift and dinner. Got it?"

"Yes ma'am," he said. "She's not staying here?"

"Rooms are just for my girls. Elsa has her own place. She just serves drinks."

Ginny called across the room. "Elsa, Honey, you just about done dinner? Walker's going to see you get home. He's got a pass to get there and back."

Why had Ginny proclaimed it to the entire room? Then it clicked. The announcement was for the benefit of the few remaining customers or those lingering out front. Elsa was off-limits and had protection.

She stacked her dirty plate with the others at the side; her full stomach ached in a pleasant way. She collected her tip jar from Wes and emptied it into her hand. It had weight and was a substantial handful of tokens. More than she'd ever had at one time. Plus the coins.

"Thanks for making sure I get home," she said to Ginny. "Can I run up and change?"

Ginny nodded. "See you before noon tomorrow. Clean up before your shift, same as today. Good work. You'll get paid at the week's end. I pay every Friday."

Elsa smiled and ran upstairs, her throbbing feet forgotten. She would make a separate wage besides the tips. There would be more coin. Was this what it felt like to be rich? She shoved the tokens in her bag but left the coins in her locker. She changed back into her regular clothes and boots as fast as possible. She didn't want Walker to wait, nor did she want to spend additional time in his company. She didn't like being forced to spend time with him, but walking the streets alone at night was dangerous. Pass or no pass, a GreenCorps patrol under Wade's command might be a problem.

"I'm ready," she said when she returned to the main floor.

Walker followed her out the door, and they headed for her neighborhood. As they left the pleasure houses and bars behind, it grew quiet.

Elsa broke the silence first. "I'm surprised you're still in town. I thought you were leaving. You can go anywhere. Why stay here?"

"Hayden likes Ginny's formula. Got us in debt because he likes it too much." He stuffed his hands in his pockets as they strolled. "Ordinarily, we would've hopped a train by now, but he wants to stick around. He's been kiting for weeks. Said it's the best he's found."

His face was invisible in the dark, but his tight voice held concern.

"Maybe it would be better for him if you made him get on a train, anyway." It wasn't her business, but Elsa couldn't help but offer advice.

"Might be true," he said. "Hard to force people to do what they don't want, though."

They walked a little farther, then he spoke again.

"I'm sorry about your grandmother. Attacking her was stupid. I feel awful that we messed up your life."

She turned her glare on him and the bitterness she carried seeped into her words. "She's a hundred. You knocked over an old lady for water tokens. It was pretty low."

"I'm sorry. I have a job, but Hayden doesn't. Thought he was making coin legit, not just stealing. He buys more drugs and adds to the debt before we're clear."

"Sorry's just a word. It doesn't mean much. I never would've taken a job like this if I wasn't desperate for credits for medical bills."

"You made good tips tonight," said Walker. "Pay your bills. Get out after a few days."

"Then do what? I've got to eat. I can't make a living without a partner. GreenCorps patrols steal my take." Her voice was bitter. She half-expected Wade to materialize as if called. The lump of tokens in her satchel might be obvious. She was aware of its bulge and the subtle clink. While this was a better way to make a living, her instincts told her that slinging drinks wasn't what she was meant to do.

"Ginny's for a few months, then. Nothing wrong with getting ahead."

"Look, my making coin doesn't let you off the hook. Walking me home doesn't erase your debt. We're not friends. Not going to braid each other's hair. One of these nights, my brother-in-law is going to force himself on me or whore me out to his brother. It's inevitable." Her voice shook with rage. "I can't stay long, no matter how much I make. Even if it's tempting to save up. If Granny dies, I'm going to do what you said and hop a train and ride out of here."

It surprised her she'd said so much to a stranger, but he'd heard Jaxon on the porch and had some idea what she faced.

"Let me know if you need some pointers," he said in a quiet voice. "With the train."

"It might be better if we don't talk when you walk me home." She stopped in front of her house. "This is me."

The house was dark, and the street was quiet at this hour.

She considered his offer while she watched him leave after she unlocked the door. Walker was hard to hate. He seemed easy-going and was respectful to women. He seemed genuinely sorry, but he'd broken her grandmother's arm. Some of this mess was his fault. She spoke with confidence, but she wasn't convinced she could hop a train, even with assistance. This was her home. Everything out in the world was unknown.

* * *

Walker
April 24th, 2195, Long Beach
Sunrise: 6:11 a.m. Sunset 7:31 p.m.

Her name is Elsa. When she turned her hawk eyes on me this afternoon at Ginny's, they blazed with fury, even if her words were polite. Wasn't more than I deserved. I wronged her and I'm sorry. Haven't felt like I owed someone in a long time. Until now. Since mom died, the only person I've been close to is Hayden, and the balance sheet tips the other direction. If I cared who did more favors, I'd have left him long ago.

Seems Hayden and I fucked up her life more than I realized. What we did almost turned out to be as bad as the fire when our lives got wrecked. She can't work the Heap and we're responsible. Working at Ginny's will rob her of her independence, at the least. May also steal her virtue and her dignity.

The squeeze is on in Long Beach over water. Heard guys were talking about striking for better conditions in the scrapyards. Rebels may have influenced their plans. GreenCorps got wind of the rumors and they have locked this place down. Train security is heightened. Wasn't hard to get here, will be harder to leave. Imagine they're going to keep tightening their grip. Keep everyone poor, too weak to fight back. This place makes a profit for GreenCorps because the raw materials they haul out of here cost them so little in wages.

Just found out I won't get paid at week's end. Somehow Hayden weaseled my pay out of Ginny in advance. Saw the "not sorry" look in her eyes when she gave me the news. She's got him on the hook. Easiest way for her to get her share is to take my wages. She might think she owns me too, but I'll quit when it's time. Pay or no pay. Haven't decided when to go, but I'm not staying here much longer.

Walked Elsa home after her shift finished near two a.m. Just some ramshackle place near the Heap. One pieced together with slabs of wood, cinder blocks, and brick with rusty old metal siding and cracked solar panels on the roof. Tried to apologize, but there wasn't much to say. But, if I'm keeping her safe from the creeps at night, I'm paying her back for what I did. It's the least I can do. Even if Ginny didn't ask, I'd continue.

Conditions in Long Beach are appalling. It's dangerous here at night and Elsa's one of Ginny's investments. Poor girl is slinging drinks right now, but Ginny's grooming her to be a whore. I can tell. Once you start that life, you never get out. Not until you're dead or too old to do it anymore. Mom said it was temporary when she started. Look how that turned out.

Chapter 9: Caitlyn

April 25th, 2195

Dearest Mathew,

The rebels sent me home after the failed mission in Dallas and gave me all your back pay. Widows get first dibs. I wanted to cash out and go. It was enough that I felt rich. By buying seeds and young animals on the black market in Salt Lake City, I stretched the funds to make a proper start. I was careful with my windfall and now I'm back at the farm. The farmhands are gone and there's a lot of work to do by myself, but I'm capable. Most of the time I don't mind, unless I'm too tired at night to write to you. I don't enjoy being around other people right now. I'm disappointed with everyone. Most of all, myself.

Everywhere I turn, I expect to see you and I'm disappointed when you're not here. Still, I'd rather be on the farm than somewhere you've never been. I couldn't take patching together injured kids anymore. They just got shot again, taking too many chances. I wish there was a way for them to balance courage and invincibility. Sometimes I can't sleep at night and feel like a coward for choosing to make a different life that is so safe. But safe is alive.

Caitlyn chewed on the end of her pen, contemplating what else to say in her letter. It wasn't like he could read it, but she'd been alone since last fall. She'd started writing to Mathew to feel less lonely, but she had little to say. Every day was the same. She got up at dawn, worked until dusk. Her medic skills were going to get rusty, but perhaps that was best. She wanted to avoid any more catastrophes.

Her muscles ached from hard work, and her heart yearned for company. There was no one to talk to and very little to break up the monotony. She stared out the window at the sunset glow on the horizon that extended to the limit of her vision. The colors bled into the overcast sky. The vibrant pink and orange sky was beautiful, but she preferred the view of the mountains to the east.

Sometimes the flat plains seemed too open, too exposed, especially if she went as far as the salt flats. It was like someone had taken a rolling pin and flattened the land. Parts of Utah were beautiful in different ways, the stark orangish mountains, the cracked plain, and the greenery on the bench near the mountains where she lived.

A scratching noise at the door diverted her attention from writing. She considered ignoring it, but she was too curious not to check.

"Better not be that egg-sucking raccoon." Caitlyn got up with a few groans and stretches to ease her muscles.

She spoke aloud because it was a relief to speak. It was almost like there was someone to hear her. She set her notebook on the kitchen table and tiptoed to the door so she wouldn't scare whatever was out there away. She grabbed her rifle from its position next to the door and checked that it was loaded. She eased the door open just enough to peer outside through the crack. Nothing. She slid the barrel through the opening and swiveled to look at the barn, the chicken coop, and the compost pile. Nothing. It also had better not be one of her neighbors snooping or spying for GreenCorps.

She opened the door another fraction. She stepped out to investigate when something scraped her boot. She looked down in astonishment. A furry white paw reached around the door and tapped her foot again. It wasn't a raccoon paw. It was white velvet with claws. A cat? So far from other houses, this was rare and unexpected. Where had it come from? Perhaps it had wandered over from a distant neighbor.

Out of curiosity, Caitlyn slid her foot to the side and opened the door another few inches. Without warning, a streak of brown and white shot into the room, the cat's body brushing her legs as it darted between. She closed the door and turned to see where the strange cat had gone—she hadn't meant to let it in.

The tabby cat hopped onto the chair Caitlyn had just vacated, turned around twice, and lowered itself onto its haunches. It stared at her with its tawny yellow eyes, as if daring her to make it move.

"No, you don't. That's where I was sitting." She stopped with her arms crossed a few paces from the cat.

The cat stared her down, not budging at her words. It acted as if it belonged here, though Caitlyn never seen it before. Mathew hadn't mentioned his parents owning a cat. It wasn't scared of her. It seemed used to people, not like the feral cats that slunk through the fields with a fat mouse or rat draped from their mouths. All the same, she approached this one with caution.

Its fur was sleek and well-groomed. It was young and scrawny, but looked healthy otherwise. She didn't have any close neighbors and didn't know where it had come from. Perhaps it had lived with someone who'd died. Her heart swelled. Maybe it needed a home, someone to take care of it.

The cat purred and squinted its eyes as it kneaded the afghan on her chair, its claws working in and out on the small paws. Its rumbly purr was the loudest sound in the room.

"No, you don't. Don't get too comfortable. That's still my spot."

Fearing for her hand if the cat's mood changed, she was careful as she picked up the half-grown cat, cradling it against her chest and arm. It was warm and its fur was the softest she'd ever known. Its purr intensified. She sat in her chair, tugging the blanket onto her lap, and placed the cat upon it. She expected the animal to jump down. The cats she'd known when she was younger wouldn't have put up with being moved to a new position, but this one didn't seem to mind.

At first, Caitlyn didn't dare move and just stroked the cat. The cat stood, turned around to curl into a ball, and rested its head on her knee. Caitlyn held her breath for a minute and then relaxed. The tabby cat had beautiful markings, with both swirls and stripes, a crooked white blaze across its little nose, and four white feet.

Caitlyn picked up her book and read for another hour until her head nodded. She slid out from under the cat, giving it the chair it had claimed while she went to clean up for bed. She grabbed her notebook from the table. She'd try to write her letter again from bed. At least she had something new to write about now.

She pumped water into the basin in the kitchen and washed, getting ready to sleep. She peeked at the cat before crossing the floor to the roomier of the two bedrooms at the back of the brick farmhouse. It showed no interest in her as it slept.

She picked up the kerosene lamp and brought it with her into the bedroom and set it down on the bedside table. She changed into her worn flannel pajama pants and one of Mathew's shirts. It didn't smell like him anymore, but she wore it for comfort just the same. She picked up her pen and her notebook. She would write a quick note before retiring for the night and added onto the bit from earlier.

April 25th, 2195
A cat has invited itself into the house. I didn't have the heart to send it away. It would be nice to have company. If it's interested in staying tomorrow, I'll find something to feed it. As long as she's here, I'll call her Mittens.
Thinking of you,
Your Caitlyn

She shut the notebook's cover, hiding the letter within, turned down the lamp, and slid into the cool sheets, the warm coverlet's weight settling over her as she closed her eyes. The expanse of bed stretched out beside her, as empty as ever.

CHAPTER 10: ELSA PLUS WALKER

The next three weeks flew by in a flash. Each day, Elsa cleaned up, worked hard, and ate proper food. Walker accompanied her home after her shift. Each night, he dropped her off as soon as she unlocked her door and left without a glance. He didn't engage her in conversation again. Her words the first night might have been a little harsh, but she wasn't looking to make friends, especially with someone temporary. He could be gone tomorrow or next week. She didn't need anyone beyond her family.

Elsa appreciated his company on the two occasions they ran into Wade and his patrol. Both times Walker stepped between her and the GreenCorps recruits. The soldiers backed off when they saw Walker, who carried a handgun on loan from Ginny and a sharp knife. With broad shoulders and hard muscles, he carried himself like he knew how to fight. It was something about his walk.

A couple of times before work, Hayden wandered across her path, staring at his hands or stumbling down the street. Was Walker still paying for his brother's drugs? It didn't seem like the right thing to do, though she kept her opinion to herself.

With her weekly wages and tips, Elsa bought a new stack of water tokens, a change of clothes for herself and Granny, as well as new, refinished boots for everyday. She stored the water tokens and a supply of food bars in the hidden safe. On Sundays, she visited Granny and told her about the stockpile of supplies.

By the conclusion of the second week, Granny wanted to move home. She disliked being underfoot and complained about being a burden on Avery. Her grandmother's ankle had almost healed, but she hobbled more than before her injury and took a nap each afternoon. She tired easily. At her age, a slowdown was a major setback, and it seemed like she was fading. Elsa wasn't certain Granny should come home yet, even if home was quiet and strange without her. Granny would be alone all day; at least at Avery's, she had company.

Despite her gruffness, Granny adored Avery's little girls. She would sit for hours and entertain the toddler. If Jaxon would let Granny stay, this was a much better life for someone well-past retirement age. Elsa couldn't live under the same roof with Jaxon, but perhaps Granny could stay.

Striding to work, Elsa thought of the conversation with Granny about her job last Sunday. Granny disapproved.

"I don't like you working there. You should quit," Granny had said with a scowl, her mouth pinched tight against the pain and her eyes glassy.

"Jaxon arranged it. It's just until we can get back to work."

Elsa had tried to keep a soothing tone.

"You stay out of Ginny's formula. Even if you're grown, I'll take a switch to you if you kite. That shit will get you killed."

"I won't touch it," Elsa had promised. She hadn't stayed long. It was challenging to see Granny like this and not be able to do something. Maybe the antibiotics she got from Marcus would take care of the infection this time.

The following Thursday morning, Elsa stopped in at Vic and Martha's. She didn't see them daily anymore, but their store was still her preferred place to check for news and to buy things for her growing stash. Vic had promised to keep an ear open for someone looking for a local partner on the Heap. Despite the advantages that coin brought, Elsa missed the freedom of working for herself. She'd paid the yearly license fee to keep their sector, even if they weren't working it right now, just in case.

"Morning, Elsa," Vic said. "You still got that mystery tube?"

She nodded, but didn't reach into her bag.

"I left it at home," she lied. She remembered how it had tingled in her hand when she'd found it. It had felt important; learning the contents had reinforced that idea, even if she had trusted no one to explain what it held. She was reluctant to sell. It represented a feasible way out, even if it was a distant dream.

"I put the word out and found someone who might be interested," Vic spoke fast, the words tumbling over each other like stones on the beach as they left his mouth. His eyes flicked to the other customer.

A burly man who stood at Martha's end of the counter buying two bottles of alcohol turned to face her. "If it's what it sounds like, I'm interested. I collect oddities and I'll pay silver coins, not plastic tokens. Enough for stacks of water tokens."

This man wasn't someone Elsa had seen before. He wore a long-sleeved shirt with a collar and buttons and dressed all in black. He must have coin because his freshly laundered clothes hadn't faded to gray, and his silver-studded boots shone with polish. Like most of the men in town, he wore a beard. His was dark, trimmed, and matched his short hair.

"Cat got your tongue, girl?" he said.

There was something off-putting about his confident manner—an arrogance. She wanted to avoid doing business with him if possible. Her instincts told her she'd regret it.

"Go on, I told him about the tube," said Vic, eager to be helpful.

She ground her back teeth. Vic's talkative nature had been to her advantage before, but now she wished she'd never said a word. She'd talked to him about selling the tube in the beginning, but she'd never been serious. She was glad she hadn't mentioned that it opened or about the key inside.

"I got a good-paying job. I'm not so desperate to sell anymore. It's a keepsake of my old life," she said, forcing herself to look the strange man in the eye.

"Is the tube plain? Or etched?" said the man, his dark eyes boring into her while he waited for an answer.

"There was a picture on it, a leaf or something?" said Vic with a slight frown as he tried to recall the details. "Not the rebel logo, but something similar."

Vic needed to stop helping. Elsa nodded, but didn't add more information. Her sense of unease grew as the strange man's interest remained.

"Since you didn't bring it, why don't we meet here later and you can sell it to me then?" the man said. "Two silver coins should be an enticement."

His persistence brought a deepening sense of concern. What did he know about the tube? Was he aware of the maps and the seed bunkers? Perhaps his interest was the rebel connection. Was he a rebel?

Despite her curiosity, it didn't matter. She wasn't selling.

"I work soon," said Elsa, attempting to keep her tone light. "If you're sticking around for a couple of days, why don't you leave your info with Vic? If I change my mind, I'll be able to contact you."

"I suppose," the man said, scratching at his beard. "How about three silver coins?"

She shook her head. Bargaining? For him to increase the price so fast, he must be very interested. He probably thought he could get the tube, that it was only a matter of time until he found her price. She ground her teeth together, more determined not to sell.

"I'll be in town for a short span for business. Consider my offer."

His gaze raked her from head to toe, giving her a greasy feeling. She wanted to scrub wherever he looked. The past few weeks with regular food had been beneficial for her. She'd never think of herself as beautiful like Avery or Annie, or like Ginny must've been, but she didn't feel as boyish as she once had. His once-over lingered longer than it should've on the gentle swell of her breasts. She balled her hands into fists in her coat pocket.

"Thanks, Vic. Later, Martha." She turned around without making her own purchases, wanting to leave. They could wait until tomorrow. "Give our best to your Granny," said Vic. "I hear she's not well again. Hope it isn't serious.

Elsa nodded. Reports had arrived that Granny was worse, but there was no solution. Elsa had paid for the medicine and had made sure her grandmother was taken care of with no extra expense for Jaxon. Avery had promised to send word of any change.

Elsa dismissed the chance meeting with the arrogant man and her worries about Granny from her mind. She hurried to Ginny's early to get ready for her shift, changing into a lavender blouse with a low neckline and flowing long sleeves with a dark jean skirt. Once, these clothes would have seemed uncomfortable, but she was accustomed to them now. How fast things changed.

When she reached the bar, she clenched her fists. Hayden stood next to the counter. She despised him for his drug use, the way he took advantage of his brother, and most of all for Granny. Her desperate need for tokens had been because of his addiction.

Walker stood in front of him, his muscular arms crossed.

"Just front me enough for another measure," Hayden said, his voice pleading with Walker. "I'm good for it and will pay you back later. I promise."

She willed Walker to turn him down, even though it was none of her business.

"With what?" Walker's mouth pressed flat, frustration clear in his tone. "You aren't working. You aren't even trying to find anything. All you do is kite."

"What's it to you?" said Hayden with an ugly sneer. "I have a lot on my mind." His narrow face flushed. "You aren't my mother or my keeper. Ginny cut me off until I pay for the next measure. Said you'd told her you wanted your wages yourself. You have coin stashed all over

Denver, Salt Lake, and Reno. You don't need this coin. I do. I need it now. C'mon bro. Just one more week's worth."

"No," said Walker. "I gave Ginny my notice. I'm leaving after I get paid. I've taken care of your debt. But no more. You want more drugs. Pay for them yourself. I'm through carrying you. I'm leaving this hellhole. You can join me or not."

His eyes flicked to Elsa by the bar.

Elsa hadn't heard anyone use those words to describe Long Beach before, but all of SoCal was a hellhole. Black grime and layers of dust coated everything, and ninety-five percent of the people were chronically poor and malnourished. The rest were one accident away from joining them in poverty. Garbage landfills, ocean flotsam, and rusted remains of old cars, no longer scavengable, dotted the area. Most people lived in shacks no better than Granny's, if not worse. Life here was limited. If her family hadn't lived here, Elsa would have left already. His words were like a gut punch. This was a place with no future. Of course, he was leaving this GreenCorps prison.

Who would Ginny get to walk her home when Walker was gone? The options made her uncomfortable. One of the other bouncers might want a cut of her tips or demand something in return. She didn't like the idea of risking the trip alone. She would have to leave her coins locked up, or she'd lose them to the likes of Wade, patrolling the streets, looking for an easy mark. Alone, she'd be a sure target.

She would even miss Walker's quiet presence. He'd never laid a finger on her or looked at her wrong. If she hadn't hated him for the incident with Granny, she might even have liked him. It was past time he stood up for himself to Hayden, so she cheered inside for him.

A train arrived that day, so Ginny's was packed from the moment the doors opened. Elsa ate her mid-day meal before her shift and was run ragged by eight when she found time to grab a quick dinner. When she returned to serving drinks, Ginny tossed her head as Elsa turned to the floor. Elsa followed its motion where her boss had indicated, and her heart sank. Jaxon sat at a corner table with three other men. They needed drinks.

Before she took a step, Annie walked past and said, "Jaxon asked for you. Be careful." She squeezed Elsa's arm and continued toward the stairs with an older man with iron-gray hair and solid work boots. One of her regulars. Annie looked back over her shoulder with sympathy.

Elsa took a deep breath and headed for Jaxon's table. Alcoholic fumes rose in waves as the men talked with boisterous voices, not caring who else heard their rambling. Jaxon faced her, and she stayed on the opposite side of the table.

"Elsa, Honey," he said. "You look fantastic. You like working here?"

His eyes lingered on her chest, never making it to her face.

"I appreciate the job."

He was reminding her he'd arranged it, that she owed him.

"I want you to meet my brother, Jace," he said, indicating the burly man on her right. She'd been so focused on Jaxon that she hadn't paid attention to his loud companions. She'd seen the other two before in their GreenCorps uniforms, Wade and one of his friends, but at this introduction, a deep pit opened in her stomach and her body clenched.

"Elsa," Jace said, drawing out her name. "I've heard about you." He pivoted his chair toward her. She tried to keep her shock from showing. He leered as he recognized her, too.

"You're the girl from the trading post this morning. You give any thought to my... offer?"

In front of the other men, he made it sound sexual, not like business. Wade and his fellow recruit elbowed each other and guffawed. She seethed and tried to control her racing heart.

"Not yet."

Jace's hard stare made her feel naked. Deep down, her senses told her she was in over her head. His sneer showed he was used to getting what he wanted. He made Jaxon seem tame by comparison. She'd assumed Jaxon was the older brother, but he was the younger. Perhaps he was looking to curry favor with his big brother.

"What offer?" Jaxon narrowed his eyes. "When did you two meet?"

"Just a chance encounter this morning in town," said Jace smoothly.

He must not want the others to know about the tube. It must be worth more than what he'd offered by a considerable margin. Was that to her advantage or disadvantage? A GreenCorps man now knew about its existence. He could be a problem if he persisted.

"What can I get you all to drink?" Elsa's stomach clenched, and she wished she hadn't eaten. Her sandwich churned inside.

"Four whiskeys. Doubles," said Jaxon. "This rounds on me. Remind me later to tell you your message from your sister."

He slurred his words. How much had he had to drink? Ginny wouldn't refuse him service unless he got rowdy. He was rich. Elsa tried not to worry about the message from Avery because it might not even be true. Jaxon might string her along for his amusement. A headache stabbed behind her eyes.

Back at the bar, Wes poured the drinks for Jaxon's table ahead of the other orders, so she waited.

"Watch yourself with them." He spoke in a subdued voice.

"Thanks. I got that feeling. They're already drunk."

He nodded. "When the brothers are together, sometimes we've had trouble."

What kind of trouble? Before she could ask, Ginny ambled out of her office. She looked pleased with the packed house and strolled around the room, checking on her girls and chatting with the regulars. Elsa didn't dare stand and talk with Wes while Ginny patrolled.

Elsa placed the drinks on her tray for Jaxon and his group when Ginny's voice materialized right behind her.

"Jaxon and Jace McCoy, to what do I owe this pleasure? It isn't even week's end." Ginny rushed forward to their table, her hot pink skirt swishing.

Jace stood and kissed Ginny, then Jaxon did the same. Jaxon whispered in her ear and she threw back her head and laughed, a coarse, humorless sort of fake laugh. Her eyes cut to Elsa, and she nodded.

She swatted Jaxon's shoulder. "You old goat. Course, you can have the guest suite upstairs for the night. Just shout if you want more company. My girls are warmed up tonight."

"We'll be fine," said Jaxon. "Business first, pleasure later. We've got plans."

Ginny laughed again and clasped Elsa's arm on the way past.

Ginny murmured as she stopped with her instructions. "You get off tonight at whatever time Jaxon says. Counts as a full day. We'll get by without you on the floor. You're going to serve the whiskey upstairs whenever Jaxon wants. That clear?"

Elsa's heart stopped, and she froze. A palpable stab of fear paralyzed her limbs. She needed to control it. Ginny's face wore the implacable hardness that always lurked beneath her sunny exterior. The older woman knew how to run a business and who was important, and it wasn't the help. Elsa thought she'd been prepared for Jaxon's brother to visit and what that might entail, but she wished she was anywhere else right now. Her plan to leave had only been a dream, but if she had seriously considered the possibility, it would have saved her.

She needed to get out of here. Her heart drummed against her chest. She tried to look nonchalant as she set a drink in front of each of the men at Jaxon's table. Where could she run?

"Have a drink with us," said Jace.

"Yeah, Elsa, come have a drink," said Wade. "You clean up good. I want a turn too."

Jace turned to Wade. "Not tonight. She's mine."

Jace sat closest to her and hauled her into his lap, his brawny arm clamping her against him. She struggled to regain her footing, but couldn't. His grip was like iron and her feet dangled above the ground, unable to gain traction. He'd surprised her with the move and an icy knot of fear interfered with her coordination.

She glanced at Ginny, who shrugged and turned with another forced laugh. "You all have fun tonight."

The faint glimmer of hope that her boss would interfere evaporated as Ginny continued her rounds. There would be no help. Elsa was on her own and out of her depth.

Jace nuzzled her neck and said, "You smell good enough to eat." He rubbed harder. His whiskers grated against her skin and left patches that felt raw.

The other men laughed and watched her discomfort while Jace shoved his hand between her thighs and squeezed her leg. He stroked her underwear with his thumb, his fingers wandering to the skin beside it.

"Fuck, your skin is smooth," he whispered into her ear.

She couldn't get loose. Deep down she was terrified, shaking inside.

"Are you that smooth everywhere?"

His hot breath when he spoke was repulsive.

He grabbed her breast under her shirt and squeezed. It hurt, and she shot to her feet. Jace snaked his arm out to pull her back, but Walker appeared beside the table. He grabbed Elsa's arm and tugged her out of Jace's reach. She'd never been so glad to see Walker.

"Elsa, get back to work. You think the goddamn drinks deliver themselves."

He sounded like a bully, but she wasn't fooled. She was grateful for his help and thanked him with her eyes.

"I'm sorry about that," he said to the men. "She just works the floor down here. You men want to do more than look. The others are here for your pleasure."

Elsa backed away but listened as she took drink orders from nearby tables.

"Son," said Jaxon, lurching to his feet again. He doubled over with a coughing spell, then said, "That one is bought and paid for. Once we conclude our meeting, my brother and I are taking the party upstairs. We plan to all get better acquainted. Stay out of our way."

Walker held up his hands. "Sorry, just doing my job."

"How about you go back to doing your job by the door and leave us the fuck alone? You'll regret it if you interfere again, boy," said Jaxon.

Wes studied Elsa's face at the bar. "You need to go on break?"

"I have nowhere to go. I'm stuck. If I run, they'll hurt my Gran." She glanced at the door where Ginny stood with her drink, her arm around one of the regulars. She couldn't get out that way. If she ran, it would only delay the inevitable. She handed Wes her locker key. "Can you look after this for me?" Her voice shook.

He nodded and tucked it in his pocket. "Jaxon McCoy gets what he wants in this town. Ginny will let him do anything he wants. She'd protect you from anyone else, but not him or his brother."

Elsa kept working, the spike of fear worming deeper. She tripped over her feet and sloshed drinks, unloading her tray with sweaty hands. Twice she went to the wrong table in her distraction. She regretted not leaving before now, for all it had been just a daydream. Her gut had told her time and again to leave and she'd ignored the warnings. The McCoy brothers and their greedy eyes watched her every move. So did Ginny— every fumble and mistake cataloged. The older woman looked resigned to Elsa's loss of composure.

The endless gropes and fondles from the patrons took on a different meaning tonight and left her trembling. Nothing was innocent. It was nearly ten when Wade and his friend left and the brothers called for another round. As she threaded her way back across the floor, she tried to feel brave. It was just sex. It happened all the time. She'd accepted Jaxon's deal.

A drink from the previous round sat on the table. Its golden liquid, untouched.

"We saved you a drink, darlin'." Jace's fingers drummed on the table. He stuck his other hand under her skirt and fondled her ass.

"No thanks," she said, stepping away from his unwanted touch.

Jaxon swayed as he lurched upward and grabbed the drink. He stopped again to cough, then swirled the glass in her face. "Drink it," he said. "You just shoot it back. You're going to wish you had. Get us a bottle from the bar. Time to go upstairs."

Elsa was terrified. Maybe it would be more bearable if she had a drink. Some of the other women didn't seem to mind their jobs. How bad could it be? She grabbed the glass and shot the whiskey, tossing it back in one gulp the way she'd seen. The harsh alcohol burned her mouth and throat, and its warmth landed in the pit of her stomach. She coughed and her cheeks flushed. Maybe it would make her braver. She lifted her chin to keep her fear from showing, though she probably didn't fool anyone.

"If you men will excuse me. I have another table to finish."

She forced herself to smile and took the drink order of the next table over before returning to the bar. Her hands shook.

"What's going on?" Wes said.

Walker shuffled closer from the door to hear her answer. She glanced up at him.

"Ginny said I'm theirs." She swallowed. "They're ready to go upstairs. I'm supposed to get them a bottle." Her voice was flat and didn't sound like hers.

Wes' dark eyes showed his pity, but he grabbed a bottle of whiskey from a shelf just over his head without a word. One of the expensive ones. She'd learned the higher the shelf, the higher the cost. Walker scowled.

"Doesn't Ginny have other girls for that?" His gray eyes bored into her.

She felt judged, like somehow she'd let him down. It wasn't like she had a choice.

"Jaxon is making sure Granny is taken care of. He found me the job." Her knees knocked together as she trembled. Walker looked concerned and grabbed her bare arm.

"You're like ice. You gonna be okay?"

"I know what they want, but not how. I've never even kissed someone."

She didn't know why she shared this information with him.

Walker's eyes widened, perhaps shocked by her forthright statement.

She would have said more, but the McCoys stumbled toward the bar.

"You got that bottle yet? We're going to Room Eight." Jace licked his lips. "You're coming with us. We wouldn't want you to get lost on your way up."

His hard eyes stared like he knew she'd considered flight. If she ran, she had no idea what would happen to Avery and Granny.

Jace wasn't as drunk as Jaxon, who looked sick as well as inebriated, with red around his eyes and nose. By contrast, Jace's dark eyes remained alert. She broke out in a cold sweat. The pulse in her neck must be visible. Jace noticed her fear and smiled.

"We'll wait. I want to watch your pretty little ass on the stairs." Jace stuck out his hand for the bottle, unstoppered it, and tipped it back for a drink. He wiped the back of his hand on his mouth. "Let's go."

Elsa glanced at the door, wondering if she could run after all, but Jace grabbed her elbow in a tight grip. "After you."

* * *

Walker
May 15th, 2195, Long Beach
Sunrise: 5:51 a.m. Sunset 7:47 p.m.

I cut Hayden off. Can't handle it anymore. He's kiting all the time. He never listens. One of these days, he'll take too much and die. He's flirting with danger. Never seen him this bad. Can't take it anymore. Gave my notice at Ginny's a couple days ago. There's a train late tonight, but I'd rather get my pay on Friday before I hop aboard.

Worry what else Hayden might do to support his habit. Ginny doesn't have male whores, but she might now. Wouldn't surprise me if he's dabbled. He'd do just about anything for her formula. There's another train in four days. With or without him, I'm leaving town. If he can straighten up, I'll see him later this summer. He knows how to find me, where I go every summer when I can.

Scouted the trainyard again. Security is tight, crawling with GreenCorps uniforms, but if I follow the tracks in the dark, well past the station, I should be fine. My stuff is packed, all but my sleeping bag. Ready to leave on short notice. This place is a bust. Lost my brother to drugs again. He's twenty, not a kid. I can't look after him forever.

(Second write)

Writing on my break as I'm fuming. Elsa's in trouble tonight. There's someone else I can't look after. She's become popular at work. Works her ass off with the drinks and looks hot as hell. The regulars like her sassy mouth. Her body is all toned and muscular from working the Heap, but now she's clean and has cute clothes. Hard to take my eyes off her. Don't want to give my thoughts away, but it must be obvious that I'm interested. But I'm not staying. She deserves better than a hopper like me.

The rich prick that arranged her job was in here earlier, bragging about calling in his dues. It disappointed him not to find her before her shift. Think tonight she's in for a world of trouble. If only I could spare her that pain. Don't think I can idly sit by and do nothing. That McCoy asshole is bad news. The other girls fear him and his brother. Don't want Elsa to be hurt. Can't stick around to watch. If not today. Another day. It's inevitable. This situation has gone on too long. There has to be a way to get her out of here.

CHAPTER 11: ELSA PLUS CAITLYN

Elsa started up the stairs, her legs shaking. The brothers walked right behind, their rancid breath dogging her every step. She couldn't bolt; she'd never get past them and she didn't dare. Despite the liquid courage from the alcohol, she didn't feel brave—a tight ball of dread in the depths of her stomach made it hard to think.

Room Eight had a small table with three glasses, four chairs, and an enormous bed, which she avoiding looking at. Jaxon swayed, unsteady, as he poured a generous measure of whiskey into each glass. He downed one in a single shot.

"You two going to get better acquainted? Or am I going to go first?" Jaxon almost fell over as he reached for the bottle again. He leaned on the chair as he coughed.

"I have an idea, brother," said Jace as he rested his meaty hand on Jaxon's shoulder. "Go home to that pretty wife at your place tonight. I like the surprise you've arranged and can't wait to play."

"I did good?" said Jaxon, squinting at his brother and stumbling back a step. He grabbed the wall for support.

"Yeah, you did real good." Jace spoke to Jaxon but stared at Elsa, undressing her with his hard eyes.

Elsa's insides clenched.

"Elsa, Sweetie, I want you to suck me off," Jace said.

She had no idea what that meant.

"That's right," said Jaxon. "Teach her that. I'm going to go find Avery. She might like it rough tonight, too." He bent over coughing and held the table for support.

He must be sick and drunk. For her sister's sake, Elsa hoped he would go home and pass out. She couldn't take everything in and felt numb. This couldn't be real.

"Get started," said Jace, unbuckling his belt. "I don't enjoy repeating myself. Won't be difficult. I'm hard now," he said with a shake of his head at his brother, who fumbled for the doorknob. "Soon as he leaves."

Elsa didn't know how to respond to Jace's words. She hadn't been listening. "I don't understand." She edged closer to the exit. Maybe she could bolt when Jaxon opened the door.

"Hold it, missy," said Jace. "You aren't going anywhere until I'm finished."

Elsa stopped moving. Her heart pounded like thunder.

"You two have fun." Jaxon stumbled from the room and shut the door.

"Smile, loosen up," Jace said. "Have another drink." He licked his lips and stuck his hand down the front of his pants.

"You're mistaken about me." Elsa swallowed so she didn't gag.

As if she hadn't spoken, Jace kicked off his boots, pulled his pants down, and tossed them to the corner. He unbuttoned his shirt, revealing a thick dark mat of hair on his chest. His erection was enormous and stood at attention. She'd never seen one and preferred to stay away. That thing was going to hurt. Her icy hands shook. She shoved them behind her back.

Several faint white and red lines scarred Jace's torso and his arms were roped with muscle. He might be rich, but he'd worked hard at some point. He looked capable of hurting her if she didn't do as he asked.

"Jaxon said you're free of charge and under this thumb. You're gorgeous like his sweet Avery, but there are things he'd never ask her to do. He tried once, and she just cried. He asked me to teach them to you. The first lesson is how to give a blow job."

He shook his penis like a stick. She tried not to watch, but didn't dare look away.

"A filthy little piece of heapster trash like you should be willing to do anything."

She saw red as he spewed additional insults, but she took them. What choice did she have? This was her life now. She clenched her jaw, refusing to cry.

"You're going to get down on your knees or spread your legs at my request. Whenever I want. I bet you're really fucking tight. I don't mind that to start, I can fix that. My brother told me about your little deal and I've been saving myself this week. When I'm done, I bet my brother sets you up in an apartment for his use on the side. You'll have it made. After a few weeks' stint at Ginny's with me, you'll be ready and willing. I'm going to ride you like a freight train. Hard and fast. My brother will feel like a vacation. Consider this training for your promotion."

Jace liked to hear himself talk. His words froze her to the core.

"I like to fuck," he said as he tossed his shirt over the back of a chair. "My brother asked me because I like it rough and can break the sassiest pieces of trash. Even you."

Elsa backed up, unsure where to look. His hairy body and muscled frame were intimidating; his black eyes were terrifying, but his words were the deadliest. They aimed at breaking her before he even touched her. He stroked himself, his fist curled around his cock.

"Get over here," he said.

"I haven't been with a man before." Her voice was unsteady, her feet nailed to the floor.

Jace licked his lips. "That's so much sweeter. I'll be your first. You can think of me every time you're with anyone. I won't be gentle, but it will be memorable."

"Don't touch me." Her voice was higher than usual. "I'm not interested."

"Interested isn't my concern. Willing is better, but unwilling is fine. Either way, I'm fucking you until you can't stand. If you struggle, I'll knock you into next week first."

She stared at him and didn't answer. Her legs became rubbery. She pressed her knees together so he wouldn't see them knock together.

"You having that drink?"

She shook her head.

"Suit yourself." He lunged, grabbed her by the hair, and yanked, holding tight.

His grip hurt. Tears welled in her eyes.

"Get on your fucking knees. First lesson, take my cock in your mouth. You can lick, you can suck, or take it down your throat, but you're going to keep going until I say stop."

The dam burst and tears streamed down her face. The back of her head burned where he held her hair tight, her scalp prickling with pain. It was frustration and rage, not simple fear, that made her cry.

He grinned as he enjoyed her humiliation.

Elsa didn't have a choice. She sank to her knees, the rough wooden floor hard underneath. She glanced up at him with narrowed eyes. He loosened his hold by the smallest margin. Tentatively, she reached out. His cock was hot and hard; it leaped at her touch.

"That's right. Grab it and stick it in your mouth."

She did as he ordered. It was difficult not to gag. He tasted like stale sweat and the salt of her tears. His grip loosened a little as he thrust into her mouth. She did her best not to retch. If she threw up, he would hurt her. He moved her head by twisting her hair and maintained pressure as he slid in and out of her mouth. He moaned, and it sounded like he was enjoying this experience. She didn't understand how this could be pleasurable; it made her feel sick to her stomach. She wanted to scream, but no sound came while he pounded into her mouth. His pleasure noises increased while she held back sobs. She wouldn't do this again. Her fist clenched at her impotence.

When he stopped, he didn't release her hair. Her knees and throat felt bruised.

"Look how hard I am." He tapped his wet cock against her face. "That's a good girl."

He stroked her hair, still gripping her head. She grit her teeth. He treated her like an animal to be trained. Next, he'd ask her to beg for a treat. The heat of anger built in her veins, replacing the numb fear.

"Time for lesson two. Take off your clothes and lie on the bed."

She scrambled to her feet and tried to bolt. He'd loosened his grip on her hair, but not enough, and he jerked her backward.

"Damn girl, you're feisty." He looked amused, but slapped her face, snapping her head to the side. It was hard enough she saw stars and her lip split open. The taste of blood flooded her mouth.

Jace held her head at an awkward angle as he tightened his grip. Without warning, he grabbed her shirt and ripped it down the front. The two halves hung from her shoulders, the skin bare below. Her buttons bounced on the floor and skittered away. Her black lacy bra left nothing to the imagination and his eyes gravitated to her chest. He grabbed her breast and squeezed, causing her to cry out in pain.

He shoved her against the bed, held her down by the throat, and bit her nipple. He bit her several times across her breasts. She gasped after each, struggling to get away. He left marks but didn't break the skin. Tooth bruises. She tried to scramble away, but he regained his hold. She couldn't think straight and her breath came in gasps.

Jace put his face right above hers. "You aren't going anywhere. We're just getting started. You make a dumbass move like that again. I'll beat some sense into you. You're just a skinny little tease with that short skirt and bare ass underneath. I've been hot and bothered since I walked in this evening. I'm going to fuck you and you won't know what's what when I'm done."

The air chilled Elsa's chest, though her face and skin were flushed.

"Take your clothes off." He slid his free hand down her hip. "If I have to ask again, you'll be sorry."

She didn't dare refuse his request in that menacing tone. With shaking hands, she unzipped her boots, unhooked her skirt, and it dropped to the floor. She still wore her bra and the scrap of underwear, but they weren't protection. Her throat closed and a tight band circled her chest, restricting her breath.

"All of it." He licked his lips. "On the bed. Now." His voice cracked like a whip.

She unclasped the bra and slid off the scanty underwear with shaking hands.

His hard cock bumped into her as they slid onto the bed, his arms on either side of her, locked like a cage. The rough fabric scratched her bare skin as he pressed himself next to her.

She trembled and attempted to cover herself with her hands. Rage guided her as much as fear. Her vision blurred as tears once again overwhelmed her.

Jace shoved her face into the bed as he bit and licked her bare skin. His oily mouth touched her everywhere and his rough whiskers scratched. She didn't know how she could bear it. Her breath became ragged as she tried to fight her terror. Lashing out, she landed a solid blow to his midsection and scrambled away.

"Fuck." He rolled off the bed with a grunt. He followed and slapped her face, snapping it to the side.

Elsa cried out and saw stars, but felt a ray of hope when his erection wavered. Maybe he wasn't interested anymore. She caught her breath when he poured himself another drink. Tossing it back, he turned toward her, a look of anger suffusing his florid face.

Her quaking returned as she stood on the far side of the bed. Too late to make a move for the door.

"This isn't over. We're going back to lesson one. I want your mouth on me again before we move on to lesson two. You'll want me good and wet, it'll hurt you less. I've got three or four times in me tonight, and I don't want you shredded after the first one. I'm not a fan of blood."

He jumped on the bed and leaned against the headboard. "You can try this on your own, instead of with my hand in your hair."

The magnanimous jackass waved his hand like he was being generous, bestowing a gift or favor. No way he was putting anything else inside her without a fight.

Kneeling in front of him, she looked up, meeting his hard eyes as he smirked. She grabbed his cock as if to start over. She put little thought into what happened next. She squeezed his nuts, twisted, and bit the inside of his thigh. She ground down and drew blood, the tangy metal taste spreading through her mouth.

Understanding swept over Elsa, and she released her hold. She was in trouble.

His roar of pain and rage was followed by a blow to her cheek. Pain exploded near her right eye. He punched her again. She scrambled away, but there was nowhere to run. She couldn't get the locked door open and circled the table to put distance between them, but he was too fast.

Fists swinging, Jace caught her. She went down in a naked, crumpled heap on the floor after a blow to her stomach and another to her ribs knocked the wind from her. He swung something hard that hit her on the side and again on her back.

Elsa curled into a ball to protect herself, but Jace kicked her several times. At least twice more in the ribs. She couldn't get away. She was going to die on this floor.

Sound came from far away as her heart pounded in her ears. His incoherent cursing and her screams seemed unreal. She tried to disassociate herself from the present and send her mind elsewhere, but the pain anchored her to the present. He aimed blow after blow to her body. It hurt to draw breath.

As though from a distance, the door crashed inward and footsteps thundered. There was a cracking smash, and the floor shook when something heavy fell, bouncing on the wooden floor. She opened her eyes after the impact and risked a glance. Jace lay unconscious, his eyes closed, his mouth slack. The side of his head was wet with blood, while a crimson puddle leaked onto the floor. Someone spoke to her, and she shook her head to focus on the voice, trying to understand the words. Her body shook and she couldn't get up. She was frozen in place.

Walker stood over Jace's prone form, holding a broken chair. He'd splintered it against the older man's head, knocking him out. Walker's strength and the rage on his face were magnificent.

* * *

May 16th, 2195

Dearest Mathew,

Mittens has stayed on the farm with me. Every morning when I wake up, she's stretched out beside me, her warmth from my knee to my hip. I can't remember what I did in the evening before she came. She's good company and follows me as I do chores all day. I'll look up and she'll be watching. She keeps me in her line of sight. Probably doesn't want to miss out on something to eat. I miss you and wish you were here. I think you'd love this cat too.

Now that it's spring, I haven't written as often as before. My days are busy and the daylight hours are longer so I'm exhausted at day's end. I've worked from dawn until dusk the last two weeks. I planted the vegetable garden with beans, lettuce, potatoes, and squash. The mama goat had twins. I'm able to milk a small amount of excess and share with Mittens, which may be why she stays. One kid is brown with white, the other is black with white. My small herd of sheep has also grown. I started with five ewes and a ram and now have four lambs as well. I love having all the young creatures to care for. I think I'll buy a pig this summer. They aren't pets, but I'll have a ready source of food, unbeholden to GreenCorps.

I'm hoping that there will soon be chicks in the henhouse. I had bought six hens and a rooster. I had a few eggs over the winter, but let the hens set on their nests the last few weeks. Two of them have sizeable clutches and a third has a smaller nest. If the others are setting, they are more secretive. I could have chicks as early as next week as I understand it takes about three weeks for their eggs to hatch. I let the chickens roam in the daytime in the outdoor pen. If I had a trained dog, I'd let them wander the farmyard, but as it is, I worry about foxes, raccoons, and coyotes.

It is quiet here at the base of the mountains, with no sign of the outside world. I think that's how I prefer it. After you were gone, I lost my heart for the larger missions and the world at large. I don't know if we made a difference, and it was so hard to be involved in seeing the misery in so many places. At home, I feel like I'm healing, recharging. I need to be here right now.

One of these days, when I'm ready, I may make an overnight hike into town for supplies, but I'm going to stay here as long as I can. I might not be completely self-sufficient on the farm, but with hard work and some luck, I won't need to buy much, other than fuel for the lamp, more seeds for next year, and assorted items I can't think of right now. I'll make a list before I go to Salt Lake.

Love you and miss you,
Your Caitlyn

CHAPTER 12: TATSUDA

Tatsuda brushed the tears from his eyes, his vision blurred. It didn't take much for his fake tears to look convincing. He'd had lots of practice. Plus, he looked younger than his almost fifteen years, which was often an advantage. Not only was he short, but slight too. He wore layers of clothes that disguised his wiry strength. Being young drew sympathy if he got caught or he needed something.

The GreenCorps security forces holding him would relax their guard if they thought he was just young and scared. It was one of his best cons.

"What are you going to do to me?" he said, his bottom lip quivering. He shouldn't lay it on any thicker, but he wanted to make his point. He was just a poor, lost kid and not a threat. He shouldn't be held responsible for his actions.

"Where are your parents, kid?" The officer drummed his fingers on the desk at the police station.

Tatsuda shrugged. He looked down, letting more tears fall to garner sympathy. He hadn't seen his parents in close to five years and didn't know if they were even alive. Last he knew, they'd been trying to drink themselves to death and had kicked him out. One too many mouths to feed. He'd been looking after himself ever since. Who needed parents? If they were still alive, they'd be in New Vegas, where booze was cheap and plentiful. Good riddance. He brushed his scruffy long hair back from his face, pretending to wipe the tears.

"Well, kid, we'll keep you overnight. You got caught trying to steal bread. We'll feed you breakfast. Then you should head back to your folks. They're probably worried about you. The streets of Denver are no place for a kid on his own."

"Thank you," said Tatsuda in a soft voice as he looked up. "I'm sorry I took that bread, but I was starving." He'd angled to get caught today because he wanted a hot meal and a soft bed for a change. Dinner and breakfast. He was tired of sleeping outdoors in alleys and eating scraps, or whatever he could steal. Tonight, was on GreenCorps.

Half an hour later, he was served hot pasta with a tomato and basil sauce with a side of toasted bread with cheese. A feast. He didn't mind sleeping behind bars. The corporation had its uses.

CHAPTER 13: ELSA PLUS WALKER

"Can you get up?" Annie's voice came from far away. It was challenging to grasp the meaning.

Her friend's hand was heavy on her sore back. Elsa flinched. She couldn't bear to be touched; her skin felt burned.

"We've got to get you out of here. Put on your street clothes. Where's your locker key?"

Elsa's mouth hurt, her eye felt like it was on fire, and her body ached. She was naked in front of Walker and flushed with embarrassment. Her breath still came in gasps. She didn't want anyone to see her like this, especially Walker. She refused to be seen as feeble.

Walker watched over Jace, his face averted, but the fallen man hadn't moved. Her attacker's chest rose and fell. He wasn't dead, which meant he'd wake up.

She forced herself to a sitting position, her head spinning. She needed to leave before he came to. She'd put Avery and Granny at risk with her actions, but she had to go. She couldn't help them if she was dead.

"Wes has it." She gagged as she spoke, but kept herself from vomiting by watching a spider crawl across the wooden floorboards.

"Can you take her across the hall and clean her up? I'll be right back."

Walker nodded in response.

Annie's eyes seemed worried and her forehead was creased. She squeezed Elsa's shoulder in support before slipping out the door. Elsa had to pull herself together. She couldn't afford to fall apart. She needed to escape.

Elsa tried to stand but trembled so hard it was difficult to control her muscles. Stabbing pains seized her chest and her ribs hurt with every breath. Walker gripped her elbow and helped her up. She was naked, bruised, and felt helpless and she couldn't look him in the eye. She couldn't believe her friends had interfered. She hurt all over. Especially her face and ribs. She must look as dreadful as she felt.

"Can you walk?"

His voice was calm and soothing, which brought her tears to the surface. She blinked to keep them from falling.

She stepped and winced at the sharp pain in her side. Walker scooped her into his powerful arms, looked both ways, and crossed the hall into the bathroom. He set her down on the edge of the nearest tub and went back to close the doors.

Returning, he grabbed a hand towel and wet it at the sink. He dabbed her face, and it came away bloody.

She looked Walker in the eye for the first time. "He's going to kill you, too. You have to run." Her voice was raspy, perhaps from screaming. She couldn't remember.

"You're coming with me. We're leaving together."

She winced at his intensity, but before his words registered, Annie returned with Elsa's key and wedged the bathroom door closed. They couldn't afford interruptions.

"It's so noisy downstairs. Nobody heard anything suspicious. Business as usual."

Annie opened Elsa's locker.

"How did you know?" Elsa said to Walker. Her mouth hurt and she touched the side of her face. The tender area by her eye socket throbbed had swollen already. Bite marks covered her flushed skin.

"Annie was next door. She came to find me." Walker dabbed at her split lip again. She took the cold cloth and held it to her face as she looked at him.

His gray eyes seemed huge and darker than before. He was in trouble, too. Annie tossed Elsa's regular clothes at him while she removed the contents of Elsa's locker. He tried to pass Elsa the pile, but she was unsure of how to proceed. Her brain wasn't working at the proper speed.

Registering her confusion, he handed the clothing to her, piece by piece. Annie slipped on Elsa's bra and Elsa slid on underwear from her locker. Otherwise, she dressed with very little help, other than threading her arms into her shirt. She ignored the pain. Wearing clothes made her feel less vulnerable, and some of her strength returned. Avoiding the mirror, she spat the blood from her mouth into the sink, rinsed, and drank.

While Elsa dressed, Annie shoved the spare clothes from the locker into Elsa's satchel, including the embroidered shirt from Avery. Annie filled the canteen from Elsa's locker and added it to her bag. Elsa had kept the habit of carrying a canteen even though she'd had water to drink at Ginny's.

"Sorry I can't help more," Annie said. "You two going to manage the window? You can't take the stairs or you'll be seen."

"We got it," Walker's hand curled reassuringly around Elsa's shoulder. He sounded more confident than she felt.

Elsa concentrated on breathing, evaluating the level of pain with each motion, each breath. She gathered her strength before she nodded.

She had trouble concentrating on the present, her mind stuck on the attack. She couldn't get warm and she shook all over. Tugging her light jacket over her clothes, she slung the satchel across her shoulder and stomped her feet into her boots. She peeked into her bag—the tube was still where she'd left it. Her stash of hard coin was there too and her locker emptied. Her thoughts were disorganized but motivated by fear.

She needed to leave before Jace woke and finished what he'd started.

"Out the window. Off the roof. To the trainyard," said Walker. "Let's go."

"Where does the train go?" Her tender mouth didn't move quite right when she spoke. She ran her tongue over her teeth. None were loose.

"Anywhere that isn't here."

"I don't know how to thank you," Elsa said, turning to Annie.

"Don't get caught." Annie squeezed Elsa's arm.

Walker slid the window open without a sound and climbed through onto the tiled roof. Elsa followed, her ribs screaming in protest, but she grit her teeth and swallowed the pain. It grew darker as they moved to the rear of the building; the roof pitch made it slippery, so going was slow. Ginny's was built near the base of the hillside and the ground sloped upward. The drop at the back was only six feet. Walker sprang down first while she sat on the edge and lowered herself toward the alley. She jumped only the last couple of feet, but landing sent shooting pains through her ribs. She took a slow, deep breath before continuing.

Walker and Elsa slunk along the outside of the buildings in the back until they came to the end of the alley. It looked like a dead end, with a high fence made from slats of wood and sheets of old metal. He slid a piece to the side and revealed a makeshift shack hidden on the other side. He stepped through and opened it.

A single candle guttered on a wooden packing crate that was being used as a table, its faint light flickering. Who'd leave a candle burning in an empty room? But then she spotted Hayden lying on the floor, muttering at the roof. This must be where they slept. It smelled like dry earth, sweat, and unwashed socks. Hayden had the same sickly scent as earlier today when he'd pleaded for coin.

"We gotta go, Hayden." Walker shook his brother's shoulder.

Hayden remained unresponsive, not acknowledging their presence. An open bag with five white powdered cubes lay on the floor. Ginny's special formula. The cubes were placed under the tongue and the user would let them dissolve. He was kiting.

"Damn, where did he get more?" said Walker in a whisper. "Ginny wouldn't sell unless he had cash upfront. Idiot either whored himself out or stole it."

He shook him again, but still received no response.

"Is it safe to leave him like this?" Elsa stared at Hayden's blank expression.

"He's an idiot, but seems to know his limits. Seen it before. Too often." Walker's face sagged. "We're going to have to leave him. He knows where I might head if we get separated. We can wait for him there."

Elsa hadn't considered that leaving with Walker had meant Hayden, too. It was hard to feel sorry for him, and she was relieved he was being left behind.

Walker stuffed a tattered sheet of plastic, a rolled sleeping bag, and a folded blanket into his waiting backpack. The rest of the room was bare. His water jug was full, and he slung it across his body.

"Why are you doing this?" Elsa's forehead felt tight and creased.

"I was leaving at week's end, anyway. I'm just a train early."

He didn't meet her eyes. Was there something he wasn't telling her?

"Why are you helping me?" She labored to take a full breath without shooting pains.

"I helped get you into this mess. If I get you out, we're even."

She nodded. "Thank you. I meant to say thank you, too."

"All night, I knew that asshole was going to be a problem." His voice came out as a growl.

"Me too," she said. "I tried to be brave, but when the time came... I couldn't let him force me. Granny would have wanted me to fight. I bit him."

Something like admiration flashed through Walker's eyes. He might have seen the marks left by her teeth.

His eyes gleamed in the pale moonlight. "You ever hopped a train?" His voice vibrated with excitement. It was infectious.

"I've thought about hopping one and disappearing, but I've never left Long Beach. You'll have to walk me through it."

"Hope you learn quick. It isn't a lifestyle for everyone."

He stepped back and closed the wall, leaving Hayden kiting in their hideaway. Walker and Elsa slid back into the main alley and through the darkness to the outskirts of the trainyard. Every noise made her heart lurch. The movement of scurrying rats and feral cats gave her a fright. Her nerves balanced on a razor's edge.

"Station guards will check everything. Security is tight. Easy to get into corporation towns, but hard to get out. Especially one on lock-down. Lucky, I know how. Have to get past the yard and down the track. We'll hop on when it comes past. You sure you're up to this?"

She nodded. The worst pain was in her ribs. Everything else was tolerable, though she would be sore for days. Despite her uncertainty, excitement shot through her at the thought of leaving. She couldn't stay and had to trust Granny's care to her sister. Her throat tightened. She shoved her hand into her satchel and wrapped it around the tube. It symbolized freedom. She might not be fully prepared, but she had this. She squeezed it for comfort, then let go. This wasn't the Tuesday train that headed southeast past Riverside. This train was headed north. She didn't know where she'd end up.

They passed the series of station buildings, then cut back toward the tracks and across to the far side. Slinking between shadows, Walker checked before they moved to the next position. Twice, they waited for security to move to a different position. A knot of fear balled inside her as she imagined a ticking clock. Jace might wake up and begin a proper search.

A sagging, rusted fence separated railroad property from the junkyard next door. They skirted the primary station and kept to the edge of darkness as they paralleled the rails heading north. The footing was uneven, with bits of rock interspersed with low bushes. She placed each step with care so she didn't make noise. She didn't speak until they were well past the station.

"How long do you think until he wakes up or someone finds him?" Elsa kept her voice low, not much more than a whisper. She couldn't banish Jace from her thoughts.

"Won't be long, I'd imagine. I didn't cause permanent damage. But he'll have a headache." Walker hesitated. "He's going to have a scar where you bit him."

"Good," Elsa said with satisfaction.

"I don't think anyone will look for him, so we have until he comes to. He didn't expect to be interrupted. Ginny planned that he'd keep you there all night. Told me I didn't need to walk you home." His voice was almost a growl again.

Heat surged up from her stomach. She'd contained the feeling, but Ginny's remark was the last straw. Elsa's adrenaline had worn off and reality was sinking in. She ran for the bushes at the edge farthest from the tracks and heaved out the contents of her stomach.

When she finished, she wiped her face, swished water in her mouth, and spat. She drank the second swallow.

"Not too much water," said Walker. "Once we're on that train, it might be hours or even days until it stops. It's supposed to stop in Sacramento, but if it's an express, it won't, and there is no way to tell. We can't get off until it does. Might carry on to Reno, Salt Lake, Denver, or Portland."

She considered his words. "Should I use the bathroom first too?" She flushed.

"Go ahead," he whispered. "Pick a bush, any bush. Just don't go far."

She moved away from Walker before choosing a place. She was embarrassed that he was close enough to hear. Her cheeks burned even though he'd carried her naked. He'd seen all of her, bones, boobs, and welts. While she'd liked how his muscular arms had felt and that he'd smelled clean and healthy, that wasn't how she wanted to be seen. He'd never be interested in her now. That thought made her pause. She used to hate him, but after tonight, he was forgiven. They weren't even—the scale tilted in his favor.

When Elsa returned, he pointed up the tracks. "There's a spot about two hundred yards away where we can hide. I scouted ahead of time. The ground is level, but near enough to the station that the train won't have built up speed. This train has the right kind of cars. I'd considered hopping this one before deciding to wait for Friday's pay."

She didn't know what the right cars were, but was glad he'd stayed.

They'd just settled in to wait, hidden by the night and the thick bushes, when Walker tugged her closer to the ground, his arm heavy across her back. Her ribs protested the pressure, but she scrunched smaller and held her breath. Gravel crunched beside the tracks from back toward the station. Two men approached, their lanterns like floating spheres of yellow light. Elsa shut her eyes, not wanting to lose her night vision or give their position away. Walker wrapped his arm tighter, huddling together and still.

His dark coat covered them both, warming her with his proximity. Her heart sped up. She breathed in his fresh outdoor scent and found it calming. Were the men specifically searching for hoppers, or for them?

The station guards passed their position and moved up the track. Five minutes later, the men returned, this time shining their light on the far side. She tried not to breathe, hoping they wouldn't be discovered.

When all became quiet, Walker removed his arm. She missed its warmth and reminded herself that she shouldn't get too attached. He was helping her, so they'd be even. There was no guarantee that they'd stick together beyond this first train ride. She couldn't count on help for long. She needed to learn to be independent out in the world. Although a part of her wondered if he could help.

"When the train leaves, we're going to wait for the front half to pass."

She nodded, a lump forming in her throat. She was lucky to have his instructions because she had no practical knowledge of train hopping.

"We're going to run beside the train and match its speed, getting closer and closer. Near the back of each car is a ladder. I'll go first and pull myself up. Your job will be to catch the same ladder and climb after me. If you miss, there will be another chance on the next car, but I won't be with you to help. I know you're favoring your ribs. You're hurt. But if you can get on a ladder, that's the first step. From there, just hold on until I pull you aboard."

"Where do we ride? Do we go inside?"

"Imagine a porch under the overhang of the covered train car at the back. That's where we'll sit. This kind of car is called a hopper. That's where we get our names."

"How do I grab the ladder?" It should be obvious, but it wasn't—not to her. This was outside her experience.

"Think hand, hand, step, hop. We're on the left. Start with that side."

He tapped each piece of her to illustrate as he repeated the order.

Her skin tingled each place he touched. His touch was nothing like Jace or Jaxon. It was warm and undemanding. She replayed his words. Hand, hand, step, hop.

"Anything else?"

"We wait."

* * *

Waiting with Elsa by the train, Walker could let down his guard and his thoughts wander; his musing returned to assholes like Jace McCoy that he'd encountered when he was young.

He'd grown up in a brothel, not unlike Ginny's. The smell had been the same: smoke, ale, sweat, and a spicy tang of desperation or lust. He'd known more about sex than most children.

An older woman named Sally ran the establishment, cut from the same cloth as Ginny. An ex-whore who'd somehow survived, one tougher than most. She hired Walker's mom when Walker was two. He remembered nothing before the brothel.

It was unusual to take someone with a kid, but his mother was beautiful and desperate. She wouldn't let her child starve and was willing to do anything. Sally gambled on her, a widow with experience enough she wouldn't be prudish or need training. His babysitters were bartenders, sick and injured whores, or puzzles in the kitchen where Hayden's mom cooked.

The first time his mom was beaten, Walker was six. She'd received the odd black eye or bruise before that, but nothing more serious. This beating took her laugh away. When she screamed, the cook had to restrain him so he wouldn't be injured too.

The second time, he was ten and his mom changed. She'd never gotten over the limp, but she'd also started using. She stopped having time for him and took pills for chronic pain. Walker knew that wasn't the only reason. He'd seen enough to know better. He tried to convince her to leave, but she laughed at him—a nasty mocking sound nothing like her old lilting one.

"If we had any options, I'd have tried years ago. This is my life," was all she said.

She was high and servicing someone rich the last time she was beaten, but her screams reached the bar where he'd been sweeping. Both bouncers and the bartender were needed to restrain fourteen-year-old Walker, who intended to kill the bastard, but they sat on him while he yelled and cursed. They told him if he laid a hand on a GreenCorps man, he'd hang. He vowed it would never happen again. Next time, he would save her.

Hayden must've heard Walker's angry shouts and came running. Sally had both boys escorted to jail to cool their tempers.

Hayden had always liked fire. That evening, he'd been playing with matches in the back alley before racing to help Walker. Nobody knew about Hayden's smoldering garbage can fire, which burned the whorehouse to the ground that night. No survivors. The next morning, the boys returned home to a smoking hole in the ground. Charred timbers and scorched stone were all that remained. Hayden's mother had been elsewhere and survived. She disowned her son, guessing from his stricken expression that he was at fault.

That day, still in shock, they hopped their first train from Santa Fe to Albuquerque. Scared to get off, they remained aboard all the way to Vegas. They stayed on the move for two years before stopping to work.

As he waited for the train in the dark, Walker wondered how different their lives would have been if they'd stayed in Santa Fe, another GreenCorps town. Would they be GreenCorps drones? Or if they'd dared to get off the train when it had stopped for an hour in Albuquerque? Probably the same result.

Hayden had been devastated that his mother had blamed him. He'd spent the first three days huddled in a ball, sobbing, broken—he'd been too scared to return. As far as he knew, she'd never forgiven him for the fire.

Tonight, when Walker had smashed the chair over Jace McCoy, it had been a victory for his soul. Something he'd wished he'd been able to do long ago. He wasn't just saving Elsa. He'd done it for his mother. If he got Elsa away and helped her find a new life, it might make up for the times he'd been young and helpless. Maybe do something that would have made his mother proud.

CHAPTER 14: ELSA PLUS WALKER

Elsa's sore muscles stiffened while they waited for the train. The night became chilly as the darkness stretched toward the paler light of dawn. Her eyelids grew heavy, but she didn't dare sleep. Her discomfort and busy thoughts kept her from true rest, anyway. She massaged her tightest muscles, ensuring she didn't prod her most acute injuries. It was tricky to judge the passage of time, but it must be three or four in the morning.

Station security patrolled the tracks several times, while she and Walker huddled in the bushes for hours, remaining unseen. From their remarks and the frequency, Jace was awake and had the station on alert. She was terrified to be found, but controlled her breathing and tried to remain calm.

Elsa's breath was visible in the late spring air. The ground where they lay was bone-chillingly cold and sucked the heat from her body. Voices and metal-on-metal of crashing noises jolted her from her reverie, indicating that at last there was action on the rails.

"Get ready. That's the slack action of the coupling between cars. Means a train is starting or stopping."

Walker tensed beside her. His muscles flexed in preparation.

"Stretch when you're up. Stay hidden until the engine passes. The drivers are the only people on board who might see or report us. No passenger cars on this train. It'll be loud so we won't be able to talk much."

Adrenaline surged through her, and her heart pounded. The noise became deafening, and the rails vibrated, then everything around them moved too. Train accidents happened all the time—images of bodies and metal spread everywhere flashed before her eyes. She couldn't believe she was really doing this.

"What if it's going too fast to get on?" She almost stuttered the question. The warmth from his hand on her shoulder gave her strength.

"Rule of thumb, if you can't count the spokes of the wheels, it's too fast. Harder to tell in the dark, but trust me."

She nodded, filing that piece of information away.

Walker's eyes shone in the faint moonlight, gleaming with excitement.

"You got this. Remember, hand, hand, step, hop."

The train's engine rumbled past and the train whistle blew. She'd heard the sound from home thousands of times, but here it took on new meaning. Elsa covered her ears and the ground vibration increased. Walker adjusted the straps on his pack as he jumped to his feet, swinging his arms and stomping his feet to get the blood flowing.

"You ready?"

She nodded and drew in a long breath. Ignoring the sharp pains in her side at her sudden movement, she too stretched to warm up her muscles. He took her hand and jogged a few steps to show her the necessary pace. They ran on the packed gravel filling by the tracks. He'd chosen the level ground well, but she had to be careful not to twist an ankle. The train's rumble built in her chest and it became too loud to talk. She counted the train cars as they passed. Two water tankers and three dozen covered hoppers passed before the second engine appeared, lights shining in the front. Another dozen hoppers passed.

"Now," Walker shouted and released her hand. He ran closer to the train, matching its speed, and she followed. Her heart lodged in her throat at each crunching step.

"Next car. Ladder at the back."

Her stomach bottomed out as Walker grabbed the next iron ladder. He was fast as he scrambled to the top, with no wasted motion. This was it. She reached for the cold metal and faltered, but increased her pace as she placed her second hand. Hand, hand. She stepped with her inside foot, as Walker had shown. Her hop didn't get high enough and, though she was on the ladder, she was unstable and felt like she was going to fall.

She hadn't grabbed high enough. Stabbing pain in her ribs prevented her from reaching higher. She wanted to scream, but Walker's hands grabbed her forearms and he pulled her up a rung where she found her footing and could take a breath.

Her heart thundered, matching the rhythm of the train as its wheels picked up speed. She climbed the remainder of the ladder and stood on the moving train, clutching the side for balance. She looked up and saw Walker's crooked grin. An answering one emerged on her lips. She was on board.

The train picked up speed. The wind whipped her hair and chilled her face. Her eyes streamed from the bracing wind.

"Over here," Walker shouted to get her attention. He moved onto the porch toward the back of the hopper, sat under the overhang, then swung off his pack and wedged it behind him.

She climbed awkwardly to sit where he'd showed. A metal flange divided the hopper's porch down the middle, but there was room for two people on either side. He'd taken the close edge of the near side, leaving the farther spot for her, the one most protected from the elements. She slid next to him, slinging off her satchel. Her jacket wasn't warm enough, and she'd been freezing for hours. A hot drink would warm her inside, but no chance of getting one.

She shivered and hugged her knees to her chest. A lump formed in her throat. She attempted not to think about Granny and how the train was carrying her away from everything she'd known. It wasn't the time to think about her family yet.

"You did good," he yelled. "Easier in the daylight, but more risk of getting caught."

Walker removed the blanket he'd shoved in the top of his pack and wrapped it around them so they could share body heat. He dug in the outside of his pack again and came up with a small tin. Inside were a dozen neon orange bits of foam. He pressed two of them into her hands. She had no idea what they were and stared at him, an eyebrow raised. He rolled one between his fingers, then stuck it in his left ear. He did the same with his right.

"Cuts the noise," he shouted.

Though it was strange to stuff something in her ears, she copied him. The relief was immediate. The train still reverberated in her bones, but the harsh whistle of the wind and roar of the wheels on the tracks became dull and muffled.

There wasn't much to see in the darkness as the train's speed increased and they left the lights of Long Beach behind. They passed other patches of light from time to time, most small, but the train never slowed.

"Next stop, Sacramento. About ten hours. Sleep if you can." He wrapped an arm around her and drew her against his side. He was gentle and seemed mindful of her injuries, and it felt too pleasant to resist. He was so warm.

It had been a long day, and Elsa was exhausted. Despite the din and the awkwardness of sleeping while sitting, she needed rest, so she closed her eyes.

When she woke with a jolt, dreading the impact of Jace's hand, the sun was high in the sky. She'd dozed more than she'd thought she would. Her heart raced, and she took a few breaths of cool air to calm herself. She was safe with Walker, where they huddled in the shadow of the covered hopper. Her cheeks flamed, and she was glad for the cold air sweeping by. She'd slumped onto Walker's chest as she slept.

Walker handed her strips of dried meat to eat, and she drank from her canteen. Remembering his words, she drank little. Already she had to pee and wasn't sure how that would work on the train. The blanket was no longer around Walker, just herself. He'd tucked it around her while she'd slept. He must have seen to his own needs already. She squirmed with discomfort.

"If you need to go, use the other side, behind the divider."

She nodded and stood, her legs unsteady as she moved forward. She refused to look at the ground rushing beneath the train near the coupling holding the cars together. There was room for her to place her foot safely on the metal floor that made up the grate as she crossed beyond the porch divider. Was the pattern of the grate imprinted on her butt from sitting so long?

Peeing through the holes in the metal grating didn't seem private or sanitary, but it was her best option. It was awkward to maintain her balance and pull her pants down, but it wasn't much different from finding a private place on the Heap. She aimed for the outside edge. Every movement reminded her of her sore ribs and tired muscles. She pulled up her pants and examined the bruises on her side. She didn't think Jace had broken anything, but her side hurt like hell.

With that accomplished, she returned to Walker's side and flashed him a smile of gratitude. She finished her jerky, and he handed her a pressed bar of oats and nuts in a sealed wrapper. Her stomach grumbled in appreciation, though the train's noise blocked it from giving away her hunger.

"I recognize where we are." Walker spoke next to her ear. "Another hour at most. We'll get off when the train stops. Our car will be outside the trainyard."

Elsa watched the countryside roll past. It looked hotter and drier than Long Beach, but much of the country was empty, without the packed slums, landfills, and the companies that scavenged and milled for GreenCorps. The spring countryside was flat, with green rolling hills above the remnants of taller, golden grass fields. Darker shrubs and sparse squatty trees scattered the plains and took her breath away. She'd never seen so much wild land at one time.

Twice the train rolled through an area that looked like it had once been a town, with the telltale lumps where houses and buildings had fallen into ruin. Once the roofs collapsed, the structures disintegrated in a matter of decades. Water and vegetation invaded and destroyed what had been abandoned. Railroad tracks were the only sign of people as they headed north. The population outside towns was often sparse, or so she understood from the GreenCorps news. The articles made GreenCorps sound like the only force keeping civilization together after the Collapse.

What had happened to the people from long ago? The ones who'd left the mountains of garbage and used up the underground water so crops wouldn't grow—the same people who'd polluted the seas with vast amounts of plastic. A plague had wiped out many, but Granny's stories said that there'd been a larger disaster of an unknown nature.

Elsa extracted the metal tube from her satchel and examined it. Should she look for the seed bunkers? Perhaps she should search for someone more qualified—someone who would use the knowledge to better civilization. To grow crops and feed people. If the seeds were still in the bunkers, it would be a shame to let them go to waste. Jace McCoy wasn't that person. Maybe the rebels? Not that she had any idea how to find them.

"What's that?" Walker shouted into her ear.

"Found it in the Heap," she said, choosing to trust him with her secret.

"Never seen anything like it. Can I see it later? We're coming into town."

She stowed the tube and prepared to disembark.

"Climb down once the train stops. I'll go first. Run like hell, then hide."

She tensed at his words. Would they split up now that they were away from Long Beach? Did she want to stay with Walker? He was going to go somewhere that Hayden might find him. How long would he wait? If she looked for the seeds, she might have to travel alone. Was she ready to leave? She didn't know much about hopping trains. She couldn't have made it this far without Walker showing her what to do. There was a lot more to it than the trip last night.

Not only did she have more to learn, but if she was going to travel the rails, she'd need supplies. She'd left without being prepared. Among other things, she needed a proper coat, a knife, food, and a hat. The list was extensive. She had a few coins in the bottom of her bag, both silver and copper. She also had the coins from her locker, which was lucky. Outfitting herself would be expensive.

Thoughts spun in her head. Too many to focus on one. She had questions but few answers. She rose to her feet as the train slowed. Train cars crashed up the line, jolting their hopper. The first impact almost sent her flying, but Walker grabbed her arm and showed her how to brace herself, taking the brunt of the lurches with her legs.

She emulated his actions as, once more, her heart thumped hard in her chest. He'd repacked. Now he threw his backpack on, tucked in the straps, and adjusted his water jug so it wouldn't get in the way. She slung her satchel across her chest and fastened it. The train crashes became more infrequent; the train had almost come to a stop. Walker checked both sides and pointed to the right. He swung over the summit of the ladder and she prepared to follow.

Several sets of tracks lined the train yard. This wasn't like Long Beach, where they only maintained two pairs. There were five or six. Two sets of tracks to the left was another train, also stopped. On the right lay a single empty set. Near the station, half a dozen workers milled—unloading and loading the other train. As Walker had predicted, their train car remained outside the trainyard, but only just. GreenCorps security teams in their black and green uniforms and rifles patrolled nearby. She and Walker would have to be quick and quiet to remain unseen.

When Elsa could no longer detect motion, Walker descended the ladder. He hopped to the ground and waited for her feet to hit the gravel, then he ran back in the direction the train had come, crossed the lone set of tracks, and sprinted toward the close edge of the train tracks. She followed with stabbing pains in her ribs and her mouth dry. She expected to hear shouts, but there were none.

A tall wooden fence lined with bushes paralleled the station beyond the railway lines. They ducked behind the fence to find a hole, like a tunnel through the greenery. Inside, the dappled light through the leaves cast a green hue on everything as the branches arched above. They continued past the engine of their train while behind the barrier.

When Walker stopped, he removed his earplugs and returned them to the tin, which he stowed in an outside pocket of his backpack. She took hers from her ears and held them out, the bright orange bits in her dirty hand.

He shook his head. "Keep them for next time. Come with me. I know a place close by where we can rest. Didn't get a lot of sleep last night. I'll need a brief rest. He pitched his voice low and leaned in close so the trainyard workers wouldn't hear them across the fence.

Grateful he wouldn't abandon her just yet, she followed.

Keeping the noise of the train station on their right, they followed the fence another couple of hundred yards before veering left into a grass-covered valley between two hills. A faint path led between them toward a treed area on the hillside, where Walker veered into the woods. The rolling hills cut most of the train noise. They came to a hidden flat area behind some boulders and shaded by trees with a firepit. Others had camped here before. Perhaps even Hayden and Walker, since her companion had known where to take refuge.

"You good if we rest for an hour or two? I'll venture into town this afternoon." He spread his sleeping bag on the flattened grass and tossed her the blanket. "You can use this until you get something better."

"Where are you going after here?" Was he planning to catch a train tonight? Was she invited? She forced herself to look him in the eye.

"I'm headed toward Salt Lake City but will get off part-way. There's a place outside Reno where Hayden will know to go, but he could be three or four days or maybe a week while he waits for another train.

Maybe two weeks. If he even decides to come. Where do you think you'll go?"

Elsa shrugged and looked at the ground. Tears pushed behind her eyes and threatened to spill. She hadn't cried about abandoning Granny yet and fought the impulse. She refused to consider how she'd let the older woman down, deserted her. When had she become so soft? She hadn't cried since she'd lost her mom when she was nine.

She didn't count the assault last night. Physical pain and humiliation were different. She clenched her jaw, refusing to break in front of Walker. She didn't know how long she could hold them back. Her whole life had been upended.

"You can stay with me if you like," Walker said with a shrug. "I can teach you about hopping trains and how to get by in the wider world. Hayden and I have been just about everywhere."

He looked nonchalant as he spoke, but there was something in his tone that made her think her answer mattered. She couldn't tell if he hoped she would say yes or no. She didn't know him well enough to read his expression.

"Thank you, as long as you don't mind," she said, keeping her tone casual. "I don't know much about anything out here."

His smile lit up his face, and his eyes shone at her answer. He may not want to be alone either and may have lost his traveling buddy. Maybe she could make herself indispensable and he would let her stick around. She could do worse than to travel with a knowledgeable companion like Walker.

"I've traveled all over the West since I left home eight years ago. We even went north to Canada once."

"Do you want company in town?" She would love to see a town different than Long Beach.

He hesitated. "You should lie low. You took a beating and look pretty conspicuous. We're better off if nobody recognizes us. GreenCorps recruits will be everywhere with the news from Long Beach."

Elsa swallowed her disappointment. Overnight, the bruises on her body had turned purple. Her face must also be vibrant. Her cheek was tender and swollen, but she'd forgotten how awful she must appear. She looked down, studying her broken fingernails.

"Hey, not your fault."

Walker touched her cheek, and she looked up. His casual contact didn't hurt. It was pleasant, as he was being gentle.

"I'm just as worried if we go into town that people will think I did it. We don't need that type of judgment from the kind people of Sacramento."

"Will you help me find travel gear? A warmer jacket, and a few things. Whatever you think I need the most." Though nobody else was present, she looked around to ensure they were alone and leaned in. "I have a few coins."

"The train we need shouldn't come through for a few days. I'll find time to shop and trade. I'll check the schedule and see about getting you outfitted."

Elsa lay down near the boulder, the rock solid and secure at her back. Her ribs ached, her face hurt, and she was worn out. The bruises were worse down her right side, face and body. Her right eye was swollen and if she closed her left, her vision was blurry. A few feet away, Walker fell asleep almost right away. His deep, even breathing was the loudest sound in their camp.

It was daylight and Elsa found it difficult to rest—for all that she was exhausted. She envied Walker his ability to sleep with ease. If she slept, she'd replay the night before with Jace, over and over. Thinking about it made it hard to breathe. She didn't dare close her eyes.

Birds chirped in the trees, the knee-high grass beyond the trees swished, and leaves above rustled. Country sounds were unfamiliar. With no one to watch, her tears flowed, and she couldn't relax. She'd held them in for hours but could no longer.

She muffled her sobs with her arm and her whole body shook. So much had happened in the last fourteen hours. She hadn't gotten to say goodbye to Granny. What would Avery think about her disappearance? Perhaps her sister would hear about the trouble at Ginny's. Would Jace hurt her, thinking she'd have information? Would Jaxon turn his wife out? Elsa had stocked the safe with most of her savings. There was enough to live on for months if a person was careful. She'd left the new license; perhaps Granny could sell it. Maybe Granny would be all right.

Eventually, Elsa's tears stopped, and she gave in to her exhaustion and slept.

* * *

Walker
May 16th, 2195, Sacramento
Sunrise: 5:50 a.m. Sunset 7:47 p.m.

Travel Log:
Sacramento Station security light, no trouble with arrival shortly after noon. Bulls in the station, crew unloading and loading parked train.

Camped in hills, usual place in the trees.

Got out of Long Beach in a hurry, hopping from north of the station despite security. Avoided regular patrols and the intensified search after McCoy must have awakened.

Hayden stayed behind in Long Beach. No idea when he'll notice I'm gone and follow. Escaped with Elsa. Helped her out of a jam. She's black and blue all down one side and may have cracked ribs, maybe broken. I didn't let on when she woke me crying. She tried so hard not to let me see her tears. Didn't want to embarrass her or make her think her efforts weren't enough. Anyone else would have cracked hours ago, been a sobbing mess. Once she fell asleep, I got up. Didn't sleep long, but it'll be enough for now.

Didn't bother with my final paycheck. Have a stash to collect here in town. Another in Reno and a third in Salt Lake. No idea where we'll end up, but I'll gather what I can. Won't hurt to carry some cash. I trust Elsa not to steal, unlike Hayden.

There's something about Elsa that calls to me. When she turns her fearless topaz eyes on me, I want to be a better man.

CHAPTER 15: ELSA PLUS WALKER

When Elsa awoke, she was alone. The sun had passed the mid-day mark overhead when they'd disembarked the train and it was perhaps mid-afternoon now. Her first panicked thought was that Walker had left her behind, but his sleeping bag and backpack remained nearby. She'd asked him to buy things, but she hadn't given him any coin. He was probably checking the departure schedule.

Her canteen was missing; maybe he was also getting fresh water. From what she'd learned, water cost less outside of SoCal. Water was also expensive in Texas and most of the south. In some places, fresh water ran above ground in lakes and rivers, though that was hard to believe without seeing it. She'd only seen that kind of water in pictures.

Elsa wandered the trail toward town a short distance, but, aware of her bruises and Walker's warning that she'd be conspicuous, she didn't go far. It was quiet here, like early morning on the Heap, before the other workers arrived. The breeze was brisk as it swept out from the trees, causing the grasses to sway, the motion mesmerizing to watch. She swallowed, nervous about being alone in this unknown country.

She stood on tiptoe and checked in all directions, scanning the horizon for danger. There was so much to see when the sky stretched so far, almost without end, disappearing on the horizon. The vast sky was unfamiliar, but peaceful. The black dust and oily grime that covered everything like a second skin at home were absent. The air smelled cleaner, with the aroma of dry grass and moist earth instead of smoke and oil.

The stench of garbage had permeated everything in Long Beach, but it became more apparent with its absence. The Texas fires had also affected SoCal. The oil refineries, wells, and tire factories there still smoldered and the predominant winds blew to the west, coating SoCal in smog. Her great-grandmother had been born before the fires started, but only just. Here the sky was fresh, a clean blue without haze. This was how Elsa had imagined spring.

Sacramento was outside SoCal and was its own city-state, a hub for trade with SoCal, Western Canada, and the pockets of civilization in New Vegas, Utah, and the Denver District. She'd learned this much from the news regularly posted in Vic's store, even if it was a corporation-run store. GreenCorps was based out of Denver and controlled SoCal and much of the West. They had influence in other parts of the country because they owned most of the trains and maintained the railroad lines. They were responsible for most of the commerce and the economy of the western land.

With nothing better to do, Elsa returned to camp and removed the metal cylinder from her bag. She took the pins from her pocket and opened it, spreading the maps on her blanket. She weighted each sheet of the precious paper with a stone to keep them from being stolen by the breeze.

One of the maps showed Davis, California, just outside Sacramento. According to the map legend, the site was less than fifteen miles to the west. The seed bunker was supposed to be located underneath the former University of California. Many of the buildings would be long gone, but those of stone or brick could be partially intact. Markers and signs might still be legible. It might be possible to find the bunker. If she found it, she would have a better idea of the value of the tube. Plus, she was interested in what she'd see if it was intact. Fifteen miles there and fifteen miles back wasn't inconceivable, even on foot.

"What's that?" said Walker.

Elsa jumped at his voice. She hadn't heard his approach. Her heartbeat slowed as she recovered from the surprise. He stood over her, his shadow cast on the map.

She wouldn't survive long if she didn't start trusting him. With a deep breath, she turned and showed him the paper.

"Maps from inside that tube. They show the location of storage bunkers with supplies and a vault with seed storage that was supposed to remain intact and climate-controlled, whatever that means, for hundreds of years."

"How could anyone store seeds like that?"

"A letter from a long ago, from the Department of Agriculture, says they were worried about the loss of genetic diversity and food shortages. I'm not sure I understand the first part, but I'm an expert on food shortage. I'd hardly eaten actual food or regular meals until I worked at Ginny's. We lived on protein bars, oatmeal with dried berries, and supplements. A few times at my sister's, I ate something different." Her mind wandered, thinking of grapes and cheese.

"That's close to here." Walker crouched beside her, looking at the Davis map. He tapped the red triangle at the center with his finger.

His proximity gave her butterflies in her stomach. She didn't want to feel this way around him. He was just a friend. Or was her reaction because he'd helped her when she'd been vulnerable?

"I could walk fifteen miles in a day." She bit the inside of her cheek while she waited for his reaction.

"We could. We have time while we wait for our train."

Elsa looked up, feeling hopeful. "You'd come with me?"

He sat cross-legged next to a bundle he'd brought from town. "Sounds like fun to explore, like a hunt for treasure."

Excitement built, along with the fluttery sensation inside. "That's how I see it. That's why I couldn't sell the tube, even when we were hungry. It meant opportunity." Her heart raced at the prospect of sharing this adventure with Walker.

"Anyone else know about the tube?"

"A handful of local heapsters. At first, I asked around, but only showed Vic. He told me to ask my Granny about it."

"Why her?"

She showed him the leaf engraved on the end. "It's like the rebel leaf, but with fewer veins. I compared the images. Granny used to be involved with the rebels before she was caught and sent to SoCal."

"Does the tube belong to the rebels?" He ran his finger along the etched leaf.

She shook her head. "They might be interested, but it's not theirs. It's older. Pre-Collapse, early twenty-first century."

She returned to her story. "Jace found out about it, but I refused to sell." She grimaced. "Nobody knows it opens. You're the only other person who's seen the maps. It took me a few weeks to figure out how to make the lid appear. The maps and key are a secret."

"Key?"

Elsa retrieved it from the metal cylinder and passed him the silver key. Walker turned it over a few times and then handed it back with a shrug. It didn't look special—nothing more than a key. She'd found dozens in the Heap that looked almost the same, but often covered in rust spots as the thin coating over the metal had corroded. This one had been protected.

"Do you think the bunkers could still be accessible?" She clutched the key in her hand, the metal warming in her palm.

"We won't know unless we try. I don't have any plans, other than to stop at the cabin hideaway for a while. I love being there in summer. Maybe hopping trains for the fall, seeing the countryside. Waking up somewhere new every few days or few weeks, leaving when the spirit takes me."

That could be a pleasant life. Different, but good.

Walker's eyes held a faraway look. Then he smiled and said, "Following the map sounds interesting. Wouldn't you hate to wonder and never check? Where's your sense of adventure?"

Walker's words rang true. She would regret doing nothing, and this was a second chance. She'd never made the journey to Riverside, despite its proximity to Long Beach. She'd been too busy with life. To be honest, she'd been afraid.

"Let's do it. Leave in the morning?" Elsa gathered the maps and rolled them before returning them to the metal cylinder. She added the key and closed the top.

"Why wait? We have several hours of daylight left. I bought food for a few days, including something for a treat, and refilled the canteens. The countryside is like this for miles around. Ideally, we can find fresh water somewhere, but if we're careful, what we have should last until we return. We can be back the day after tomorrow."

Walker tossed her a navy-blue woolen jacket, then a brown, brimmed hat of flexible material. It should be waterproof from the feel.

"Thanks. What did this cost?" Elsa wanted to pay and not have it awkward between them. She didn't enjoy owing people.

"The hat is a present. I didn't pay for the coat."

"You stole it? Then I don't want it." She couldn't take something she hadn't paid for. Someone had made it or bought it and deserved compensation. She dug in her bag and found a couple of coppers.

"Can we take the coins into town and leave them for the jacket?" She couldn't condone stealing, even if she was the one who benefited.

"I'm not going back to pay. It's too risky." He folded his arms across his chest. "If it makes you feel better, the coat was in a corporation store, used."

Elsa felt rotten because Walker had been helpful and kind. She had no right to judge. He was looking out for her, but stealing was wrong. It reminded her of that day on the Heap. The only thing he'd ever done to her was the day he'd attacked Granny. She pushed it from her mind. He'd helped her, and she should just take it, but she'd worked hard all her life to survive and couldn't benefit from someone's loss. To accept the coat went against her principles.

"I appreciate your help, but I can't take it."

"Your loss then. Leave it here. Maybe someone will find it, someone, that needs it." His jaw flared and his eyes narrowed.

"I'm not taking stolen goods." She was being silly. She hated GreenCorps too, but she didn't like her values being tested without a discussion. She wouldn't have stolen it. She wouldn't wear it. The weather looked nice enough, so she wouldn't freeze and perhaps she could buy another when they returned.

"Your loss. You'll be cold tonight." He grinned, daring her to take the coat.

She ignored him while he rolled his sleeping bag and stuffed it in his backpack. Inside, she seethed but settled and stopped talking. She detested wasting anything, yet she refused to back down. So little in her life was in her control right now.

She folded the blanket, which he also stuffed in his pack. It wouldn't fit in her bag, but she wouldn't mind carrying it. She would need to buy something bigger to carry her belongings when they returned, so she added a backpack to her mental list.

"The map showed a railway line as a direct route to the old University campus. We can find it and follow." His voice remained calm.

She was glad he'd changed the subject and didn't seem to hold a grudge.

"The iron rails will have been scavenged, but long ago, the engineers built the land up along the rail lines and should provide a path. It'll keep us going in a straight line out here. Without it, it would be easy to get lost. If we're going to try for a few of these bunkers, I'll buy a compass. Unless Hayden joins us; he has one."

Elsa was excited about the plan and chose not to react to his mention of Hayden. She didn't like him or find him trustworthy. He might never come and he wasn't here right now.

They didn't have many belongings, so they packed their campsite in minutes. She tossed the jacket onto the rocks. Someone else could have it.

They skirted the edge of the nearby hill, then angled north, using the town below as a reference. They found the elevated railway line without the metal rails, just like Walker had said. It headed east to west, so they turned toward where the sun would set and the former town of Davis. She'd never heard of it, so she didn't know if it had been resettled or abandoned and reclaimed by nature. They'd soon find out.

The sunshine warmed her skin, and Elsa was grateful for the hat's protection for her face. Her heels and toes had been coming through the scruffy old boots before her recent job, and these weren't much better—the coin from Ginny's had paid for a different, nicer pair—but these wouldn't last if she did much hiking. Thinking of the boots made her consider her time at Ginny's. It had been good for one thing: coin. But the coin had been a trap. It had prevented her from leaving to find a job with fewer risks. She now understood how Ginny always found willing workers, despite the dangers of the job.

Elsa had slept for a few hours on the train, so at first, she was fresh and the hiking easy. Her ribs must only be bruised, not cracked as she'd feared. Her side ached, but wasn't excruciating. The sharp stabbing pains were absent unless she moved too fast or took too deep a breath. If she had to run, they'd hurt, and walking was uncomfortable but tolerable.

Elsa had never been anywhere so open and empty as the plains. While she saw how that might bother some people, it was an adventure. It was almost like she'd journeyed back in time or to somewhere much farther than a ten-hour train ride from home. She recalled a tattered old book she'd read. Following the railway line was like traveling the yellow brick road to seek her fortune. Would she meet more fellow travelers to share her quest?

* * *

Walker
May 16th (second write)
Sacramento station.

The train we want leaves in two or three days. Snagged a coat for Elsa, who doesn't have proper gear for riding a train or sleeping outside. Bought her a hat. She refused the coat and left it in camp. Stubborn fool. Said it wasn't right to steal. I've never felt bad about stealing from GreenCorps. Still don't. She might regret it, but I won't say another word.

She'll be cold overnight without a jacket since she doesn't have a sleeping bag either. But it's spring and shouldn't be dangerous. Maybe when we come back, she'll reconsider. A couple of nights of freezing her ass off shouldn't hurt. Seldom been over the mountains toward Reno and Tahoe without storms, even snow in July 2189. She'll need something warm, as that's where we're headed after Davis. The high mountain passes are a different weather system than down here. At least summer is coming soon. Won't be long until we can count on pleasant weather.

Leaving Sacramento Station on foot for Davis and the old University of California site. Elsa has maps that could be worth a fortune. Says she's up for a fifteen-mile hike. Not so sure, but we're going to try. She's battered from the trouble last night, but if she's game, so am I. Better than sitting in camp for two or three days with nothing to do but think. Good to get her away from the rail line for a couple days in case they expand the search. Keen to see unfamiliar country and go somewhere I've never been.

CHAPTER 16: ELSA PLUS TATSUDA

Elsa and Walker traveled on the old rail line where grass had grown through the gravel and the railroad ties, leveling the ground so it was easier to walk. The sky stretched in all directions with few clouds and Elsa spent much of the afternoon drinking in the sights. The land was open and exposed, and at times the wind blustered around them, but her new hat kept her hair from blowing in her face. She hadn't appreciated the gift enough, as the stolen jacket had distracted her, but she hadn't received many gifts.

"Thank you for the hat," she said belatedly, breaking the silence.

Walker turned and winked. Their argument, forgotten.

Their path cut through the rolling hills where the breeze lessened, but they spent much of the journey crossing the plains. They didn't see signs of modern habitation, though twice they passed the lumps that held the probable remains of buildings. The scavenger in Elsa itched to excavate, to see what she would unearth, but she reminded herself of their new mission. They only had a few days, then they needed to get back to the train. She didn't have time to stop.

Noticing the potential excavation sites made her think about Davis. What they would find? Would the bunker be accessible? If they had to dig to find the seed bunker, she had her trowel, though a shovel would have been useful.

A line of tall leafy trees crossed near their path as evening approached. The trees created three sides of a square that faced the former train tracks. The sun was near the horizon and brilliant colors spread through the western sky. She'd never seen such a stunning sky. Her feet throbbed and her ribs ached. She was running out of energy, though she refused to complain.

"Let's stop here for the night," said Walker. "There might be clean water or shelter."

Elsa looked around, not seeing either. Other than the trees, it looked as windswept and uninhabited as the rest of the country.

"What makes you think there's water?" She tilted her head to the side. She wasn't doubting, but was curious and wanted to learn.

"The trees," said Walker. "When the trees grow in straight lines, often they were planted as windbreaks. Once there would have been houses or farms here, even if it's barren now. If there were homes, there might be water."

He squinted as he pointed. He didn't wear his goggles. Out here, away from the smoke, she hadn't often wanted hers either, despite their protection.

Elsa considered how many people were rumored to have lived in pre-plague California when it was all one state instead of a few towns, like Sacramento, and the trash heap sprawl of SoCal. There wouldn't have been much empty land. Most of the people had died of viruses long ago or been decimated by the disaster. The following generations of survivors had fought over water and resources.

It hadn't been until GreenCorps emerged as an industrial power, that people could make a living and became re-organized. According to GreenCorps, they'd shipped water and supplies to the workers via rail and exported scrap metal, plastic nurdles, and excavated goods of value. They sold the Heap licenses, operated the railroad, and employed the people in SoCal and beyond. Seeing this empty land, she wasn't sure she believed the corporation version of history where they claimed they'd saved everyone.

"This wasn't big enough to have been a town, so anyone living here would've had their own well with water for drinking, washing, and growing crops," said Walker as they left the earthen bank and approached the row of leafy trees.

Their light brown bark was thick and jagged, with deep grooves and ridges. The ground was littered with seed pods and knobby branches. Drifts of white fluff collected in thick clumps at their bases and in the bushes. As the wind picked up, white cottony fuzz floated through the air. Elsa's eyes itched, and she suppressed a sneeze.

"What kind of trees are these?" They were higher and narrower than most of the trees that had dotted the hills. Few trees at home had roots deep enough to find water.

Walker laughed. "Cottonwoods."

He brushed some of the cotton from her hair. When he stood close, he seemed taller, towering over her. Her heart fluttered. Flustered by his proximity, she distracted herself by asking more questions.

"Wouldn't wells be filled in or dried up? The people have been gone for almost two hundred years."

"Sometimes they've been reclaimed. We should check."

A search of the area around the first mound in the square yielded nothing, as did the parcel next to it. Behind the trees were another three lumps. The line of trees was thicker than she'd expected, no longer a single line, but filled with trees of all sizes and saplings shooting from the edges. It had become a tangled stand of trees, a narrow forest, with layers of debris that crunched underfoot. Beyond the trees, they found a structure, about three feet high. It couldn't be seen from the tracks or the front of the trees, but there was a hidden well.

Scrawled on the nearest side was a list of dates.

"The well was opened and recovered in 2165. They checked it in 2193," said Walker, scanning the writing. "Water was good only two years ago. Should be fine."

"Should we boil it?" She'd read underground water could be contaminated.

"We could, just to be safe. Sometimes that isn't an option, but I'd like a fire tonight. There's plenty of wood from the trees. A fire would keep wolves away from this area. There didn't use to be this far south when there were more people, but as their prey moved into open land, the wolves followed."

"Do we need to take turns sleeping to watch for them?" Elsa bit her lip, afraid he'd mock her for her question. She didn't have experience with animals, other than dogs, cats, and rats.

"People are more likely to be a problem than wolves. But not out here. Haven't seen smoke, roads, wagon tracks, anything. This is quiet country. Also haven't seen signs of wolves. They're a remote possibility, but don't worry. Unless they're starving, they'll ignore us."

Glad to be with someone who knew things, she gave him a shy smile that he returned. Working together, they uncovered the well's heavy wooden lid. A stainless-steel bucket sat just below the top on a narrow platform. A sturdy rope was attached to the bucket and tied around the platform. It was dark inside.

Walker dropped the pail, and it splashed several yards below before he hauled it up.

"Water smells fine," he said, setting it near his pack.

Elsa took a long drink from her refilled canteen. She'd only sipped throughout the afternoon and now felt free to quench her thirst. Walker drank from the bucket. So much for boiling. She was familiar with flat tanker water with a faint metallic aftertaste. Unboiled water straight from the ground was delicious.

"Look for a fire pit. Should be one nearby. This is an excellent camp." He nodded as he scanned the area. "We can't be the first travelers to want to stay near water."

They located a campsite not far away, in a grove of trees. Someone had constructed a shelter with a slanted roof of slabs and three rough walls. It wasn't waterproof but would cut the wind. The open side faced a rock-lined fire pit and someone had stacked a pile of firewood against an outside wall.

"We should gather firewood. We'll leave some chopped wood behind. I don't want to use the entire supply. I don't have an ax, just a hatchet, but we can replace some of what we burn."

It amazed Elsa that his guesses had been so accurate. "How did you know this would be here? Have you been here before?"

He shook his head. "The west is covered with campsites and shelters like this. A lot of us vagabonds wander. We have a code. *'Use what you need. Leave what you can.'* We help each other."

"Don't you have a home to return to? When you're tired of traveling?" She wouldn't like to wander forever. Someday, she wanted a new home. With a pang, she thought of her family that she'd left behind.

Walker shook his head.

Elsa moved around the grove, collecting branches. She was careful how she bent, accommodating her sore ribs. Was his code another reason he was helping?

"What about a new home?" She worried at her bottom lip with her teeth.

"I haven't found anywhere yet, besides Jim's cabin. Never had a reason to settle. Maybe when I'm older and hopping trains gets too difficult."

"You mentioned that you've been on the road for eight years," said Elsa. "How old were you when you left home?" He must have been young; he wasn't much older than she was.

"Fourteen. Lived down south, but we were burnt out. My mother died, so I had no reason to stay. Santa Fe was a lot like SoCal, a low-income town controlled by GreenCorps." His voice was steady as he shared. "Only way out was to become one of their recruits, or hop a train and escape. Hayden lived next door. His mother threw him out. He didn't have anyone either, so we decided to be each other's family."

"What if he doesn't follow this time?" Gathering wood was easy when most of it was so dry. There must not have been much rain this spring.

"He will. It's just a matter of when. Once we spent the summer apart, but he waited for me near Reno. We have a typical route, even if this was our first stop in SoCal."

Walker dragged a thick branch toward the firepit.

"His drug problem comes and goes. He's fine if he can refrain from using. He's better company when we're poor. We worked the mines in the mountains near Denver last winter and made good coin. He suggested we go where it was warmer before heading back on the road, so we hopped a ride to SoCal. He spent all of his coin on drugs and couldn't work."

"You didn't." He didn't seem the type to need an escape. He seemed present.

Walker shook his head. "Never touched that stuff. Believe in living in the real world, not kiting my way through life. Plus, I'm a saver. If I ever find somewhere I want to stay, I'll have a payment for a home or for whatever I need to make a living, not just a shack that can barely be patched together."

Her cheeks flamed at the offhand comment. Not a home like hers with Granny, which fit that description; it had been more patch than house. There had been little of the original building left and they'd never had coin for improvement. Granny had lived in that house for close to fifty years. Elsa's chest tightened. If she hadn't left, she probably would have become just like her great-grandmother in time. Tough, jaded, but with fewer life experiences beyond the Heap. She wished she'd asked more about where her grandmother had grown up or about the rebellion. That would have been interesting.

Elsa didn't ask Walker where he'd stashed his money. He said he'd hidden it, that he didn't carry his wealth. He wouldn't tell her, nor should he. In his place, she wouldn't tell anyone either. She felt relaxed around him and it was easy to forget that they weren't much more than strangers. Had he ever been close to anyone, besides Hayden? She hadn't. While Janna was a friend, they'd drifted apart due to limited free time and responsibilities. Elsa had also never been in love. The thought gave her a funny twitch in her stomach. It was easier to look after herself and be alone, but that wasn't what she was doing. She liked Walker's company and hoped they had more time together. Examining the thought made her uncomfortable.

"How are your ribs?"

She jumped at his sudden question.

"Okay, but sore." She downplayed how stiff they felt. Compared to her initial fear they were broken, they were fine. She could deal with the pain.

"I was afraid McCoy had cracked them. I got there just as he kicked you."

"He kicked me a few times. I'm just thankful he'd taken off his boots." The lump lodged itself in her throat, and she inhaled, noticing where the pain increased.

"Picked up some balm in town that's supposed to soothe sore muscles. Made by someone local. Figured after walking today, you could use some. Want me to put it on your back and ribs?"

He was being so nice.

"Please, I would appreciate that."

Walker used a wooden match to light the fire just as the sun dipped below the horizon. With the sun gone, the temperature dropped. Bands of pink and orange streaked the sky and stretched across the horizon. Elsa had grown up with smoky gray skies, banks of mist, and soupy fog off the filthy ocean. Haze obscured the sun and moon—nothing like these spectacular colors. She was speechless at their beauty.

"Let's get you fixed up," said Walker. "Then I'll cook."

The fire crackled and popped and the air smelled like smoke, but a cleaner version than she was accustomed to—more wood than chemical. This scent was almost pleasant. She hoped the dim light hid her blush at the idea of Walker touching her skin. At least he wasn't like Jace and only wanted to help.

Elsa stood next to him and lifted her shirt on the right, exposing the bruises decorating her ribs, including the one larger purple patch the size of her hand in the center where the last impact had been. Another area on her back felt sore, too, but she couldn't see it.

He whistled. "Shit, those must hurt."

"A little." She sucked in her breath as the first tentative touch of the cream was cold. Walker's touch remained gentle as he rubbed the balm on her bruises. Her skin warmed, becoming hot on her sore muscles as he massaged it in with his fingertips. Her side and back tingled, and his hand lingered. "If you hadn't interrupted, he might have beaten me to death."

"He bragged all evening that he was going to break you, ride you all night. I despised him from the moment he opened his mouth." Walker's voice was tight.

She glanced behind her and saw that his jaw was clenched and his eyes had darkened.

"He'd have continued, even with bite marks. He just wanted to make sure you wouldn't fight anymore." His mouth twisted at the end.

From his tone and the strength of his dislike, Walker had taken the attack personally. Had there been something similar in his past? He'd never mentioned a father. Something like that would explain his willingness to do so much to help her escape a dangerous situation.

His hands had stopped applying balm, though his fingers still traced the outside edge of her bruises. Elsa swallowed a lump in her throat. His hands felt pleasant on her skin and her face warmed at the continued contact. He moved to put the cream on bruises she could've reached in the front.

"Annie said he'd hurt four other girls in the last year. That's why Ginny was pleased to spare them. She didn't want you hurt, but she was saving one of hers. That's why his brother's arrangement was advantageous to her."

"I didn't know," Elsa said. "The other girls didn't talk to me. Except for Annie."

Walker finished doctoring her ribs, and she covered her injuries again.

He paused and cleared his throat. "Annie didn't want to scare you."

That made sense. She'd been terrified anyway.

"Want some on your face too?" Walker touched her cheekbone, a featherlight graze that shot throughout her body. "Not by your eye. It might burn. Besides, the swelling around your eye is going down. It was worse this morning." His voice was softer than before and he stood close enough that his heat warmed her.

Elsa appreciated his direct approach regarding her injuries. He didn't lie and say she looked fine. She knew she looked awful.

"Why are you being so nice to me?" She meant to keep her questions to herself, not ask aloud, but she was off-kilter, standing so close to him. Her gaze wandered upward to his lips. His scent reminded her of the outdoors, like a tree with a hint of something sweet.

"Told you, I owe you." He dropped his gaze to the ground. "I never should have gone along with Hayden's stupid plan. For two weeks, he'd talked about that crazy lady who'd shot him for no reason. Said he wanted to scare her. His elbow was swollen, and he needed the medic. He was angry about spending coin he'd rather have spent on drugs."

She clenched her fists. "That's not what happened."

"I gathered that," he said, his lips pressed together and his voice rougher than usual. Walker passed her the container with the soothing balm and the lid.

He seemed angry that Hayden had lied.

"I wouldn't have helped him if I realized what he was up to. Or if I'd figured out sooner who he meant to scare. It was a stupid plan. I wouldn't have hurt you or your grandmother."

Elsa met his gray eyes with a warm smile. He'd remembered her and Granny from the first meeting, too.

"The day after you arrived, Hayden tried to steal from us. Only Granny was above ground while I was digging. She yelled at him and I came to see what was happening. He thought we were weak, I guess— an easy target. Granny fired wide, but close enough to chase him off.

She seldom needs a second shot. She shot Wade three times when he was younger, before he gave up robbing solo and joined GreenCorps. Course, he was a slow learner."

"He's that brute that made you nervous when I walked you home from Ginny's?"

She nodded. "My next-door neighbor. He propositioned me a few times and stole my take from the Heap. If he'd caught me outside and alone, he'd have raped me." Her voice shook.

"He's a shit person. I overheard stuff around town. He sold his own sister south to the slavers. She's probably working in southern Texas fighting fires or part of the sex trade by now. I wouldn't wish that on anyone."

Elsa's breath caught, and she stumbled back, feeling off-balance. Walker reached out a hand to steady her.

"That's the job he got for Janna?" Bile rose in the back of her throat and her chest constricted. At Walker's nod, she said, "If I didn't hate him already, that clinches it. I feel sick."

His warm gray eyes looked sympathetic, though the line of his mouth looked angry.

"She was a friend?" He held out the small jar he'd been using. "Hang onto the cream. I can put it on for you in the morning. It'll be easier for me, then you don't have to bend or strain your ribs. I meant to earlier, but got distracted by the maps."

Elsa nodded as she dropped the container into her satchel. She was shaken by what had happened to Janna. She'd heard the expression, "Sold south." From the stories that filtered back to SoCal, it was always horrible.

"My father talked about selling Avery south when she turned twelve. That's when we ran away to Granny's." Elsa's voice shook. Some people were horrible. It was painful that she hadn't known about Janna, yet there was nothing she could have done. Her friend was gone, and it was too late. She'd been missing for weeks.

Walker squeezed Elsa's arm and grabbed his backpack. "Let's cook. I'm starving."

He wrapped four potatoes in crumpled foil and half-buried them in ashes near the fire's embers to roast as he added more firewood. Elsa stared at the hypnotic dance of the flames and the twirling sparks as they ascended into the night while she waited for dinner. She let them soothe her aching heart.

When the food was ready, they ate a quiet meal of roasted potatoes with a small sprinkling of salt. She wasn't sure if she'd ever had anything so delicious to eat, not even the lavish meals at Ginny's. The fresh air and exercise added to her appetite and the flavor. She shivered as the night became cold. In the distance came the yipping from a group of animals, causing her to head to jerk up in alarm.

"Coyotes," said Walker with a partial smile. "Not wolves. They won't bother us."

She'd seen the dog cousins hunting rats in the daytime. They weren't dangerous.

When it was time to sleep, Elsa paused to watch the sky beyond the trees just a little longer. It was pitch black but blanketed with a multitude of stars. Her breath caught at the beauty. She'd never seen the sky like this, reinforcing the idea that out here, away from SoCal, was like another world where anything was possible.

When she lay down in the shelter on the hard ground, she wished for the abandoned jacket and that she hadn't been too stubborn to accept it. She wrapped herself in the blanket and, though it was cold, she fell asleep in seconds. Her sleep was fitful, and she tossed and turned all night, waking several times, her heart racing and a scream on her lips. Jace starred in her dreams, his fists and feet landing blows. Sometimes she couldn't fight him off and he'd finished what he started.

After the first time, Elsa wished she dared to reach out to Walker and ask for comfort. She didn't want to wake him, so she lay staring out into the dark until her body calmed and she returned to sleep. She was used to handling things on her own. Not long before dawn, she awoke to find she was no longer cold; Walker had wrapped around her, his arm heavy and comforting. His even breathing helped her return to sleep, feeling safe.

* * *

Tatsuda slid his hand into the pocket of a nearby brown woolen jacket. He enjoyed working crowds around Denver's shops in the evening after payday at the mines. The business sector was guaranteed to be busy Friday night. He extracted a wad of paper money, Canadian currency. He couldn't spend it himself, but he knew a guy who could exchange it, for a cut, of course. Wandering downtown, he avoided the banks and GreenCorps headquarters. He couldn't get picked up again so soon, or he might be recognized or remembered, but in a city this size, there'd be new people doing the job in a few months and he'd be forgotten. He liked living here, the center of the modern world.

The city nestled in the mountains that surrounded it like a blue bowl with a layer of fluffy clouds on the edges that balanced on the gray and snow-tipped peaks behind. They'd restored more in Denver than most pre-Collapse cities. Close to a hundred thousand people lived and worked here.

Tatsuda moved between neighborhoods, keeping his head down, while he tried to slide through life unseen. He'd lived on the streets for years and tried not to be noticed. It had been over three years since he'd left New Vegas. He'd followed a group of youths that hopped trains. They'd ditched him when they got to the city and didn't have any use for him. He was just glad they'd let him tag along to show him how to get on and off the train.

He was near the station now, and the cars bashing into each other reminded him of the first day he'd come to town. The train ride had been cold and much longer than he'd expected.

Pick-pocketing was easier in Denver with so many people. People with coin supported businesses by spending. This was a working city, and one of the few places that forced GreenCorps to pay living wages. Their economy was based on the wealth gathered from others, but disproportionately from the nearby mines for silver, gold, gypsum, marble, and iron. If the miners stopped working, GreenCorps suffered.

Tatsuda pulled his wits into focus. It didn't matter how he'd gotten here, just that he was here now. He peeked around the corner and wandered into the next block, toward the gambling halls and brothels. They were always near the train station for the workers and those with good pay. He watched the crowd, looking for someone distracted or busy, and found his next mark.

A young woman sat alone on a bench overlooking a park. This was a rough neighborhood, and she didn't fit in. She wore nice clothes and shiny shoes. She'd tipped her head back and the May sunshine lit her face. Her eyes were closed, unwary.

Tatsuda sidled toward her bench on silent feet and unclasped her bag. She remained oblivious as his hand lifted her coin purse out of her larger satchel. His heart raced as he kept the coins from jingling when he transferred his take to the deep pocket of his long jacket. He kept moving and found three more people too busy to notice his dexterous fingers dipping into their pockets—a profitable afternoon.

CHAPTER 17: ELSA PLUS WALKER

The rest of Elsa's and Walker's journey to Davis was uneventful. They approached the former town at mid-morning after continuing on the old rail line to a former university campus which was now uninhabited. Old university buildings made of brick and stone stood in ruin, their walls partially intact, the roofs gone. Trees grew inside, their roots crushing the rocks further. One day, nothing would be left of these structures.

They followed the map and searched the ruins for about an hour before they found what they were looking for in an old garden. A building made of stone and partially covered in thick vines decorated the middle of the garden beside a dried-up pond, thick with weeds. The map indicated they needed to locate a pole with the leaf emblem, which they found as part of the doorjamb of the stone building. Elsa and Walker circled the stone hut and returned to the front. The roof looked intact, as did the windowless walls, which must be constructed with quality materials and craftsmanship to be still standing.

The door was the only way in. It was made of heavy, once painted metal—probably steel or galvanized iron. Flecks of ocean blue paint remained. The overhang of the roof and the stone walls had protected the building from the worst of the weather. Excitement shot through Elsa. She glanced at Walker to see if he shared her enthusiasm. Wearing a toothy grin, he set down his backpack to remove a candle lantern and his matches. He lit the lantern in preparation.

"What are you waiting for?" he said, his eyes shining. "See if your key works."

Elsa's hands trembled as she put the key to the lock. It slid in with no trouble. A green light appeared above the keyhole. A thrill raced down her spine when she turned it and there was a faint click. The door wouldn't budge even after she tugged the handle. She bit her lip and tried again. She held back tears of frustration. In desperation, she yanked and jarred her ribs, but the door slid only an infinitesimal amount. It appeared to be wedged.

Crushing disappointment filled her lungs as she tugged again with the same result. She couldn't pull harder without hurting herself. She'd invested a lot of hope into what they might find inside.

"Building may have settled, changing how the door will open," said Walker. "The hinges may have bent just enough to be crooked. Can I try?"

She stepped back. They'd come all this way, and she wanted to see what was inside. He passed her the lantern.

Walker tugged, and the door creaked but remained closed. He stepped back to examine it. He moved closer again and lifted the handle and door upward as he pulled, groaning. Beads of sweat appeared on his forehead and the corded muscles of his forearms bulged. This time, the door scraped and squeaked, moving as he applied additional pressure. Elsa's heart raced once more. She felt like cheering his efforts.

When the door was half-open, he stopped and mopped his brow with his sleeve.

"That's wide enough for us to get through." He wiped his hands on his pants and shared a rare, lopsided grin with her. The smile sent jolts throughout her. He wasn't just handsome, he was also smart and kind. She felt a sudden, strong physical attraction.

When she went to return the candle lantern, he shook his head.

"You should do the honors," he said with a faint smile. "It's your discovery."

He gestured to the doorway and the dark room beyond. Courtesy was rare in her experience, so his consideration stood out.

Elsa paused at the threshold. The air emanating from the room smelled damp and musty with overtones of mold. Thick sheets of dusty cobwebs draped through the air. She removed her trowel from her satchel and stepped forward, breaking the cobwebs with her tool. She sneezed several times but didn't stop her advance. About eight feet into the cold stone room was a second door. She used the same key to unlock it.

This door opened with ease. Walker crowded close behind, his warm breath on the nape of her neck. Beyond this door, a set of stairs descended underground. The air wasn't fresh, but it no longer smelled of damp or mold, just stale. It must have had a better seal, as there were no spider webs here. Everything looked clean. The metal stairs and the blue handrail seemed solid with no rust, which made sense as it had been sealed away from the elements. The treads were made of metal grating, similar to the train platforms. With holes in the stairs, it was dizzying to look down. She couldn't see the bottom, and she kept her eyes averted.

"What are we waiting for? Let's go," said Walker.

His voice echoed down the stairwell. It was tough to tell how far down it went.

"What about the doors?" Elsa bit her lip, looking back. "I don't know if the key works from inside." The candle lantern's faint glow created a small puddle of light that pushed against the enveloping darkness.

Walker trotted back outside and collected rocks. He wedged them in both doorways so the wind couldn't lock them inside by accident.

"Good idea." Her voice sounded unsure, creating an eerie echo throughout the cavernous space. She was familiar with being underground in the Heap, but didn't like the idea of being trapped somewhere unknown. She stowed the trowel, so she'd have one hand for the light and another for the handrail. The steep staircase below was swallowed by the darkness.

She extended the light as far as possible for a better view, but the first flight disappeared around a sharp corner. She breathed deep and stepped down, Walker right behind. Their feet clanged on the metal and echoed unnaturally loud in the cool darkness. As she rounded the corner, the lantern revealed another flight of stairs. She stepped onto the first stair. There was a click and a popping sound, then a whirring noise started below. She jumped back, Walker steading her elbow, but the noises were only lights and a fan turning on. Pale strips of yellow light appeared below the handrail, illuminating the treads better than the candle.

Elsa was tempted to blow out the flame but continued to let it burn. What if the lights shut off? The unrelieved blackness beyond the circle of light seemed total.

They descended thirteen flights of stairs before they came to a dusty concrete floor at the bottom. Fresh air circulated throughout, the moving air cool on her face. She shivered and goosebumps rose on both arms from both the chill and anticipation.

A third door at the bottom of the stairs barred the way. This too opened with the same key. This door's motion was smooth and quiet. Their footsteps on the gritty floor created the only noise. Her heart beat so hard it should be audible in the silence. Walker's breathing, too, seemed magnified by the surrounding quiet. She bit her lip and stepped inside the seed bunker.

A second set of lights switched on inside the room, perhaps triggered by motion. This time she didn't startle at the popping sounds as the lights turned on in a wave, starting near and continuing away from them for several seconds. The room before them was immense and filled with racks of shelves, as far as they eye could see. The dry air was colder here, probably to prevent the seeds from growing or decaying. The closest shelves held survival gear. Beyond, the racks contained identical brown boxes with white labels—the seeds.

The near space was stocked with supplies Elsa couldn't have afforded, especially new or in pristine condition, like these were. More than a dozen sleeping bags lined the shelves—stuffed in oblong sacs of eye-popping fire red, sky blue, and grass green. To someone used to the grays and browns of SoCal, and faded fabric or plastic clothing, the bright colors almost assaulted her eyes. She found assorted backpacks in small, medium, and large.

Further investigation revealed hundreds of boxes of dehydrated rations that said, *"Just add water."* On the opposite side of the entryway were shelves with lanterns, ropes, containers marked as battery packs, and small boxes with portable camp stoves. There were matches, lanterns, knives, an ax, a collapsible shovel, and more. She'd never seen so much that was new in one place. This was better than the large GreenCorps trading post.

"Looks like you don't need to buy gear," Walker said. "You got lucky." He slid a flaming red tube off the shelf with the sleeping bags. "I'm upgrading." He shot her another grin that set her heart racing.

She placed the candle lantern on the floor by the door. When her hands were free, he tossed a sleeping bag tube to her as well. The slippery fabric was sturdy, flexible, and probably water-resistant.

"Choose a pack," he said. "You're not that big, so get one your size. You want to be able to carry it."

For a fleeting instant, Elsa felt reluctant to take anything. The gear on the shelves wasn't hers and she didn't want trouble. But this had been left here a hundred and seventy-five years ago to help people. And this was her discovery. She could choose some gear and nobody would miss it. They wouldn't take it all. It was like Walker's vagabond code: Take what you need.

In the end, she chose a medium black and forest green pack, filling it with the sleeping bag, a multi-purpose tool with several blades, socks, gloves, a change of clothing, a jacket, and a pair of durable-looking pants. She removed her worn plastic clothing and slipped on a second set of dark brown pants from the shelf. At the last minute, she added a box of water purification tablets to the front pocket with matches and a solar-powered flashlight. She'd never owned so many possessions at once.

Walker packed rope, a tarp, more matches, a compass, a portable stove with fuel, and a first aid kit in a nylon pouch, while she filled the excess space in her pack with dried rations, stackable cooking pots, and thick but light-weight plastic dishes and cutlery. She lifted the pack several times to judge its weight.

Near the end of the shelves, she found pairs of the nicest boots she'd ever seen. They were solid and had good treads on the bottom. She looked at them for several minutes, biting the inside of her cheek, before grabbing a pair. While she wore newly refinished boots, the best she'd ever had, these were pristine and never worn before. She tried several pairs until she found some that fit. She paced the room, trying them out. They were stiff but didn't rub. Walker watched for a minute and also tried on a couple of pairs until he found some.

"We'll have so much new stuff, we'll need to be careful not to be targets," he said. "First chance you get, muddy your boots and smear your pack with dirt. Make them appear used. That's why I'm keeping my old pack."

Elsa didn't want to destroy something by taking it from the bunker itself, but she wanted something as proof that they'd been here. It wasn't just about supplies, but the seeds. A discovery like this could change the lives of so many. She wandered to the shelves where the seed collection began. Inside the boxes, there were hundreds of foil packages with the same types of seeds. She made a note of the kinds of seeds stored here. Most were things she'd never heard of: almond, apricot, sweet cherry, fig, kiwi fruit, olive, persimmon, pistachios, plum, pomegranate, and walnuts. The familiar ones were peaches and grapes. Remembering the sweet fruit tastes, her mouth watered.

In the end, she chose two different packets, labeled "Almond" and "Apricot," and took a handful of each. Both were something new. They showed pictures of trees on the packet and held notes on the back with instructions and information. One was a nut, and the other was fruit.

Food. If anyone would be interested in the maps and key, it would be because of food plants.

While she might get the best price from the GreenCorps president in Denver, she couldn't imagine selling to the corporation. People like her wouldn't see any benefit from the results. GreenCorps would plant them and sell the produce at prices regular people couldn't afford. Maybe she should check if the other bunkers were also intact. She didn't know who else she could tell about the bunkers, but there had to be someone out there who would do the right thing.

When they'd collected and stowed everything they planned to take, Elsa estimated that they'd been underground for a few hours. Down the hall, there were bunk beds in several rooms where they could have stayed, but there was no reason to sleep here except novelty. There should be hours of daylight left, and she didn't wish to remain so far from the trains. She needed to be further from SoCal, so she'd never be found. If they left now, they could return to the campsite where they'd spent last night and be back near the trains in Sacramento by midday tomorrow.

"Time to go?" She wondered how Walker would react. The seed bunker was incredible, and they hadn't explored all of it, but they had survival gear and proof of its existence—that was enough.

He nodded. "Aim for the trees where we spent last night? There was shelter and fresh water, and we can try out the sleeping bags?"

"I don't think I'll be cold this time."

"You were cold last night?" A crease appeared on his forehead.

She hadn't meant to complain. After each round of nightmares, she'd lain awake cold, unable to sleep until the last time when she'd woken up next to Walker.

At her reluctant nod, he said, "Next time, move closer to the fire or closer to me. I won't mind. I'm always warm. Probably wouldn't even wake me."

He wasn't offering more than body heat, but she flushed anyway. He might not know he'd slept next to her. He must have wandered in his sleep. At least he hadn't reminded her of the jacket she'd left behind.

"Thanks." She appreciated the offer.

She locked the door at the base of the stairs. From within came the snapping sounds as the banks of lights shut off, once again moving in waves as sections turned dark. Walker took the candle lantern and led the way up the steep metal stairs. The light strips seemed pale after the bright lights of the bunker.

The underground damp and cold, left Elsa's hands icy, so she welcomed the warmth as they ascended. When they reached the surface, nothing had changed. The stones Walker had set to hold the doors open were still in position, and she sighed with relief. Kicking the rocks aside, she locked the doors behind them, a red light flashing above the keyhole. The lock used the key, but it had an electronic component. She tried the handle to be sure the door locked. Satisfied, she turned to go.

Outside was sunny and warm and she breathed in—fresh air filling her lungs. Even with the pain in her ribs, it was worth it. The sky was the bluest she'd ever seen, with a smattering of fluffy white clouds in patches—beautiful and clean. SoCal seemed a world away. If it wasn't for family, she'd never consider returning. What would her nieces think of the blue sky? A pang filled her at everything they were missing.

Elsa and Walker reversed their path and trudged along the rail line to the campsite in the trees where they'd slept the night before. As predicted, her new boots were stiff as boards at first, but she didn't get blisters. Her feet were cushioned and didn't throb as they had the night before.

"We should try everything new," said Walker when they reached the shelter. "Charge the stove, battery packs, and flashlights in the sun. Cook on the stove tonight and see how it works." He set out the battery packs to charge while they still had daylight.

"Try out the new rations instead of protein bars?" she asked with a cheerful smile. He'd run out of potatoes. They'd been too heavy to carry many, but they'd been special. She'd had enough protein bars to last a lifetime and looked forward to something different.

His answer was a crooked grin.

* * *

Walker
May 17th, 2195, Halfway back from Davis
Sunrise: 5:50 a.m. Sunset 7:48 p.m.

The seed bunker was a windfall. Almost felt guilty about the riches within. Could have taken three times what we did and left enough for another three dozen people. Elsa mentioned possibly selling the key and maps. Not to GreenCorps though. None of my business, but I like the idea that she could share the wealth. Someone should plant and tend the young trees. Trees take a long time to develop. It would take years to make a difference.

If GreenCorps gets the seeds, they'll plant and tend them for the wealthy. They already control water, most animal and dairy farms, and staple crops, such as corn, potatoes, and wheat. The rebels have it right when they say the wealth should be redistributed and other companies should be allowed to compete.

Elsa had bad dreams again, restless all night. She isn't getting much sleep and woke me twice, screaming in her sleep. Slept near her after that, so she would be warm and comforted. If I could go back and hurt Jace worse, I would.

CHAPTER 18: ELSA PLUS WALKER

The next morning, Elsa and Walker completed the last leg of the trip and returned to Sacramento and the hidden camp in the hills near the train yard. Walker expressed surprise at how quiet it was for the time of year. He'd expected to see other hoppers, but she was glad they were on their own.

"I want to confirm the train schedule in town," Walker said. "The train should be either tomorrow morning or the next day."

"Still think I should stay here?" She wanted to see a town that wasn't Long Beach.

"Your bruises are healing, but you're too distinctive. Just keep an eye on the gear. Mix some mud to dirty your pack, at least to take the shine off. Walking back made our boots dusty."

"How long will you be gone?" She would be lost if he never returned and she didn't know enough about hopping trains. She hoped nothing delayed him. A friendship was growing between them and she could learn from him. She hated feeling helpless or like she might owe him. If they were together, they could be partners.

"Ninety percent of train-hopping is waiting," said Walker. "I won't be more than a couple hours. I'm going to buy food and scout the trainyard. Want to make sure nothing's changed since Hayden and I went through a couple of months ago. See if we can use the front end to hop on or if it's too exposed. See if there's news from SoCal."

He headed for town.

Elsa chewed inside her cheek, trying to set her worried thoughts aside. He'd be back.

Quiet descended after Walker departed, though the peace was disturbed soon after by the distant crashing of slack cars in the trainyard, as a train either started or stopped. She couldn't tell which from here. A small yellow-brown bird with white stripes on its wings landed on a tree branch and sang for a while. She held her breath and listened to its song, relieved the train had stopped making noise, which grated on her nerves.

She spotted two more birds in nearby trees. Returning her gaze to the first bird, she couldn't take her eyes off it sitting amidst the pale green of the spring leaves. She was familiar with only seagulls and crows. This bird was tiny and beautiful. The world was full of new colors she'd seldom seen.

Bored with waiting and tired of figuring out the overwhelming prospect of what to do with the seeds now that she'd found them, Elsa walked back toward the train station and chose a vantage point on the hill where she could watch the trains arrive and depart. She hadn't been there long when a train arrived from the south. She watched as a boy, maybe fifteen or sixteen years old, hopped off the train. Not past the edge of the trainyard, like Walker had taught, but near the station. She covered her mouth in horror as a trio of recruits in their uniforms captured the boy.

The recruits asked something, but the boy shook his head. One of the GreenCorps soldiers must not have liked the boy's answer. The soldier smashed the butt of his rifle on the boy's head. His head snapped back. The other soldiers joined in, pummeling him to the ground. The boy's screams cut off, but the beating continued.

She slunk back to camp trembling all over and was sick by the trees. That might have happened to her without Walker. GreenCorps recruits were often violent. It wasn't the first death they'd caused.

"You want the good news or the bad news?" Walker dropped a bundle on the ground.

Elsa jumped when he spoke, her heart racing. There'd been no noise on the path; he was as quiet as a cat. Either that or the ground absorbed sound and didn't crunch or rattle like the dry gravel in SoCal. She should have watched better. What if it had been someone else entering camp?

"Bad?"

"There are Wanted posters all over town with your likeness. There's a reward of ten gold coins for your capture and return to Jace McCoy and GreenCorps."

Her mouth fell open, speechless. She swallowed and winced at the painful tickle in her throat. Recovering from the surprise of the massive reward, she said, "The reward is too high. That doesn't make sense. I didn't hurt Jace much. It was just a bite, nothing permanent."

"It's not for biting him. This is for theft." Walker's eyes bored into her own.

"I didn't steal anything." Her forehead tightened as she frowned.

"Posters say you stole a metal cylinder. Says it was property of GreenCorps."

"He offered me two, then three silver coins. I wouldn't sell."

Walker raised an eyebrow.

"When would I have stolen it? I didn't leave the floor after Jace came into Ginny's. I was working and didn't have a chance. If he'd paid me, the tube would have been with his stuff in his hotel room, not in my locker. You carried me out naked. Where was it hidden?"

His shoulders relaxed, and he smiled. "I don't believe his version, but I wondered where it came from."

"Jace McCoy is a lying ass." Her anger caused her words to come out in a hiss.

"When did he try to buy it?" Walker's head cocked to the side.

His question didn't contain an accusation or doubt, just curiosity, so she calmed her voice to answer. There was no reason to be defensive.

"Just before my shift. I went to Vic's to buy new boots for Granny. I'd been stocking our place for when she returned because I was going to quit Ginny's as soon as Granny came home. To hell with Jaxon. Jace didn't like that I refused to sell. I left without buying anything, which is why I had coins in my bag. Normally I don't carry cash or tokens."

"When did you find the tube?"

"The day before I met you," she said. "When you first came to town."

"You've held onto it a while."

"I could tell it was important." She didn't tell him about the feeling she'd gotten, but their trip to the bunker had proven to her she should continue to trust her instincts. She hadn't shared how she tried to live by her gut, as she feared he might be dismissive. For now, she'd go along with Walker and his plans, but before long, she'd have to look for the rebels, to see if they could help her with the seeds. She wasn't ready to leave Walker or strike out on her own.

"I'm still not sure of something," he said, stepping closer.

Disappointment lanced through her. Didn't he believe her? "What?" She looked down, and he tipped her chin up. Sparks shot through her at the contact.

"How am I going to turn you into a boy?"

"Turn me into a boy?" Confusion pulled her face into a frown. Her eyebrows scrunched together and her mouth pressed down.

"Hide you in plain sight. You're about to become my kid brother. From a distance, people who've seen us might think you're Hayden."

"I already look like I'm fifteen. Now a boy. That shouldn't be hard." Her voice cracked on the words. She didn't want to be mistaken for Hayden. But, if they were looking for a young woman, she'd be best off not to match the description. "What about you? Are they looking for you?"

"I'm mentioned on the poster, but the description is so general I'm not worried. There're hundreds of big men. Doubt anyone will know it's me. The reward is for both of us. Alone, I'm not worth turning in. You're the thief. I'm the accomplice."

"I'm sorry you're in trouble because of me." Despite their unpleasant start, they'd become friends in a short time. He probably had friends all over with his easy-going manner and good looks, people he could trust not to turn him over to GreenCorps, even if they recognized his description.

He shrugged. "It's not the first time GreenCorps has wanted me."

"I don't look like Hayden."

"You're both slim with dark hair, though he's taller. You aren't side-by-side, so nobody can compare. Next to me, you both look short. I'll cut your hair as part of your disguise. Keep your hat low, over part of your face. Our next train will come through in daylight. Tomorrow morning, so we'll be visible. We'll get in position before it gets light, hide behind the fence, and run once the train starts. But you never know who'll be watching. It's crawling with recruits today. Jace may have increased security. Could be bulls keeping watch all over. Might be why no other hoppers are around."

"When you were gone, there was a boy who hopped off the train." Her voice caught. "They caught him by the station. I don't think he survived."

Walker was quiet and rested his hand on her arm.

She glanced at his face, only inches away. There was a tightness by his eyes. "You look worried. Is it about the reward?" Maybe he regretted staying with her.

"It's complicated getting to the next train," he said. "They're unloading it tonight. It's three tracks over from the near edge. Another train will be in front of it. A third one is heading into SoCal and is expected on the fourth track. A busy station is good in some ways, but hard in others."

Her forehead bunched, and she shrugged.

"In daylight, with heightened security, we have to run through the train yard and climb over one train to get to the next. We can't approach from the other side because of the third train. We run a greater risk of getting caught, or at least seen by the bulls."

"Why don't we slide under? It's sneakier. We'd be harder to see."

"More likely to be crushed, too. Never go under a train, even if it's stopped. Never hop a knuckle to ride, and never jump from a moving train. Unless your life is in danger, then the risk of death is no worse. You'll end up broken or mangled."

"How do they know I hopped a train?" She'd been wondering that since he'd returned. It wasn't a gigantic leap in logic, but she could have gone anywhere. There wasn't another way to travel to leave SoCal except on foot. Where else could she go?

"Me, I expect," said Walker. "They must know we're together."

That made sense. Her cheeks flamed.

"No secret that I smashed Jace with the chair. He saw my face as it connected and recognized me. Plus, a room full of people heard us have words downstairs. And many folks know I'm a hopper."

An image flashed through her brain of Walker, pretending to send her back to work. She hadn't thanked him for that. A lump grew in her throat. He kept talking.

"I walk you home at night. It isn't a stretch for them to know we're friends, or think we're more. Especially if they talk to Daisy."

"What does Daisy know?"

"She wanted me to stay."

Elsa's eyebrows rose. This was news to her, though she'd suspected he might have been friendly with some of Ginny's girls. "You were involved with Daisy?" Her heart sank to her feet, and it was all she could do not to drop her eyes. It shouldn't bother her, but it did. She didn't want Walker to be in love with someone in SoCal. Or anywhere else.

"Not involved, but she asked me to stay. Told her I was interested in someone else. She wanted casual fun, but I said I couldn't just be casual. I'm not made that way. Can't pretend to be in love."

Walker's words were slow to penetrate her brain. He couldn't pretend. That made two of them. She'd never fallen in love either. Maybe their hearts were made of stone. But he said he couldn't have sex with just anyone and that he was interested in someone. She hated the idea that the attraction she felt was one-sided. He'd never expressed he was drawn to her and she might be misunderstanding his attention. This was outside her experience.

"To save herself, Ginny would have given me up. Told them I was leaving town," he said.

"Maybe Hayden talked," Elsa said with a shrug as she took a step back. She found it difficult to have a serious conversation with Walker within reach. Her reaction to him was a distraction.

"Hayden would never tell where I'm going."

Walker sounded confident, but he wasn't considering his brother's addiction. Hayden would do anything for more drugs. She'd seen it before. Ginny had her hooks into Walker's brother now. But Elsa didn't want to argue. Walker had been with Hayden a long time and knew him better than she did. Maybe she was wrong.

Walker smiled and despite the danger, her mood calmed. They'd figure it out.

"Come on," he said. "Let's cut your hair."

Although Elsa often kept her hair short, it was only in the last couple of months that it had gotten long enough to feel feminine, with ends that curled by her neck. She liked it. She also liked how she'd filled out with a regular diet of healthy food. Just when she'd started to feel like a woman, she was going to masquerade as a boy. It figured.

She ran her comb through her wind-snarled hair and handed it to Walker. He found scissors in his pack and patted a rock.

"Sit."

She sat where he pointed. Walker gathered her hair into a bunch at the nape; his fingers warm where they brushed her skin and the rush at the contact zinged through her. He cropped her hair as close to her head as possible and she winced as the dull scissors tugged. He tossed the loose chunks of hair toward the trees. Perhaps the tiny yellow songbirds would take it for their nests. He used his fingers to measure how short the rest should be to make it match. It took a long time while he moved around, cutting on each side to make it even.

When finished, her hair was the shortest it had ever been, little more than stubble that tickled her hand when she rubbed it. Her head would be cold. He'd left it a little longer on top, but it was shorter than any girl's hair she'd seen. Granny had never been as careful as Walker to keep the ends of her hair even, but the flattering haircut Annie had given her was gone.

"Your eyes are the exact shade of whiskey, or like a hawk's. I've never seen eyes that color." Walker said. "With your short hair, they stand out even more."

His voice was soft and her heart skipped. Maybe he was interested in her after all.

He cleared his throat and continued.

"Nobody is going to believe you're a boy if they get a close look at your face. Keep your cap pulled low. Walk tough and confident, like you did in Long Beach. It's a good thing you're not very girlish or this would never work."

His words weren't meant to wound, but cut all the same. Her hopes of attracting his interest were dashed.

Walker wouldn't meet her eyes as he finished. Had he done a poor job? She rubbed her head again, feeling the short lengths of fine hair. It would be easier to keep clean this way. Better for traveling. In the summer, it would be cool.

She was uncertain of the source of her disappointment. "Thanks." It felt ungrateful, but her words were little more than a mumble.

The haircut would help her disguise. She couldn't imagine anything worse than being returned to Jace for the reward, besides death. She wouldn't make it easy for GreenCorps or whoever was offering the gold. Guilt shot through her as she remembered the threat to Avery and Granny with her absence. Her throat felt like she'd swallowed blades. She sneezed. She hoped she wasn't getting Jaxon's cold.

"No problem. We should eat, then get to sleep. We have to be up early. I'll set a timer so we don't miss our train. We're far enough from town that nobody else will hear."

Changing the subject was good. Anything besides the stupid haircut.

"Where's the next train headed again?"

"Reno," he said. "We'll hike into the mountains toward a lake. I know a place in the woods."

A lake. That amount of water was hard to imagine, even though she'd lived near the ocean. The idea of fresh, still water was different and exciting. But that night, she dreamed of drowning, about Jace lurking in the dark blue depths. Nightmares where he pulled her under. When she woke, she couldn't shake the thought that she was meant for something more. A cabin in the woods would be fine for a while, but she had to figure out a way to use the wealth of seeds.

* * *

Walker
May 18th, 2195, Sacramento
Sunrise: 5:49 a.m. Sunset: 7:49 p.m.

Train security upped. At least double the usual number of bulls with GreenCorps recruits scattered among them. Elsa saw a kid hopping who didn't know what he was doing. He didn't make it out of the trainyard. Reassured her I have experience. Reno security tends to be high. Hayden and I were locked up overnight, twice. Once when we were young and inexperienced, again later when Hayden was kiting. He passed out when we tried to catch a train. Thought for sure we'd be transported to Texas that time. See notes June 2193.

Elsa kept sneezing and coughing tonight and fell asleep fast. Startled awake once already, but went back to sleep. As I'm writing, she's restless and flushed. Might have a fever. Not surprised that she's getting sick. She's rundown from no sleep.

Wanted posters for Elsa all over town. Jace may have come through on the train this morning. They put posters up while we went to Davis.

Isn't a close likeness, except her eyes. Posters say she's a thief. GreenCorps are liars, but what did I expect?

Disguising Elsa as a boy was a good idea in theory, but I figured something out tonight. She thinks she's unattractive, and that's a shame. Never considered that she doesn't know how beautiful she is or how much it affects me. Difficult to maintain a distance between us when we're traveling together. Don't really want to and I won't try anymore. I'm no great catch, but we could be good together. I like her and she isn't indifferent to me. She has a tough exterior, but I want to know the real Elsa.

Excited to hike out to Jim's cabin on Lake Tahoe. It's a long hike, so we'll have to camp partway. Might have to do some repairs on the cabin roof. Only there once or twice a year and I wouldn't want it to fall apart. If we're lucky, Hayden can join us and we can stay for a month or two. Long enough to get him clean again and for Elsa to see his good side. She's only seen him at his worst. I miss the cabin and the solitude whenever I'm away. There's nowhere else I feel at peace, like I belong.

CHAPTER 19: ELSA PLUS CAITLYN

When Elsa opened her eyes, Walker still held her shoulder after shaking her awake. She sat and stretched as he smiled and winked before he moved away. The sun had not yet risen in the east, but soon would. Bands of pale pink and yellowish-orange with banks of gray and white clouds broke up the color as they waited for the sun. There was just enough light to see the camp.

Since leaving SoCal, the colors around Elsa continued to amaze her. It was tough to wrest her bleary eyes from the sunrise. She and Walker gathered their belongings in silence and packed for the train. Her new sleeping bag had been warm, and the tarp had protected her from ground moisture. Despite that, she ached from sleeping on the ground. She didn't ask Walker to put the balm on her. Knowing she looked boyish again made her reluctant to feel his hands on her skin and the tingly sensation they caused. She applied some in the areas she could reach. Her back could wait.

She shaded her face with her hat, as much for warmth over her newly shorn head as for disguise, and followed Walker onto the path through the knee-high damp golden grass. The pale light gave the landscape a bleached quality. Her pants proved to be water-resistant because the dew beaded on the fabric rather than soaking in when she walked the narrow path.

Near the trainyard, they ducked into the tunnel greenway, returning the way they'd come only a few days ago. A chill breeze picked up, tickling her bare neck. It was colder than the pleasant weather of the last few days. She swallowed again, a tightness in her throat hard to dispel.

Ominous dark clouds loomed over the brilliant morning colors as a storm front cruised in from the north. Cloud gray differed from smoke. The clouds crept with flowing tendrils that stretched and followed, almost like something alive.

"We're going to get wet." Walker frowned at the sky.

The breeze ruffled his hair as he leaned in and whispered. His breath was warm on her cheek. Elsa's heart rate increased, and she bit the inside of her lower lip, worrying it between her teeth. It seldom rained in SoCal so the prospect should be exciting. However, lying in the grass, they would have no protection and she didn't want to get soaked.

"Your earplugs handy for the train ride?" He kept his voice low, sending shivers throughout her body. He touched near her ear with his icy hands.

She nodded. A gleam appeared in his eyes as he prepared. The anticipation seemed like his favorite part of train hopping and was contagious.

"You remember what I said about the train blocking ours?"

"Over, not under. Follow you. Aim for a few cars from the end, so we stay out of the main part of the trainyard."

"Right. We've got an hour, maybe two. The train goes when it's ready, not quite on a set schedule."

Her hands grew clammy as they followed the fence to the other end of the trainyard. Instead of hiding behind the barrier, Walker took her hand as he led her past its final section while he watched the station over his shoulder for security and patrols. It remained quiet, though the station yard buzzed with activity, nobody looked their way. They lay in the tall grass, peering through the clumps of thick stalks. From this vantage, they watched the trains for movement—ready to run.

Conditions at the station yard were just as Walker had explained. He was a patient teacher, smart and competent. Three trains waited at the station. Two were headed north and one south. The far train headed for SoCal was short, with fewer than two dozen cars. Up the empty tracks sat three tanker cars they'd detached from the southbound train, identical to those used to carry water.

Elsa's brow furrowed. One train faced SoCal, but in the dim light, it didn't look like it had more than three cars with water. If they had the tankers and water available, why withhold the supply?

Anger surged through her. She'd worked herself to the brink of exhaustion for weeks to save water tokens as the price had soared. GreenCorps was playing games and keeping people downtrodden and thirsty on purpose. Granny was right. Elsa ground her teeth in aggravation. It was unfair that Granny and the others suffered when water was available. She seethed until she ran out of energy.

She yawned and smothered the next with her arm. It was too hard to rest without nightmares. Each night since they'd left the train, she'd awakened several times and had trouble getting back to sleep. She hated that Jace invaded her dreams, turning them into nightmares.

The spring air had a bite this morning. She shivered, the sting in the back of her throat more persistent; it was scratchy and sore. She suppressed a sneeze, not wanting to risk the noise. Her frame quivered with the effort. She wasn't freezing, but her shoulders and collar bones ached. There were no injuries there, and she didn't think it was from wearing her backpack.

Heat radiated off Walker beside her. Her bruises, except the worst ones on her ribs, had seemed less this morning, fading to pale green and dull yellow instead of varying shades of purple. Stiff muscles and lying on the ground bothered her ribs, making them hurt once more. She fidgeted to find a more comfortable position and settled on her elbows as much as possible. Her muscles seemed sluggish as she couldn't get rid of the ache and she hoped nothing was wrong.

It was the fourth morning since they'd left SoCal. Her swollen eye wasn't as tender; her vision had improved and seemed almost normal. Tired from cold, sleepless nights and early mornings, it was hard for Elsa not to doze while they waited. She was startled awake by the first drops of icy rain as they splattered on her face.

"You okay?" Walker said in a quiet whisper as he rested his hand on her back.

The tightness by his eyes and mouth had returned. She nodded.

"Everything will be slippery. Grab the ladder, get a solid grip. We're getting on from the right this time. Right hand, left hand, right foot, hop with your left."

He touched each in turn as he had the first night, imprinting the feel on her brain. She ran through the sequence again, and bobbed her head to show she understood.

"Grab higher than last time if you can, so you have room for your feet."

He must have sensed faint train vibrations as the engine started, because as he finished his last instructions, the slack action crashes started in the yard.

"We're behind the train. We've got to go now."

His voice quivered and his eyes shone like polished coins. Rising to his feet, he checked his backpack and tucked in the loose straps. He scanned the area, watching for security, but nobody noticed the two hoppers standing close to the train tracks, well behind the main station. She poked at her straps, but Walker found another loose piece and looped it into her arm strap with a quick flash of a smile.

He tossed his head and indicated it was time to go. He crouched and hunched over as he ran, so she did the same. He aimed for a boxcar-to-boxcar knuckle of the nearest train, just ahead of their position. He climbed on the edge, not the joint-clamps where it was lower—avoiding the knuckle. Elsa followed. The metal knuckle looked like clasped hands holding one car to another. Walker paused and looked in both directions before he jumped to the ground, landing with a soft thud. He reached a hand back to help her. She took it and winced as she landed, clutching her side at the jolt without meaning to. Walker's eyes cut to her injury. She nodded and took a deep breath. She could do this.

Their train slid forward as it left the Sacramento station. Slow-moving, but increasing. She could still count individual wheel spokes. Adrenaline surged as Walker jogged across the trainyard, gravel crunching under his feet, the sound covered by the train's movement. They crossed the empty set of tracks to the northbound train. The noise was considerable as additional train cars smashed into each other up the line.

Elsa chewed the inside of her mouth and a muscle below her eye twitched. The station workers and bulls worked on the far side of this train. Any one of them could end this venture if they caught her before she hopped the train. Ten gold coins was a fortune. It was a wonder Walker hadn't turned her in for that amount. She'd followed her gut and trusted him, which, in itself, was a marvel.

They were in luck. Walker pointed to a covered hopper, the fourth car from the end. He picked up the pace and ran next to the chosen car, letting it move past until he was beside the pale gray ladder at the back. She stayed at his heels. The train was close enough to touch if she reached out her fingers. Though she focused on him, she almost missed his ascent; he was quick.

With the instructions running through her head, Elsa took a deep breath and grabbed. Hand, hand, step, and hop. The ladder was cold on her hands and her foot slipped sideways on the chosen rung, but she was on as the second foot landed, sliding against the ladder's uprights.

This time, she spaced her hands and feet better but had to adjust her grip higher to feel stable before climbing. She was too short to reach higher rungs from the ground. Walker had suggested she settle on the close side as soon as possible, not to linger. One of the most important rules of train hopping was, *"Don't be seen."*

She threaded her way across the platform and sat, but not before two workers at the station noticed her. The first waved. The second yelled, though she couldn't hear what he said over the roar of the train. Fear surged through her veins. She wiped her red, wet palms on her pants and tucked them into her armpits. The storm had arrived and the rain outside increased, coming down in sheets, which soon changed to frozen white balls that pinged off the train and onto her head, arms, and legs.

What could the men who'd seen her do? Report to the next station?

"Do they have radios on board?" she shouted.

"Just phones at the stations," he said. "They saw you?"

She nodded, and her shoulders slumped. The train was moving, picking up speed. They might have recognized her. Security knew someone had climbed aboard. She slid farther into the overhang, hidden by the flange as the train became too fast to make out details on the ground through the grated floor.

The porch provided partial protection from the frozen balls of rain. The roar of the train reverberated in her chest, and she hugged her knees toward her chest. Icy chunks peppered her legs and feet as their speed increased. Safe for now, she shared a grin with Walker. Water ran down his face and his gray eyes gleamed.

When Walker produced his tin as a reminder, she extracted her earplugs from her pocket and inserted the bits of foam. The relief was immediate. The noise of the trains was worse than the waiting. The train car blocked most of the damp wind and flying bits of ice. The grasslands on the sides looked wet and scattered patches of white littered the ground. Was this snow? Her brain felt foggy. She had a feeling that snow was softer; this was something else. The rain poured down in white sheets while clouds and mist seemed to hug the ground toward the almost invisible town.

"Hail." His voice was loud enough to be heard over the train when he cupped his hands by her ear.

She nodded. She'd read about hail.

"Four hours to Reno. After that, we hike."

Walker grabbed the tarp, which was as blue as yesterday's brilliant, cloudless sky. He unfolded a section and wrapped it behind them on one side and draped it across their legs. It was large enough to cover their packs, too.

"Traveling in style," he shouted.

Sacramento sprawled larger than Long Beach, with brick buildings spreading from the edge of the train tracks at one edge as far as the eye could see in the other directions. The builders had used repurposed brick, resulting in a collection of colors on the same house or shop. Electric street lights glowed in the early morning rain and hail. The town gave way to fields of dark earth with thin green spears of baby plants poking through the ground.

Walker handed her a breakfast bar, and they munched in silence as the plains rolled by. Her throat remained scratchy, and she'd lost her appetite, but she forced herself to eat. She didn't want to get more run-down. Her thoughts turned to Granny as the train carried her farther away. Was she home with the goods stored in the safe? Or had she stayed with Avery? Perhaps Jaxon had thrown them out. The not knowing made Elsa's heart ache.

Elsa watched the faint outline of Sacramento pass by from her hiding place. She couldn't see much to the sides and nothing forward from her position, but she watched what unfolded behind the train.

Further from Sacramento, scattered houses dotted the landscape, some surrounded by lines of trees like those she and Walker had found on the walk to Davis. A couple of buildings were abandoned and falling into ruin. They rushed past tall cottonwoods and scrubby oak trees, like those she'd seen most of her life, but larger. The hail subsided and became a slow drizzle that was not much more than cold mist.

The civilized country dropped away, and the train became the only sign of people, though a curl of dark smoke sometimes rose from a distant chimney. Unexcavated mounds dotted the area through which the train traveled, hinting that once the land had been more populated. Why were there so many unscavenged mounds? Perhaps usable items had been stripped before the houses fell apart, their components making up other houses. As they left the plains, the mounds became intermittent.

The slow rain fell and the color of the land changed to a dull, unrelieved brown on the flats, with hints of new green seeping through in patches on the hills. Elsa guessed as spring became summer, there'd be more green—at least until the summer sun scorched it golden brown. The trees grew in clumps or stands. Perhaps there were enough in places to be called forests.

The track climbed a steady uphill grade, and the hills grew steeper, still rolling, not rugged like the mountains she'd read about, but stacked next to each other, rising higher in rows and buckled levels. Higher rocky peaks surrounded them; the train aimed for the pass between them.

Elsa shivered, despite the tarp keeping off most of the water. Her head pulsed in time to the roar of the train's wheels on the iron rails beneath. Walker draped his arm behind her shoulders and pulled her against his solid warmth.

"Sleep on me." He stroked her frozen head. "I'll keep you warm."

She rested against his shoulder and chest, too tired to analyze his actions. She nodded off despite her pounding skull.

* * *

May 18th, 2195

Dearest Mathew,

I've been thinking more about our years with the rebels. We worked so hard to fight GreenCorps and I'm not sure they even noticed. We weren't much more than fleas to them, our efforts irritating but insignificant, unlike the previous generation who freed thousands and liberated hundreds of train cars' worth of grain and supplies. That's also why their punishment was so severe, the work camps in Texas and SoCal filled with hundreds of rebel captives with life sentences.

I doubt GreenCorps noticed we diverted the odd tanker of water or boxcar filled with rations to Texas, or helped smuggle out a portion of the prisoners sent there to work. It was small scale to them, even if it was worthwhile to us.

It wasn't until we talked the miners in Denver into striking for better work conditions five years ago that they took notice. After that, it was *simply a matter of time until we were quelled. We should have left the front-line sooner. If we had, we'd still be together and I wouldn't have to miss you the way I do. My heart is lonely without yours next to it.*

If only I had the courage to do something to help people again, but I don't. I want to hide here on the farm and let the world pass by without noticing me. Sometimes I feel like I've given up, that our cause was too important and I've done something wrong. The hold GreenCorps has on the west is unfair. Other times, I feel smart to have left that life behind. Grady said I'd be bored on the farm if I stay forever. Time will tell what is true and if he is right, or if I am.

All my love,
Your Caitlyn

Chapter 20: Elsa plus Walker

"Elsa, wake up," Walker shouted, his voice punctuated by gentle shakes. "Wake up."

She blinked and swallowed. It seemed as though knives lodged in her throat. Her chest was tight, and she labored to take a full breath. She lifted her throbbing head and looked around. It was cold and rainy and the train was nearing a town, with buildings appearing on both sides. Time to get off and run. It was challenging not to grumble at the idea.

Walker frowned at her, a deep crease between his brows. She didn't know why, and it was difficult to concentrate.

He rested the back of his hand on her forehead and she closed her eyes, leaning into the cool sensation on her skin. His hand was icy, yet soothing. She was disappointed when it moved.

"Elsa, honey, stay awake. We get off the train soon."

Her eyes popped open. She hadn't meant to close her eyes again, and she avoided swallowing, as it was painful. She helped Walker refold the tarp after he shook off most of the water and tied it onto his pack. Stowing her pillow, she flexed her legs and feet, attempting to get her chilled muscles ready to run.

Walker's frown persisted as they readied to jump. Was something wrong? The slack action crashes started, the cars jolting into each other as the train slowed. She held on, the wet metal chilling her hands while Walker moved to the right, his eyes scanning their surroundings. He moved to the left and repeated the motion, methodical and precise. It was too much effort to ask about it now, but she had a feeling it was important. She wanted to learn why he did things a certain way, in case she was ever on her own.

He'd started on the right and returned to it a second time, this time nodding. He pointed in that direction and she stood, swaying with the train's motion as it reduced its speed. She held the train and braced her feet, adopting a wider stance to avoid falling as the crashes became more violent and frequent. He stood close behind, giving her additional support.

Walker waited until the train came to a complete stop, then, quick as lightning, he climbed down the ladder. Her arms and legs were sluggish and her butt numb, but Elsa followed as fast as she was able. She stumbled as she hit the ground but caught herself by touching one hand down. Her balance was off.

She removed an earplug and heard distant shouting. She looked up. A burly man in a black and green GreenCorps uniform was barreling toward them.

Bulls must have been waiting to meet their train. He was more than a hundred yards up the train, but coming fast. With his earplugs in, Walker might not have realized the danger. She tapped his shoulder. Walker looked, grabbed her hand, and ran. The initial lurch almost pulled her off her feet. She sprinted without looking to see if security followed.

"Train hopping trash, get back here," said a gruff voice running toward her.

"Those two jumped off a hopper at the back," said another voice, joining him by jumping through from the opposite side of the train. "The two Sacramento station said to watch for."

At least two, maybe three sets of feet pounded the gravel behind them. She and Walker jumped over another stationary train, side by side. He kept her hand in his as they raced for the eight-foot chain-link fence. Walker threw his pack over, then hers, and boosted her onto the fence before he leaped up and over. She struggled to pull herself higher, hoping she wouldn't be caught from below. The ground swam beneath her in a dizzy spell and she couldn't move, afraid she would fall.

Hands reached for her foot and she kicked someone. Grasping hands claimed her ankle while she struggled. She panicked; afraid they'd pull her down. Images of the boy beaten to death outside Sacramento filled her mind.

"Listen, kid, we've got you. Stop fighting," said a deep voice. "We won't hurt you. They want you alive."

She kicked again, and her foot connected with a crunch. The hand released her leg as someone cursed. She climbed the last section of the fence, heaving herself over the top and letting herself drop to the ground. She doubled over in a coughing spasm. Stabbing pains shot through her ribs and made breathing difficult.

She straightened when the coughing stopped and grabbed her pack from the wet grass and slung it onto her back. Walker fastened his while he waited. He could have left her behind. He took her hand again without a word and they fled, straight into the neighborhood near the tracks.

"Don't look back, just run," Walker said.

The small brick homes were cleaner and neater on the outside and in better repair than most of the houses she was used to seeing. It was mid-day and there were few people on the streets—a couple of women with young children and someone who reminded her of Granny. Elsa felt conspicuous as they raced through the quiet streets until they found a deserted lot between houses.

Walker zigged, and they bolted into the vacant lot and through the tall grass and thick bushes. They hid behind a lump in wet shrubbery while her heart raced. They crouched deep in the tangled bushes and waited, listening to determine if anyone followed. Her chest heaved, the sharp pain on her side. She suppressed a cough, though her body shook with the effort as she caught her breath.

They didn't have long to wait.

"Just a couple of lads," said one voice. "I've seen them before. I recognized the big guy."

"The other one's no lad," said the deep voice, the owner of the face she'd kicked. His voice had a muffled quality. She peeked out. He held his sleeve to his face, his nose dripping blood. "I got a good look at her face. Eyes like an owl. She might be the one for the gold on the poster. Saw bruises on her face like the Wanted sheet."

Elsa shivered and remained still, hoping her loud breathing wouldn't give them away.

"Doubt it. Anyone could have bruises. I swear that was the kid that likes to kite. He was with the other one a couple of summers ago. Picked him off the tracks once when he collapsed. They spent a night in lock-up. I remember them 'cause the big one is faster than you think and sneaky. He could have escaped then, just like today, but he stuck with his partner."

"I'm coming back to search more later," said the deep voice. "I know what I saw."

Their voices faded as they continued up the street. Her heart raced, each thump stabbing pain through her ribs.

"Give it time. They won't search nearby for long." Walker whispered. His foam earplugs were in his hand. She took out her second one and stuffed them in her coat pocket.

"We're off GreenCorps property. They can't even agree if you're even the one for the reward."

She nodded and swallowed, her throat fiery and swollen. She drank from her canteen, hoping the water would soothe the ache, but the pain intensified.

They waited in the bushes for maybe twenty minutes before Walker said, "All clear."

Elsa's clothes were soaked through, but they'd have to dry as they hiked. It wasn't safe to stay in Reno.

She and Walker cut through the lot and climbed a short wooden fence into the yard of the house behind and then onto the next street. The houses here were twice the size of those at home and many had raised boxes of black dirt behind them that looked like gardens. Maybe the people here were used to growing some of their food to supplement their diet. The limited range of seeds available might still be expensive, but ordinary people must be able to afford a few to vary their diet.

"My hideaway is a cabin, thirty miles from here. It's a safe place to wait for Hayden. If he hasn't come by summer's end, we'll move on to the next place on our route."

Now that the scare was over and they hadn't been caught, Elsa's head pounded and it was all she could do not to groan at the prospect of a long hike. He couldn't intend to go the entire distance today. Could he? It was almost noon, and it seemed like she'd been on the road all day.

Walker skirted busier sections of town where the GreenCorps shops were open. Posters of her face would be everywhere. They headed south until the buildings thinned, then stopped. Even on the edges of town, they'd pasted her posters on brick walls. They couldn't stop, resupply, or find a place to rest without the risk of being recognized. They hiked onto a flat, grass-covered plain. The rain stopped, but the chill wind continued with little to break it. It bit through her sodden coat, but she couldn't take it off; she'd freeze without it.

"This used to be a road," said Walker as they trudged. "For cars, once upon a time."

She'd seen rusted cars and pictures in old books, but never one that worked.

Walker pointed out crumbles of black rock littering the ground—remnants of a road, now crumbled into useless pieces that grass, weeds, and bushes grew through. Scattered signs and reflective markers lay hidden in the grass, relics of a previous age, as they followed the long-abandoned highway south. They passed several partially concealed rusted remains of vehicles now engulfed by vegetation. The chrome and tires had been stripped, the metal was corroded and full of holes; now they were orangish-brown chunks, their innards unrecognizable piles of junk.

The morning's storm caught up to them, pelting them in an unrelenting torrent. She hoped there wouldn't be more hail. The wind whipped Walker's hair behind him and the back of Elsa's neck froze, making her miss her longer hair. It chilled Elsa to the bone. The ache in her back and shoulders intensified and the band around her chest grew tighter. She stopped to cough, a deep rattle that she tried to suppress, with limited success.

Somehow, her feet moved onward. It helped to focus on small goals, rather than to think of a thirty-mile journey. She chose something in the distance in the direction they walked, like a tree, a sign, or the crest of a hill. When they reached that landmark, she chose the next, forcing herself to continue. The elevation climbed, though the hills didn't feel steep. In the thin mountain air, it became harder to breathe. She was slowing Walker down, and she was grateful he stayed.

Her energy reserves hit rock bottom, and she needed a distraction.

"How'd you find this place?" she said, breaking the silence.

"Hayden and I found it six years ago. We helped an old guy named Jim outside Denver. A pair of GreenCorps soldiers beat him and took his pack. Left him at the side of the tracks. We helped him board and took care of him. When he recovered, he shared the directions to his cabin. Told us to come anytime we needed a place to hole up. We stop in every year."

"Will he be there too?" She bit her lip; she didn't want to intrude in a stranger's home.

"Jim died two years ago." Walker's voice was quiet.

"I'm sorry."

He waved off her condolences. "He was good to us, but was old, in his nineties. Far as we could tell, he died of natural causes one winter. Buried him in the forest after we found his body."

"Tell me about the place." Her breath became increasingly labored, and it was challenging to keep moving when her muscles screamed for her to stop. If she looked up, everything lost focus. She watched her feet, no longer caring about distant landmarks that were too daunting. One step at a time.

"The cabin is on a beach and overlooks the lake, which is so colorful it seems unreal."

Walker's voice softened as he talked about the beautiful setting.

"The water is every shade of blue and by the shore it's turquoise. Other times it's dark like a storm or silvery like the clouds. The lake is deep, but not so wide you can't see across to the other side. There's a trail all the way around and several campsites. We'll have to take the path around for fun sometime. Jim built his place in a grove of ancient pine trees that smell like fresh sap in the summer sun. The forest stretches behind and is filled with deer, rabbits, and owls."

"It sounds like paradise." She'd never been anywhere with forests and such a variety of animals.

"You know how to swim?" His face broke into a smile.

She shook her head. It jarred her headache, so she clenched her jaw. Everything hurt.

"Too bad it isn't warm weather yet, but if we're here long enough, I'll teach you."

She couldn't imagine immersing herself in water. She'd lived next to the ocean her whole life, but the wild currents and surf were dangerous, shark-infested, and full of trash. She'd never wanted to swim, but he made this lake sound appealing. Maybe they could stay longer than a couple of weeks.

Elsa's questions started a flood of memories and stories. Walker entertained her for several miles and a few hours, providing the much-needed distraction. His voice trailed off as she fell behind. She doubled over, coughing. She wanted to stop.

"You've been a real fighter. We'll find a place to stop for the night soon. We're more than halfway."

"Fighter?" she croaked. Her voice had seized up with her throat.

"You worked hard to get here. You're sick, but you haven't complained. You're tough. Been worried about you since I woke you up. You have a fever. Hayden would have whined all day."

"I'm okay." It came out a mumble.

"You're glassy-eyed, feverish, and aching. I don't like the bark in your cough. Top that off with being chilled for hours. I need to get you somewhere safe, where we won't have to worry about the authorities or someone looking to cash in on that reward. I'll make us a fire. I'm sorry it's taking so long."

She had no idea he'd noticed her struggle. He cared enough to notice. She almost burst into tears of relief.

"Can you make it to the next set of trees? There's a lake with fresh water and I can rig a shelter. We can stay a few days if we need to. We shouldn't be bothered, and you can rest."

Elsa nodded. It was a relief to acknowledge how awful she felt. Tears still threatened, but they didn't fall. They walked at a slow pace until they arrived at the flat lake, its shallow edge lined with leafy bushes. In all likelihood, Walker knew what type they were, but she was too sick to ask.

"Why don't you wait in the dry patch under the biggest tree? Out of the wind."

Under normal circumstances, she would've helped, but she was done. Drained and needing rest, she slumped down where he suggested. It took all her remaining willpower to stay upright; she wanted to curl up and sleep.

Elsa shivered. She'd stayed warmish while walking, but her reserves were gone. Without movement, she was chilled and spent.

The hill and a stand of bushy trees sheltered the campsite, but from the way the treetops tossed, the wind had picked up. The storm wasn't over.

Walker dragged over lengths of dry wood and knocked the branches from them with his hatchet. He took a handful of spike nails from his pack, built a wooden frame, and lashed the blue tarp onto it—making a homemade tent.

She doubled over with wracking coughs. Walker stopped building and looked up, the telltale crease between his brows.

He opened his pack and removed an older, worn tarp of dull orange with slits and holes in a few places. He spread it on the ground inside the shelter.

"You can go in now. This is home tonight."

Elsa got to her feet and took two steps. The ground swam beneath her and the trees and shelter spun. She pitched forward as everything went black.

* * *

Walker
May 19th, 2195, Washoe Lake
Sunrise: 5:48 a.m. Sunset: 7:50 p.m.

Elsa was sick all day. I pushed hard to get out of Reno, where it wasn't safe. Close call at Reno station. They were probably called to be alert to our arrival. I recognized the bulls. One almost caught Elsa on the fence. She kicked him and we got away. If she'd been healthy, she'd have scramled up and over that fence, no problem. Perhaps I miscalculated. Should have run the other direction and gone around the station, even if the distance was farther. Don't know if the bulls will report that they recognize her. Made sure they got a good look at me to help with her disguise as Hayden.

Made it to Washoe Lake, but Elsa blacked out. Scared the daylights out of me. Took off her wet clothing and tucked her into bed in the shelter. Made willow bark tea to reduce her fever when she wakes. Wish I had something to help her cough or honey to soothe her throat, but I have nothing. Her deep cough must be agonizing with sore ribs.

Her fever is worse than I thought. She's ranting in her sleep. Fighting off Jace again. Makes me angry enough that I'd kill him if he was here. Hate seeing her so fearful. She rests better when I lie beside her. She wouldn't let me that close if she was awake, but asleep she reaches for me.

She's my injured hawk, but her strength will come back. Lesser people would have given up long ago. It's clear that she has a will of iron.

CHAPTER 21: ELSA PLUS WALKER

When Elsa woke, she was warm and dry and in her sleeping bag. The air had a blue cast, and she didn't remember how she'd gotten there. She'd been cold and drenched to the skin. Now, she wore dry underclothes and a clean shirt, and had been tucked into bed. She flushed hot at the idea that Walker had undressed her. He'd seen her naked before, but she didn't want rescuing her to become a habit. Shouldn't she be strong enough on her own? A coughing spasm shook her, and she sat, waiting for it to pass.

A fire popped and snapped, drawing her gaze to the opening of the makeshift tent. Walker sat on a round length of wood, his feet stretched before him at the entrance of the shelter. He'd made a firepit, and a pot was at a boil while he cooked, the steam rising. The sky was dark blue, with a smattering of stars scattered throughout a hole in the clouds as the storm passed. She didn't know if she'd slept a few hours or all night. Was it twilight or dawn? A heavy weight squeezed her chest, and she coughed as she tried to speak.

Walker spun around. Was that relief in his eyes? "Good, you're awake."

"What day is it?" Her voice sounded raspy.

"It's the same night we camped. You've been asleep for about four hours. I made willow bark tea for your fever."

She didn't feel like drinking tea, even if it was thoughtful. Walker brought her a mug and crouched beside her, resting a cool hand on her forehead. The drink was warm, but not hot. It must have cooled while she slept. She grimaced at the bitterness of the reddish liquid.

"It's good for your headache, too. Drink it all."

She stared at him over the rim of the cup. His tone was all business, and she didn't have the energy to argue.

"That's better," he said with a small smile. "Elsa with attitude."

She drank, sipping small amounts each time, so there wasn't much to swallow or gulp. The taste didn't bother her after the first few sips.

"You hungry?"

She shook her head and placed the empty mug on the ground. She shivered again. Now that she was sitting and not in the cocoon of her sleeping bag, she was chilled. Goosebumps pebbled her arms, and the cold seeped into her aching bones. How could shoulders be so painful? She touched her collar bones. They always ached when she was sick.

"You're shaking. Lay down, cover up."

She followed orders and stared at him. Though bossy, he'd been kind and more talkative than ever before. She enjoyed spending time with someone her own age. She loved Granny, but it wasn't the same. Even Avery hadn't filled her need for a friend; they'd been so different. Elsa had been lonely for so long she'd forgotten there was any other way. Maybe Walker could be an actual friend. When she moved on with the seeds, perhaps he would come.

Walker returned to the fire, removed the pot, added wood, and collected his dinner. He sat next to her and ate.

"Sure you're not hungry?"

She shook her head and picked up her canteen.

His spoon clicked the side of his bowl as he scooped pasta and held it out for her, but she waved it away. Her head felt fuzzy again, and his form floated in and out of focus, so she lay down. Her eyelids grew heavy, and it became hard to keep them open. Her eyes fluttered several times before she gave in and let them fall. The last thing she felt was his cool hand on her forehead.

The next time she woke, she was yelling and trying to stand. Her throat ached from the exertion, and she was hot and covered in slick sweat. Walker held her arms and kept her from rising, hugging her from behind, his arms and legs wrapped around her. In her dream, Jace had been beating her again. She'd fought back instead of balling up on the ground.

Walker made soothing noises. "I've got you. I won't let Jace hurt you."

Tension leached from Elsa's body and she ceased her struggles. Taking a couple of breaths, she evaluated the ache in her chest. It wasn't worse. The pain reminded her that Jace was far away. It was dark and almost impossible to see more than an arm's length away, but she and Walker were alone and safe. The tightness in her chest loosened.

Walker grabbed a mug, his eyes and teeth reflecting the pale light. It was full of steaming liquid, a fresh batch. Shouldn't he sleep too? It had been a long day. She glanced back at him, not understanding what he wanted until he held the cup to her lips. She shivered with cold, her teeth chattering as she drank.

She sipped tea until he was satisfied, and then he placed the cup on the ground, away from where she might flail and hit it. He coaxed her into lying down, then he lay down behind her, spooning her while wrapped in his own sleeping bag. His hard, muscular arms held her against his warm chest and body. He shared his heat, helping her chills subside.

"Go back to sleep. It was just a bad dream."

Stroking the side of her head, he smoothed her short hair, soothing her to sleep. His hand was so nice. She felt cared for and safe with him so close. She couldn't stay tense and as her muscles relaxed, she drifted back to sleep.

* * *

Walker
May 19th, 2195, Washoe Lake
Sunset: 5:47 a.m. Sunrise: 7:50 p.m.

Elsa's nightmares continued most of the night. Her trouble reminded me of Hayden's fear of fire after we left home. The first year he woke up screaming almost every night. That's why he started using drugs. So he wouldn't think or dream of the flames. He wasn't there when the brothel burned, but in his imagination, everyone died horrific deaths.

She slept all today while I fished from the shore and listened for her nightmares. Made a stock of willow bark. Not sure we should leave tomorrow. It won't hurt to stay another day. Or even two.

* * *

The next time Elsa woke, the mouth-watering scent of roasting meat filled the air. She shifted, and Walker turned from his seat at the entrance.

"You're awake." His genuine smile melted her heart. "How do you feel?"

She assessed how to answer his question. She didn't feel hot or cold, but normal. Knowing she'd asked before, she said, "Is it morning or evening?"

"You slept all day. It's the second evening since we camped."

"I feel weak, but no fever or chills."

"That's an improvement. Dinner and tea?"

Shadows ringed his gray eyes, and he needed to shave. He must not have slept much. She had a vague recollection that each time she'd woken in the night, he'd been there. What would she have done if she'd been alone? A stab of guilt rushed through her; she hated to be a bother.

"What's cooking?" She sat up and sniffed. The smell was intoxicating.

"Caught fish today. They're almost ready."

Though Elsa had lived by the ocean, she'd never eaten fish. Judging by its aroma, she was certain she would like it. Real protein was expensive. Plus, the local fish in Long Beach were full of plastic and inedible. Thinking of fish reminded her of Janna and the fish farm project she'd mentioned before her disappearance. Which brought

Elsa's thoughts back to home and those she'd left behind. What could she do to help Granny and Avery? She reached into her bag, her fingers tracing the shape of the tube. Her help may be indirect, but she needed to keep trying. She needed to figure out how to use the seeds, if she could keep them away from GreenCorps.

Elsa's burst of energy waned after the delicious trout. Her stomach was satisfied and though her fever hadn't returned, she was tired. Perhaps Walker could be convinced to sleep too.

"I'm more tired than I thought. I'm sorry my bad dreams disturbed you, but thanks for taking care of me."

"I don't mind," he said with a weary smile.

"I mind. I hate being helpless." His answer and his care made her aware that he hadn't looked after her out of obligation. It gave her hope. She wasn't quite ready to act on it, but it was there.

"A lot has happened in the last few days. I promise it'll get better."

She hoped that was true. He handed her another mug of reddish tea.

"If we sleep well tonight, do you think you'll be up to trekking tomorrow?"

"Then you have to rest, too." She flushed at her words.

He smiled, which made her heart lurch. It wasn't made of stone, after all.

"I'll clean up from dinner. I won't be long. I promise."

She lay down and pulled her sleeping bag up to her neck. Her eyelids were heavy, and she yawned. At some point, she registered Walker joined her and wrapped her in his arms. She fell into a deep and dreamless sleep. It helped, knowing that he was there.

CHAPTER 22: ELSA PLUS TATSUDA

"Up for hiking today?" said Walker as they ate oatmeal with dried red berries for breakfast. "It's about eight hours. If it's too much, we can stop partway. The first half is the hardest. After that, a lot is downhill."

Elsa nodded, feeling more like herself and eager to be underway.

They trekked through forests of evergreens with pale green tips on older greenish-blue growth and stands of thin leafy trees with smooth, pale bark. Their pale new leaves rustled in the breeze. The mountains were beautiful and the quiet solitude peaceful—so different from SoCal—that she was in a constant state of awe.

"What kind of trees are these?" They rested in a whispering grove with dappled light.

"Poplar. They're stunning in the fall; the leaves turn bright yellow."

She imagined the forest in shimmering gold, the pale bark shining like silver; like an enchanted forest from the fairytales Granny used to tell.

The mountain water from a rushing stream was ice cold and tasted somehow fresh and wild, so different from lukewarm tanker water or flat boiled water. It was more refreshing, plus it was free. Walker smiled when she shared that revelation.

Hours later, he pointed out the immense lake below. "There's Lake Tahoe."

Excitement surged through her. So much freshwater made her breath catch in her throat. Another smaller lake of sparkling blue that matched the sky nestled in a valley to their left.

By mid-afternoon, they emerged from the forest above the lake and scrambled down one last steep trail. A sandy beach stretched in both directions, with a cabin against the face of a cliff. The log cabin had a foundation made from rounded grayish stone slathered with mortar. The logs had weathered to a pleasant silvery gray, though the overlapping slabs on the roof were a different, newer color. Her heart caught. This looked like a proper home.

The cabin door wasn't locked. Perhaps it was remote enough that nobody would find it in order to steal. So much of the land they'd crossed seemed empty of people. Perhaps if you stayed away from the railways and towns, it would be possible to live a life independent of GreenCorps. The seeds would help with that. Would there be a way for her family to escape SoCal? She couldn't imagine them train hopping. Nor would Avery leave Jaxon.

A kitchen and living area made up the main room. A water pump stood over a stainless-steel kitchen sink and a cast-iron wood stove for cooking sat nearby. Two bunks sat beside the far wall, with a large metal trunk pushed against one end. There didn't appear to be solar panels, but sunlight poured in the glass windows on three sides. Candles and lamps sat at various locations. It was a far cry from the tiny dark room she'd lived in with Granny, which had been only a few paces across.

Elsa swung her pack off her back, relieved to be freed from its weight. Her knees ached from the long descent. She was excited to be somewhere they would stay for a few weeks, even if they were waiting for Hayden. She banished him from her mind, not wanting to sour thoughts of staying, if only for a reprieve from her primary objective of finding someone to help distribute the seeds.

"Can I look around?" The cabin's interior piqued her curiosity. What would she find? "Be my guest. I'm going to check outside to make sure there's no storm damage to the buildings and see if there's enough chopped wood. Others may have stopped here since Hayden and I stayed last summer."

"What's in the other building?" She pointed to the smaller shack that sat in the cabin's shadow.

"Wood, tools. Should be a boat in the rafters. Tomorrow, I can teach you to canoe."

She hadn't heard of a canoe, but nodded. She wanted to see and try everything.

Walker left while Elsa poked around inside. A thin layer of dust sprinkled the wooden countertop, the windowsills, and the furniture. A door in the back corner of the main room was wedged open with a wooden block. She found a bedroom with a full-size bed, blankets stacked on the end. The mattress was covered in a thick woven cover, similar to the finely woven plastic from home. Why wasn't there evidence of chewing by rats and mice? The cabin had been vacant for months.

In SoCal, it had been a constant battle to keep the rodents out. They'd stored everything important in metal cases or brick structures.

The air was dry and stale but didn't smell musty or moldy, just like dust. She sneezed and crossed to the window to open it for fresh air. With the window up, a screen covered the opening.

Startled by a faint mewling noise from the closet, Elsa found a nest made from old clothes and ripped towels with four kittens. Their slate-blue eyes glared up at her. Two of the kittens hissed when she extended her hand toward them. How had they gotten here with the door and windows closed?

She moved closer to see a rectangular hole cut into the floor of the closet into a crawlspace below. It must be how their mother came and went, and it explained the lack of mice. The kittens looked healthy and well-fed, with tight, round tummies. Two were black and white, one was gray, and another was a tabby. They looked about three or four weeks old. Too young to be on their own, but big enough to wander.

She wished she could hold a kitten and feel its soft fur, but she left them alone and returned to the main room to continue her exploration.

Elsa had seen cats on the Heap, hunting rats. Here, they probably ate mice and squirrels instead. She hadn't noticed rats since leaving SoCal. There must be some, but they weren't as prevalent. Strange that she hadn't thought of it until now. It was interesting what you took for granted.

The kitchen was stocked with cooking pots and dishes in drawers and cupboards—things she could have sold for weeks' worth of food and water. One cupboard contained large glass jars, one with a few cups of flour in the bottom. She'd wondered what they'd eat here at the cabin, assuming mostly the dry rations from the seed bunker. Maybe they could supplement with other things. Walker seemed resourceful.

"You like it?" Walker jammed his hands in the pockets of his jeans.

She hadn't heard his quiet footsteps. She hadn't quite been able to figure out what was different about him today. It was seeing him here that brought it together. He'd lost the wary, tense look he'd had in SoCal and most of their travels. He didn't have to act tough or be on guard. This was a place where he could relax.

"There are kittens in the bedroom closet." She smiled as he grinned. "Four of them."

"Again? Jim's cat has a litter or two every year. This is her cabin now. Even though it's often empty, the furniture and mattresses are still good because mice can't nest in them. She keeps it clean. We make sure we leave the bedroom wedged open when we leave."

"That's smart."

"You finished looking around?"

She nodded. The cabin wasn't so large that there was much more to discover. She turned and caught an image out of the corner of her eye, something she'd missed, a framed picture on the wall. She walked closer for a better look as her heart rate increased. The photo was old and faded, but one she recognized. It was the same group photo she'd seen in Granny's box.

Walker pointed to a man at the back with dark hair. "That's Jim. He didn't look like that when I knew him. He was old and broken, with burns all over one side."

"That's Granny," said Elsa, pointing to her great-grandmother, standing next to the tall man that she would marry. A lump formed in Elsa's throat. "From her rebel days."

"Shit. That's why your grandmother looked familiar. Jim was with the rebels until explosives they rigged went off too soon. His grandson leads them now." He pointed to the child with an ax-like birthmark. "That's him, Ryan Grady."

Walker's warm breath on her neck sent shivers down her spine. She wasn't confident she was ready to deal with those feelings. If she was wrong and Walker didn't return her interest, it'd be awkward. She stepped back.

"What were you going to say before I interrupted?" She needed time to think.

"Want to come fishing? Maybe we can catch some dinner. There's a stream down the beach. Lake fishing is better with the boat, but we can try that tomorrow."

She wanted to think about this connection to her grandmother, tenuous as it was. The man who'd lived here might have been Granny's friend.

The fish last night had been delicious.

Walker grabbed two long poles and a bucket from beside the door. "Let's go then."

His happiness was infectious and her smile emerged.

They strolled up the beach, her feet sinking in the soft sand, and set up where a creek rushed down the mountain and joined the lake about two hundred and fifty yards from the cabin. Walker dug in the earthen bank with a small spade and found squiggly pink earthworms he dropped in a can with a scoop of dirt. Fishing didn't appear to need many supplies. Or cost tokens. She smiled at the idea of catching their own food for free.

Walker showed her how to thread a worm onto a hook with a small barb and cast the line into the deep pool at the creek's mouth. The current made the hooks jiggle and dance in the water. They sat on the warm rocks by the water channel and Elsa tilted her head toward the sun. Walker's presence was calming and steady.

She'd never had so much leisure time during the daylight hours; she was used to working. Their time now wasn't unproductive; they might catch dinner. Her eyes adjusted to the water, light, and shadows as she stared. Some of the flickering shadows underwater were fish and her heartbeat quickened with this realization.

The first time a tug came on the end of her line, it was like a nudge, and she flinched. She held her breath, not knowing what to do. The shadow moved away and her heart sank.

"It left." She hushed her voice as she turned to Walker.

"Next time, hold still and wait. Let a fish take a few nibbles, a solid bite on the hook. It might stay on when you yank."

Soon Walker yelled, and his line jerked three times in quick succession. He flicked the rod hard and spun it away from the water. At the end dangled a glistening fish as long as his forearm, shimmering silver with light pink and green. It flipped back and forth, staying on the hook.

"You got one!" Her heart thumped even though he'd been the first to catch a fish, almost as excited as if she'd caught one.

"Another couple, and we have dinner." His silvery gray eyes danced.

He unhooked the fish and dropped it in the bucket before he got a new worm, re-baited his hook, and returned to fishing. It was her turn next. The line tugged, tugged, then pulled hard. Her heart raced with the thrill.

"I've got one." She maintained her calm and jerked the rod, like Walker had, swinging it toward land. Suspended on her line hung another fish, flashing in the sunlight.

"Nice one." He unhooked her fish and added it to the bucket.

They spent another hour fishing, each catching a second. Fishing seemed to consist of quiet waiting, followed by bursts of energy and excitement.

"We won't eat more than that tonight," said Walker after his second catch.

He laid them in a row on a piece of bark and showed her how to clean them.

"That one's browner." Her eyes were riveted on the process as Walker gutted the fish.

"The three silver are rainbow trout. The brown is a brook trout."

"How did you learn about all this?" She waved her hand at the woods and the lake.

"Jim taught me." He rinsed his hands and the fish, then tossed the guts into the lake. "The first three summers Hayden and I came, we stayed for four months. Jim built the bunk beds, so we didn't have to sleep on the floor."

She caught a note of longing in his voice, and it tugged at her heart. He was caught up in his story, so she stayed silent and just listened; perhaps later she'd ask why.

"Jim taught me about the fish and animals that live here. I can snare rabbits, and I might shoot a grouse with a slingshot. If it was winter and I had a rifle, I could shoot a deer and live here until spring. He showed me which plants are safe to eat and others that are poisonous. I can show you those, too."

"What's a grouse?"

"A bigger bird you can eat, like a chicken. You can get close because they're not smart."

"I ate chicken once at my sister's. I liked it." They collected everything and strolled back toward the cabin.

"Your sister's rich?"

"She's married to Jaxon McCoy and lives in one of the big houses above Long Beach."

"How did that happen? No offense, but it doesn't seem like your family and his would often mix."

She shrugged. "Avery hated the Heap and never belonged. She worked there to pay back Granny."

"Pay her back?"

"Our mother died when we were nine and eleven. Our father had gambling debts. He borrowed coin he couldn't repay to someone who was going to hurt him. We overheard his plan to sell Avery south to pay off his loan."

"Your father? What a loser." He glanced at her, perhaps waiting for a reaction, but she had nothing to add and just shrugged, so he continued. "Mine died when I was young. I don't remember him. He was a rebel and died in Texas. I'd rather not remember my father than have one who wanted to sell their child."

The disgust in Walker's eyes at her father's action was clear. She didn't blame him. There was a lot of common ground in their past. He didn't say he'd been lonely, but she felt it in his tone.

"What did you do?" His slanted glance warmed her inside.

"I ran to Granny, our mother's grandmother, and told her the plan. She cashed in her life savings and paid his bills. When she took us in, Avery and I promised each other we'd pay back the debt because we wanted Granny to be able to afford to keep us. We were extra mouths to feed and didn't want to be a burden. Father had complained about how expensive we were to feed. We didn't want to go back to him."

"Still doesn't explain how your sister met Jaxon."

"It's a long story."

"We've got time," he said with a slow smile. "I'm not in a hurry."

From his smile, she didn't think he was talking about her story anymore. She gathered her thoughts as they dropped off the covered bucket of fish on the porch outside the cabin, and Elsa walked with Walker to the shed. He loaded her up with a small armload of split wood. He gathered another much larger load for himself and they carried them to the house.

"After the first couple of years, Granny's Heap partner died, and Avery and I worked full shifts."

They unloaded the wood into a box inside by the stove.

"Granny taught my sister to shoot and stand guard because the shaft gave my sister nightmares. Avery hated it underground and had claustrophobia. Granny was the excavator, and I worked the pulleys, though I'd help with the digging as needed. She taught me what had value and what to watch for. Anyway, my sister detested the Heap. She tried to keep the stink off. She practically wore off the lines of her hands, always scrubbing with sand. She bought herself fancy soap and gave up part of her drinking water to be clean."

"She wasn't as practical as you," said Walker with a sidelong glance, like he was gauging her reaction. He built a fire in the cookstove.

"Oh yes. But she's gorgeous and was clean and wore nice clothes. She didn't fit with us. Jaxon noticed her five years ago, when she was seventeen. He became obsessed, following her around. Everywhere we'd go, he'd show up. For once, he couldn't just take something he wanted, and it made him more interested."

"Granny threaten to shoot off his balls?" Walker lifted an eyebrow with his question.

Elsa laughed. "Something like that. He's an ass, but stays. Sometimes he hits her, but she forgives him. I don't visit too often because it makes my blood boil. I'd never put up with that. He's unfaithful and abusive, but Avery chose her life. I asked once. She says she doesn't regret marrying him."

"They have kids?"

"Two little girls. Rose and Charlotte. They don't let me see them. They're ashamed of me." Her voice caught, and she tossed her head, missing her longer hair. "Jaxon thinks I'm trash. He pursued Avery like she was a princess, but I was nothing." Being called trash always hurt.

"I can't imagine being ashamed of you." He rested his hand on her arm. "I've never seen anyone with more spirit."

It was difficult to meet his gaze, but she held it until he dropped his eyes. Her arm tingled where he'd rested his hand. It was nice.

"Let's cook these fish," he said with an easy smile that made her heart skip. What was she going to do about this attraction? It wasn't going away; it was growing stronger. Was she courageous enough to take a chance?

* * *

Elsa woke in the dark, not knowing where she was. Her throat ached from screaming and she'd tossed her blankets aside. She couldn't catch her breath and the sobs hurt her chest.

"You okay?" Walker's sleepy voice came from the doorway. He'd given her the bedroom and insisted on sleeping in his old bunk, which must be a tight squeeze for someone his height. He'd probably slept in the bedroom since Jim died.

She wanted to reassure him and took great gulps of air but couldn't speak.

"Can I come in?"

She nodded, though it was doubtful that he could see. Without moonlight or candles, it was pitch black.

His footsteps shuffled across the floor.

His weight settled on the bed beside her as he sat beside her and wrapped his arms around her. He slid behind her, an arm and a leg on either side of where she rocked in the middle of the bed. He was warm and solid and smelled like the wood he'd chopped tonight after dinner.

"I've got you." His voice was soft against her hair and he squeezed her tighter, though not so much it hurt her ribs. Just enough pressure to feel him surrounding her. Her back against his powerful chest. With his proximity, the tension drained out of her and her breathing slowed. The awful nightmares crept in and made her feel weak.

"I'm sorry," she said when she got the sobs under control. She still trembled, though she was enveloped in Walker's hug. He wore only underwear, and she became hyperaware that his warm skin was pressed against hers. The light stubble of his cheek rubbed against her neck.

"It's okay," he repeated.

"He's far away. I shouldn't feel this way. I'm sorry I wake you up every night."

"Logic isn't a big part of nightmares," said Walker, loosening his grip, but not moving away. "Want me to stay?"

It was too dark for him to see her blush, but she hesitated before she answered, and his weight shifted as he started to leave.

"Stay, please." The words flew from her mouth before she analyzed what he'd think or what it meant. She wanted him here.

"Of course. I was shorter when Jim built the bunks. Don't fit as well as I'd hoped."

His amused tone was clear.

"We can trade." He should have the bedroom. She'd clear out.

"Or we can share, and I'll guard your dreams. When you were sick, you rested better when I slept beside you. I don't mind."

Her heart lurched and her pulse quickened. He hadn't offered more than comfort, but where might that lead? He didn't act like he was seducing her, but it wasn't a flippant offer either. She wasn't experienced in matters of attraction, but she'd noticed things about Walker that she'd hadn't before their train ride.

In the last week, he'd turned into someone she depended on. Someone she liked. It was challenging to keep her hands to herself because she wanted to touch him, to smooth his messy hair, to grip his hard muscles, and to feel his muscular arms around her. Before she'd drifted off to sleep tonight, she'd wondered what it would be like to kiss him. Her face burned.

She slid under the covers and rearranged her pillow. Walker lifted the quilt and slid in next to her. He was long and warm and his arm around her was solid, but comfortable. If she dreamed the remainder of the night, they were peaceful.

* * *

Tatsuda slipped into one of the seedier gambling halls close to Denver station. His eyes darted from side to side as he determined if it was safe. He slid into an unoccupied table near the corner where he could watch the patrons. He wasn't there for food or drink, or to place bets. He was hoping for someone rich and drunk enough not to notice when he lifted their coin.

Men were free with their coins here. It was a profitable place to sit and observe. Unless one of the older thieves kicked him out. This was their territory, but he'd heard the guild of thieves had a meeting of their senior members somewhere else tonight, so they'd be busy right now. He wasn't welcome at the meeting any more than he was welcome here. But, if they didn't know, they couldn't catch him. Tears wouldn't work on the bosses if they caught him here. He'd have to be gone in less than an hour. In and out like a shadow.

Tatsuda scanned the dim room with caution, trying to fit in and look normal. He wouldn't be allowed to remain at a table without spending coin, so he ordered an ale for cover.

"I'm waiting for someone." He glanced over his shoulder toward the door as if expecting an arrival.

The hard-eyed server evaluated his tipping level and thumped the mug of ale on the table and stalked off. Tatsuda watched the entrances, on high alert for anyone who would take an interest in him. Even with his attention divided, the voices of the men to his right in the darkest part of the corner were hard to ignore.

"Fucking bitch. She stole the map cylinder."

"Get the bloody thing back."

Tatsuda risked a glance to determine who'd spoken.

A burly man with dark hair and a short dark beard spoke to his older, well-dressed companion, who wore a navy-blue suit. Dressed like that, the second man must work for GreenCorps. His guess was that the other was a railroad man. He was big, carried himself like he was educated, and dressed better than the miners.

"How did she know about it? She's just some born and raised SoCal heapster," said the corporation exec. "And keep your voice down. We don't need to broadcast this problem to the lot here. Bunch of thieves and degenerates. Next time, I'll choose where we meet."

"She's the one who excavated it from the Heap," said the first man. "I offered her three silver coins."

"Three silver was a bargain price, my friend," said the well-dressed man. "Let me help you get your story straight. Keep it simple. She stole it. Now we're out ten gold to get it back. We need that tube. The letter in the Corporation's archives said it should have maps to all six other locations and a key. We've never found them, so they could be anywhere. It's worth five times the reward. Maybe ten. Hard to put a value on its worth."

More than ten gold coins? Tatsuda's heart raced. It was hard not to react. He sipped his ale and strained his ears for more.

"I'll have to go back to SoCal to pick up more information or find someone to track her. She left with a hopper. I thought she might come here to sell the cylinder a second time. Greedy bitch."

"I don't care what you do, just get it fast."

"I'm working on it. My brother will keep me posted if there are leads."

"We located the Denver bunker ten years ago, but it didn't have types of seeds we're missing and there'd been extensive water damage in the records area. Everything was destroyed. We need the maps and that key."

"Ten gold coins ought to tempt someone. They'll turn her in."

Yes, they would. Tatsuda wished he could ask the questions. There was so much more he wanted to know. His hand shook.

"So I know what to tell your father, how long has she been gone?"

"She hopped a train to Sacramento on the sixteenth. I was two days and a train behind. A bull in Sacramento reported a possible sighting on the nineteenth. Nothing since. She could be on foot or have hopped another train. Just in case, I have men scouring Reno. If she even goes to a store for supplies, I'll get word. I thought she would travel here, but nobody saw her in Salt Lake City. I'll spend a few days searching in Denver before I head back. She wanted to sell the tube once. She'll try again. She had the stink of desperation."

"Search Salt Lake on the way back. That's a perfect place for young women to disappear. The rebels and the cultists love helping them."

"They causing trouble again?"

The GreenCorps man made a clicking noise that Tatsuda couldn't interpret as his mind raced at their conversation.

"She could have gone anywhere from Sacramento. Don't waste my time. Let me know if there's actual news. Spread the word about the reward." The well-dressed man left while his companion ordered cards and a woman.

Ten gold pieces? Such a vast fortune was beyond imagination. Tatsuda visualized what he could buy with the gold. He'd be set for life if he collected the reward. The seed of a plan formed in his mind, and his pulse quickened. If he could find the missing thief, he could steal the tube from her. That part would be easy. Then he'd claim the ten gold pieces. GreenCorps wanted this thing and sounded desperate. Perhaps he could name his price. Fifteen gold? He had faith in his ability to steal anything. He doubted the girl was in Denver, but he'd wait a few days to be certain. Reno wasn't far. He'd hopped trains before. He could again.

Tatsuda would do some research. He couldn't read, but he recognized numbers. He'd go to the train station and check the reward posters. From them, he'd get a likeness of the mystery girl and try to pick up her trail. He might hear something the burly man wouldn't. He was just a kid. People might answer questions they wouldn't for a rich man, or a GreenCorps bully.

Tatsuda stayed in the gambling hall and enacted his original plan. He found two marks and liberated their coin before he slipped outside. He meandered toward the train station, alert for where to get today's free meal. A solid day's take and a prospect of a challenge. A chance to make his fortune. Not bad for an afternoon's work.

CHAPTER 23: ELSA PLUS WALKER

Three nights in a row, Elsa slept without repeating bad dreams; when she woke with her heart pounding, Walker was there. She caught up on sleep, becoming healthy and well-rested. Her bruises faded, all except one patch on her ribs that remained a sullen purple and sore to the touch. There was no pain unless she breathed deep.

The fourth night before bed, she decided to talk to Walker.

She dried the last dish, her hand shaking. "Would you like me to sleep out here tonight?" She watched him with her peripheral vision.

He set down the last of the clean dishes and his head jerked in her direction. "Why would you say that?"

Elsa looked at him, gathering her courage around her like a blanket in order to speak. Her cheeks warmed, but she dove in. "You sleep with me out of pity, but I'm feeling better. You've been great, but I can't depend on you being there every night."

"Yes, you can." Walker crossed the room without seeming to move his feet, took the dishtowel from her hands, and hung it up. He stood close enough that she had to tip her head back to see his face.

"I enjoy sleeping with you. If you'd been healthy, I'd have been tempted to do more than sleep. It has nothing to do with pity. I like you. You know I do."

His words shot heat to her core.

"I'm not sick or injured now." She locked her gaze on his while her heart skipped and fluttered. She bit her bottom lip and his eyes followed the motion. Granny had always said if you wanted something, you had to act, not wait to react. She stepped closer.

"You told the bartender at Ginny's that you've never been kissed. Did you want him to kiss you? His tone had changed, his voice was huskier.

Walker's proximity quickened her pulse, her eyes drawn to his lips like magnets.

"Wes? I never wanted to kiss Wes."

"Would you like to kiss me?"

Her palms grew sweaty, and she swallowed. Bravery wasn't easy.

"Will you teach me?"

"Damn, woman. Of course. It's all I've been thinking about for days. If I kiss you, I'll want more, but I'll stop if you tell me to." Walker cupped her jaw with one hand and current raced through her.

Her whole body blushed. She was on fire with desire and embarrassment. She wanted more too and believed in telling the truth.

"I didn't understand half of what Jace wanted to do. I couldn't stand his touch. He forced me to do things I didn't want. I'm lucky it didn't go any farther. But others do these things for pleasure. For fun. Do you know how to make them pleasurable?" Elsa fought the impulse to look away and held contact with his pale gray eyes.

His eyes remained locked on hers. "I grew up in a whorehouse. I've seen or heard just about everything you could imagine. But I left home at age fourteen, so I haven't had much practice." His eyes darkened.

His revelation about his childhood didn't surprise Elsa. He looked calm, but beads of sweat had appeared on his forehead. He swallowed at the end of his words. It made her feel better he was nervous too. His thumb stroked her cheek; tendrils of heat spread.

"Will you teach me not to be afraid?"

Walker caressed her lower lip with his thumb and the bottom fell out of her stomach and her breath hitched. He stroked her lip again and heat licked through her, a current that shocked her core, like the jolt she got every time they touched, only stronger because this was deliberate.

"How do you do that?" she asked, trying not to tremble.

"It's because you like me." He moistened his lips as he bent toward her with a smile.

He was much taller than she was, but they fit together well. She liked his strength and size. When his lips met hers, her knees sagged, and she grabbed onto the front of his shirt for support. He chuckled and wrapped his arms around her. The first touch of his mouth to hers was tentative and soft, but she relaxed into the kiss.

Elsa swayed against him and he tugged her closer, his hand splayed on her lower back. Its warmth seeped through her clothes. He was hot. She wound her arms around his neck, and his tongue moved into her mouth as he deepened the kiss. Her body understood more than her brain as she hungrily returned his kiss. Its electricity traveled through her from her head to her toes, tingling as it spread.

They kissed until they were both breathless. Walker's cheeks had a hectic flush and his lips were red. He cupped her jaw again, maintaining the electricity between them. He kissed the side of her neck and she stretched it sideways to allow him better access. She gasped when he slid a hand beneath her shirt and stroked her the underside of her breast.

"Are these the kinds of lessons you were thinking?" His voice had a husky quality. "Because I think you're an excellent student."

"Teach me more."

He took her hand and backed up, leading her to the bedroom. Her heart raced, and she ached in sensitive places. She'd hoped this might be how their evening developed.

"Should we take off our clothes?" he said.

"You've seen me naked. More than once."

"Not like this. I want to look at you like the beautiful woman you are."

Warmth shot through her. She hadn't thought those words would be possible; they were unexpected.

"Or we could practice what you've learned already if you would rather?"

She wanted more and let her actions speak as she stripped, dropping her clothes to the floor. His gaze grew more intense. He removed his shirt, placed it on the chair in the corner, and his other clothes followed. She watched, enjoying his deliberate movements that allowed her to admire how he was put together.

Walker's muscles were well-defined, hard planes across his chest and stomach. She'd watched his powerful muscles shift when he split firewood with his shirt off this morning and it had given her the idea to speak. Desire rose inside her. His arousal was also obvious.

"Can I touch you?" Her hand stretched toward him even before he answered, but she stayed where she was.

"I'd like that. But I'm not worried about feeling pleasure and you are. Maybe we need to practice more kissing."

His lopsided grin put her at ease.

Elsa stepped forward, and suddenly his heated skin was against hers. His lips captured hers and she was swept up in the sensation of being touched with his mouth and hands, while his cock tapped against her, surprising her by adding to her excitement. With Walker, nothing was scary. He was glorious, muscled, and powerful, but his touch was gentle. Her hands were tentative at first, but she wanted to touch his skin, to explore him. She grew bolder, her hands more sure.

Her heart drummed against her ribs, and it became difficult to think. She enjoyed touching and kissing Walker, but it led to a feeling of urgency. They'd avoided the most intimate touches so far, but her body wanted more and she had trouble holding still. One of his hands slid between her legs and she moaned as his fingers found her most sensitive bundle of nerves. It was slippery there, dripping. When he discovered her secret wetness, he sucked in a breath. His fingers slid into her again, parting her nether lips.

"Do you trust me?" His voice was calm, despite his excitement.

She nodded, speechless and beyond words, trembling where she stood.

"Come on the bed," he said. "With me."

Elsa followed his directions and he lay beside her, stroking first her cheek and jaw, then her breasts, then her hip. He left a trail of desire in his wake. His hand returned inside her legs and this time he slid a finger inside her. She gasped. This was nothing like before. He moved it within her and her hips bucked off the bed. Her breath came faster and when a second finger joined the first, the sensation was incredible. It should have been uncomfortable or embarrassing, but it felt right.

Walker slid them in and out while she moaned and arched her back, her small breasts jutting into the air. He captured one of her nipples in his mouth and she moaned. She'd never imagined she could feel this incredible. She reached down and touched his cock, sliding its silken hardness into her hand. He groaned, and she stopped, worried she'd done it wrong.

"You can touch me as much as you want," he said. "You wanted to know about pleasure. How much more of a lesson do you want tonight?" His voice was strained, his longing in his voice. "We can stop whenever you want."

"I want more. Unless you want to stop?"

He kissed her, erasing her worries.

"It might hurt the first time, but you're so ready, it won't be for long."

She bit her lip and nodded. He rubbed her wet, swollen mound and her reservations dissolved. His tongue slid into her mouth in the same slow swirling rhythm that increased the tempo like his hand. Her breath became ragged, and she whimpered as a tightness expanded inside her, needing release. The world fell away and went dark around the edges. Blossoms of sparks exploded in her brain with intense pleasure.

Elsa cried out at the height of it and Walker's mouth claimed hers again as he held her to the earth while she soared above, riding a wave of ecstasy. When she returned to herself, she shuddered in his embrace.

When she stopped shaking and her vision returned, Walker's arms tightened around her. She stared, lost in the depths of his eyes, gray but lit from behind with a silver light. She'd never seen them so pale.

"Is that everything?" she said, her voice husky and low.

He hadn't experienced pleasure, only given, and she wanted to give as well as take. She put her hands on his chest and the rapid-fire thump of his heart matched her own. He swallowed as he looked down at her.

"More." Her hand reached for his swollen cock, which leaped at her touch. She'd said the correct thing.

He rolled on top of her, supporting his weight with his arms, and positioned himself at her entrance. She stiffened in anticipation, but when his lips caught hers again, she lost her nervousness. Walker wouldn't hurt her. There was a moment of awkwardness, then wild heat as he thrust inside. She pulsed around him and there was a flash of pain when he pushed, but it was replaced by a warmth that spread outward and expanded throughout her body. This wasn't just for him as the heat grew again with each movement.

Walker thrust into her, slow at first, then faster and deeper. Her release was quick, and she shook, crying out with pleasure.

His body stiffened, and he cried out. He pumped inside her a few more times before he collapsed. His cheeks were flushed and his heart raced like a train, faster than ever, against her chest. His forehead rested against hers while he caught his breath, and she attempted to regain her composure through the aftershocks of their lovemaking. He tilted his head toward her—his kiss thorough and deep.

"Thank you."

"Thank you too." Her limbs were relaxed and softer than usual, heavier. She didn't want to move. "How soon can we do that again?"

He laughed. "We can try again soon."

"Good, I want more." She didn't think she'd ever get enough of him now that she'd started down this track.

* * *

Walker
May 28th, 2195, Lake Tahoe
Sunrise: 5:37 a.m. Sunset: 8:16 p.m.

Arrived at the cabin just over a week ago. Feel like a different person here. This is where I belong. It's never been clearer. Always loved being here, but not like this. I've gotten to share what I've learned with Elsa, who absorbs everything like a sponge. Her mind is incredible. Soon it will be warm enough that I can teach her to swim. Find myself thinking about her day and night. Not just her body, which is incredible, with its combination of smooth and soft, hard and muscular, but how she wants everything I can teach. She's thirsty for knowledge, in the bedroom and outside. I'm lucky to have met her. She's gained a foothold in my heart. Haven't ever been close to anyone like this. I've fallen for her. Never known anyone else to say exactly what they think and want. Don't think she knows how to lie. It's refreshing.

Can't believe I'm thinking this, but if Hayden doesn't catch up, I won't be as sorry as I would have thought. Still worry about him. But it's a relief for him to clean up his own shit. Not leave me to cope and get him out of trouble.

This is the first time since the first summer here six years ago that I've dared to dream that I could stay, make a life unbeholden to GreenCorps. Elsa and I could have a life together.

CHAPTER 24: TATSUDA PLUS ELSA

Tatsuda jumped off the train in Reno that had arrived via Salt Lake City, where he'd chased leads. He'd followed a system to eliminate the towns along the track where the girl from the Wanted poster could have gotten off. He'd found no clues and didn't think she'd been to Denver or Salt Lake. He had a suspicion he'd find her trail in Reno.

The air here seemed thinner, though it shouldn't differ from the mountain city he'd left. The weather was warm, and the air was clean and quiet. It hadn't been as smooth a journey as he'd hoped. He'd had trouble with a creep in a green jacket who'd followed him from the station in Salt Lake City, pinned him against the wall, and threatened him at knifepoint with the shaking hands of addiction.

The guy with pinched features had taken everything Tatsuda had brought. There had been little of value, but it'd included his coin. He'd tried to pretend he was part of a larger group of passersby that would protect him. The ragged young man with his sour smell hadn't believed him. After that encounter, Tatsuda kept to himself and skulked in deeper shadows. He changed his look to be more pathetic, less worth robbing. His small size was often an advantage, but not when he was overpowered.

He landed on an inner track, dropped to a low crouch, and dashed toward the rear of the train, using the parked train cars as cover until he'd left the main trainyard. With a quick glance up the track, he checked that nobody had followed, then was up and over the outer fence. He looked back twice as he headed for a neighborhood, but it appeared he'd slipped through security.

In downtown Reno, the Wanted posters for the girl and her boyfriend papered the fences and decorated every window. He wouldn't recognize the man—the description matched half the men in town—but the woman was more distinctive. She wouldn't be able to go anywhere without being caught. The scale of the search was larger than he'd expected, but for ten gold coins it was worth it.

While his wandering through town might appear aimless to someone on the outside, he was searching according to his plan. He listened to conversations, hoping to glean the right information. The girl had last been seen headed here; this was where he'd find the trail.

For the next week, he lurked near the workers in the station's public section. He offered to do odd jobs for the kitchen staff for meals. He became part of the scenery, hoping it would pay off. Then one day, Tatsuda overheard two bulls talking while they ate. They disagreed about what had happened. One man claimed it had been two young men who'd jumped the fence, the other said it had been a young man and a slim girl with bruises. She'd been dressed as a boy.

"He was holding her hand," he argued with his friend.

The conversation had the feel of something debated several times without a solution or agreement.

"Could have been his brother. The big guy helps him when he's a mess."

"You should have seen the eyes on her," said the guard with a deep voice. He shook his head. "If you'd seen her eyes, we wouldn't be having this discussion."

Tatsuda smiled. She'd been here, with a big guy, and evaded capture. Smart of her to find protection. Her large, serious eyes were her most distinctive feature. She'd been here and left the station rather than hopped another train. She must have had a haircut if she'd been mistaken for a boy. He listened to how she'd gone over the fence and disappeared into the neighborhood to the south of the station.

He would concentrate his efforts on that neighborhood. If she wasn't there, she might have gone beyond Reno into the mountains to wait for the search to die down. That's what he would have done. Perhaps she would return to the tracks here when the search slowed. Maps showed few settlements south of Reno within walking distance. It was probable that she'd return to Reno for the train; it was too far to walk to the other cities along the railway line.

After, he'd go somewhere by rail that GreenCorps wouldn't expect, maybe Vegas. Maybe Salt Lake. Maybe Western Canada, where she'd be beyond GreenCorps' reach, but she and her boyfriend would have to start again in Reno. He would watch and wait. With a little luck, she would come to him.

It wasn't hard to find food in Reno, since he wasn't particular. He would play a waiting game. He became a ghost, slipping in and out of shops and pockets, seldom seen but always present.

* * *

After more than a month of sunshine, Elsa woke to the sound of steady rain tapping on the roof and dripping from the eaves. The air in the cabin was cold, their cookfire long since extinguished. Walker's naked body wrapped around her, sharing its heat. She'd rather stay in bed this morning than get up. As she stirred, he nuzzled her neck and his arm tightened.

"Don't go. I'm not ready to let you up yet."

"We'll get hungry."

"I'm already hungry." His hand slipped between her legs, and he stroked her dampness. She pressed against him and he rolled her to face him and his mouth connected with hers. They hadn't been able to get enough of each other for the last month. All it took was a look, and they were kissing or touching, their clothes abandoned. The heat between them hadn't subsided, but had intensified.

When they emerged later that morning, the rain was slowing. It had been an ideal stay at the cabin, but Elsa had become restless. For more than a week, her gut had been telling her it was time to leave. She hadn't confided in Walker because she didn't want to disappoint him. He loved it here, and she had no intention of asking him to leave, but the feeling had eaten away at her happiness. She refused to feel guilty about having her own happiness this past month, but she wasn't the only one who deserved this life. Thousands of others deserved a life free of GreenCorps tyranny.

She'd found the maps for a reason, and sitting by a lake and hiding weren't enough. She was meant to do something about the seed bunkers. She needed to find someone who would distribute the seeds and help grow trees and crops. The feeling had become urgent. She would talk to Walker today.

Most days they left the cabin and spent it outside, but she wasn't in a hurry. It was still wet outside, so she decided to poke around in Jim's trunk. She was curious to see what it held. There might be something related to the rebels, something that might help her find them and convince them to aid her cause.

The metal trunk wasn't locked, so she threw back the lid and examined the contents. There was a shotgun, a handgun, several boxes of shotgun shells, and a half-full case of shiny bullets. A handcrafted blanket was folded on one side. Underneath was a box with a stack of photographs—most were of a dark-haired woman and two boys. There was one of Granny, standing with her grown daughter and two younger men who looked so alike they must have been brothers. On the back, in faded ink, it read, "Aki, Avery, John, and Mark." The date was 2145, the same year GreenCorps had sent Granny to live in SoCal.

A large yellow envelope at the side contained brittle documents that Elsa peeled out with excruciating slowness to avoid having them crumble to pieces. A glance at his birth certificate showed Jim Daniels had been James Grady, born in 2097 in Salt Lake City, Utah. Another document was a land title deed to the property where the cabin was built, including hundreds of acres of the mountain and beachfront of Lake Tahoe. A newer, hand-written letter, signed and witnessed, left the land title to Walker Sullivan. The cabin was his, in truth. She set that aside to show Walker.

At the bottom of the trunk was a mission statement by the rebels, signed by Aki and Jonathan Lee, as well as James and Elspeth Grady.

"We have taken it upon ourselves to break the chains of GreenCorps' domination. They cannot and should not control the dairy farms, corn and wheat production, and the majority of the orchards in the central and western regions of what used to be America. People should be free to live and work in order to feed their families. GreenCorps has no right to control our education, jobs, and welfare. Food and water are basic rights. Everyone should have access to clean water and affordable food.

We dedicate ourselves to the cause of freeing our people from corporate tyranny that has replaced a government dictatorship."

Perhaps the rebels would help her with the seed bunkers after all. The idea wasn't preposterous. Their cause had been about access to food, which could be why they'd taken the Department of Agriculture leaf emblem as their symbol. It made sense. Her gut told her she needed to find them. She needed to tell Walker.

Dread filled her. What if he didn't want to leave? He loved it here. This was the closest place he had to a home, and she wasn't certain she had the right to ask him to leave.

She replaced everything in the trunk and joined him at the table to eat breakfast.

"Find anything interesting?"

Elsa told Walker about the guns, photos, and documents.

"The cabin and the land are yours. Jim left an official paper." She retrieved it from the top of the trunk.

"He said he would." Walker's hands shook as he read it. "We should put it back. It's safer here than with me. Thank you for showing me." His voice broke. "The cabin's really mine."

Seeing Walker respond with such powerful emotion about the deed, Elsa balked. It didn't seem like the moment to explain what she'd found about the rebels. She wanted to process the information, knowing she had to find them, but leaving would be dangerous. GreenCorps was out there, waiting for them to return or try to hop another train. But she needed to act. Today. She'd talk to him today. Later.

After chopping and stacking firewood, Elsa and Walker spent most of the day on the water. They explored further down the lake than usual; fishing late that afternoon after the sun broke through the overcast skies.

Without warning, Elsa's stomach clenched as they pulled the canoe onshore at their beach; she was surprised by the intensity of the reaction.

Something was going to happen.

She glanced up to see movement on the forest trail above the cabin, a flash of green. Her chest became tight. Had they been discovered?

Walker threw his paddle into the boat and charged past her, running up the path. He didn't go to the cabin and the weapons, but to the trailhead. There was only one person who would make him react that way.

"You made it," he shouted.

It had been six weeks since they'd left Hayden in SoCal. Just last week, Walker had expressed doubt that Hayden would come—it was taking too long. Elsa took a deep breath. She'd been dreading this moment, but for Walker's sake, she would try to forgive Hayden. The image of him rifling through Granny's pockets while the old lady lay crumpled on the ground flashed through Elsa's mind and she grit her teeth. It was going to be difficult.

"We thought you weren't coming." Walker pulled Hayden into a hug after he stumbled down the last section of the trail.

From the expression on Hayden's face, he hadn't expected an exuberant welcome.

"I knew you'd come here," said Hayden, stepping back. "But I didn't expect you to leave me behind."

"We had to leave town in a hurry." Walker smiled. "I'm surprised you took so long. Did you have trouble?"

"Heard you left someone for dead and helped that thief escape. I didn't want anyone to follow me here. This is our private place."

Hayden's eyes cut to Elsa at the shoreline.

"I didn't hit McCoy hard enough to have killed him," said Walker, shaking his head. "Elsa didn't steal anything. That's a lie."

"There are Wanted posters of the two of you that are supposed to be posted from here to Denver. Maybe beyond. Probably everywhere the train goes. You'd be fools to get back on the trains."

"You weren't followed?" Walker looked up the cliff side trail.

"I spent a couple of weeks in Salt Lake City, throwing them off track."

"What else did you do? It's been six weeks."

Hayden's eyes flicked past Walker, returning to Elsa. "What's she doing here?"

Elsa didn't like the way Hayden avoided answering the questions, instead asking his own. Despite his decision to let Hayden stand on his own, Walker was too accepting of Hayden's non-answers. He must want to hope for the best. She unclipped her life jacket and let it fall in the boat, straightened the paddles, and grabbed the basket of fish. There was ample to share with an extra person. She steeled her nerves to deal with Hayden and walked toward the reunion.

Walker stepped back from the path; a wide grin on his handsome face.

"Hayden, you remember Elsa."

Walker threw his arm around her and tucked her into his side. She enjoyed the possessive feel of it. It was one way to explain their relationship status without words. She looked up at him.

Hayden's eyes darted to the side.

"Elsa, you remember my brother?"

Walker's eyes begged her to give Hayden another chance.

"I'm glad you found us," she said, attempting a smile, though her whole body was rigid. "Walker was concerned when you took so long."

Had Walker noticed the way Hayden's eyes narrowed at the sight of his arm around her? Jealousy oozed from Hayden in waves. She would try to ignore it. Perhaps he needed time to adjust. She wished he hadn't come, but she wouldn't be rude. Besides, she couldn't stay much longer.

"I'll take those." Walker reached for the basket of trout. "I'll clean them for dinner. You two start a fire and get acquainted. I'll be up in a few minutes." He raised an eyebrow, checking that she was okay.

She nodded.

"I'll make the fire." Hayden stalked toward the cabin with angry strides.

"I'm glad your brother is okay. You were concerned." Elsa kissed Walker before following Hayden. Maybe tonight wouldn't be the best night to talk about leaving. She swallowed her disappointment.

Inside the cabin and away from Walker's eyes, Hayden's demeanor changed, becoming more aggressive. He snapped around and stalked towards her.

"Don't get too comfortable," said Hayden, his face in hers.

She wanted to slap him, but stepped to the side.

"You're not McCoy's whore now, you're my brother's. Don't expect that to last."

"I wasn't a whore at Ginny's. Not for the McCoys or anyone else." Elsa tried to keep the heat out of her voice, clenching her fist at her side, but his nasty comments made it difficult.

Hayden shrugged and raised an eyebrow as he scanned her from head to toe. "You look like a whore to me."

Her blood boiled, and she saw red. She took a couple of deep breaths so she didn't punch him. "You still look like a drug-obsessed thief to me." She spoke in her sweetest voice, then let her voice show its heat. "But Walker's been good to me, so for his sake, I planned to give you another chance—even if you broke Granny's arm and put us out of work. Now, I'm not so sure. Every word from your mouth confirms that my first impression was correct. You're a creep."

"Your glares don't scare me," said Hayden, though he'd taken a step back, perhaps at the vehemence of her words. "When we go back to the real world, my brother and I are going to leave you behind. He'll see that he doesn't need you. He's my brother and you're nothing but easy trash from the Heap. He'll tire of you soon enough." His mouth twisted on his words.

Her eyes stung, and she lifted her chin and turned away. To distract herself, she kept busy, tidying the morning's clean dishes they'd left in the dish rack. Walker's footsteps scraped against the stone walkway as he returned.

Her jaw clenched as she rinsed the greens they'd collected earlier, keeping her eyes averted as Walker brought over the cleaned fish. He kissed her temple and squeezed her arm as he moved about the kitchen, helping to prepare the food. If he noticed the thick tension in the room, he gave no sign.

Elsa was quiet that evening as the men told stories of their time on the road. "Remember when" was a common phrase. Hayden brought up a dozen stories when the two of them had a close shave, a fun time, or seen something special. She enjoyed hearing about their adventures, but found it hard to relate. She was sure it was deliberate on Hayden's part.

Whenever Walker tried to steer the conversation to the last six weeks, Hayden guided it away again without explanation. Nor did he seem interested in their journey. His plan to leave her out was effective, but she tried not to let it bother her. Walker squeezed her hand under the table a few times, letting her know he understood. At least he wasn't oblivious.

The moon rose over the lake, creating a silver trail on the inky water. It was late.

Elsa stood. "You two enjoy catching up. I was awake early listening to the rain. I'm going to get ready for bed."

"I won't be long," said Walker with an amiable smile; the one that made her heart catch.

She got ready for bed, washing up outside at the pump and brushing her teeth by the lake. After using the outhouse, she headed back to the cabin but stopped as angry voices carried through the open window on the breeze.

"I can't believe you left me there. Instead, you brought *her* here. This is our refuge."

"Can't believe you're being such an ass. Jace McCoy beat the shit out of her and tried to rape her. I couldn't stand back and let that happen. We tried to take you with us, but you were kiting so high you couldn't talk or walk, let alone hop a train. If they'd caught us, we'd have been forced onto a GreenCorps work detail or deported to a Texas work camp. I trusted you to catch up, which you did. It just doesn't look good. You took so long and you won't say anything about where you've been."

"You act like you don't trust me," said Hayden.

"I don't. You have to earn trust, and lately, all you've done is break it."

"Well, I'm not traveling with her. You're going to have to make a choice. I understand if you feel obligated to drop her off in Reno, where she can catch her own train. Or she can disappear into town. But, I won't hop a train with her; she's a wanted criminal, a liability. She'll get you in more trouble than you're in already. What were you thinking? You attacked a rich man. She's using you."

Elsa stood frozen, waiting to hear what Walker said.

"I'm not leaving her."

She almost collapsed in relief that he wasn't swayed by his brother's ultimatum.

"You'll leave me again? After everything we've been through together?"

"I didn't say that," said Walker. "I'm happy to travel with you both. I won't send her away or leave her behind. If you decide not to be with us, that's your choice."

"I won't be your third wheel. You like fucking her. You've been drooling all night. I saw those steamy looks between you. It has been a long time since you had any action. A man has needs. I get that. But that doesn't mean she has to stay with us. You got some, now you can move on."

"I'm not using her like that and you're a jackass to suggest that I would. I care about her. She's willing to give you a chance. Can't you return the favor?"

Elsa shouldn't be listening, but stayed in the shadow below the window. Despite Hayden's crass words, Walker's words warmed her inside. She hadn't been wrong to let him close to her heart.

"Did you tell her what kind of people we are? The kind that burned the house down and killed everyone, including your mother."

She covered her mouth with her hand and bit her lip. Walker hadn't explained what had sent them out on the road hopping trains, but she'd known it had been serious.

"That was an accident. We were kids. We can't blame ourselves forever."

"That's right, it was my fault. I was the one who started the fire." Hayden's tone was nasty, cutting.

"That has nothing to do with Elsa. We can talk about it another day. I've had enough of this for tonight. Take whichever bunk you prefer. We've got the bedroom."

Elsa headed for the beach and sat on the sand, looking out at the lake. Seconds later, Walker stormed out the front door. His shoulders remained tense when he joined her a few minutes later by the water. He'd washed too and smelled clean.

"How much of that did you hear?" His voice was soft.

"Most of it."

"He'll come around. I'm not leaving you. You're important to me. He isn't used to sharing, and he's being unreasonable."

Her heart grew heavy at the idea of leaving. This was the moment. "I don't want you to feel obligated to be with me, but I have to talk to you about something."

Walker took her hand and hauled her to her feet. He clasped his hands behind her back. "Do I seem like someone forced to spend time with you?"

Elsa shook her head, but her words stuck in her throat.

"Let's get out of here. Go look at the stars. We can talk out there." He gave her a quick kiss.

She nodded. She wasn't willing to go back into the cabin either. The urgent need to talk to Walker about leaving took precedence over her distrust of Hayden in their house and the way her gut clenched at the thought.

"Let me grab something." Walker jogged toward the shed and returned with a picnic blanket from the clothesline.

Taking her hand, they walked until they couldn't see the lights of the cabin. They left the beach and scrambled up a bluff overlooking the lake, where he spread the blanket.

"Words can be difficult, but maybe I can show you how I feel."

Their lovemaking was intense from the beginning, both of them fervent and needing to connect. She called out over and over, while he took more care for her pleasure than his own, putting off his own release until she was incoherent and shaking.

Afterward, he touched his lips to hers as they lay naked under the multitude of stars. "I didn't think I'd ever meet anyone like you. I had no idea there was anyone out there I'd care about, but you, Elsa, you woke my heart. You make me whole. I want to know everything about you. Please stay with me. I won't lose you because my brother is an ass. Please. We'll figure it out."

Elsa loved Walker. His words like lightning, zapping a realization.

It shocked her; her thoughts echoed his words. They belonged together, which made the conversation about leaving more heart-wrenching.

He held her, warming her with his heat. The breeze danced across her naked flesh, giving her goosebumps. She'd do anything for him. For Walker, she'd put up with Hayden's animosity.

"I'll try to like Hayden. You care about him, so I'll try, but I've been meaning to speak to you about something for a week now. It's so wonderful here at the cabin that I didn't know how to start." A lump formed in her throat and she bit her lip.

"You can tell me anything." His voice was quiet.

"I have to search for the rebels. I love it here and I want to be with you more than anything, but I feel compelled to do this. I found the tube for a reason and I have to do something about it, or I'll never rest. My gut has been screaming that it's time.

"It's dangerous out there," Walker said, his eyes not leaving hers. "How soon do you want to go? I can be packed tomorrow, if that's what you want."

She let out her breath. "You'll come with me? What about your brother?"

Walker kissed her again. "You and I belong together. It doesn't matter if it's here or out there. I'm putting you and this cause first. Which means I'm living for myself instead of Hayden. This mission is for us."

Elsa's heart swelled. A few tears escaped as she returned his kiss and hugged him hard, feeling his solid embrace. "Three days. Let's take three days, then we go."

When they returned to the cabin, Hayden was sitting on the porch. He would have heard their echoes across the water, but he didn't speak when they stepped past him on the way inside.

"See you in the morning." Walker clasped his brother's shoulder on the way by. "I'm glad you made it. It's good to have you here."

Hayden nodded but said nothing. Elsa found it hard to read his face. This time, his jealousy was well-hidden.

Afterward, when she and Walker lay naked and entangled on their bed, he tilted her chin to him, his lips soft on hers. Walker wanted to stay with her. That was what mattered. He didn't think she was casual or trash. He loved her and believed in her mission. She fell asleep in his arms, ignoring the hard lump in her gut that said there would be more trouble.

CHAPTER 25: ELSA PLUS WALKER

The next morning, Hayden accompanied them as they gathered wood and hiked by the lake. He said little, but he acted polite. It gave her hope that maybe they would find a way to work together. However, Elsa wasn't surprised when he begged off fishing in the afternoon. Maybe he'd spent enough time in their company for one day.

"I'll dig bulrush tubers to go with dinner. You going to Emerald Bay?" Hayden said.

That was the shallow bay with the best fishing. She wished to accept that nothing was awry with his words, but something about the way he asked roused her suspicions. What was his agenda? Maybe he wanted to start dinner or know where they were headed in case he changed his mind. She couldn't put her finger on what made her uneasy.

"We'll be gone for a couple of hours," said Walker. "Depends on how the fish are biting. Hope you don't mind."

"I don't mean to interfere with your routine," said Hayden. "I'll head to Marlette Lake when I'm done digging tubers. I'll leave some for you and camp overnight. Do my own fishing and come back tomorrow."

Walker's eyebrows lifted in surprise.

"You just got here. Everything ok?"

"I'm fine. I just thought you two might like your privacy. Last night was awkward. I felt like I was interrupting."

"I'm sorry. We want you here," said Walker, his cheeks flushing pink. "We'll keep the noise down."

Hayden waved him off with a shrug and a smile. He seemed to be in a better mood today. Was it genuine?

"I'll see you tomorrow. Happy fishing." Walker laughed as Elsa turned away with her own blush.

She'd been too loud. Embarrassed, but pleased Hayden wasn't joining them, she climbed into the boat and Walker shoved the canoe out onto the lake, hopping in at the back. When Elsa looked over her shoulder, Hayden stood on the beach until they rounded the corner and were out of sight. A creeping sense of unease swept over her again. Something wasn't right. The thought that had been niggling at her since they'd gotten in the boat became clear.

She never should have left him alone with the tube. She was out of the habit of carrying it everywhere she went, because there'd been no need to hide it from Walker. She stopped paddling and twisted in her seat, her eyes straining in the direction of the cabin.

"What is it?" said Walker.

"You'll think I'm silly." Her brow furrowed.

"Tell me anyway."

"Sometimes Granny knew things, things that kept her alive. It's how she survived her rebellion years. Said she sensed things in her gut. When I was little, I didn't understand, but it happens to me. My gut clenches and I get a feeling about something. When I met you, I knew you would be important. It was like I recognized you. Or that the job at Ginny's was no good. I took it anyway, because I had no choice, but ignoring it got me in trouble."

"On the Heap, I could always tell when I scavenged something valuable. When I found the tube, my entire arm tingled. My gut told me it would change my life. I was too scared to do anything about it, but it was significant. The sense that it's time to leave is another instinct."

"You have good instincts." Walker's face set in a frown, his forehead wrinkled. "What does that have to do with right now? We're leaving in a couple of days."

"Something is off with Hayden."

"You just don't know him. He's moody. You said you'd give him a chance."

Walker's strokes became harder and the canoe shot through the water. This was why it was tricky to explain. His brother was a prickly subject.

"I want to, but I just know he's up to something. Sending us off and offering to be away tonight. It doesn't make sense. Yesterday he was jealous and called me your whore. He said I was trash."

Walker's head jerked up, his eyes blazing, but she didn't let him interrupt.

"He was clear that he didn't accept my presence. Today he's considerate and giving us time alone. It's too quick a turnaround. It's suspicious."

"I hope you're wrong." Walker stopped paddling.

Elsa watched while he waged an inner struggle. "I hope so too."

The canoe drifted to a stop, becoming still as Walker frowned. They floated, the water lapping against the boat. She said nothing.

He nodded and his expression cleared. "Let's go back," he said, turning the canoe. "I trust you. Hayden can be a weasel."

Hayden's absence was notable on the beach, nor could they spot him down the beach at the marshy area with the bulrushes. He wasn't anywhere. They hadn't been gone long—no more than thirty minutes.

Elsa ran into the cabin. Every day since they'd arrived, they'd left the door wedged open so the elusive cat with whom they shared the cabin could patrol. Last night, with Hayden sleeping in the other room, was the first time they'd closed the door. Elsa had slid the wedge under the door this morning, propping it open.

The door to the bedroom was closed.

Hayden had been in their room.

Opening the door, her first glance showed nothing amiss. On a second sweep, her gaze latched onto the strap from her old satchel, where it stuck out of her backpack. She hadn't left it that way. Hayden had rummaged in her backpack.

Her stomach clenched, this time with fear, and she broke out into a cold sweat. Dread sat cold and hollow in her gut.

The tube was missing.

She lifted everything out of the backpack and searched with shaking hands. It wasn't there. She double-checked the outer pockets, dumping the contents to the floor. Nothing. She scanned the floor all around in case it had fallen, her chest tight, her breathing fast. The tube was gone.

Hayden had stolen it. He must have come here looking for it. He'd known it was valuable. Not only had he seen the Wanted pictures, but he'd probably talked to Jace. He wanted the reward. He wasn't heading to Marlette Lake; he was headed back to Reno and wanted a lead. He must know they'd pursue because the tube was important. He'd counted on them not noticing until tomorrow. Her jaw clenched.

"Walker," she called, running back to the beach.

He was partway down the shore, headed for the marsh.

Elsa ran toward him and shouted. "Hayden took the tube." Her voice was high and upset and carried along the water. She wouldn't cry.

Walker ran back and took her shaking hands in his solid ones. Her fingers were ice cold. The maps and bunkers represented the future. It wasn't just a tube he'd stolen.

"What? Why would he do that?" He answered his own question as soon as he'd uttered the words. "For the fucking reward, of course." His face turned deep red as he bit off each word.

"We can't let him give it to Jace. He'll turn us in. Tell them where we are if he hasn't already. GreenCorps will take everything." Her voice was too loud.

"He must have taken it as soon as we were out of sight. He had it all planned. I'm going after him. I'll make him give it back." Walker's lip curled as he spoke.

"Should I come?"

He shook his head. "I need to talk to him alone. If you're there, he'll be too defensive. I'll be back tonight, with or without him. We'll pack, leave tomorrow, and go somewhere he won't expect. We'll find a way to contact the rebels."

Walker's fists were clenched, and he took a few deep breaths.

"I'm sorry. My brother is a jerk who can't think beyond his next high. He either wants the reward or to sell it to the highest bidder. I'll get the tube. Either way, you were right. We have to move on." He slung his canteen across his chest and said, "I'll see you tonight."

He kissed Elsa and strode to the cliff trail, scrambling upward, moving fast. Elsa watched until he disappeared from sight. The tight ball in her stomach didn't dissipate. Something was still wrong, so she packed while she waited.

To keep her mind busy, she carried the canoe to the shed and used the ropes and pulleys to return it to the rafters, where it would be stored out of the weather. She locked up the tools they'd used in the hidden wall cupboard in the back. She felt like she was saying goodbye to the cabin.

She packed their belongings and cuddled the now-friendly kittens one more time; the small furry beasts had helped the cabin feel like home. She hoped they would be here if she and Walker ever returned.

The packs were lighter than before as they'd eaten some of the food. She folded the blankets on the bed and put away the dishes. She filled her canteen and took a last look around. Putting her pack over her front, she hefted Walker's larger pack onto her back. It was heavy, but she wasn't trying to catch up fast. Her instincts screamed that they'd need to continue, not come back. Someday, but not this summer.

Elsa wedged the door to the bedroom open for the cats, and left, pulling the outside door closed. She wouldn't sit and wait to find out what happened. That wasn't her style. She wasn't weak or helpless. She was going after Walker.

The tight feeling moved to her chest as she scrambled up the steep cliff, hoping she would remember the way; she would watch for the trail markers. She climbed for two hours, her calves burning and her lungs heaving from exertion and altitude. While fit, she didn't think she would catch up to Walker unless he and his brother stopped to argue. She was a few hours behind, but had faith that Walker would find his brother. She might meet him on his return.

Progress was steady, and she was almost to the ridge near the mountain pass when she heard a shout in the distance. Her blood ran cold as the sound echoed from the surrounding peaks. She couldn't locate its source.

They had seen no one else in the mountains; the voice was Walker or Hayden. She didn't know which. She hurried forward, watching for signs of movement.

She scrambled to the top of a steep slope beside a scree of loose stone blocks. She glanced down, back the way she'd just come. Blood smeared one of the jagged rocks below her feet to the left. Dread filled her. Her eye followed the smear to another, and below.

Walker lay motionless in the rocks and bushes at the base of the cliff. He'd fallen and lay below, hidden from the path.

Or been pushed.

Her heart stopped. She didn't know if he was unconscious or dead. She unclipped the packs, leaving them at the top, and started down. She didn't need to worry, as Hayden would be long gone.

Elsa felt like throwing up, but controlled her fear and clambered down the scree with a lump of fear in her throat. Forcing her way through the thick bushes, she didn't care that thorns scratched her hands and arms.

"Walker, can you hear me?"

He didn't answer as she dropped to his side.

Blood trickled down his forehead and covered the side of his face. None of his limbs looked broken. She touched his cheek, her hands trembling. He was still warm and breathing. A moan escaped his lips, but his eyes were closed.

"Elsa." His voice was weak. "Smart girl, not to wait."

"I'm here." She checked his pulse. His heart was racing and his skin was clammy. "What happened?"

He opened his eyes but didn't move.

"Hayden denied stealing the tube at first. Didn't believe him. Told him I knew why. Offered to help him get clean. We fought for an hour. He said awful things, and in the end, he admitted what he'd done. That's when he screamed, shoved me, and ran. Not sure he realized the cliff was so close. I hit my head when I landed, but shielded it as I rolled down."

"Can you move?"

"Bruised my back, and I feel sick when I move. Gathering my strength to try again."

Walker pushed up to a seated position while she examined the cut on his forehead.

Elsa cleaned it with water from her canteen and a rag from his pocket. "Hold this on it. It needs pressure. Can you make it back up the slope? I'll help. We can camp near the spring."

Walker stood, using her to support his weight. At the second step, he said, "I'm going to throw up."

She maintained the cloth's pressure against his forehead while he threw up. When he was finished, she handed him his canteen.

"Thanks." He gave her a weak but grateful smile.

Beads of sweat rolled down his pasty face. A purple lump had developed on his forehead where he'd bashed it on the rocks. He was lucky to be alive, and she wanted to assess his injuries, but he was on his feet, so this was the best chance to get up the cliff. Rage against Hayden lent her strength. Going back to the cabin was risky. It was too far and might not be safe. They would camp off the trail where they would be hard to find.

Elsa supported Walker until they reached the top, where she'd dropped the backpacks. Her arms and legs shook with the exertion and she lowered him to sit with his back against a massive pine. The scent of warm sap filled the air.

She pressed the damp cloth to his wound. The bleeding had almost stopped, but the bash on his forehead had swollen further. One eye socket looked scraped and tender. She crouched beside him.

"What hurts the most?"

"My head. If I don't look up, I'm less dizzy."

"Is your vision okay?"

"Double," he said with a grimace. "I can't get back to the cabin tonight."

"We don't have to. I stowed the boat and brought everything. We can camp here while you rest. Then we're going to follow Hayden and take my tube back. Where do you think he's going?"

"We can't stay. When we were arguing, Hayden let it slip that he has a buyer in Salt Lake."

* * *

Walker

June 22nd, 2195, the mountains above Lake Tahoe

Sunrise: 5:34 a.m. Sunset: 8:28 p.m. First day of summer.

Can't believe Hayden pushed me over the edge onto the rocks. Our conversation was heated, but I wasn't expecting him to be out of control. Never seen him so angry. Should have known his good mood this morning was false. He was seething about Elsa, which I missed. He feels betrayed as well as replaced. Never meant to make him feel that way.

He doesn't understand that his choices have been difficult for me for years. Watching him self-destruct is too hard. Can't keep doing it. I have to live my own life.

He was furious I'd caught up so fast. Surprised him. He thought he'd be on the train and safe from confrontation before I got to Reno. Don't know if anyone from GreenCorps is coming for us. Camped off the main trail where we won't be seen.

Lucky Elsa came when she did. Surprised we got up that slope. I weigh so much more than she does, but she wouldn't let me fail. I admire her inner strength. Worried a day or two of recovery won't be enough. Hayden is getting further by the hour. He'll sell the tube before we can catch up. He has a buyer arranged. My guess is Jace McCoy. He's gotten himself mixed up in more trouble than he can handle. We'll have to scour the city to get it back. I'm not sure we have a chance, but we have to try.

CHAPTER 26: ELSA PLUS CAITLYN

Elsa and Walker reached the outskirts of Reno after hiking for three and a half days. They'd kept the pace slow so Walker didn't jar his head or over-exert himself. He'd refused to sit on the mountain and wait until he felt better, so was plagued by headaches and double vision. He'd said little beyond the original assessment, but she could tell the blow to his head affected him. He was also covered in bruises from the rocky slope. He was lucky nothing had broken or been crushed.

She applied the balm he'd bought for her in Sacramento. It soothed the bruised and scraped skin, though he claimed it was her gentle hands that helped most. She enjoyed looking after him, returning the favor from their first few days together.

It was afternoon when Elsa snuck into Reno. Walker had given her strict instructions of whom to avoid at the station and how not to be seen. The train to Salt Lake City left every other day. There was no trace of Hayden near the train station and she checked the hiding places Walker suggested. Nothing. It was hard not to be disappointed, though it was what she'd expected. Hayden must have already left.

Twice while searching near the train yard, Elsa sensed she was being watched. The sensation made her shoulder blades twitch. At first, she shrugged it off as paranoia, but it felt too real. As a wanted fugitive, it was also realistic and dangerous. The second time, she spotted a furtive movement when she scanned the shadows. It might be someone looking for the reward, someone who'd recognized her or suspected who she might be.

Instead of leading them back to Walker, she rested in a quiet place out of sight, hidden enough that her follower should think she felt safe, but not so hidden she would be trapped if confronted.

Before long, a boy with shoulder-length black hair crept close. He was perhaps twelve years old and silent on his bare feet, placing them with care. His face was dirty, etched with mud and grime. He'd either dirtied it on purpose or didn't wash very often. His tangled hair was snarled enough that she suspected it hadn't been combed in weeks.

She almost relaxed her vigilance, but her shoulders tightened. Was this her watcher? He appeared small and harmless. At his age, she'd been strong and capable and too often dismissed or underestimated. For that reason, she maintained her pose and her guard.

The boy kept his eyes riveted on her face as he slunk closer, perhaps uncertain if she was sleeping as she watched with slit eyes. He reached into her backpack without seeming to move the zipper. It was silent. He must be an excellent pick-pocket. She let him grope around inside while her heart rate quickened and she waited.

When he dropped his eyes, she pounced, grabbing his wrist. She held on while he struggled without sound. Tears streamed down his dirty cheeks. She didn't believe they were real. Crying on demand would be useful for a young thief.

"Please Miss, do you have something to eat?" His voice emerged as no more than a whisper.

"I doubt that's what you're looking for," she said, maintaining her firm grip on his wrist. "You look too well-fed to be starving, for all you need a haircut and a bath." She could guess what he was looking for. She'd kept away from the Wanted posters, but they named her a thief. Her gut said he might be looking for what she'd 'stolen'?

His tears stopped, and he narrowed his eyes. Upon closer inspection, she decided he looked older—perhaps fourteen—despite his small stature. His size made him appear young, but his eyes showed his true age.

"If you're looking for the tube, it was stolen. Four days ago."

He didn't bother to deny it. He sat back on his heels in the dirt with a sigh.

Elsa released her hold.

"How?" His wary brown eyes searched her face, perhaps trying to determine if she told the truth.

"My boyfriend's brother took it. He would have come through here two days ago. Maybe early yesterday." She tilted her head to the side. "There haven't been many hoppers. Perhaps you saw him."

She watched while he seemed to process this information.

"Did he have a green coat?" The boy chewed his thumbnail.

She winced at his grubby hands and the dirt under his chipped nails.

"He did. Did you see which train he caught?"

His eyes narrowed. "He was here the day before yesterday. Denver or Salt Lake," said the boy without hesitation. "I don't know if it was an express or one that stops."

His eyes were downcast.

"I ran into him in Salt Lake a couple of weeks ago when he stole my supplies. I recognized him, and let him leave without checking his stuff." He grimaced.

Elsa guessed he wished he'd checked. "You were watching for me?"

He shrugged. "Ten gold coins."

"Walker and I are following him. We want the tube back. Perhaps you'd like to help."

"What's the point? He'll have turned it into GreenCorps for the reward. Today, or maybe yesterday."

"We're going to get it back. Maybe you'd like to join us in keeping it from GreenCorps. For your information, the posters lie, I didn't steal it. I found it in SoCal in the Heap. It's mine."

"What's inside the tube?"

His intent eyes bored into hers. He'd figured out the contents were what was important, not the tube itself. How had he connected that information?

"Something to do with food and making a better life. I'm tired of starving, aren't you?"

"Food?" He licked his lips.

She nodded, wondering when he'd had his last meal. At his age, she'd been hungry all the time. She would be sure to offer to feed him.

"If you turn me in for the reward without the tube, they won't pay. They don't want me. They want the maps and key from inside." It was plausible, but she wasn't sure if that was the whole truth.

Elsa watched him, weighing her words. She shouldn't trust this ragged boy. He was a thief and had been about to steal from her. He wanted the reward money, but her gut told her the boy could be trusted. If he believed the reward was for the tube and not for her, it might work. With his stealthy feet and light fingers, he would be useful if they hoped to recover the tube.

"What's your name?"

"Tatsuda." It came out as a mutter.

"Come with me Tatsuda. I'm Elsa. I'll introduce you to Walker and get you something to eat. I might need your help to get him on the train. He was injured a few days ago."

* * *

The next train from Reno to Salt Lake left that night after dark. They followed Tatsuda's lead to the train yard; he used a circuitous route without fences to climb. Elsa's heart raced as they used the cover of darkness to slip into position. The three of them waited closer to the trains than Walker was comfortable, but she deferred to their young companion's suggestion. He said he had a plan.

While crouched in the bushes, Walker shifted position several times and rubbed his temples and jaw, yet there was nothing she could do to assist. She would check him over again after the train. Riding hunched over in the cold all night wouldn't help his condition.

Walker hadn't argued much about Tatsuda joining them, another sign that he wasn't feeling well. When she'd introduced the youth, she'd explained how they'd met and that he'd seen Hayden, twice. Walker had nodded, trusting her judgment.

It was approaching midnight when Tatsuda disappeared. He was gone long enough that her heart rate increased and her palms grew sweaty. Maybe asking for his help had been a mistake. He could've changed his mind and decided to turn her in, even if she didn't have the tube. Perhaps he didn't believe that she was worthless to GreenCorps.

Elsa strained at the darkness, her ears trying to catch sounds of stealth or force. Any kind of footstep or motion. Security didn't seem alarmed and the work team loading the train continued, calling out to each other and joking in what she'd learned was a normal fashion for the railroad workers. In the distance, a coyote yipped, perhaps playing with a rodent it had caught or calling to a pack member. There were no noises that seemed out of place.

The train inched forward. Its silhouette changed, and up the line the slack action crashes began, becoming louder and more frequent. It was time to go. Her heart drummed against her ribs as they stood, stretching their stiff muscles. They slunk onto the darkened tracks, crossing three sets of empty tracks. She and Walker crept forward faster, the darkness masking their movement as they prepared to climb onboard.

When a hand tapped her shoulder, Elsa smothered a scream. Her heart skipped and her frame trembled with the energy to remain silent and keep her legs moving.

Tatsuda's eyes gleamed in the moonlight right behind her. He rested his finger against his lips and grabbed her hand. She took Walker's and Tatsuda led them at a partial run farther up the train as it departed. The moving train blocked them from the view of the men who worked at the station. She expected an outcry, but there was nothing out of the ordinary.

She and Walker had aimed farther back, but seeing the change in direction, Walker whispered, "Good idea, kid."

Elsa didn't understand what was intended, but she appreciated Walker did. They ran alongside the train, just behind the engine in the middle. Tatsuda scrambled up the ladder first and opened a door at the rear of the car. Walker went next and Elsa came last. She caught the cold steel of the ladder better than she had the two previous train rides, but was glad for Walker's steadying hand as she stepped onto the moving train. The night was overcast and black as old rubber.

Inside the train car, a dim light came on with their motion at the door. A long narrow car stretched ahead of them with an unoccupied seat and controls at the front. She released the breath she'd been holding as Walker closed the door. The train noise was still apparent as the speed increased, but muted enough for regular speech. They didn't need to yell or use earplugs to muffle the sound.

"What is this place?" She looked around.

"Electric engines have an entire cabin," said Walker, slinging off his pack. "Trains have two or three drivers in the primary engine at the front who take turns on long hauls. Ones like this in the middle are here for extra power but are almost always unmanned. Hayden and I risked it a couple of times in winter when it was frigid, but the doors are often locked."

"How did you know we could get in?" said Elsa, turning to their newest companion.

"I unlocked it," said Tatsuda with a shrug. "I wasn't sure I'd get back to you in time."

"It was smart," said Walker.

The boy looked down and shuffled his feet. He didn't look comfortable with the attention or compliments. "Since Walker is hurt, I thought a proper bed would be best." His voice was soft.

Elsa didn't see beds, but spread out on the floor would be superior to crouched outside behind the hoppers.

"Thanks. I'm impressed with your quick thinking." Walker squeezed the boy's shoulder along with his words of praise.

Tatsuda's eyes widened, and he stood straighter.

In the dim cabin light, Walker was pale and sweating again. Her concern spiked. Head injuries were tricky. She remembered the medic talking about them after Granny's accident. Walker strode to the wall and unclipped a section with straps, then another. He folded down two padded shelves. Beds. She would've had no idea they were there. She wished a car like this had been an option on the day with her fever and the hail. She remembered little of that day; it was such a blur, but it had been a nightmare riding outside.

Walker opened cupboards until he found one with blankets and pillows. He tossed one of each to the boy and two more onto the lower bed. Tatsuda scrambled up to the top bunk, rolled himself in the gray woolen blanket, and lay down. He looked to be asleep in a matter of seconds. His face relaxed when he slept. The rest of the time, it was guarded. How long had the kid been on his own?

"Is it safe being here?" Elsa was reluctant to relax despite its comfort. They hadn't traveled this way before.

Walker sat on the lower bed and unlaced his boots and took them off. Her eyebrows rose, surprised that he felt safe to do so. He set them on the floor, open and ready to be slipped on at short notice.

"While the train's moving? We're safe enough."

"Is the pain in your head worse than before?"

He pushed as far back on the fold-out bed toward the wall as possible without answering. The bunks were made long enough for men of his stature, and he stretched out to his full length with a sigh. He lay on his side and patted the space beside him.

"I'm fine. Just need to sleep."

Elsa smiled, though she didn't quite believe him. She placed her boots like his and lay next to him. It was a tight fit, but comfortable. Sleep was more likely to come when they were together. Nestled beside him, she faced into the room.

"It's a ten-hour ride. Get some sleep. I'll be okay." He stroked her hair.

She snuggled against him, glad for his warmth and for the security that his presence brought.

"You didn't sleep much last night. You were restless. Today you looked tired." He paused when she said nothing. "I'm sore, but my headache was less today. Only had double vision a few times. I'll be fine."

"You've been quiet. What were you thinking while we waited?"

"If we can't find Hayden or get the tube, maybe we could go back to the cabin. You want the tube back and I'm in favor of that, but I don't wish to endanger us. I don't want them to take you away. We don't know that he gave up the cabin's location. We didn't see anyone on the trail out." Walker's arm tightened.

Tears pricked her eyes. She wasn't keen on doing anything risky, but the tube could improve so many lives. She wasn't giving up. She relaxed into him as the train thundered through the night, the motion lulling her to sleep.

* * *

June 26th, 2195

Dearest Mathew,

My garden is flourishing with tall potato plants and ripening tomatoes. They will go nicely with the fresh lettuce, peas, and beans. I'm proud it's doing so well since it's the first year I've done it on my own. I'm grateful we worked together for a couple of years so I could learn. I'll freeze or can much of the bounty, so I will have it to eat through the winter. Last winter, my diet seemed bland and monotonous without the variety of homegrown food. We were spoiled when we lived here before. Everything tastes better when you grow it yourself. My food last year was all freeze-dried and prepackaged. At least in Salt Lake, I could buy from non-corporation stores.

Tomorrow, I need an early start as I'm going into the city to buy supplies, including a young pig, if I can afford one. I'll raise it this summer and butcher it when the weather turns cold. I'll be gone overnight, but the animals will be fine for that short amount of time. I wish you were here so you could go to town instead. I'd prefer to stay at home than mix with people again. You never know who you'll see.

Love,

Your Caitlyn

CHAPTER 27: ELSA PLUS WALKER

Elsa woke before the others and enjoyed some quiet time, sitting by the window for several hours as the train rolled through the flat, barren country. The earth was packed hard, cracked and bone dry. Heatwaves rose in the distance, though it was only mid-morning. It didn't look like it had rained in years—the colors appearing bleached and dust-covered. It was far too much like SoCal for her liking. The comparison brought her family to the forefront, along with her worry for how they were faring.

By the time Walker woke, the landscape had changed, with distant mountains and odd bits of dark green shrubbery.

Tatsuda, who was awake now, said, "We're getting close to Salt Lake City."

He slid off his bunk while Walker folded the blankets and put away everything they'd used. She helped stow the beds, and they collected their belongings. No sense flaunting that they'd been here.

Mountains rose in the east and a belt of green lined the bottom with leafy trees and vegetation. A couple of canyon mouths emerged from the rocky cliffs that looked like they had streams at their base. Thick bushes lined their sides in stark contrast to the surrounding stone.

Many of the rocks had a reddish hue. The lumpy remains of buildings and houses littered the plain. Lots of people had once lived here. Smoke rose from chimneys near where the town was visible. Brick buildings in a grid pattern with straight streets filled the view as the train slowed.

An enormous lake stretched as far as she could see. Wide bands of yellow, white, and light brown ringed the near lakeshore. The water level looked lower than in other years. The strip of green was sandwiched between the mountains and the lake. Even if it wasn't often, it must rain here, unlike home.

"The lake is salty like the ocean," said Walker, as if reading her thoughts. "I suppose that's obvious." He paused. "Saltier even. Almost nothing lives in it except miniature brine shrimp, and they're inedible."

"So much water when everything else is so dry and barren is shocking."

"People live both north and south along the mountains and into the canyons. Many aren't interested in GreenCorps. This is an area where the corporation has the least control. People here didn't need as much to restart after the Collapse and have maintained more independence. They were used to doing for themselves. Their church tells them to stockpile goods in preparation for an emergency." He paused. "Or that's what Jim said. His family was from this region. There are still folk that follow the old religion and the rebels have a stronghold, though I don't know how to get in touch. I've never been in contact with Jim's connections. He didn't talk much about those days."

"Neither did Granny." Elsa swallowed to keep her tears at bay.

They checked their boots and straps to prepare for disembarking.

"The problem with riding in this car is that we're going to be in the heart of the station, in the thick of the action as they load and unload trains," said Walker. "The bulls might not see us if we're lucky. We'll have to see where the workers are occupied, then run."

She liked when he shared his experience to explain what she should expect. He looked better this morning, but still had the tightness between his eyes.

"Have you been here much, kid?" said Walker to Tatsuda. He jerked his head toward the window, indicating the town.

"Twice." The boy bit his nails and glanced out the window.

"When we get off, we might get separated," said Walker. "There's a massive building in the middle of town. A church. They call it the temple. Meet near the western gate."

"I've seen it. Why do you want me to meet you?" Tatsuda blurted. "In Reno, I was going to steal from you or turn Elsa in for the reward."

Taking a leap of faith at what she had seen behind his tough façade, Elsa stepped forward. "You can help us, and maybe we can help you, too. It's a rough world out there on your own."

"I get by." His eyes hardened.

Another leap. "I'm sure you do, but don't we all want to do better than that?"

Tatsuda looked thoughtful but didn't reply.

As the train slowed, Walker stood straight, while Tatsuda and Elsa crouched below the level of the windows.

"What's our best strategy? You okay to run?" Elsa glanced up at Walker. He stood next to the window, watching the train's entry into the station as the speed decreased. She grabbed a bar on the wall to brace herself as the train jolted several times in rapid succession.

"Slept nine hours. Just a low-level headache left. I'll be fine."

She hoped that was true. He wouldn't like her fussing, especially in front of the boy. She dropped the subject and took him at his word.

"When we exit, run left. The fence is closer. We're on a middle track and will need to get over a train. Remember not to use the joint of the knuckle, but on and off after a quick look. Don't stay between for long. No idea how long that train will be parked. It could be ready to leave or need to be unloaded. This is always a busy station. If you see anyone, run like hell. Get anywhere hard to follow. Bushes, a fence, or put a train between you, even if you have to cross and recross. Keep moving."

Elsa nodded. His words were directed at her, but she watched Tatsuda take note as he nodded several times.

"Okay, now." Walker eased the door open.

He looked right while they filed past. She peered up and down the track to the left. It was clear, so she climbed down the ladder and jogged between the trains. The parked trains extended as far back as she could see, making a long tunnel between the train cars with about ten feet between. She ran toward the rear of the train, her visibility limited to the expanse between the two trains. Waves of heat emanated from both sides.

Walker and Tatsuda followed, their careful footsteps crunching the gravel. When she hoped she'd gone far enough, she stopped and climbed the low place between two cars.

She scrambled across and peeked to check if it was clear, and her heart almost stopped. The previous boxcar and several others she'd just passed were being loaded. A group of at least five men worked together, and they'd brought several large crates on a low cart with wheels. The cart was almost empty, with several crates stacked on the front edge of the boxcar while the men moved them deeper inside.

Up the track, a second group looked to be loading as well. She filled her lungs with air and tried to calm herself, willing the uniformed men not to notice. Her heart raced while she tried to think. She took a breath and remembered Walker's instructions.

She eased back the way she'd come. She wasn't supposed to linger. Walker or Tatsuda were nowhere to be seen. They may both be between cars as well. She debated for a moment if she should wait. She'd just continued further down the trains when Walker popped out from between the next two cars. She pointed toward the back of the train and raised an eyebrow.

He nodded, and they walked, instead of running, trying to be quiet enough to avoid detection. Her heart drummed double-time against her ribs and her palms dripped with sweat.

Elsa expected Tatsuda to materialize. Instead, shouts and curses came from the far side of the train. The workers had seen him. Her throat tightened. She didn't want him caught and prayed he was a fast runner.

"Hey, kid. Stop."

"Get him."

"Watch close, there might be others."

"You looking to catch a ride, boy?"

Elsa couldn't hear Tatsuda's answers, and she didn't stick around to listen. It was only a matter of when someone decided to check where he'd come from.

With a surge of adrenaline, she ran, Walker sprinting at her heels. They tried to put distance between themselves and the railway workers. She couldn't hear anything over the roaring in her ears.

"Gotcha. Nothing like a trip to the work camps to make you rethink your life choices," said a growly voice on the far side of the train.

"You alone, kid?"

"Always," said Tatsuda. "I don't trust anyone."

His petulant words stuck daggers in her chest as her heart sank at his capture. He hadn't given them up.

It had been close. Tatsuda must have run in the same direction on the opposite side before they'd caught him.

"It's Texas for you, kid. You hopped the wrong train."

"Make sure you get them all. We have orders to deport anyone we catch."

Walker pointed to the next low place. He and Elsa clambered aboard so they couldn't be seen from either side if someone checked between the trains. She held her breath and froze like a statue. They were still too close to the work crew to dare to run. Her heart pounded and her eyes felt wide. Walker squeezed her hand, then released it as he slid to the edge and peeked out.

He lifted his hand with five fingers extended. She nodded. That's how many men she'd seen in the closest group. The crunching footsteps returned toward where the men had been working and became more distant. She waited until her chest ached with the effort. The sound of cart wheels moved away before she breathed.

Up the line, the train upon which they perched crashed several times. Elsa grabbed the metal guard rail for support as she stumbled and almost lost her footing. The train inched forward. They had to get off before it picked up speed. Whether the rail yard men were far enough away or not, it was time to go. Walker jumped, and she followed. They ducked behind the nearby bushes, finding the usual hidden passages within. When they slowed down and caught their breath, they shared a glance.

"We have to help Tatsuda," she said, her voice one of determination. "We can't let them send him south."

* * *

Walker
June 27th, 2195, Salt Lake City
Sunrise; 5:57 a.m. Sunset 9:02 p.m.

Travel Notes:
Security light today, late morning arrival. Slept in second engine cabin.

Workers present and busy. Loading and unloading a northbound train.

Eight tracks, four occupied. Arrived on track five in the center engine after a ten-hour overnight trip from Reno.

Elsa and I weren't seen getting off the train, but our companion got pinched by the workers. They'll have taken him to security. Regular train security, not GreenCorps recruits. Not sure if he'll talk. Feel like he won't. We have a decision to make. The kid helped us. We should help the kid.

Lied to Elsa. Said I was fine, but my head still isn't right. Damn thing hurts like hell. Running was bad. She has enough to worry about, and I'll be fine. Need a little more recovery time. Can't afford to slow down right now. It's our only chance to recover the tube. Can't let her down.

Grateful the kid thought of the engine cabin even if getting off in daylight was complicated. Needed the rest.

Hope we find Hayden quick. An extra person searching will be useful. Have a feeling the new kid doesn't miss much.

CHAPTER 28: ELSA PLUS WALKER

"How will we get Tatsuda back?" said Elsa, staring at the train station.

"I'm going to walk into railroad security and ask for my runaway farmhand," said Walker.

"What can I do?"

"You need to stay away from the station and the shops. You aren't safe here either. A lot of them are still run by GreenCorps. If it hadn't been necessary because of my injury, I wouldn't have let you risk yourself in Reno."

"Let?" Her eyebrow raised. "I haven't let people tell me what I can and cannot do since I was a kid."

"Fine. I'm asking you not to do anything stupid to get yourself locked up. Where would we be if you end up in GreenCorps custody?" He shot her an apologetic look. "Sorry. I'm just frustrated."

"You'll get Tatsuda, then we search for Hayden?"

"I'll do my best," said Walker with a wink.

Elsa still frowned. He smoothed her brows with his thumb and kissed her. Her irritation faded. It was nice to have someone who looked out for her, even if she didn't always need it.

"I'll be safe. I promise. They don't want me and my description is too general. I've been inside before, so I know what to expect."

She nodded; he made sense. She could agree without liking it. "I hate waiting, not being involved." She let out a deep breath.

He laughed. "Know how you feel. C'mon. There's a quiet place we can stay."

Taking her hand, they veered away from the trains toward a neighborhood on their left. After a couple of blocks, Walker ducked into a back lane, then into the overgrown yard of a dilapidated house. It was more run-down than the remaining houses and the yard was filled with dirt patches and thick bushes. The windows were boarded up from inside and it didn't appear as if anyone lived here. The wood siding was dry and cracked like tinder, but Walker lifted the covering of a boarded-up basement window on the side, revealing a basement entrance.

"Careful where you step."

He lit his candle lantern and held it aloft as he ducked inside. He held out a hand which Elsa grabbed, then she stepped across the window frame. They stood on a long, narrow piece of furniture, either a table or a bench, though she couldn't see which in the dim light. It was stable, perhaps fastened in place. She jumped down, and he passed her the lantern as he replaced the window cover.

It was cool inside and musty enough she wrinkled her nose. After the bright sun outside, the cellar seemed dark with only the glow from their lantern. Shadows lurked in the corners and she couldn't see beyond their immediate vicinity.

"Stairs are this way," he said, taking the lantern back to lead.

"Is there anywhere you haven't been or don't have a hideaway?"

"No. Except Texas. Never wanted to go there." He paused. "We always found places to stay. We weren't always on the move, but we didn't want to attract attention. Fixed up what we needed to."

She didn't know what made the crunching sound beneath her boots. Perhaps sand, crumbled brick, or bug carcasses. Tiny rustlings in the corner made her think of rats with their tiny claws. She wouldn't be surprised to see the rodents here. Twice she stumbled over mystery objects on the floor. Maybe chunks of wood or broken bricks. Spiderwebs caught on her arms and a couple drifted onto her face, though she appreciated Walker going first and enduring the brunt of the cobwebs. She wiped her skin several times, hoping it wasn't covered in spiders.

The cinder block stairs looked newer than the house, as though they'd been repaired.

"Did you make these?" said Elsa as they climbed the narrow stairs.

"Found it like this. Thought it was someone's safehouse at some point. Maybe rebels.

Doubt it was like this when the house was occupied. You can see from the dust and spider webs that this place isn't used often. If at all. Was two years ago when Hayden and I stayed."

He opened a creaky door at the top of the stairs. The upstairs windows were boarded up, but light streamed through cracks between, making it easier to see. The floor was rotten and unstable in places, but functional. Walker led her to a room with a few dusty chairs and stacked wooden crates as a table. Another smaller crate sat by the window, perhaps for a lookout.

Walker strolled to the window. "The station is that way," he said, pointing. "You'll be able to watch me leave and come back, but I'm going into town for food and water first. Then I'll go to the station and try to get Tatsuda."

She stood at his side, looking down the street.

"Will you stay here?" He cupped her jaw and stroked her cheek. Despite the weeks of intimacy at the cabin, her body still reacted to his touch.

His eyes pleaded with her to stay safe.

Elsa nodded.

His smile lit the room, and he kissed her, a kiss with a promise for more later.

Walker was gone about an hour on his first foray with the canteens. She met him in the basement to take them. He passed his heavy pack inside.

"There's a water pump in a park a few blocks north, but this should be enough for tonight. I'm leaving everything here. Nothing says 'traveler' like walking around with a pack and a canteen."

"Thanks." She preferred knowing where to get water, just in case. If security nabbed him too, it would be a long night.

"Got vegetables, a loaf of bread, and a jar of peanut butter." At her blank expression, he said, "You've never had peanut butter?"

She shook her head.

"You'll love it. We'll have sandwiches. With luck, all three of us."

She nodded, frustrated that she was of so little use when she had to stay hidden. Maybe they should work on a better disguise.

Walker left again, the board thumping when replaced as he exited. She resumed her position at the window and watched him saunter toward the station. The first time Walker had gone out, she'd counted the tumbleweeds that rolled past, seen three cats and a dog, and watched a couple of kids on rusty bikes race back and forth in a never-ending loop. Now the kids and animals were gone and there was nothing to see or do. The boring afternoon crawled.

Elsa wished she had a book to help her pass the time. He'd been gone for less than half an hour when her stomach clenched. Her instincts told her she needed to go somewhere else. Something important was going to happen. She'd promised Walker she'd stay, but ignoring her premonition wouldn't help them find Hayden or the tube.

Taking a deep breath, she slid her canteen over her shoulder but left everything else behind. She went down the cinderblock stairs and out. She placed the lantern in front of the basement window where she exited, where Walker would see it upon his return. She was careful to extinguish the light first. A fire would be like a beacon to the residents.

Looking toward the station, she hoped Walker and Tatsuda would arrive so she wouldn't have to break her promise. When they didn't come, she sucked in a deep breath and closed her eyes. She needed to go to the train station, too. What if they were in trouble?

She neared a side entrance and was wondering if she should sneak inside when voices came to her from the lane behind the building. One sounded familiar. She sidled up to the corner and peered around the corner. Kegs lined the wall in a stack, and she slid behind them, crouching near the ground. She peeked again and her blood ran cold. Jaxon and Jace McCoy stood several yards away. Jaxon faced her direction, and it was his voice that she had overheard. She ducked out of sight, her heart racing.

"That was a stroke of genius, brother," Jace said. "Using the addict that traveled with the bouncer. He was most cooperative."

She clenched her fists. Hayden had talked with Jace. She'd suspected, but it was maddening to hear it confirmed. It was also dangerous to stay and listen, but this was her chance to reclaim the tube. Luck had brought her here and she would be careful.

"We're meeting tonight. He said he'd be on a train, either two days ago or today at the latest. He had orders to lie low and keep his mouth shut until I got here. The boy was confident he could find his brother and the girl. It involved hiking, so I sent him alone. I'd told him to bring the whore who bit me too, but that might not be possible. I'd like to make her pay. I had to take antibiotics. Stupid bitch."

"How much you paying the kid?" said Jaxon.

"You bring the package from Ginny, like I asked?"

It sounded like Jaxon rummaged in his bag and passed something to his brother.

"This much," Jace said.

"That's nowhere near the value of ten gold. That's worth less than a silver," said Jaxon with a nasty laugh. "You think the kid's stupid enough to have waited for you? Or do you think he might have found a different buyer?"

"If he crosses me, he'll regret it," said Jace, his tone flat.

His voice sent shivers up her spine.

"I let him think he could do other jobs for me, earn a steady supply."

Elsa unclenched her fists. She had indentations from her nails on her sweaty palms and hers stomach roiled. Hayden had stolen the tube for drugs. Not even for coin. The McCoys were taking advantage of his addiction. She almost felt sorry for him. But he'd done this to himself. Nobody forced him to use. She'd been right to trust her intuition; hearing this meeting had been fortuitous. Its position was close enough to the station that this was where the brothers must be meeting after arriving on separate trains.

She would follow Jace when he went to meet Hayden. She wouldn't confront him; she didn't dare face another beating, but if she learned where he was staying, then with Tatsuda's help, they might retrieve the tube. She might be able to contact the rebels about help with the bunker. Things were coming together.

She angled her hat to shadow her face and hid until the brothers strolled toward town. She kept them in sight, her heartbeat still erratic. She hoped Walker wouldn't be angry and wished she'd been able to leave him a note. With luck, she wouldn't be gone long.

* * *

Walker marched up to the front desk in the station. It was best to approach with confidence. He'd scouted the building and confirmed where Tatsuda was being held. Just the regular overnight lock-up, nothing too secure.

"Excuse me, sir. My father sent me to check for our runaway farmhand. The new kid we just hired. Signed on for the season. Split before he'd fulfilled his commitment. Been gone a few days, living rough. We wondered if he might have tried to hop a train."

Two men behind the counter looked at one another. "Can you describe him?" said the taller one.

"Long, tangled dark hair, about twelve years old. Sulky air. He's lazy and didn't want to do a full day's work."

"Yeah, we found him. Come with me," said the older man, who produced a set of keys on a ring from his pocket with a jingle and beckoned to Walker. "We didn't know if he'd come off a train or was getting on. He wouldn't say. If you hadn't arrived, we were shipping him to Texas tomorrow morning."

They ducked down the hallway, their footsteps echoing in the clean, quiet building. The security man unlocked the door on the left, but stopped. "They found him on the tracks, jumping between train cars. Probably looking for a place to hide, hoping security would miss him. What's his name?"

"Told us it was Billy, but I doubt it's his real name."

"He hasn't said much, except asking questions about his brother."

"That's why we thought of the station. He mentioned his older brother was a hopper. Probably already skipped town, leaving the poor kid behind."

"Stupid kid. He's too young for that kind of life." The security man opened the door into a room containing three cells with steel bars.

"Where's your farm?"

"Near Provo. Hoping to get the kid and head home tonight."

Tatsuda sat slumped on a bench in the far cell.

"Billy. You can't get away that easy," said Walker. "Your brother sold your labor to us for the season. We're counting on you. You can't cut and run just because you don't like it. We gave you clothes and food. You owe us the work."

"I don't like working for your family," said Tatsuda with a sneer. "You don't feed me enough."

"If you worked harder, we'd feed you more."

The security man laughed. "Can't argue with that." He had Walker sign some papers, then opened the cell. "Time to go, kid. We got things to do."

` Walker grabbed Tatsuda's arm and shook him. "You'll regret it if you run off again. I had to waste two full days to get you back. Let's go."

He hauled the boy toward the exit, a firm grip on his upper arm, and half dragged him down the street. He continued the charade until the railroad building was out of sight.

When they made it around the corner, the boy said. "Thanks for coming. I miscalculated how fast the workers would be, but they talked about your brother. At least I think so. They saw another kid on the tracks a couple of days ago that sounded like him. With the fuss about Elsa, it's been lonely hopping. A lot of bulls and GreenCorps stiffs."

"You took an enormous risk, but you did good, kid."

"Where's Elsa?" the boy said, his head cocked to the side.

"Close, come on. We've got peanut butter sandwiches for dinner."

Walker led him to the safehouse, looking up and down the lane before entering the yard and removing the board from the window. When he caught sight of the candle lantern sitting in the middle of the workbench, he got a sinking feeling. Elsa wouldn't have left it there if she were inside. She'd said she'd stay, but something must have changed her mind.

He lit the lantern and sent the boy inside while he fixed the board. It was as he feared. All their stuff was there, but Elsa was gone.

CHAPTER 29: CAITLYN

Caitlyn wiped the sweat from her brow as she neared Salt Lake City. She'd gotten up early to beat the heat and had taken care of her animals, leaving them plenty of feed and water as she'd be gone overnight. After a day's walking, her feet were sore and her throat was parched. She could use a drink. Glancing at the sky, she estimated the time as late afternoon. She wanted to make her purchases today, find a place to sleep, and leave at first light. The sooner she left town, the better. It was crowded, dangerous, and full of painful reminders of who she used to be. Maybe she shouldn't have come.

Salt Lake was okay, as far as cities went, with limited GreenCorps influence. It had a population of about thirty thousand in town and about the same number spread around the outlying area, most on the benchland sandwiched along the base of the mountains. Between the church and the rebels, it was growing fast with all the young families who'd settled here.

She wandered the dusty streets until she came to the downtown business area. Like most towns, they'd rebuilt it on the rubble of the old city. Concrete block, red rock, and brick had been reused with new mortar. The city was old, but most of the buildings were only a couple of generations in age. The new town was laid out like a grid with the Latter-Day Saint temple at the center—one of the few original buildings that remained from before the Collapse. She aimed for the outdoor market in the town square.

It was mid-week and bustling in the afternoon's desert heat radiating from the streets and buildings. She was thankful so many vendors had set up tents or awnings over their wares to provide shade. It didn't take long to buy more seeds and the odds and ends she wanted. With a minimum of speech, she arranged to pick up a young pig tomorrow morning.

"Mind if I come back in an hour?" Her voice was scratchy as she spoke to the shopkeeper and passed him her grocery list. She was unused to speaking, and it was still rough despite her earlier transactions. "Left my empty pack in the corner." She needed that drink more than ever.

"No problem, ma'am." The clerk tucked a pencil behind his ear. "That gives us plenty of time to put this order together."

Caitlyn returned outside and strode across the square, her feet moving toward the old meeting place before her head had time to consider. It wasn't long before she found what she was looking for. A green door was set into an alley and had a small leaf etched into the edge near the frame. You had to know what you were looking for to find it. The rebels were tolerated by the church but despised by GreenCorps.

She looked back toward the market, then pounded on the door before she changed her mind. Two hard thumps with her clenched fist. She grimaced, unsure if she was already regretting her decision.

An older man with short iron-gray hair opened the door. Squinting at her, he broke into a wide grin. "Caitlyn, that you? You look like a farmer. Oh, that's right. That's what you are now. Get in here." He threw his arms wide.

She nodded, a lump in her throat; despite her hesitation, she was glad to see Darren. He'd been like a second father to Mathew. She blinked back tears at his hard hug.

"Come have a drink. Like an oven out there, even though it's only June. You walk all the way in from your place today?"

She smiled and followed him inside. Relieved she'd come after all, the tightness in her chest eased and her shoulders relaxed. There were no windows in this bar, which kept it cool, and it had the familiar stench of cheap ale and sweat. Just what she'd expect in this heat. Most of those who frequented this bar spent little time worrying about cleanliness. They had more important concerns than regular baths. She'd been an anomaly.

Licking her lips, she stepped up to the bar.

"Look who I found." Darren drummed both hands on the counter.

"Knew she couldn't stay away," said a lean man seated at a round table behind them.

Caitlyn turned to face him. His wire spectacles sat pushed up on his head near his ax-shaped birthmark, while he sipped a tankard of ale. Grady looked the same, too. Still dressed in jeans and a buttoned denim shirt. A more unassuming leader she couldn't imagine. Time here stood still.

"You got coin, Honey?" said the barkeeper.

He must be new. She fumbled at her pouch.

"This is Mathew's widow," said Grady. "It's on me."

"Sorry to hear about Mathew." The barkeeper filled a foaming mug and slid it to her across the scarred wood of the bar. "He was one of our best."

A lump swelled in her throat. Of course, that's how he'd know her. Mathew had been one of them his whole life. She'd been a relative newcomer despite the years she'd given to the cause. He'd died a hero and left her behind. She wasn't sure why she'd come to this particular bar, but her feet had led her here of their own volition. Perhaps there was a reason. Even just to be around others who'd known him for an evening made her heart lighter.

"Anything exciting in town this spring?" She faced Grady.

He shoved a chair out for her with his foot, an invitation.

"Come sit. Chat. This is a timely visit." He paused. "It is a visit, right?"

He had a shrewd, calculating look in his blue eyes, as usual. She sat and took a long drink, draining half her beer, while she considered. She hadn't meant it as a return, but she could use a little excitement.

"You enjoy farming?" He tapped the end of his pencil on the table.

Caitlyn watched him over the rim of her mug as she raised it again. The thick glass masked her wary expression.

"I like taking care of things," she said at last.

Grady nodded. "You always did. We've missed having another trained medic."

She jumped at the pounding on the outer door. Darren trotted down the hall and came back to talk to Grady.

"That kid is in the market again."

Grady looked at her. "There's a kid asking questions around town. Claiming he has something GreenCorps wants, and he's looking to sell. Supposed to have a leaf on it. Might be something old. We might need someone to get a look."

She lifted her empty mug. She could use another.

Darren laughed and gave it to the barkeeper, who filled it without comment.

"The kid says he's meeting someone from GreenCorps this evening. If it has our leaf, we want to know what it is. This might be something that could use a woman's touch."

Grady's gaze was steady. He wanted her to do a job. She'd just arrived.

Caitlyn didn't answer, but her thoughts whirled like a spinning top. This wasn't why she'd come here. Or was it? She missed the rush of adrenaline when on a mission, even something small. But she'd wanted out. No more jobs. Nothing risky. That's what she'd told herself. Then, the first thing she did when she had a moment was stroll into rebel headquarters. That didn't sound like someone content to be a farmer, for all she liked the animals.

"Just want me to get a look? Follow him?"

Grady raised an eyebrow and shrugged.

"Why a woman? Anyone here could do that." She looked at both men for answers. She needed more information.

"There's a reward for a certain dark-haired girl. A thief. Ten gold," said Darren.

She whistled at the sum and tugged on her long blonde braid.

"We think these two things are related. The boy with something and the girl thief. Maybe they're working together. You'd be a distraction while we follow the kid. Hide your blonde locks and play decoy," said Grady, sipping his beer. "See who takes the bait."

He looked amused.

"When?"

"Pretty much right now. Hurry and finish your free drink." Grady motioned to Darren and two others at the far side of the room. "The guys won't let GreenCorps harm you. If it gets hot, fade into the crowd. Meet back here later. We've got a room upstairs where you can stay tonight. No charge. You're family."

Caitlyn drained the rest of her beer, wiped the froth from her mouth with her sleeve, and banged the mug on the table. She hoped she wouldn't regret this. She stood, wound her braid around her head like a crown, and stuffed it under her hat.

"Fine. Let's go. I've got groceries to collect in a half an hour."

The men laughed as she followed them out the door, her hands shaking and her heart racing. She hadn't done anything like this in over a year.

"Just talk to the kid, then walk away when his buyer shows up. See if anyone follows," said Darren. "Someone confirmed the leaf on the metal tube the kid has. That was the update at the door. Kid was flashing it around the market. Follow, see who he talks to."

Caitlyn made her way through the crowded streets and wandered the market until one of Darren's men sidled up and whispered, "On your left, shaky kid in the green coat."

She continued shopping, keeping the boy on her left, four or five yards ahead. He must be too hot in that coat. She wasn't surprised this was the target. He looked like he was waiting for someone, looking around and no longer pretending to buy or sell. His skin was sweaty and his hands trembled. Was he just nervous or was he sick?

Caitlyn approached when he stood at the end of a table with carved wooden bowls. He was alone, nobody in earshot. This was her opportunity to talk without being overheard. She stepped closer but didn't look at him. Picking up one of the smooth brown bowls as though inspecting its craftsmanship, she said, "Heard you've got something for sale."

The skinny boy and startled at her voice. She got a better look at his face and placed his age at eighteen or twenty, more than a kid, but not much. His eyes looked haunted, sunken, and rimmed with red. His trembling hands made a different kind of sense. He wasn't sick; he needed a fix. A rush of shame washed over her. They shouldn't be watching this kid—they should help him. He was too thin and a strung-out mess. Something tugged at her, reminding her of Mathew's middle brother. Another kid she hadn't been able to save.

"What do you know, lady?" he said in a hiss.

"I know someone who might be interested in what you've got." It wasn't a lie, just not quite what she'd been instructed. She made things up as she went along. Grady would have counted on it.

"More than ten gold interested?" His beady eyes darted back and forth while they moved to the next table. She picked up a jar of honey and paid, passing over a couple of coppers.

Ten was the magic number. Their instincts were correct.

"Too rich." No way Grady had that kind of money, no matter what the kid was selling. "Three gold. Cash in two minutes, plus a hot meal."

He shook his head. "GreenCorps will pay ten, but I might get a better deal. You're just about out of time." He took a few steps and turned his back to her, scanning the crowd. Her instincts told her he was watching for someone specific that he'd recognize. He stiffened and his gaze fixed on one place as he found who he was waiting for. Time to set her trap.

Caitlyn looked in the same direction. A burly man with a black cowboy hat and beard was shoving his way straight toward them. She grabbed the boy's arm, making sure the newcomer would see it, and leaned her mouth close to his ear.

"Thanks, kid," she whispered.

He frowned. He must be confused. She squeezed his arm, released it, and darted in the opposite direction. She hid her face and hunched her shoulders to look small. She glanced over her shoulder, a fake nervous check to see if the newcomer had taken the bait.

"Who was that? Was that her?" the big man shouted as she veered away. "Get back here, bitch," a deep voice called.

Several shoppers jumped, startled at his yell, and her heart rate increased. She broke into a run, her boots pounding the red cobblestone courtyard, weaving her way as she dodged through the crowd. Several cries of outrage and a crash showed that he'd followed. Judging by the noise, he was losing ground.

She ducked into the store where she'd left her list and stuffed her hat in her pocket as soon as she slipped through the door. Ripping off her dusty coat, she tossed it toward her backpack. Out of sight. Her blonde braid tumbled down her back. It was as much disguise as she could improvise on short notice.

Stepping up to the counter, she pretended to be waiting and calm, a normal shopper. Her blood thrummed in her ears and her adrenaline was pumping, but she tried to look composed, despite the sheen of sweat on her face at the sudden exertion. Her armpits were damp and her heartbeat seemed erratic.

The door burst open, the bell jangling with the rough motion. The door crashed into the wall on the inside.

Conversation stopped and all eyes, including hers, turned to look at the big man in the doorway. He wore all black, including shiny black boots with silver studs. His chest heaved from running as he stared. Those were not work boots; this was a man with money.

"Where'd she go?"

He sounded like he expected answers, but his demand went unanswered as he scanned the room. His harsh voice wasn't winning any friends. One of Darren's friends stood outside the door, watching.

The shopkeeper stacked her piled goods in front of her.

"Here you go, Mrs. Dawson." He hadn't mentioned her name earlier, but he recognized her now. Everyone had liked Mathew.

Caitlyn turned to the shopkeeper with a gentle smile. "Thank you so much. It's a pleasure doing business with you, as usual." She made her voice as sweet as possible. Her shoulder blades spasmed at the angry man's stare, but she moved in a slow and unconcerned way. She grabbed her backpack from the end of the counter where she'd stowed it and packed her goods.

Some quick-thinking clerk had moved her coat, keeping it out of sight. Odds were it would be at headquarters within the hour. That's how things worked in Salt Lake. She'd check in with Grady and be on her way at first light. The rest was none of her concern.

* * *

Back at rebel headquarters, Caitlyn set her pack on the floor and ordered stew for dinner. It came with a piece of rye bread and she tucked into her meal—ravenous from her journey and the afternoon's excitement. Darren and the guys returned soon after she'd finished eating. One tossed her jacket over the back of a nearby chair and she grinned at him.

"Thanks. Took long enough."

All three men laughed, nodded to Grady, and made their way to his table. She stayed to listen to their report instead of going to her room.

"The buyer was Jace McCoy. Works for the top bosses at GreenCorps in Denver. His father is one of the elite and this Jace handles tough jobs for the higher-ups, things they don't want to take care of themselves. Whatever he's buying is big. They must really want that tube," said Darren, rubbing the bristles on the top of his head. "Maybe we should have tried to buy it."

"Kid wouldn't sell at a reasonable price," Caitlyn said.

They turned to look at her.

"You tried?" said Grady with a faint smile and a nod.

"He was holding out for the minimum ten gold." She shrugged. "The big guy showed up quick."

"No way McCoy will give that junkie ten gold," said Grady, leaning back in his chair. "He won't pay him ten copper."

"Probably give him a fix or kill him. Take what he's selling," said Darren.

Her blood ran cold at her old friend's statement. He didn't sound upset. He was stating facts.

"He's just a kid," she said. "Anything you can do about it?"

Ryan Grady shook his head. He looked like he was going to say more as he pointed his pencil in her direction, but Darren interrupted.

"There's someone else following McCoy. The girl from the posters. The real one. I didn't recognize her at first, but it's her. Dressed as a boy. Thought she was one until I got a good look. She might be worth something, but she doesn't have the mystery tube, which I'm betting is what they really want."

"Wouldn't be the first time GreenCorps lied," said Grady.

"You still have someone watching the kid?" said Caitlyn, reaching for her jacket.

"Of course, but we aren't interfering."

"You aren't, but I'm going to help him. Everyone deserves a second chance." Nobody said anything. Grady shifted on his chair and wouldn't meet her eyes. She sighed. "Can I still leave my stuff here?" She stood up.

Grady gave her a long stare before he nodded once. "Try not to come in hot. I don't want McCoy here."

She shot him a slanted look as she strode toward the door. She wasn't stupid.

"Darren, fill her in," said Grady.

Darren followed her toward the exit.

"It's probably too late. The kid waited in the market for McCoy. When the man lost you, he came back and dragged the kid toward the rough part of town. That was an hour ago."

"I have to try." She checked her pouch with coin. She'd have to make a stop.

"You're a softie, Cait. A sucker for the young ones. Are you sure you want to get involved? McCoy's a tough customer. You don't want to cross him."

Her answer was to open the door, and she left without a backward glance.

CHAPTER 30: ELSA PLUS WALKER

Elsa followed the older McCoy brother from the station, keeping to a safe distance as he crossed the unfamiliar town. She caught sight of her own face on Wanted posters only twice. At no time did she walk without others between her and her quarry. Jace entered a hotel called the Seagull's Rest, where she didn't dare follow, and she wasn't sure how long she should wait.

After ten minutes, she was debating whether to give up and return to the house when Jace stepped outside. He no longer carried his baggage and may have rented a room. Without looking to either side, Jace headed toward the market she'd glimpsed on the way here, past the temple in the middle of town.

Elsa skirted along the edge of the buildings to assure she wasn't seen. It became more crowded, but she kept Jace in sight. He picked up speed as he crossed the busy square full of laden tables, shoppers, and casual townspeople. He didn't shop, walking with purpose.

It was tricky to concentrate on following him with the variety of goods for sale in this prosperous town. And the people. She'd never seen so many at once. Reaching the perimeter of the crowd, she moved along the side. She looked beyond Jace and glimpsed Hayden's green coat. Even from this distance, his pinched face and wide-eyed stare were distinctive. A woman whispered in his ear and ran.

Jace yelled, "Get back here, bitch."

He gave chase, perhaps thinking the other woman was her. Elsa melted into a quiet doorway and hugged the shadows. She watched Hayden, her heart pounding. She considered talking to him, but Jace might return any second. She didn't have much time. She couldn't demand the tube back. It wouldn't be that easy; he hated her. She wasn't confident she could overpower Hayden to take the tube. Most of all, it wouldn't be smart to give her presence away. He would turn her over to Jace and GreenCorps. She was at a crossroads, with no straightforward answers.

McCoy would soon realize the other woman wasn't her. Perhaps he'd return to his hotel. She could guide Tatsuda there and help him recover the tube. She trusted the kid on instinct, and she and Walker had seen nothing to indicate he might double-cross them.

Hayden looked terrible. His hands shook, and she doubted he'd eaten in days. His cheeks were sunken and his movements jerky. Was he tormented by what he'd done to Walker? Did it keep him awake at night? It was no more than he deserved for pushing his brother down a rocky slope. Jace's return startled her from her reverie.

His face was purplish-red and his jaw set. Every muscle in his powerful frame radiated frustration. She wouldn't want to be Hayden. The woman he'd chased had eluded him, to Elsa's satisfaction. She angled her body to remain hidden as she crept closer within the crowded market. She needed to be close enough to hear what the men said.

"Useless hopper," Jace said to Hayden as he grabbed the boy and shook him. "You couldn't keep her here for one minute. Where would she go?"

Jace hadn't discovered the other woman's identity. Elsa didn't know if that would help or hinder her plans. She felt sorry for Hayden, despite everything he'd done. This meeting was stupid and dangerous, and he was going to get himself hurt. Despite the distance, the rattle of his teeth was audible as Jace berated him. Hayden couldn't speak until the older man released him with a final shake.

"It wasn't her," Hayden gasped. "I don't know who that woman was, and I don't know what she wanted. I've never seen her before until she appeared a few minutes ago. Maybe she was interested in me. Or a whore and you scared her off."

Hayden wasn't a good liar. Deception was written all over his face with his shifty gaze and lack of eye contact. Jace didn't appear to believe him any more than Elsa had. The woman must have said something about the tube. Maybe she'd been another potential buyer.

"You sure it wasn't her?" His lip curled in a sneer.

Jace's florid face appeared angry and cruel. He grabbed Hayden, his gigantic hand closing around the smaller man's arm. He growled something in Hayden's face that Elsa wasn't close enough to hear. Hayden paled.

"I've got it, I've got it," Hayden said. "I didn't let you down. I told you I could get it."

Jace looked around, perhaps realizing how exposed they were. Elsa ducked down to adjust her bootlace, her heart pounding. She was too close and dripped with sweat.

"We can't do this here," the older man said, taking a deep breath. "If I pay you out in the open, the toughs in this town will steal it before you've gone three steps. A strong breeze could knock you over."

Elsa agreed with his assessment but didn't believe that was the reason for his suggestion. Her gut told that Jace couldn't be trusted. She sensed this. Shouldn't Hayden? Hayden was asking for trouble by going off alone with the man. Her instincts told her to watch for a chance to help Hayden.

"I hadn't thought of that." Hayden shuffled his feet and looked at the ground.

She wanted to groan at his stupidity.

"I know a place that will be much quieter," said Jace with a nasty smirk.

Jace towed Hayden as the older man pushed his way toward the northwestern corner of the town square, back toward the train station.

Elsa stayed far enough back that she could see Hayden's coat, but not so close either of them would see her. Hayden was in trouble. Her instinct was to help, perhaps cause a disturbance so he could run, but in all probability, he would stay until Jace paid him. She ground her teeth.

Following wasn't the best plan either, but she didn't dare let Jace out of her sight. Her stomach clenched, and she stayed unseen, always keeping the crowd between herself and those she followed.

The buildings changed as they left the main market square, becoming older, more run-down. They passed the temple where Walker had said to meet after the train if they got separated. Guilt rose inside her in waves. She'd left when she'd promised to stay inside. Walker might be angry, but she couldn't go back and leave Hayden to the mercy of Jace. She hoped the plan to get Tatsuda had been successful.

Jace turned a few streets before the one that led back to the train. She followed onto the noisy street. Bars and brothels lined both sides— more than two dozen—many with their doors open. Competing yells and music spilled outside, blaring and creating a cacophony. It was more raucous and run-down than the street where his hotel had been located. It seemed an odd place for a private word, and more dangerous. She added a swagger to her step she didn't feel, trying to look less conspicuous.

Elsa fell back, still keeping Jace and Hayden in her sights. This close to the railroad, the bars would be busy as soon as the railroad workers finished for the day. Business should pick up any time.

Jace dragged Hayden into an alley between two large brick buildings by the end of the street. A single peek into the dark space showed that it was empty. She crept forward, her heart thudding in her chest. Her footsteps were slow and measured while she maintained a readiness to flee. She stopped inching when she reached the next corner. Jace's loud voice carried to her position, even if she couldn't see him. She froze. This was close enough.

"Here's the first installment of what I owe. A show of good faith."

"I want my coin. I worked hard for that," said Hayden's whiney voice.

Jace must have offered him drugs first.

"I don't carry ten gold on me, kid. That would be a death wish. If anyone suspected I had that, they'd kill me to take it. We have to go to Denver to get the rest."

"I don't want to go back to Denver. You said when I brought it here, you'd pay."

"Just take this kid. You know you want to."

There was a pause, and she wished she could see what was happening. Was the stupid kid going to kite right here, right now? She worried her bottom lip with her teeth.

"Thank you," said Hayden with a sigh. "I wasn't sure there would be more of these."

He inhaled and though she didn't know him well, the longing was apparent in his voice. Ginny's cubes were fast-acting. Hayden would be kiting in seconds. She was uncertain why she cared, but she did.

"Take two, kid," said Jace.

"That's too much at once," said Hayden, his voice thick and dreamy.

"You earned it. It'll feel great."

"I earned it," said Hayden. The bag rustled.

Anger surged through Elsa. She didn't expect the wave of red that clouded her vision. Hayden had hurt Granny and then Walker and that was hard to forgive, but what Jace was doing was reprehensible.

That's when the beating started. Her heart thumped hard, and she risked a single quick peek around the corner, jerking her head back.

Fifteen feet away, Jace had Hayden pinned against a building. The sickening sound must have been when he'd smashed the boy's head against the wall. Jace had twisted one arm behind the boy's back and wrenched his shoulder when he slammed him into the bricks. He held him with one arm and punched with the other. The boy whimpered, but Hayden didn't scream. He must already be beyond resistance.

She peeked again just as Jace released him and kneed him in the groin. The boy slumped to the ground and Jace let him fall. One side of Hayden's face was bloody and scraped. Jace kicked Hayden several times; his hard black boots inflicting damage to the unresponsive boy lying on the dusty ground.

Elsa felt sick. She had to do something. She disliked Hayden, but he was a human and Walker's brother. She couldn't let him be beaten to death. Jace's leer when he'd tried to kill her flashed through her mind. This time she needed to act.

She stepped out of the shadows. This had to be stopped.

She spun around the corner and shoved a garbage can, knocking it to the ground. As it hit the ground with a clatter, she stumbled and caught herself. She looked up. Her eyes met Jace's, and she froze.

He narrowed his eyes in recognition, the look penetrating her flimsy disguise.

"Leave him alone." Her voice came more confident than she felt inside.

"You." He pulled a knife from his belt, lurched in her direction, then skidded to a stop. He glanced back at Hayden and grimaced. He reached into the boy's backpack where it lay on the ground.

Jace removed the tube and shot her a look of triumph.

Not caring who might recognize her, she fled because her life depended on it. Her breath caught in her throat and her feet pounded the hard-packed earth and cobblestones. She wasn't sure she could outrun Jace in a strange city. She didn't know where to go, but her gut told her to keep moving. She'd find somewhere.

Elsa dodged through several alleys on the other side of the street, praying she didn't run into a dead end. Jace ran past the mouth of the alley, and she ducked behind a stack of crates. He was close. When she crept out of hiding, he spotted her again. She zigged back across the street. In the next alley, alone once more, she rattled doors and shook knobs. Nothing opened. She couldn't find a place to hide. Everything was locked.

While she crouched behind some garbage cans, Jace's heavy footsteps rumbled nearby as he searched.

He cursed. "Elsa. Get out here. What makes you think you can get away you stupid slut?"

She crouched lower, sweat soaking her clothes.

"Bitch. Get out here. This is your last chance." He kicked several containers of refuse, the cans clattering to the ground, one rolling past her and coming to a rest beside the building. Her chest heaved and the noise of her pounding heart thundered in her ears, but she remained quiet. When at last he turned, she dashed the other way, toward the market, hoping to get lost amongst the shoppers, but the crowd had thinned.

Her eyes scanned the buildings, looking for somewhere to hide. She closed her eyes and tried to listen to what her instincts said. Her gut told her to go south. She sprinted toward the far side of the square, dodging through the remaining vendors.

A light flickered in a nearby lane, where it caught her attention. She bolted in that direction, praying to find somewhere safe.

Ducking into the quiet street, she saw a green door. She turned the knob.

It was unlocked.

Elsa eased it open and stepped inside, closing it without a sound. She slid the deadbolt closed and looked around, wondering what kind of place this was. It was dim and looked like a storage room with rows of cluttered shelving, but the hall led deeper into the building. Electric lights hummed above her, but only one was lit, casting a bluish-white light. She ran her fingers over the front of a shelf and they came away dusty. It wasn't a store, a home, or a restaurant, though she smelled food. Something spicy with meat. Her stomach gurgled.

Quiet, even voices came from a room deeper in the building. But she didn't think she'd disturbed anyone. She'd just have to remain unnoticed until she was safe, then slip out the door. Walker must be worried by now. If the situation was reversed, she'd be concerned.

"Seems we've attracted a listener," said a voice behind her.

He'd come from the shadows at the back.

She grabbed for the deadbolt, but the man pounced, holding the door closed. She broke out in a sweat. His hand was tattooed with a leaf in the webbing between his fingers and thumb. A rebel? She turned to face him, questions on her lips.

"I wouldn't leave yet," he said. "There's quite the reward on your head and someone here who'd like to meet you."

* * *

Walker had positioned himself with Tatsuda where he watched the Temple's western gate. He hadn't known where to go to find Elsa, and this was where they'd agreed to meet if they were separated. He shaded his eyes against the bright light of the setting sun. There wasn't a whisper or rumor about her capture. If someone had claimed her reward, there would have been talk. He balled his hands into fists. Where was she?

He and Tatsuda had looked everywhere. Near the station, the park with the water pump, and the nearby neighborhoods, but she'd vanished. He wasn't sure she could find her way back to the house, since she didn't know Salt Lake. She must have gone beyond the neighborhood, but he didn't know where. He alternated between feelings of anger and concern, debating whether he would strangle her with his bare hands or kiss her senseless.

Maybe she would come to the meeting place. The Temple was the largest building in town. She couldn't miss it. As long as she wasn't hurt or injured, she'd come. He didn't want to consider what else might happen. With the price on her head, she would be shackled until they transported her to Denver. Not somewhere like the small holding cells where the bulls kept vagrants overnight, but somewhere more secure. He wasn't confident he could pull off that kind of rescue operation, but he wouldn't let her be sent to Denver as a prisoner or sold south.

He grit his teeth, grinding his molars until they ached. His chest remained tight with worry. He'd been trying to keep her safe, not restrict her freedom. She valued her independence, and that's what he loved about her. But her continued absence made him concerned. She'd promised to stay inside. He inhaled and exhaled twice and then relaxed his fists. The sun set and the light dimmed, but the city remained hot as heat rose from the cobblestones in waves. He was sweating buckets.

Walker's heart stopped cold when he spotted Jace McCoy striding across the square. He hadn't expected to see the man here. Walker tugged his cap, covering his face, and assumed a slouched posture to hide his distinctive height. The last time he'd seen the GreenCorps man, he'd been unconscious on the floor at Ginny's. Walker clenched his fist again. He owed Jace for Elsa's nightmares, if nothing else. He'd like nothing better than to hit that asshole, but he wasn't that rash.

"That's McCoy," he said under his breath to Tatsuda. "He's the one who beat Elsa and accused her of theft."

The boy nodded. "He was in Denver several weeks ago."

Walker shot him a hard look. "That's what made you come looking for her."

The kid nodded. "I didn't know his name, but he said he could get the metal tube. I thought I might find it first."

"Shit," said Walker.

Jace's knuckles were swollen and bloody. His injuries looked recent. He'd either used them to deliver a beating or he'd been in a fight. There was no sign the man was hurt anywhere else. If it had been a fight, he must have won. Walker couldn't see Elsa, but if she'd seen Jace from the hideout, that would have given her a reason to leave. Walker scanned the emptying square. She wasn't following Jace now.

Jace shook one hand as if it stung as he stalked past their position. His jaw bulged, and he didn't glance left or right. He didn't notice Walker. The GreenCorps man turned toward the section of the city with high-end brothels and hotels. Walker's heart lurched. He scanned the people in the square, his heart in his throat, still hoping Elsa would appear. He hoped it wasn't her blood on the man's knuckles.

Walker looked over to ask the kid his opinion, but Tatsuda was gone.

CHAPTER 31: TATSUDA PLUS WALKER

Tatsuda slipped into the flow of people moving away from the market as it closed for the night. He recognized the burly man Walker had pointed out as the man from Denver, the one who'd met with the GreenCorps suit. He would steal the tube if the other man had it. He wasn't sure if he'd sell it back to GreenCorps or return it to Elsa. He liked Elsa and Walker—they'd been kind and helped him out of jail. He wasn't sure what he'd do. Ten gold was a lot of coin.

His hands twitched to claim such a prize. The man in black had punched someone or something. More than once. Tatsuda didn't know if it was Elsa or the thief, or someone else, but the man carried a bundle wrapped in cloth about the right size to be the tube Elsa had described.

The man entered a two-story brick hotel halfway down the street; the painted sign above the door had a seagull with outspread wings. Tatsuda couldn't read the lettering, but that didn't matter. His target was inside. He nodded to a kid a couple of years younger than he was, also dusty and long-haired, while he waited to see if McCoy came out. He guessed the boy was a lookout—perhaps for the rebels.

Tatsuda decided to see what was taking so long. Perhaps the man was drinking or with a woman.

He walked toward the hotel entrance but stopped when the dusty kid said, "They won't serve our kind in that one."

Tatsuda assumed that meant young, or perhaps homeless. He needed to look different.

There was no reason for McCoy to remember him from Denver, but Tatsuda stood in the hotel's shadow at the side and straightened his hair. He tied it back, smoothing it with his hands, attempting to look less desperate—like someone with a family to care about how he looked. He brushed most of the dust from his clothes. It was the best he could do without water. He stood straighter, put on his cap, and whistled while he walked.

Striding to the hotel's front door, he said to the bouncer, "My dad might be here tonight. It was payday. I've been sent to bring him home."

"I know nothing about that, kid," the bald man with bulging muscles said. He crossed his arms across his chest, looking forbidding. He didn't crack a smile.

"May I check?" Tatsuda said. "If he's here, I'll take him and go."

The barman looked at him for the first time.

"You don't look like trouble. See that you aren't."

"Thanks, mister." Tatsuda nodded and darted inside. His eyes took a minute to adjust to the change in lighting. He spotted Jace right away, but was careful not to let his gaze rest on the older man. It was a standard barroom with tables, a bar, and a wall of alcohol. The guest rooms must be upstairs. He watched a little longer before proceeding. Several well-dressed women circulated amongst the male patrons and he corrected himself. This was definitely a brothel. He was tempted to ask for an ale to slake his thirst and check the kid's words, but he needed to focus.

Tatsuda didn't want to talk to Jace or be memorable. This was a scouting mission. It was best to be unremarkable. Ordinary. Jace sat at the bar on his own as the bartender poured a drink from a bottle into a glass in front of the man. The cloth-wrapped bundle wasn't in sight. Perhaps Jace had taken it to a room, or it was in a pocket.

Tatsuda took several more steps, scanning the room as though looking for someone. He allowed his shoulders to droop, giving him a dejected look. He spoke to the bartender.

"Excuse me. My father is supposed to be here. If he isn't, he should be here soon. May I wait?"

The bartender hesitated. "Half an hour, kid. I'm not serving you alcohol. Other places might, but I won't. Make sure you stay out of my way."

He waved to a seat at the far end of the bar, three seats past McCoy. Tatsuda sat on the indicated stool and the bartender slid him a glass of cool water.

"No charge. It's a hot one."

"Thank you, sir." Grateful for the drink, Tatsuda sipped, watching the door but following everywhere else with his peripheral vision. He was waiting for an opportunity to get upstairs. There was an argument in the corner and a drunk customer at the bar. He waited, but nothing happened. No distractions; this was a boring bar. He sighed.

McCoy ordered a second drink and watched the working women. Not in an urgent way, more a patient shopping. Choosing someone for later. McCoy shifted position to better watch.

He didn't have deep enough pockets to hide the tube. Tatsuda determined McCoy didn't have it on him. He might have a room.

Tatsuda gave the bartender a nod and slid off his stool. "Guess my dad's not coming here after all. Thanks, I'm going to keep looking."

The man nodded while he dried beer mugs. Tatsuda nodded to the bouncer too, on his way out. A regular, polite kid. He ambled down the street past four additional hotels, then ducked into the dark space between the buildings and slid into a more familiar role—burglar.

He returned to Jace's hotel the back way. He shimmied up to the roof between the chimney and the brick wall, using the cracked mortar as hand and footholds. He dropped onto the tiles, keeping his feet quiet so it wasn't obvious to those inside that someone was on the roof.

Tiptoeing to the nearest open window, he stayed low and peered into the room. There was nobody inside. The bed was made and a red suitcase sat on the floor. The window wouldn't open farther, perhaps designed that way. He crawled through the window, though it was a tight fit. He wouldn't want to try it at full speed.

A quick examination showed two dresses hanging in the closet. Not Jace's room, though he hadn't expected it to be. He eased the door open to the hallway and stepped out. As he moved to the next door, he left the door closed but not latched. He might need to return this way in a hurry when leaving. His heart accelerated as he checked both directions and listened hard. He was alone in the carpeted hallway. He removed a thin piece of wire from his pocket and a shearing wrench to unlock the next door in the empty hall.

This room was empty, with no baggage. Voices came from within the next two, and he avoided them. He opened the fifth. A black duffle bag sat on the bed. Beside it lay the shiny metal tube, halfway unwrapped in a piece of cloth. It was smaller than he'd imagined.

Tatsuda cleared his throat and looked around. This room faced the same direction as the one where he'd entered. He darted forward and grabbed the tube, its metal surface cool in his hand. He shook it. A faint metallic object clinked inside, but without an obvious way to open it. No lid, no seams. He had to take the whole thing.

Voices approached from the stairs, getting closer. He froze to listen. The man sounded like McCoy. Tatsuda looked for a place to hide, his hands sweaty. There was nowhere and he couldn't get back to the other exit. Tatsuda leaped toward the window and shoved it open, his hands shaking as he pushed the frame upward. It stuck in the same low position as the other. He wriggled through the small opening just as the door moved. Whoever opened the door wouldn't have seen his face, but would see the motion and his feet as they slid out.

"What the hell?" the brawny man said.

Tatsuda heard him getting closer and gave a hard push, lurching outward.

He slid onto the roof just in time. He slammed the window on the big man's fingers as he turned to run, careful of his footing on the steep roof. He tucked the tube into his front pocket so he had both hands for balance.

He had a matter of seconds before McCoy came after him.

"Stop, thief!" Came the call through the reopened window.

Tatsuda scrambled faster. The window opening was too small for McCoy to follow. The man turned, probably running for the stairs. Tatsuda needed to get off the roof. Climbing would take too long. At the back of the building, he grabbed the edge and swung himself down. He closed his eyes and clenched his teeth. This might hurt. He dangled and dropped to the hard-packed ground. His knees buckled and hit the ground. One ankle rolled. It hurt like fury, but he was down.

He sprinted away as cries of "thief" hit the street from the front. He dashed from the alley, not daring to watch if they'd followed. He headed away from the hotels, zigzagging his way toward the Temple.

Running through the central square, he passed Walker, still waiting for Elsa, though the light had faded and it was almost dark.

"Run," Tatsuda said as he sped by, his breath coming in gasps. His sore ankle was becoming a problem.

Walker looked startled, but ran. They stopped at the neighborhood park, close to their hideout. Tatsuda didn't know how long ago he'd lost McCoy, but there were no longer signs of pursuit. He limped the remaining steps to the water pump, where he put his hands on his knees while he caught his breath.

"I think I lost him." His lungs ached and his chest burned from the chase. Now that he'd stopped, he inspected the damage. His ankle throbbed and his pants had ripped at one knee.

"Where the hell did you go?" Walker had already caught his breath.

"I got it." Tatsuda held up the tube with a shy grin.

Walker returned his smile for an instant. "Good job, kid. Did you see Elsa or my brother?" There was concern in his voice.

Tatsuda shook his head. He would have liked to have found Elsa.

"It's a start. You did great." Walker looked around, but they were alone. "Think we're safe. Let's go back to the house and have something to eat. Elsa will have to find us. We can't search for her in the dark."

* * *

Walker and Tatsuda returned to the hideout. His hopes that Elsa would be there were dashed when he found the candle lantern unlit and waiting. He made dinner, his ears straining as he listened to every movement that could mean Elsa's return. He remained disappointed.

Tatsuda gave him the tube before they ate. The kid could steal it back any time. Walker had no illusions that it was safe, but he jammed it into his pocket. He would find a hiding place after Tatsuda fell asleep. If the boy slept. There was no way for Walker to be sure he wasn't faking. He hoped the boy was another person to trust. His list was short: Jim and Elsa. He supposed he would have to trust Elsa's feeling about the kid. It was close to midnight when Walker sat on the zipped sleeping bags and leaned against the wall with his journal. He would write a quick entry, then try to sleep.

June 25th, 2195 (second write)

Can't sleep. Elsa's disappearance and Jace McCoy's presence must be related. Worried that her independence or her instincts have gotten her in over her head. Tomorrow I'll follow the direction we saw Jace come from and leave no stone unturned. Have to find her. She could be injured. She isn't helpless, but McCoy is bigger and stronger than she is.

I want to be where she is. We make each other's lives better. We fit together. I hadn't expected to depend on anyone, but I do. We're a team.

Walker hadn't been writing long when faint scratching noises came from outside. He might have missed them if he hadn't been awake. Someone had removed the board that covered the basement window. He held his breath. Elsa? Or had McCoy followed? Walker crept to the top of the stairs and waited in the dark, his heart pounding. There was a single set of footfalls.

It seemed to take an eternity for the person to creep upstairs. Despite their stealth, the steps were too heavy to be Elsa's. He handled his disappointment as he unsheathed his knife and tightened his grip.

A man's shadow detached from the inky darkness of the stairwell from the basement. In the pale glimmers of moonlight streaming in through the slits in the window, he didn't recognize the balding man. Walker rushed him without a sound and pinned him against the wall, his blade at the intruder's throat.

Walker didn't want to make a loud noise in an unoccupied house, hoping he hadn't woken Tatsuda. The man against the wall showed no surprise at the attack and offered no resistance.

"Put your hands where I can see them," Walker whispered.

The man held his hands beside his chest, palms out in surrender. He seemed to wait for Walker to speak.

"Who are you and why are you here?" Walker's voice was filled with menace. His disappointment that this wasn't Elsa was sharp.

"We're trying to figure out how you fit into this mess that occurred today."

"We?"

"The organization I'm with."

"GreenCorps, Saints, or rebels?" Walker didn't relax his hold on the other man or reduce his vigilance. He didn't like to mix with any of those organizations.

"GreenCorps?" the man spat. "How could you even ask? Also, not the Church."

"Can you prove who you are?" said Walker.

"Name's Darren, I work for Ryan Grady. Leader of the rebels."

Walker had heard of the man in his travels, not just from Jim. Grady was reputed to be an expert judge of character and a moderate, or voice of reason, among the rebels. He'd also been an elusive man for GreenCorps to track. They'd been looking for him for a long time. It wasn't surprising that he was here in Utah.

"Where's your tattoo?" said Walker.

"Left hand," said Darren, making no move to show it.

"What mess?" Walker dropped the topic to return to the more important issue, his knife steady at the man's throat.

"The young man in the green coat," the rebel said.

"My brother." Walker wasn't sure if he was relieved or angry. He took a deep breath. He loved Hayden, but the idiot had stolen from Elsa and shoved him down a cliff. Hayden had left him to die. His head ached at the thought. Damn drugs. Walker would like to thrash his brother, but he didn't want him to come to actual harm.

"He sold something to Jace McCoy of GreenCorps. McCoy may have killed him."

"May have?" His voice came out a snarl. It became harder to keep his hands steady and his heart banged against his ribs.

"McCoy isn't one to leave loose ends, but he had a follower. She might have interfered. Dark-haired girl, yellow eyes. I don't know what happened because they sent me for you before she told most of her story. One of ours went to help your brother."

"You have Elsa?" Walker's voice changed to a growl as his grip on the knife tightened.

"Easy big guy. Ya, I saw the girl. Brave out there in the wide-open, considering the price on her head. Or foolhardy. Maybe both."

"Did McCoy hurt her?"

"Relax that knife a little? I'm all for answering your questions, but I don't like to bleed."

Walker glanced at the man's neck. A narrow stream of blood trickled down the rebel's throat. He pulled the knife back infinitesimally, so he was no longer cutting him.

"Answer the question."

"McCoy chased your girl, but she gave him the slip. By coincidence, she found her way into our headquarters. Lucky for her, someone left the door unlocked. She's having a late dinner with Grady. He hasn't decided what to do with her. She refused to talk until Grady sent me to get you."

"Any proof?" Walker growled.

"Well, I'm here. You guys are staying in one of our bolt holes, so I knew where she meant when she described it. She said to tell you that Grady was in the picture too, whatever that means."

The picture of Jim and her Granny. The rebel leader might be older than Walker had imagined because he'd been one of the four children. At last, Walker could breathe again with her message. Would the long-ago connection between Elsa's Granny, Jim, and Ryan Grady be an advantage? Was Elsa sending him another, deeper message? He wasn't sure, but he sure as hell didn't trust strangers. His thoughts raced as he considered Darren's words.

"Damn," said Walker, lowering the knife and stepping back. He kept his guard up and the knife drawn, but a weight lifted from his chest. If this was true, then Elsa was unharmed, at least for now. "Why didn't she come back herself?"

"Grady wasn't finished. The price on her head makes her very interesting. Even the rebellion needs money."

"Can you take me to her?" Walker's muscles tensed again. Over his dead body would they sell her out.

"Sure. What about whoever's sleeping in the other room?"

Tatsuda had created a disturbance, too. Walker didn't want to share more information than needed with a stranger.

"I'll let him know where we're going and that I'll be back."

Walker didn't like turning his back on an unknown rebel. It made his shoulder blades itch as he walked into the room where Tatsuda slept. The boy looked like he was asleep. Deep, even breaths came from his corner of the room, but Walker wasn't fooled. The boy had been listening from beside the door until seconds earlier.

"Elsa's been detained by the rebels. She sent me a message. I don't think they've hurt her. I'm going to get her and it might take a while. You want to wait, or come?"

"I'm sleeping," the boy said without opening his eyes.

"We'll come back later or send word tomorrow. We're not leaving. You're with us as long as you want to be. You've earned that."

Tatsuda sat up, his eyes opened wider than Walker had seen before. The boy nodded once. "I'll look after the backpacks."

Walker squeezed Tatsuda's shoulder and left. He read people pretty well and had faith in the boy to be here when he and Elsa returned.

"Take me to my girlfriend," he said to the man in the darkened kitchen.

CHAPTER 32: CAITLYN PLUS ELSA

On her search for the green-coated kid, Caitlyn ran into some kind of chase in the bar and brothel district. She spotted McCoy searching for someone. She'd seen the girl from the poster pass by just moments before, and Caitlyn guessed that was his target. He cursed and stomped, roaring like a madman. Residents and rebels kept out of his way while subtly hindering him. Carts rolled in into his path and people were slow to move. They despised GreenCorps in Utah. Their presence was a reminder of unwanted interference and outside oppression.

The girl gave McCoy the slip, and he stalked off toward another part of town. Caitlyn crossed the street to avoid another encounter with the man.

It took a while for Caitlyn to locate where he'd left the boy. She had to find somewhere quiet that Jace McCoy might have taken the kid to dispose of him. Dark now, only the front street was lit, leaving the lanes and alleys in shadow. Luckily, she carried a flashlight or she would never have found him.

Rats scurried along ahead of her in the darkness as she sidled down the side of a building. Something larger slunk away at the edge of her vision. Kid, coyote, or raccoon? It didn't matter.

His body was sprawled against the back wall around the corner and behind the last bar on the street. She spied the ridiculous green coat first, the color gleaming in the flashlight's yellow glow. When she saw the boy's body, she worried she was too late. McCoy would have left the boy for dead.

Caitlyn sighed. It was fortunate she was a medic, as one side of the kid's face was covered in blood so dark it looked black. She jumped. It looked like his hands and feet were moving until her directed light showed more rats. She shuddered. The rodents hadn't been feeding yet—they'd been investigating. As far as she could see, he wasn't bitten. The creatures scurried away as she knelt beside him.

With two fingers, she checked his pulse on the side of his neck. His pulse was erratic and slow, and she leaned closer—the whisper of his shallow, thin breath on her cheek. He was in terrible shape. Her preliminary examination determined that his left arm was broken, his opposite shoulder was dislocated, and his face was scratched and bloody. But his sickly-sweet smell and his sweaty unresponsiveness had her the most concerned. With his injuries, he should have woken when she prodded.

Expecting the overdose, Caitlyn had stopped at an apothecary for supplies and came prepared. She crushed activated charcoal in her shallow mortar and pestle, then forced some of the fine powder between his lips. She dripped water into his mouth and he automatically swallowed. She repeated the procedure a dozen times, hoping she got enough into him to prevent him from dying.

He was so high he wouldn't be feeling pain from his wounds, but he would later, if he woke. The shoulder needed to be reset and the longer she waited, the more it would swell. She wasn't convinced she could do it alone, but she had to try. The procedure was painful for the patient; it was for the best that he was unconscious and wouldn't fight.

She repositioned his body and gripped his arm by the elbow to get the proper angle. She put her foot on his chest near the shoulder and used the pressure of his arm, her foot, and the hard ground to guide the ball of his humerus back into his shoulder socket. The swelling made it difficult, but it went with an audible clunk. The boy just flinched when he should have screamed.

She tore off his shirt and bound the shoulder and chest with medical tape for stability; she had to move him and didn't want it popping back out. She washed the blood from his face. The cuts and scratches were superficial, except a deeper one by his ear. She applied an antiseptic, then salve. He needed antibiotics to be sure to remain free of infection but needed to be conscious to take them.

Caitlyn worked on his broken arm, which wasn't the same side as the dislocated shoulder. Wincing at the difficult movements, she positioned his hand and arm in the proper alignment, trying to be gentle. He twitched while she worked, but remained unconscious. With two broken slats she freed from a wooden crate, she fashioned a splint, and bound it together. It wasn't pretty, but it was a decent field dressing. She gave him another dose of activated charcoal and checked his pulse. It wasn't better, but at least it wasn't worse. He was still alive.

She repacked her supplies and crouched on her heels while she considered her options. She didn't have a stretcher or partner, and nothing with which to drag him. She wouldn't leave the same way she'd arrived. She'd stick to alleys and dark places. The fewer people who saw them, the better. She still planned to travel home tomorrow—she had animals to feed. She wasn't involved with the rebels long-term. Not anymore.

Breathing deep, she heaved the boy over her shoulder like a sack of grain, his head and arms flopping down her back. She stood up, appalled by how scrawny he was. A young man should weigh more. A pang of sympathy filled her. While not as heavy as she'd feared, his dead weight was awkward and it wasn't easy to walk. She readjusted him and staggered down the alley, her flashlight tucked in her armpit providing dim light. She was glad for the muscles she'd gained farming as she trudged through the night.

In her head, she mapped out a route back to headquarters. Her way wasn't the most direct, but it would be the safest. She would sleep, collect her pig, and leave town. Her involvement with the rebels would be over until her next visit. This had been enough excitement.

* * *

Elsa leaned back in her chair and pretended the room wasn't full of armed strangers, but tension remained in her shoulders. She'd recognized Grady as one of the children from Jim and Granny's photos by the birthmark on his forehead. He had leaf tattoos between his forefinger and thumb on both hands and from what he said, she guessed he was a rebel leader. He'd been polite, but it was clear that she wasn't free to leave.

She hadn't revealed the connection to her Granny yet. She was waiting for Walker. Her chest tightened as she tried to speak without giving away too much personal information. At the back of her mind, the events of today repeated. She'd failed to retrieve the tube and had lost Hayden, even if she'd distracted Jace for a moment. Grady told her that a medic had gone to help him, but hadn't returned. Would Walker blame her if his brother was dead?

When the door from the alley opened, she stood, her chair scraping the floor.

"Elsa, are you okay?" Walker ran into the room.

She strode to meet him and he scooped her into an embrace, burying his face against her head and neck, his racing heart against hers. Tension drained from her body. She never would have thought anyone could come to mean so much to her in such a short time, but he had.

"I'm sorry I left when I said I wouldn't." She met his concerned gray eyes.

"Jace was a good reason. I trusted you, but I worried." Walker released her, but took her hand in his larger one and squeezed.

"This is Ryan Grady," said Elsa, indicating the middle-aged man seated at the table. "And this is Walker."

"I've heard a lot about you, sir. Nice to meet you."

Grady inclined his head.

"Has someone come with Hayden or sent word?" Walker said to the leader.

"Hayden? Ah, your brother. We expect them anytime. I must warn you, your brother put himself in serious danger and he may be beyond our medic's care. Your Elsa distracted McCoy and led him away, or it would have been worse. The boy was alive last she saw him, but I have no doubt McCoy would have killed him. Beaten him to death. He's not a kind man and likes to take care of things like that himself."

Elsa touched her hand to her ribs, where her bruises had been. "I have experience with that."

"You saw it happen?" asked Walker, turning to her.

"Some of it. I didn't want Jace to see me at first, so I watched from the shadows. He gave your brother drugs instead of the reward and grabbed the tube. Hayden took two cubes and was wasted within moments. He couldn't fight back and Jace probably thought he'd done enough to finish your brother before I interrupted. I yelled for him to stop and Jace chased me." Her hands shook as she spoke. Attracting Jace's attention had been difficult, considering their history.

"Thank you for trying," said Walker. "You didn't owe Hayden anything."

"I'm curious about two things," said Grady.

Elsa had almost forgotten they were in rebel headquarters and that Grady was there.

"Just two?" said Darren as he pulled up a chair and sat. "Slow night for you, boss."

Grady smiled. "Like I said, two things. The first is what is the mystery tube with the rebel leaf?"

Elsa started to answer, but he put his hand up and she stopped.

"The second is, I'm interested in what picture you might have seen. I've tried to stay out of pictures most of my life."

Elsa and Walker looked at each other, and he nodded. He squeezed her hand, which she took as moral support. She turned to Walker. "I told him about the Heap and Ginny's while he sent someone for you. I explained how I'd found the tube and that I didn't steal it, despite GreenCorps' accusations."

She turned to Grady and lifted her chin. "The tube has maps inside and a key for six seed bunkers. The underground bunkers were filled with seeds in the twenty-first century before the Collapse. Food plants and trees that are extinct now, the kind that reproduce and live for years. Survival gear and freeze-dried rations were added during plague times."

"So, almost two hundred years ago," said Grady. "Why is it relevant now? Why does it have the rebel leaf?"

"I don't think the leaf means it belongs to the rebels." Elsa chose deliberate words as she strung her thoughts together like beads on a necklace. "A long-ago rebel may have owned it and added the leaf. Someone etched the design before the tube ended up in the Heap. I found a mission statement drafted by the early rebels. They adopted the leaf because they were interested in fair growing practices and food for everyone." She checked to ensure she hadn't offended Grady. She didn't want to insult him. She imagined herself walking a line between truth and avoidance.

"How do you know the seed bunkers still exist?" said Grady. "Two hundred years is a long time. GreenCorps would have found and taken everything long ago."

"We went to one and checked it out." Elsa's palms became sweaty. Her instincts had brought her here, and her gut told her that Grady could be trusted. Part of her wanted to keep this information secret, but if it was ever to mean something more, she needed help. She might be a survivor, but she wasn't a revolutionary. She wasn't even part of the rebellion. Even if it would be beneficial for everyone, she couldn't imagine changing the world or reducing GreenCorps control, at least not on her own.

Grady's eyebrows rose to his hairline. "You went inside one. Where?"

She wasn't sure he believed her. Her story about the bunkers sounded improbable.

"About fifteen miles outside Sacramento. At the old University of California site where it was deep underground and secure. We took some of the survival gear. That's why Walker and I have matching pants and boots."

"I noticed your boots. Not what I expected for someone from SoCal," said Grady with a nod. "Any other proof?"

"I took a couple of foil seed packets. They're at the house where we're staying."

"You were a scavenger. Why didn't you sell the tube to GreenCorps in the beginning? I imagine you needed the coin, living in a place like that."

"It seemed special." She met Grady's steady gaze. "I didn't want to sell it for next to nothing. I had a gut feeling that it was important."

"What about after you saw the key? You could have charged much more."

"So GreenCorps would keep everything? Grow the crops and sell them at prices only the wealthy can afford? They control almost all food supplies and clean water already. It would be like cheese, milk, grapes, and apples. Like so many things. They have a monopoly. It's not fair. More food for the rich." She slapped the table for emphasis and looked down in surprise at the angry sound that matched her mood. She sounded like one of the rebels.

Grady nodded. "What about us? Would you sell it to the rebels?"

"I don't know much about what you do. Hard to learn much in SoCal except the bit in the GreenCorps news and they made the rebels seem like criminals."

"Can she think about it?" said Walker. "It's late to decide something so fast."

"Where's the tube now?" said Grady. "McCoy still has it?"

Walker squeezed Elsa's hand. "It's safe. We got it back."

"Tatsuda stole it?" said Elsa with a laugh. At Walker's nod, she said, "That's great." She frowned. "Unless he's halfway back to Denver." She was astonished that she was happy about someone's theft.

"I want to hear about the picture," said Grady.

Elsa took another deep breath. "This is more of an interesting coincidence."

"My great-grandmother in SoCal raised me. She broke her arm and developed an infection this spring, and muttered in her fevered sleep. Otherwise, I wouldn't know much about her past. I've pieced this together from clues, what she let slip, and information I found later. She raised me but refused to talk about the rebellion, but it sounds like she was involved for a long time. Years. It's where she met her husband. Their daughter grew up and joined their efforts. It went wrong when they attacked a train to free a transport of people who'd been sold south."

Her voice was full of emotion as she talked about Granny's secret former life and her throat became tight. She wished Granny was here to explain.

Elsa took a breath. "The rebels leading the raid were caught and executed on the spot, including my great-grandfather and his daughter. This left my great-grandmother with her infant granddaughter to raise. Somehow GreenCorps caught up to her and Granny was banished to SoCal, leaving the rebellion behind."

"And the picture?" Grady's brow was furrowed as he leaned forward, his palms clasped together.

Perhaps the story seemed familiar. Such a disaster might be part of rebel lore.

"Granny had three photos in a box in the safe. You were a child in one." She shifted, hoping the man wasn't sensitive about his birthmark. "I recognized the mark on your forehead."

Grady peered at her face and thumped the table, making her jump. "All night, I've been trying to figure out who you reminded me of. I should have recognized those eyes. You're Aki Lee's kin?"

She nodded, hoping it wasn't a mistake to reveal Granny's identity.

He sat back. "In 2145, I was eight years old and not allowed to take part in the train raid. We were betrayed. My father never discovered who the traitor was, but GreenCorps never would have caught Aki without help. She was a wily one. My father admired her and worried about filling her shoes as leader."

"That's not all," said Walker. "Hayden and I helped an old man on the train six years ago. He'd been beaten and his supplies stolen. We gave him food and water. To repay us, he revealed the location of his mountain cabin near Lake Tahoe. His name was Jim. My brother and I spent summers with him until he died two years ago. We found out his name was James Grady. A framed copy of the same picture hung on his wall."

"So. both of you have connections to the rebel's glorious past. Maybe you were drawn here for a reason," said Grady.

"So, you aren't turning me in for the reward?" Elsa preferred to be direct.

Beside her, Walker tensed, watching Grady's reaction, though the rebel leader seemed to keep his emotions close.

"We could use ten gold," said one of the two men who'd listened from bar stools.

"We're not cashing her in for any reward." Grady's voice held absolute authority. His men didn't argue. "My father's twin brother died in the same raid, leaving an infant daughter."

Elsa put her hand on her stomach as it clenched. Before she had time to ask, Grady continued. "Jim was my grandfather. My father's twin married Aki's daughter, which makes him your grandfather. Your mother was my baby cousin. We're kin."

She couldn't speak or breathe. A hole inside her she hadn't known existed filled in.

"It never occurred to me I might have relatives beyond SoCal."

Walker clasped his arm around her waist. She gazed up at him and smiled.

"The rebels could use you. We're always looking for the right kind of volunteers. Like the kind that have ties to us already or would help an injured old man."

"I'm not sure I'm ready to join." Her voice seemed calm, unruffled on the outside, but inside she quaked. This man was family. "I need to find someone who can use the key and the maps. Do the rebels have a way to get the seeds distributed and planted?"

Grady grimaced. "Not right now. One day perhaps."

"Someday never seems to come." She had difficulty keeping the bitterness from her voice.

"You can't, but do you know where we might find someone who can?" said Walker.

Elsa took his hand and squeezed.

"Western Canada. Go north. We have allies there. Part of their country used to be America, the same country that included Texas, California, Utah, and many others. Washington and Oregon joined Western Canada in 2035."

She looked at Walker, who nodded. He'd been to Canada before.

"I can send word to expect you," Grady said. "If you're serious."

"I'd appreciate that," she said. "But we have to talk. I can't decide for everyone."

She was about to suggest that they meet again tomorrow when someone kicked the door outside. Two loud thumps.

"Probably Caitlyn," said Grady. "Darren?"

Darren hopped up, knife in hand, to answer the door.

From where they sat in the main room, they heard a woman's voice.

"Can somebody take him? Is there a room we can use?"

"Bring him into the bar. His family's there."

Walker strode toward the door and Elsa followed. He crossed to the tall blonde woman who carried Hayden slung over her shoulder and took his brother's limp body.

Caitlyn stretched and let out a deep sigh.

Walker's voice shook. "Is my brother alive?"

CHAPTER 33: WALKER

June 26th, 2195, Salt Lake
Sunrise: 5:57 a.m. Sunset: 9:02 p.m.

The medic who returned with Hayden said if he makes it through the night and stays off the drugs, he might live. She destroyed the rest of his stash, at least what he had on him. He might have more somewhere else. Can't force him to stop, but maybe this time he'll realize it almost got him killed.

He's resting on a cot in her room. She'll watch him tonight. Said his heartbeat was regular again and is hopeful he'll live. She gave me a jar with cream for the cuts and scrapes on his face to keep them from scarring. She wouldn't accept payment. Grady has teased her about taking care of strays. They act like old friends, which helps me trust Grady more.

Left Hayden at rebel headquarters under Caitlyn's care for the night and returned to the house and Tatsuda. She's leaving in the morning. Hayden's weak, but can stay until we collect him. Grady wants to see the maps and key. The bunkers intrigued him. The tube was in my pocket, but I wanted to give it to Elsa first. Despite them helping Hayden and the information that Grady is supposed to be Elsa's kin, the rebels might have their own agenda. We need to learn more.

Elsa poured over the maps tonight, turning the key over and over in her hand, scared to let it go again. Asked me questions about Canada.

Walker closed his journal, his eyes bleary. He rubbed at his temples. His head still ached, but it seemed better tonight despite his exhaustion. He'd been too wound up to sleep when they'd gotten back. Elsa was curled up next to him. Her face was relaxed, softer at night than during the day. Tatsuda slept in the next room. Only a few hours remained until dawn. He put his journal away and lay down. Still unable to sleep, he replayed the conversation when they'd returned tonight. When they'd shared the maps with Tatsuda and discussed the trip north.

"Oregon isn't that far," Elsa had said.

"It might not seem that far, but getting across the border into Western Canada might be difficult. While there are bunkers in Washington and Oregon, we should aim for Vancouver, the capital. That's where decisions get made."

Thinking of the long journey, picturing routes in his head, was something he could do. No final decision had been made, but they'd be going to Canada; he could feel it.

On that thought, he drifted off to sleep.

It couldn't have been more than a few hours later when Walker woke with a feeling of unease. Elsa was restless, tossing and turning, but that was common. He put a hand on her arm and she settled. That wasn't it. Something was wrong. He listened until the silence hurt his ears. No feral cats or trains at the station.

Outside was too quiet.

This close to morning, there should be some activity. Walker dressed and packed everything except his sleeping bag, which was zipped together with Elsa's. No more sleep tonight. He glanced out the window, searching for the source of his concern.

Elsa sat bolt upright; her eyes wide.

"What's wrong?" She sniffed the air. "What's burning?"

His heart lurched. The air held a faint undercurrent of smoke. Somehow, he'd missed it.

"Pack." He ran for Tatsuda in the next room. "Something's burning. We gotta go."

The kid moved like lightning. He rolled from his blankets fully dressed and slipped on his shoes. He crammed his blanket into his pack in seconds. Elsa moved almost as quick. Her boots were on and she was closing the flap of her backpack; the tube and sleeping bags jammed inside. She grabbed her backpack and Walker collected his with a last glance at the room. They converged in the hall where the smoke hovered thicker now. He coughed, his throat raw, and covered his mouth and nose with his elbow, as did the others.

He hesitated, assessing the situation. "Stay low."

The thickest smoke rose from the basement up the staircase like a chimney. Walker shut the door at the top of the stairs, but black smoke furled underneath, filling the upstairs. They had nothing to block it to buy more time. Elsa coughed, and he frowned, motioning her lower. The usual way was obstructed. They needed another exit. He couldn't lose anyone else to fire.

The boards covering the front door were nailed shut with spikes. Walker fumbled for his hatchet. It would take too long to chop their way out, but it was better than choking from the acrid smoke or burning to death.

Tatsuda grabbed his arm. "My window."

The boy must have prepared an emergency exit. Smart. Walker's eyes streamed as the smoke worsened. They crawled to Tatsuda's room, where they flung off the loosened slats. The nails rested in the holes but were now loose.

Walker nodded. "Bags first, then you, then Elsa. I'm last."

Smoke filled the room, swirling down from the ceiling. Here too, it became hard to breathe. Walker ripped the last few boards from the edges to enlarge the opening and threw the backpacks out. They landed with a succession of thumps. The sound would draw attention to their exit, but there wasn't an alternative. He boosted Tatsuda up. The boy sat on the windowsill, then jumped, favoring his sore ankle. He landed, rolled, then dragged their bags out of the way. Elsa landed on her feet.

Walker hit the packed dirt of the yard, his head and knees jarred by the impact. For a second, he saw double. Damn concussion. He took a deep breath, exchanging looks with Elsa. She was disheveled but unhurt, and Tatsuda was brushing the dirt from his pants. Walker wasn't sure how the fire had started, but he guessed it had been deliberate. They were out and needed to figure out their next move. He turned to lead them down the alley.

"You have something of mine," said a familiar voice from the shadows.

Walker spun; his fists clenched.

Jace McCoy stepped forward in the moonlight. He snatched Tatsuda and pulled him back. He held the boy across the chest, a knife to his throat. Walker flicked a glance to Elsa, who paled.

"I want the tube back. I'm sick of chasing you across this fucking town. No more games. I paid more coin than you're worth to find you assholes. Now that I've smoked you out, you've got nowhere left to go."

The tinder-dry interior was engulfed in roaring flames illuminating the yard. The outer bricks looked solid, but the wooden interior had become an inferno. They'd gotten out just in time. Standing close to the house became unbearably hot.

"Where's my tube?" Jace took another step.

"It isn't yours." Elsa's posture stiffened, her eyes intent. "I found it in the Heap."

Walker loved when his hawk was fierce.

"The strong take what we want. That makes it mine." McCoy's hard eyes narrowed.

The knife pricked Tatsuda's throat and a red line opened beneath the knife edge. The boy whimpered; his eyes huge as he watched Elsa. A tear leaked from his eye and his lip trembled.

Elsa put her hand on Walker's tense arm. "We won't let him hurt you."

She reached into her backpack, removing the metal cylinder. Clenching her fist around it, she bit her lip. Perhaps considering. Walker held his breath while she hesitated. He didn't want her to give it up, but it wasn't his call. Its silvery-orange sheen captured the reflected light from the fire. McCoy's dark eyes fixed on the tube.

"The kid for the tube," the man said.

Walker was afraid Elsa's heart would shatter to relinquish it again.

She tossed the tube to McCoy who caught it with one hand. He shoved Tatsuda. The boy stumbled, off-balance. McCoy's smile was cruel as he pocketed the tube and flipped his knife over, the blade pointed down.

Walker's tight jaw ached. Maybe there was still a way to avoid a fight.

McCoy advanced, looking to attack. A fight then. This wasn't over.

Elsa and Tatsuda backed toward the lane while Walker unsheathed his knife.

"You didn't think you were going to get away from me, did you, sweetheart? We have unfinished business. The boys can go."

Walker ground his teeth and braced himself. This asshole wasn't taking Elsa. McCoy would have to go through him.

"Like hell," said Elsa.

When she stepped forward, Walker's heart skipped. It was challenging to protect her when she fought her own battles.

Tatsuda slipped into the darkness—smart kid. This wasn't his fight.

McCoy lunged, and Walker fought a wave of dizziness. He didn't have time to be unwell. Elsa dodged, and Walker charged forward to protect her, his knife ready. Walker pivoted but stumbled on the uneven ground. His unreliable vision made it difficult to remain steady.

Tatsuda reappeared, tripping McCoy with a slide maneuver, knocking the burly man from his feet. McCoy's knife slipped from his grasp, falling to the packed earth. Elsa grabbed the fallen blade while Tatsuda darted away on silent feet.

McCoy slid a second knife from his boot with an ugly leer. Walker became desperate to get between her and McCoy. She looked fragile compared to the muscular railroad man. Walker's hand became slippery and his knife harder to hold. He tightened his grip as the three of them circled, each looking for an advantage.

Sweat dripped down Walker's forehead, but he kept his eyes trained on McCoy. The man was agile for someone so large. He feinted toward Walker, but spun and flung himself toward Elsa. Walker stiffened when he couldn't follow the man's knife; two blades sliced through the air instead of one. His breathing hitched. He blinked to clear his double vision. He was no good to Elsa when he couldn't see.

The silver blade missed, but McCoy crashed into Elsa and he pinned her to the ground, his free hand grasping her throat. Walker lurched forward, but too late.

Each split second etched itself into his brain as he scrambled. McCoy's blade gleamed in the firelight as he stabbed Elsa's shoulder. The knife slid in deep. Blood welled, pooling around the wound. Crimson soaked her shirt as it spread. Her strangled scream echoed in the pale dawn and tears streaked her cheeks. Perhaps McCoy had aimed for her chest, but her struggles had prevented a clean stroke.

Walker shook with rage and grabbed McCoy's arm, preventing a second strike. He wrenched the man's arm behind his back, immobilizing him and freeing Elsa. With a flash of silver, Elsa plunged her knife low into her assailant's side. She stabbed his kidneys four times before McCoy went limp. Her knife aimed higher, sliding between his ribs with a whooshing sound.

Elsa collapsed.

Walker shoved McCoy away, prying him away from Elsa's sprawled form.

McCoy's face froze in a rictus of shocked pain, but he was beyond sound. A crimson bubble emerged from his mouth and popped. He didn't move.

Walker knelt by Elsa and applied pressure to her wound. His hands became slippery, covered in bright red blood. His chest constricted, making it hard to breathe, and he pushed harder. She'd collapsed after her exertions and his stomach churned with fear. He had to keep her from bleeding out. He wouldn't let her die.

"Tatsuda." The kid appeared at his side—his eyes wide. "If I give you directions, can you find the rebel headquarters? We need their medic."

The boy swallowed and nodded.

In terse words, Walker explained how to get to the alley and find the green door. "Ask for Grady, Darren, or Caitlyn. Say Jace McCoy came for the tube and Elsa's been stabbed."

Tatsuda took off running, his long hair trailing.

Walker's stomach churned. Elsa's eyes had closed, but he maintained pressure on her wound. Her eyes fluttered open.

"Did I kill him?" Her voice was weak, but she was conscious.

Walker glanced at McCoy. His face remained frozen, the blood by his mouth the same, and his eyes vacant. Walker stretched one hand, but couldn't reach into the man's pocket to retrieve the tube. He held his breath, straining for another inch, and retracted his hand when a fresh pool of blood appeared, reapplying pressure. If he had to choose the tube or Elsa, he chose her.

"You did."

"Good." She attempted a smile and his breath caught at the pain her effort caused.

"Hang on. You won't die." He hoped saying it, would make it true. Agony filled him, watching her struggle while he could do so little. His vision blurred, this time probably not related to his head injury. He wanted to hold her and tell her he loved her, that he wanted her with him always. The words lodged in his throat. He didn't want to tell her just because she was dying. He needed her to live. Help would arrive. They would have a chance at forever.

The colors of sunrise stained the sky, in stark contrast to the dark smoke pouring from the burnt wreckage. Blood covered his hands and drenched his clothes. Her skin was clammy and her lips were blue. Her pulse was weak from loss of blood and her breath labored. He cataloged everything about her condition.

"I love you," Elsa said. The distant look in her fierce eyes broke his heart.

Was she brave or giving up? Walker needed her to stay. His face froze, giving nothing away. She knew how he felt. He'd called her his other half. He didn't want her to think he'd given up and was saying goodbye if he returned the words now.

Elsa's topaz eyes looked gold, reflecting the flames. Help seemed to take an eternity while she bled on the hard ground. The sun slid above the horizon. His hands shook as he pressed. He didn't dare move or speak.

"I don't feel so good." Her voice shook and in the morning light, her skin resembled the color of milk.

His hands trembled as he held on.

Her eyes rolled back, and she lost consciousness.

His heart stopped and his breath caught in his throat. She had to hang on. He hadn't told her. Hot tears filled his eyes as he pressed her wound, still trying to staunch the flow of blood.

Darren appeared from the lane with two other men from the rebel headquarters.

"Grady sent us. We've got a cart."

Walker was having trouble paying attention to anything except Elsa, but he looked up just in time to see Grady's men toss McCoy's body into the basement inferno through the window entrance.

Tatsuda scooped their backpacks onto the wagon at the corner of the street. A mule stood connected in the traces. Darren and one of the other men lifted Elsa while Walker maintained pressure on her wound. He climbed into the cart and settled her on his lap. He watched every rise and fall of her chest as he prayed she would live.

"Let's go," Darren said. "The neighborhood has eyes."

The cart moved forward as the mule headed into town, its hooves clip-clopping through the still empty streets.

It had all gone wrong. Walker hadn't had time to tell the rebels about the tube or to have Tatsuda go through McCoy's pockets. Disposing of the body was important too. Someone would have seen what happened, but this might slow a GreenCorps investigation. The tube was better destroyed than in the hands of GreenCorps. None of that mattered now.

Would his Elsa live?

CHAPTER 34: CAITLYN PLUS ELSA AND WALKER

Caitlyn woke to a knock on her door. It took her a moment to remember she was in town and not on the farm. She rubbed her eyes and yawned as she glanced at her patient. Hayden still slept, but he no longer looked sick. She rested a hand on the boy's forehead. His temperature seemed normal. The danger from the overdose was past, but he needed to heal.

The sharp rap on her door came again, harder than before. She padded on her bare feet across the chilly floor to the door and opened a crack, just enough to see through, keeping the chain on to prevent the door from fully opening.

"What? Is it morning?" Her face split with another yawn that made her jaw creak.

Grady stood outside her door, his weathered face serious. She was surprised to see him, rather than one of his men if this was a wake-up call. Her sense of unease grew. Something was wrong.

"Can you get dressed and come down? Bring your med kit. Please."

"Who's hurt? Is it morning?" With no windows in her room, there was no way to judge the time, other than her body, which told her it was still tired.

"Sunrise was half an hour ago. I need your help again. One last favor. You've already done more than you bargained for on this trip to town, but I don't have another option."

She nodded and closed her door, dressing in a hurry. She left the boy sleeping. If he woke, the only way out was through the main room downstairs. She'd placed a glass and pitcher of water nearby if he needed a drink.

"We have a problem," said Grady when she arrived downstairs. "I need you to treat someone before you leave."

"I guessed that."

"Can the boy go to your farm to recuperate?" asked the rebel leader.

He was blunt this morning. Grady may not have slept. He looked older than usual, the lines in his face etched deeper, and his eyes bloodshot.

"Any particular reason?"

"I want him out of town and away from us. We might get some heat but will deny having seen any of them. I'll explain everything before you leave, so you aren't left in the dark about what's happening. But we have another patient who needs urgent care. My cousin."

The girl with the yellow eyes from the Wanted posters. Caitlyn had been surprised to learn Grady had additional family. As far as the world knew, he'd always been alone—though he'd once confided that he had a grown son. It may also have taken Grady by surprise to learn of the girl's connection.

"Where is she?"

"I'll take you."

Caitlyn rushed to follow.

Grady led the way to his room on the main floor behind the stairs. The girl lay on Grady's bed, her lover cradling her from behind with her head propped on his lap. He held her wounded shoulder with both hands and was covered in blood. This was Hayden's brother. She'd met them last night, though Caitlyn couldn't recall the young woman's name.

Walker looked up. "I wasn't fast enough. McCoy stabbed her but she got him. She killed him." His voice shook with emotion and tears filled his eyes.

What were they mixed up in that someone had beaten his brother half to death and attacked the girl with a knife? Grady had just met them; they weren't even rebels, but Caitlyn was willing to help anyone GreenCorps tried to bully.

The girl's skin was milky white—so translucent her veins resembled purplish-blue trails inside her arms and chest. Her lips were pale purple. She must have lost a lot of blood.

"You're going to have to let me look," Caitlyn said in a soft voice. "I can't help if I can't see how she's injured and what the blade may have hit."

Walker removed his hands and new, bright red blood bubbled to the surface of a cut in the shoulder that had a deeper well where she'd been stabbed. It didn't spurt but oozed dark reddish blood. Caitlyn grabbed a gauze pad from her bag and pressed. She pulled it away for another look. The wound was at the top of the girl's arm in the front, near her chest and shoulder. While serious, it must have missed her artery.

"It missed her brachial artery. You saved her life with your quick thinking. It's serious enough that she may have bled out without you." From the bleak expression on his face, he knew she was still in danger.

Caitlyn doused the wound with antiseptic and it bubbled and fizzed with a faint hissing sound. The girl cried out, her topaz eyes flying open. Walker smoothed her dark hair from her forehead. The big man's face was soft and his hands looked gentle.

"We're safe. You need to hold still. Caitlyn is taking care of you."

"How?" Her voice wasn't much more than a whisper.

She licked her dry lips. She needed water.

"What's your name?" said Caitlyn.

"Elsa."

"Okay, Elsa. I'm going to stitch your arm and bandage it. I need you to drink water. Small sips, but constant. Your body needs it to make fresh blood. This is going to hurt, but you're going to be okay. After I sew you up, all of you are coming to my farm to heal." The words flowed from Caitlyn's lips before she considered, but they felt right. Once she patched someone up, she had a certain responsibility for their well-being. These people needed her, and she could keep them safe.

Walker gave her a startled glance, but adjusted his partner to be closer to him.

"Why are you helping us?" Elsa's yellow eyes focused on Caitlyn. "You don't owe us anything."

The girl was direct, much like Grady.

Caitlyn bit her lip. "Someone needs to help you."

She smeared a numbing agent on Elsa's shoulder, one she'd made herself from boiled nettles. Allowing it a minute to take effect, she filled a glass of water. Walker boosted Elsa higher and took the glass while he held the gauze pad in place with his other hand. Caitlyn nodded, and he moved the pad. The wound stood out dark purple against Elsa's pale flesh and swollen. It would need to be disinfected daily. Caitlyn hoped her meager supply of antibiotics would be sufficient—the knife that had penetrated Elsa's arm may have been covered in bacteria. Infection remained a dire possibility. Caitlyn needed Grady to purchase more medicine to replenish her supply before they left.

She threaded her needle, aware that the others watched. She took a small breath and stitched; her work quick and efficient, her hand steady. The ability to focus on a wound came back to her. The last person she'd stitched had been Mathew, though he hadn't made it. He'd died later from his wounds. She didn't want to think about it and blinked away her tears.

She glanced at her patient, impressed by the way the girl remained still, though it must be painful. Elsa clamped her lips together and clenched her jaw, but the girl was tough. Her other hand was white-knuckled as she squeezed Walker's arm. She didn't flinch or cry out. Caitlyn had stitched enough people to know that wasn't common. Most called out. Many preferred to be numb from drink, which made her job easier.

After fifteen stitches, she tied off the black thread.

"I'll remove them in five to seven days. Keep it dry and try not to use your arm or it might break open. It's deep. We'll put a sling on before we leave." She tucked her suture kit away.

"Thank you," said Elsa.

Her voice sounded stronger, but she looked like a ghost.

Caitlyn cleared her throat and washed her hands in the basin, her thoughts turning to what else was necessary. She needed to report to Grady and make arrangements for what she'd need, including medicine and food for at least three more mouths.

"What is the best way to leave town?" said Walker. "The sun's up. We can't use the cover of darkness. McCoy will be missed."

"Grady will have a plan. I told him to collect my pig. My guess is he'll send us with a cart, rather than on foot. We can load up the patients and travel. Hide in plain sight. I'm just a simple farmer heading home from a supply run."

She looked at him. "If you have a change of clothes, put on something else. We can wash those at my place."

He glanced down as though he'd forgotten that he was covered in blood.

"I'm going to need your help," she said. "You're unhurt?"

He nodded. "Just headaches. I'll do whatever you need. I owe you. First for my misguided brother, and now for Elsa. Can our friend Tatsuda accompany us?"

She nodded. "Both of you can help me on my farm for a month or two. I could use the extra muscle. I didn't do this for money. It's just what I do."

* * *

Elsa's left arm ached, a fiery burning pain despite being immobilized in a sling. Her skin felt too tight, and she had no strength. She sipped water from her canteen through a long tube fashioned into a straw. She and Hayden lay shoulder to shoulder, bundled into a compartment hidden under a false floor of a wagon bed with a high-walled box for transporting livestock. She'd been assured the floor was lined so pig urine wouldn't leak into their hiding place. Caitlyn had intended to buy a pig. Her cargo leaving town had increased. It now held three piglets and four fugitives.

If Elsa had been claustrophobic, this hiding place would never have worked. Who would've guessed working the Heap would be helpful? Hayden had still been asleep when loaded into the wagon. As suspected, GreenCorps security staked out the train station in force, inspecting each car before the train left and adding extra bulls to beat the bushes and watch the departing trains. She pitied any hoppers they found today.

Grady's men reported that GreenCorps had constructed roadblocks on all roads leading out of town. Elsa had to trust their new acquaintances—difficult, but the only way to remain safe.

Walker no longer matched the description of anyone they were looking for. He'd changed his appearance by rounding his shoulders and walking with a faint limp. Grady had provided a wide-brimmed straw hat so Walker looked the part of a farmer. She'd been surprised at how different he looked.

He'd promised to open the sides of the wagon for fresh air once it was safe. Hayden woke up with a start at the worst possible time, after the wagon departed rebel headquarters but before they'd cleared a checkpoint. His eyes popped open and his breath caught. Elsa clamped her good hand over his mouth, hard enough he couldn't speak. He squirmed beneath her hand, his eyes wide.

She raised a finger to her lips and pointed upwards. Faint lines of light streamed in through the cracks, but she couldn't make out shapes beyond the slats. Anyone might be outside. Was this what it was like to be buried alive? The hidden box, a coffin for two. The compartment was stuffy and hot, though still morning. Hayden's hands rose to the rough planks, and he placed them flat above his chest, as though he wanted to shove his way out. It was a tight fit, with only four inches of extra space above their heads. At least it was long enough that her legs lay straight.

The motion of the cart made Elsa's stomach turn. She hated being unable to see outside while the wagon moved, but she didn't have a choice. She kept her hand over Hayden's mouth until his breathing slowed and he nodded, his eyes glaring. He seemed to recognize her and remember that he didn't like her. She didn't enjoy the prospect of being trapped with him for the next several hours, either. He was one of her least favorite people. He cocked his head at the sound of snuffling pigs above them. Before she whispered an explanation, the wheels ground to a halt. Her stomach lurched and her heart pounded a fast rhythm against her ribs.

"Is there a problem?" came Caitlyn's even voice. "There are GreenCorps guards everywhere."

"There's been a killing, ma'am," said a voice standing to the front left of the wagon. "We're searching for the criminals responsible."

Caitlyn gasped in horror. "That's awful."

"We're checking everyone leaving town. We have a description of the suspects."

"Of course," Caitlyn said. "Who died?"

"We're not at liberty to say. Official GreenCorps policy during an investigation. I'm going to need you to let us search your wagon. Make sure no one is hiding."

"Of course," Caitlyn said.

There was movement and a creaking sound as Walker climbed down on the right. His limping, uneven footsteps crunching on the gritty asphalt. He opened the back.

Elsa held her breath, noticing Hayden had frozen at the mention of a killing. He, too, lay stiff like a statue beside her.

"Nice piglets," came the guard's comment. "Who's the kid?"

The rebels had disguised Tatsuda by forcing him to take a bath and cut his hair. He no longer looked like a wild street kid, but a regular farm kid. Underneath the dirt, his skin was fair like Elsa's.

Tatsuda had opted to ride with the pigs rather than on the wagon seat. Three backpacks and boxes of groceries were stacked beside him. Walker's bloody clothes lay beside Elsa's feet in case they searched the bags.

"That's my farmhand."

"And the big guy? He been with you long?"

"My younger brother," Caitlyn said.

Elsa's chest tightened, hoping the story they'd concocted would be believed.

"He usually stays at home to watch the farm, but I wanted his help to select the pigs."

The gate at the rear of the wagon closed with a thud, and Walker's uneven footsteps returned to the front. The wagon dipped a little as he climbed aboard.

"Have a safe journey home," said the guard.

He must have waved them through their checkpoint as the wagon surged forward. Her stomach remained unsettled until they left town, expecting to be stopped again. Twice more she held her breath as the wagon was searched, but each time they directed the wagon to proceed. At last, they left the city. The wheels sounded different on the packed dirt than the stone or asphalt of town as she let out a sigh of relief.

Elsa fell asleep as they traveled. When she woke, they'd taken the sides off the wagon and it was late afternoon. She took a deep breath of the fresh air. Hayden, too, had fallen asleep, perhaps from the rocking motion. On her near side, high rock walls rose past where she could see. They were closer to the mountains than this morning. The cart lurched to the side, and she slid to the right as they forded a shallow stream issuing from a canyon with steep sides. Water sprayed up from the wheels, but she didn't mind. The water droplets were cooling.

It wasn't much longer before the wagon pulled into a farmyard. Everything she saw was tidy and neat. There was a barn and several animal pens on the side. She didn't recognize all the animals, but several made noises, perhaps calling for food. Clucking chickens roamed an outdoor pen enclosed by wire near the barn made from weathered gray planks.

Steps creaked above as Tatsuda opened the back and passed the boxes and bags to Walker.

"We'll get this unloaded first," Walker said, leaning down with a tired smile for Elsa by the wagon's edge.

She nodded. Her arm ached, but the pain was a small price to pay for freedom.

Caitlyn collected the piglets one at a time and carried them to a pen, depositing them over the fence. "I'll take care of the stock while you get settled." She strode out of Elsa's sight with boxes of groceries.

After they'd emptied the wagon, Walker cleared the soiled straw to the side and released the catch for the door in the wagon floor. He helped her sit up and slide out. Her legs almost gave way. She was still weak from blood loss. She looked up at him, grateful for his supporting arm. Hayden scooted over and climbed out. He looked down and avoided Walker's glare until Walker turned his back.

Elsa looked past the side of the wagon where there was a massive garden filled with new young plants, most of which she didn't recognize. Beyond them, stood a square brick house with white shutters and yellow curtains at the windows. A tabby cat trotted out from behind a building to twine around Caitlyn's legs as she came back outside.

"We're home," Caitlyn said, bending to scratch the cat behind the ears.

* * *

Walker
June 27th, 2195. Dawson's Farm, Ogden, Utah.
Sunrise: 5:57 a.m. Sunset: 9:02 p.m.

We've arrived at Caitlyn's farm. The town near here was once called Ogden. The town is long gone, but farms lie scattered on the bench between the lake and the mountains. There are no close neighbors and we are free to wander in sight of the house or into the mountains.

Caitlyn needs help with her garden, her livestock, harvesting enough food for her animals for the winter. There used to be farmhands, but they're gone. She's lived here alone since last summer when her husband died. She must have been exhausted every day from the amount of work.

Elsa, Tatsuda, and I will work the farm in exchange for her help. We arranged it on the ride from Salt Lake. Hayden may stay, he's undecided. He will be safer here than in town, with no access to drugs. He understands. It's in his eyes when we talk about our plans. Offered coin to Caitlyn after collecting my stashes in Sacramento, Reno, and Salt Lake City. She refused. Said to save it for our trip north. She let me put it in her safe, as I don't trust Hayden.

Hayden cried when he apologized to me in private tonight by the barn. First, I've seen of genuine remorse from him in a long time. Years. At last, I have hope he can recover and forgive himself. Accidents happen. I've never blamed him for my mother's death. I don't blame myself either. It was just unfortunate.

Elsa and I were invited to share Caitlyn's home, given the second bedroom in the back. Tatsuda and Hayden prefer the hay-filled loft of the barn to the hard floor of the living room. Don't blame them, but Caitlyn assured us we won't be an intrusion. Think she was lonely and truly won't mind.

Apologized to Elsa for losing the tube, for its loss in the fire with Jace. Couldn't check his body before they disposed of it. All I thought about was saving her life. Her mission had become improving lives for all those in SoCal, like Granny and her sister, or the oppressed in Texas and many others in GreenCorps controlled territory. GreenCorps holds a monopoly and an unjust stranglehold on food and water. She was on the verge of doing something great. Was obvious when she spoke of going to Canada. Her dream was destroyed. Hope we can find something else that gives her life meaning. She is meant for more than a life of obscurity and drudgery.

Walker set his journal down when Elsa entered their new room. Her color was better tonight, with pink in her cheeks. He'd been terrified of losing her. They were alone, but she checked the window and latched the door. When she turned, she held her finger to her lips. Her topaz eyes met his straight on with no guile. Her look went straight to his groin.

How he loved this woman and her straightforward manner.

She slid her hand into her pocket and produced the bunker key, holding it flat on her palm, its silver shining in the lamplight.

"Look what I found. I couldn't show you sooner. I didn't want Hayden to see."

Walker's heart quickened. Her dream wasn't dead. She must not have returned the key to the tube after showing the maps to Tatsuda before the fire. No wonder she'd been willing to give the tube to Jace. She'd kept the most valuable part on her. His heart swelled as she trusted him with knowledge of what she possessed. This woman was something else. He burned for her.

"I thought Jace had destroyed your dream." He kept his voice low.

"Our dream. We can still do this. Next year, we go," she said, her voice quiet. "I've got the real treasure."

"The maps were lost, and it'll be difficult."

Elsa tapped her temple. "We know where the bunkers are and how they're marked. We can still accomplish this."

She was right. His heart skipped a beat at her radiant smile. His hawk had a mission and come spring, they'd fly from here, together.

EPILOGUE

A loud knock at the hotel room door summoned Jaxon McCoy from a deep sleep. Last night, he'd had too much to drink with the boys from the station. He'd spent the next several hours with his mistress before passing out. She wasn't as pretty as his wife, but she was sweet, soft-spoken, and hadn't woken him when she left. Glancing outside, he squinted at the bright sun and grimaced. He'd lost track of time and missed his meeting with his brother this morning. He might still have time to catch the early afternoon train to Denver with Jace as planned, but he'd have to hurry.

Jaxon dressed and strode to the station, skipping breakfast. It was almost noon, but he wasn't hungry. The sun seemed too bright overhead and scorching hot already. Dust flew at his brisk steps. There was no sign of his older brother behind the station. He entered the station office, and the buzz of voices stopped. He became uncomfortable at the silence.

The head of security stepped forward.

"Mr. McCoy, I'm afraid we have unpleasant news," said the officer in charge.

"Do you have a message from Jace? We were supposed to meet."

The thin man in his black uniform with green trim shook his head. "It's your brother, sir." The man wrung his hands.

"Where's Jace?" Jaxon turned, looking around the office. "He's never late. Did he leave for Denver already?"

"He isn't late, sir. I'm sorry to have to be the one to tell you, but they murdered him early this morning."

Jaxon took a step back as though someone had punched him. He examined the man's face to be sure he hadn't misunderstood. The man's voice and hands shook and his face glistened with sweat. It had to be true.

"Who did this? Who killed my brother?" Jaxon snarled.

The man before him winced. "The girl from the posters and her boyfriend. We've got the city locked down. We'll find them. Should we increase the reward for her capture?"

Elsa was nothing but trouble. His jaw ached as he clenched his teeth together. He wished he'd let her starve to death. "Double it. Where did it happen?"

The man started to give directions, but Jaxon stepped closer and interrupted. "Take me there." His muscles quivered with pent-up rage. He wanted to hit something. Someone. Most of all, Elsa.

They walked a couple of blocks to where the remains of a house smoldered. The roof was gone, and the inside gutted, leaving a deep hole. Soot-stained bricks formed partial walls as the contents leaked pale plumes into the air. Everything reeked of smoke, reminding Jaxon of SoCal. He needed to move out of that cesspool. He might even bring his family. Avery was pregnant again. Maybe this time she'd have a son instead of another worthless girl.

"The girl and her friends stayed in this derelict house."

Jaxon paced the site looking for clues or something that would help him understand. He winced. A pool of blood had soaked into the packed earth of the backyard, a rusty stain.

"Neighbors saw them fighting. That's not all your brother's blood. He stabbed the girl, but she killed him, and then they threw his body into the fire to dispose of the evidence. We weren't able to recover his remains." The man glanced at the ashes in the burnt basement. "With that kind of blood loss, she might die too."

Jaxon's breath became rapid and his face burned. It was challenging to see straight through the crimson fog that clouded his vision. He clenched his fists until they ached. He kicked the ground and his gaze followed the clump of dirt as it flew through the air. A glint of silver in the trampled dirt and scraggly weeds caught his eye. He stalked over and picked it up, turning it over in his hands. It had to be the silver tube Jace had tried to buy.

Jaxon ground down again, his molars aching.

"Elsa. I'll fucking kill her." He shoved the tube into his pocket and marched toward the train station to make arrangements to travel to Denver. This wasn't over. The ungrateful bitch was going to pay.

ACKNOWLEDGMENTS

I wouldn't be me, if my acknowledgments didn't start with a story.

When my sister and I were young, we traveled (a two-day road trip) with our parents to Utah every year to see our grandparents. My parents divorced when I was eight and we stayed with my mom's parents, the Calls. For a couple of precious days and nights, my sister and I would also stay with our Jennings grandparents—without a parent. This changed the dynamic.

Our grandparents dropped everything else to visit. We would be treated like special company and served cold drinks in tall stained-glass glasses heaped with ice. We'd sit on the patio and talk for hours. We were the guests of honor and they wanted to hear everything about our lives.

Once I turned thirteen, my grandma would take me downstairs and load a huge bag of books for me to take home—a summer-to-summer loan. That's how I first read The Thorn Birds, Evergreen, the Shell Seekers, Kane and Abel, Roots, and Christy. She also sent some spicier selections that I hid from my mom. The next summer, I'd return the books, we'd discuss them, and she'd make a new set. Eventually, she gave me copies of the ones I wanted every year.

My favorite part of our visit was when my grandparents would tell stories about their youth or from the early days of their marriage. My

Grandma Carrie told about growing up in Alberta with her hoard of rodeo-riding brothers and about her sisters. I heard about when she had scarlet fever and was quarantined alone in the attic for several weeks, which is when she learned to love reading. Through their stories, my grandparents became people, not just Grandma and Grandpa.

The original kernel of Switching Tracks, the inspiration, came from listening to my Grandpa Rollen's stories of the Great Depression. His family lost their farm in Kansas, loaded up their car, Grapes-of-Wrath-style, and moved to Utah to live with cousins. My grandfather and one of his brothers were young men and didn't want to live off charity. They soon left, riding the rails to California, searching for work so they could send back their wages.

Also, a shout out to my Grandma Call, for being smart and tough. I learned recently that she once wanted to be a writer. She was the inspiration behind Granny Lee. She grew up on a ranch in Wyoming with seven brothers and lived through the Depression. At 80, she was shoveling snow off roofs and walkways for other people (which is a whole other story). When a freak tornado came off the Great Salt Lake and ripped the roof off half of her house, she stayed inside to keep the water out of her living room. She's 95 and still a force.

My Grandpa Call was a born entertainer, often reciting poems and stories learned by heart long ago. I practiced several of them when I was young, especially my favorite, about two frogs who fell into a deep bowl. Thank you to all of my grandparents for sharing their stories.

In order to write Switching Tracks, I had to learn about trains. They were something I knew little about, though I'd become familiar with the crash of the four o'clock train during a year-long bout of insomnia. So, I put a post on Facebook, asking for help.

Three main sources appeared.

The first is Vancouver author, Owen Laukkanen, who loves trains. He sent me to Reddit and provided info to connect on Instagram with a couple of his friends that are modern-day train hoppers. I would also like to thank foamers and hoppers everywhere for their accounts on Reddit that helped me to write the train scenes.

The second was my cousin-by-marriage, Eric McGovern, an engineer who drives trains for a living. He patiently answered my questions and didn't seem to mind when his answers spawned a new round of questions. His information was invaluable.

The third is a small-world coincidence that I like. A former colleague replied that her son, Mathew loves trains, works for the railroad, and volunteers at a railroad museum. She was sure he'd be happy to talk to me. So, Train Mathew and I emailed back and forth about two dozen times. He related stories about hoppers and working train security, about bodies he'd found, and the dangers of hopping. Soon after we finished emailing, I saw a picture that his mother posted on Facebook… Train Mathew was someone I know from my karate class and a long-time friend of my Sensei. Train Mathew was Karate Mat. In honor of his contributions, I named a minor character after him. Thank you, Mathew Kreiser.

As always, I want to acknowledge the contributions of my beta readers for Switching Tracks: D. Lambert, Lynette Van Steinberg, and Ben Brockway. Thank you as well to my critique partner and editor extraordinaire, Tracy Thillmann. She is amazing. I also want to thank my early readers, my mom, Julie Beyea, and Eileen Cook for taking the time to read Switching Tracks in 2021, when I first wrote the story.

A huge thank you to the Black Rose authors, which includes Karen K. Brees, Dave Buzan, K.J. Fieler, Carolyn Geduld, Gary Gerlacher, Cam Torrens, and all the others who have used their precious time to read and review Switching Tracks: Out of the Trash. Your positive words make me love my story anew. Along the way, some of these writers have become friends. Also, thanks to everyone at BRW for their help and support. The team is incredible.

Thank you also to authors Angera Allen, Michele Amitrani, and the BRW Book Club. A special thank you to all my friends, co-workers, and readers everywhere. I wouldn't be here without you.

As always, I've saved my family for last because they are the most important. Thank you to my wonderful and patient husband Rob, who is better than any book boyfriend. Thank you to my daughters Laurel and Hayley, Kayla, my mom, my sister, and my cousins who have supported this crazy writing thing I'm doing, and to all the rest for buying my books.

In case you can't wait for
The Long Haul: Pursuit of Hope by Lena Gibson,
keep reading for a sneak peek.

TRAIN HOPPERS – TWO

THE LONG HAUL

PURSUIT OF HOPE

Chapter 1: Elsa plus Walker

There used to be a city here. Several in fact. They'd hugged the edge of the mountains north and south of Salt Lake City, with a combined population of over two million. While Elsa could imagine brick buildings and shops, she couldn't fathom the idea of so many people. With seventy thousand inhabitants, Utah was one of the most populated areas remaining in what had once been America.

Elsa had once seen a map from the early twenty-first century, cities and towns bleeding together in continuous dots. Nothing like Salt Lake City and the outlying scattered farms of the present. For all the space in this sparse land, there were too many people on this particular farm.

At least one too many.

The five occupants tripped over each other daily; everyone was used to being solitary. Elsa glanced toward the house, relieved for the current peace outdoors. Walker and Hayden—brothers by choice who'd traveled together for eight years—weren't on the best of terms, and Elsa would rather be on the road than stuck here impotent to move forward with her plans. She clenched her jaw. Everyone might get along better without so much time in a confined space, but it wasn't safe to wander off the Dawson farm.

Elsa scanned the landscape for the hundredth time today. The limitless sky seemed immense and made her skin crawl. The plains were exposed with nowhere to hide. She maintained her guard and always worked with her back to the solid mountain range which stood like a fortress guarding that approach, allowing her to focus westward. The idea that she might be taken by GreenCorps and sent south haunted her daylight hours. Without the view, she felt trapped, so she always volunteered for outdoor chores.

She crunched a chunk of dry soil that turned to powder between her dusty hands and stood to stretch the cramped muscles in her back. Rotating her sore shoulder, she grimaced at the lingering pain from her fight with Jace. Taking a break from gardening, she stared at the empty countryside with a sigh. Everywhere that wasn't irrigated was parched, dry, and dull—the dust motes floating in the air shimmering in the intense afternoon sun. Too much like SoCal, but brown instead of gray. She'd escaped the Heap, but she couldn't escape the heat. On the other hand, working with her hands and growing things instead of scavenging in old trash seemed worthwhile. She loved the idea of helping to grow their food.

Beyond Caitlyn's farmyard with its barn, corral, and pigpen, the neighboring farms spread out—too distant to see with the naked eye. Solitude might be an illusion, but so far nobody had reported their presence to the authorities. If discovered, they'd be back on the run, or worse, incarcerated. Even gardening, Elsa couldn't let her guard down.

Despite the sun's glare and baked land, it would be peaceful here if it wasn't for Hayden. She glanced over her shoulder toward the house where he'd gone to find food two hours ago. What was taking him so long? At least she'd long since hidden her valuables, keeping the most important item on her person. Trying to put Hayden from her mind, she searched once more for signs of travelers. Other than the crowded farm, they seemed alone.

Swaths of building-sized mounds adorned the horizon. The earth's way of disguising the past to make way for the present. Remains of the previous civilization had been buried underground or repurposed as part of new structures.

Utah wasn't like SoCal, where Elsa had grown up in an endless garbage heap where women and children toiled to scavenge reusable items from trash to scrape out a living. Men worked the scrapyards, or if they were lucky, joined GreenCorps. Here there were options, possibilities. A chance to fight for a better life where everyone would have freedom to move and afford adequate food. She just needed to get back on the road and get on with her mission. She'd found a purpose, and waiting here until she withered wasn't it. Her gut told her she should leave soon. They'd been here almost two months; she was inclined to listen.

Maybe after her mission to the north, she should join the rebels in their canyon strongholds. She sighed. How much longer until she could travel? What if they got stuck here for the winter? She'd go stir-crazy trapped for months in such close quarters. She and Walker should go. The idea made her stand straighter. Heading out was the beginning of making a difference.

"Want help with the wheelbarrow?" Walker's voice interrupted her thoughts.

Elsa smiled, her heart fluttering as he approached; she never tired of his lopsided smile and warm gray eyes. She didn't need physical help with gardening anymore—he just liked to look after her. "It's almost full, but I can take it to the compost. My shoulder's better. Good as new." She lifted her arms above her head as proof. "It's healed. Really." It ached at times, the odd twinge while working the farm, but she kept that to herself.

Walker raised an eyebrow. "I got it."

For the first weeks after her knife wound, she'd needed Walker's help to get dressed, washing dishes, and pretty much everything. He'd coddled her, which had been a novel experience. It hadn't been easy to learn to garden one-handed, but she'd insisted on doing her share from the first day. Caitlyn had taken them into her home, stitched Elsa's stab wound, and paid for the expensive antibiotics.

As soon as she was able, Elsa insisted she be put on the rotation for farm duties. Elsa didn't like owing anyone.

"You push too hard." Walker's gray eyes twinkled as he ran a hand through his wavy brown hair, smudging his cheek with dirt from his leather work glove, which made her grin.

Squinting, she passed him her canteen and pulled up her Uvee goggles. She'd taken them off when she'd been weeding in the shade. There wasn't a lot of shade, except where Caitlyn's late husband had planted and cared for a dozen trees near the house. Now the aspen grove had grown large enough to sit under. Perfect in the afternoon as a respite from the mid-August sun. Maybe a brief rest wouldn't hurt.

This part of Utah wasn't full desert, but dry enough that water was a limiting factor on this bench of farmland. The hot air sucked all the moisture and left her skin looking like one of the numerous small lizards that skittered among the rocks. Taking back the canteen, she took a long pull. Even warm, it was refreshing. It took getting used to, but Caitlyn's well was deep and Elsa could drink as much as she wanted. Best of all, the water was free.

"Caitlyn back yet from her rounds? She's been out all afternoon." Elsa didn't hide the worry in her voice. She didn't keep secrets from Walker.

"Not yet, but she's safe; this is her land. Want to walk the fences with me tomorrow with her repair list? Take a picnic lunch?" Walker raised an eyebrow.

She grinned in reply and shook her head in mock dismay. "The perimeter is a long walk. It might take all day." Warmth surged inside that she had someone who found time for just the two of them.

Walker winked and hoisted the overflowing wheelbarrow with ease. She kissed him, leaning into his tall, muscular frame. He dropped the handles to return the kiss, one arm wrapped around her waist. Every touch, every kiss, left her wanting more.

It didn't hurt that he was tall and strong, and his touch sparked electricity between them. His strength made her feel safe, like she didn't have to be the only strong one. He'd rescued her from being beaten to death and cared for her when she'd been sick. It hadn't been easy, learning to depend on someone else, to trust them, but he'd earned it.

"You two sicken me," Hayden sneered, his pinched features set in a scowl as he trudged past.

Elsa's hackles rose at his remarks. If Caitlyn or Tatsuda had made the same remark, it would've been teasing, but Hayden's hostility had worsened. Elsa had tried being nice. She'd tried ignoring him. Other times, she'd been confrontational, and she wasn't proud of those moments. She'd resolved to do better.

His left arm remained in a plaster cast and would for another week or two. The same night Elsa had been stabbed, Hayden had been beaten and left for dead. If she hadn't interrupted, he'd have been killed. Not that he seemed grateful. She grit her teeth but stepped back from his brother. Hayden's broken arm was his sole remaining visible wound, but his bitter tone made it clear he still struggled with other demons.

She clamped her lips tight to keep her mouth under control, though she'd rather speak her mind. It was difficult to pretend she'd forgiven him for attacking Walker and her Granny. It was equally difficult to forgive Hayden for stealing the tube with their best chance of making a better life for everyone. At least she'd saved the key. She was careful not to look at it or touch it when he was nearby. He didn't know that it still existed.

"Did you collect the eggs and feed the scraps to the pigs?" Elsa bit her sharp tongue. That's all Caitlyn had asked him to complete before she'd gone to inspect the fences and make note of necessary repairs.

"Nope." He didn't turn around.

She shouldn't bother, but his idleness got under her skin. Her whole life she'd worked herself to the bone to survive. Farm work and gardening seemed easy by comparison, especially with so many available hands.

Walker grimaced, lifting the wheelbarrow again. "I'll be back with this in a few. Try not to injure one another." He lowered his voice. "If you need me, just yell."

Retreat was a smart option. He didn't like it when she and his brother fought, but he'd have her back if the situation worsened.

Hayden opened the rope hammock where it swung between two of the larger trees at the edge of the garden and climbed in. He stretched out in the shade with an exaggerated sigh. "I'm a prisoner. Prisoners don't work. Plus, I'm injured." He closed his eyes and folded his hands across his chest. It was all she could do not to kick his ass. She pictured his fall to the hard-packed ground with satisfaction.

Elsa's jaw ached, and she turned away so she didn't have to deal with his indolence. Prisoners worked plenty. She'd been born a prisoner and had always worked. He was trying to bait her. Again. He insisted he wasn't here willingly because he'd been unconscious when they'd been smuggled out of the city. If they'd left him behind, he might have died of his injuries, or died of another overdose. He was free because they'd brought him. Hayden was in debt to Caitlyn as much as they were, he just didn't seem to notice—or care.

Elsa and Tatsuda had weeded the extensive vegetable garden this morning, picked raspberries, and fed the chickens. While they'd done this, Hayden slept in. They'd watered the goats, pigs, sheep, and the mule and herded all but the pigs out to pasture. Walker had organized the tools in the barn and repaired the pigpen. Earlier this week Walker had cut and gathered hay with Caitlyn and split firewood for the cookstove. Everyone worked hard all day, pitching in with whatever was needed. Except for Hayden, who lounged in the shade.

While Hayden had been sick from withdrawal, nobody had expected him to contribute. Now that he was clear-headed, he pouted and sulked, saying he wanted to leave. It was a shame he hadn't followed through. But he wanted Walker to leave with him, to go back to their old life as vagabond train hoppers.

Walker wouldn't, not without Elsa and not knowing that there was something he could do to better the world. That battle was one Hayden always lost. One of these days, she and Walker expected to wake up and discover Hayden had given up and disappeared. She wished him good riddance.

Tatsuda, who'd been in the house, emerged with a basket; probably going to collect the eggs. He seemed happy to try his hand at something besides pick-pocketing. Although, a few times they'd discovered any odds and ends that went missing were in his possession—spoons, spools of thread, or the set of folding scissors Caitlyn left on her table.

He was like a crow, forever collecting shiny things. He returned everything he was asked for with a shrug. Elsa smiled as the scamp came outside. He probably had a stash of items not yet missed that kept him satisfied. Maybe she should ask him to empty his pockets every evening before bed, as she felt responsible for his good behavior.

Walker returned with the now empty wheelbarrow, and they loaded another gigantic pile of weeds and garden trimmings. This load could feed the goats. Elsa took another drink from her canteen and she choked as her breath caught when a figure came into view.

Her shoulders relaxed when it was only Caitlyn who strode into the farmyard, headed for the well. Caitlyn drew a bucket of water and drank with the communal cup left nearby and wiped the back of her hand across her mouth, sighing with satisfaction.

Their host's hair was blonder now than when they'd met—bleached by the summer sun—and wisps had escaped from her long braid. Despite her ever-present straw hat, her fair skin was covered in freckles. Caitlyn had the build and the kind of beauty that stopped men in their tracks. Elsa had become more confident in her own skin the past few months, but was still a little envious. Luckily, Walker appreciated her slim build, sharp tongue, and loved her how she was.

"Cloud of dust on the horizon. Rider headed this way." Caitlyn was red-cheeked as she joined the group beside the garden and she panted to catch her breath. "I ran to get back first."

Elsa nodded and then she, Tatsuda, and Walker hurried to the hidden room behind the feed locker in the barn. Despite her calm demeanour, her heart hammered—any rider was an unknown. Walker had built the hiding place the first week of their stay. It was shallow, but wide enough for all of them to stand or sit on the bench against the wall. They barred it from their side, remaining invisible from inside the barn.

Hayden stayed behind. He didn't like the enclosed space or being so close to Elsa.

His voice carried on the late afternoon breeze as he talked to Caitlyn.

"Let's see what they want," Hayden said. "Might not be anyone that has anything to do with me." He yawned. "I'm not a wanted criminal, unlike some." His cutting tone, once more, directed at Elsa—who had the staggering sum of ten gold on her head. Maybe more, as rumor had it that with Jace's murder, the reward had doubled.

Elsa kept her mouth shut. Caitlyn could decide how to handle Hayden. It was her farm, and the former rebel was in charge. More words were exchanged, but Elsa couldn't hear them.

They waited in their dusty hiding spot for a stifling hour, sweat pooling between Elsa's breasts and running down her back, making it itchy. She tried to distract herself from the discomfort and her mind wandered back over the last few months and how she'd gotten here, hiding in a sweltering secret room.

Back in the SoCal work camp where she'd been born, Elsa had found buried treasure in the Heap, treasure that had brought her here to Caitlyn's farm in a roundabout way. Last spring, scavenging the Heap for trash to trade for subsistence rations, she'd unearthed a metal tube. Inside had been two-hundred-year-old maps and a key.

After a vicious beating by Jace McCoy, the man she'd later killed, she'd left SoCal by hopping a train with Walker and followed a map to a pre-Collapse bunker filled with seeds of edible plants and tree varieties long thought extinct—seeds that weren't sterile terminator seeds like those purchased from GreenCorps. She hoped to take the key north and find someone to help grow and distribute the seeds. With those future crops, they could supply food for the masses and break the GreenCorps monopoly and their stranglehold on the population.

Though the maps had been destroyed with Jace's body after his death, she remembered the bunker locations and was confident she could find them, as she would recognize the marker near the entrance. Her deepest secret was possession of the key.

She clutched the heavy metal, with its curves and jagged edges, around her neck. It was proof that a better life could exist. It just might take some work. No longer lost in thought, cooler air rushed in when Caitlyn knocked to retrieve them and Walker opened the door.

"Come on out. Just a messenger. There's a note from Grady for Elsa."

Elsa's heart quickened, and Walker squeezed her hand. She'd discovered she had long-lost family out here in the wide world, not just her great-grandmother, sister, and nieces in SoCal. Ryan Grady—the leader of the rebels that resisted GreenCorps, the corporation that controlled food, water, and the railroad—was her great-uncle. He wouldn't risk a message without good reason. It couldn't be good news. Her stomach lurched as confirmation that something was about to change.

They returned to the house, passing Hayden still slouched in the hammock, his eyes closed. The farmyard was deserted, the horse and rider gone, but inside a brown envelope lay on the table. Elsa washed her hands at the kitchen sink with a small hand pump, dried them, and picked up the letter. She turned it over in her hands. There was no name. She raised an eyebrow in Caitlyn's direction.

"That's it. The rider referred to you as Grady's niece."

Elsa slid out the letter on thick homemade paper. Her hands trembled as she read the contents. The message was brief, and she read it twice. The first time it was difficult to comprehend the words. Her skin became clammy, and she shivered, her skin breaking out in gooseflesh. One hand rose to cover her mouth, like she was pressing her emotions inward. The news wasn't unexpected, nevertheless; it left her shaken. Despite her chill, her face flushed, and the room spun. The dizziness passed. She got to the end the second time and her eyes swam with tears.

My dearest niece,

I hate to be the bearer of bad news, but find I must be. Earlier this summer, I sent a note to your great-grandmother to let her know you are

well. Your sister replied that Granny passed soon after your departure.
She urges you to continue your travels. It isn't necessary for you to return
and she sends her love.

Her words cannot be a surprise, as travel is difficult and we live in
dangerous times.

I'm sure this isn't easy to hear. Take care of yourself. If you need
anything, don't hesitate to ask. I make no promises, but will do what is
in my power to assist your endeavors.

Uncle Ryan

P.S. I also sent a letter to my friends in the north. They are interested
in your project and will render assistance if you reach them in person and
provide proof of your commitment.

In the letter, Grady used no names other than his own, but just his
first name and not the name the world knew him by. He gave no
specifics or details. Should the wrong eyes see this innocuous letter, it
would raise few alarms. "Proof" meant the seed packets she carried
from the bunker she and Walker had visited in Davis, California. They
were still tucked safely in her backpack. Or would she need additional
proof?

She passed the letter to Walker, her hands still shaking. He scanned
it, giving her a look of concern. A tight band constricted her chest even
when Walker pulled her into a hug. Her Granny had died while she was
gone. Abandoned. It wasn't Elsa's fault; her great-grandmother had
been over a hundred years old, but Elsa hadn't said goodbye to the
woman who'd raised her and taught her how to survive. A lump of
sorrow persisted, leaving her hollow. Safe in Walker's arms, her tears
overflowed.

"That isn't all," said Caitlyn with a gentle voice from where she
stood by the stove feeding wood to the fire. "Grady's sending someone
here to stay. He should be here in a few days. Mason's coming from

Texas and needs somewhere to lie low for a couple of months. He can sleep in the barn with the boys."

Something about her tone told Elsa that their host was unimpressed.

* * *

Walker
August 8th, 2195. Dawson's Farm, Utah.
Sunrise: 6:30 a.m. Sunset, 8:35 p.m.

Elsa, Tatsuda, and I have worked on Caitlyn's farm for almost two months while she's healed. Didn't know if I'd take to the settled life, but I've enjoyed staying in one place, even if it isn't the cabin. One day, I hope Elsa and I can have a place like this where we can work together, grow our own food, and live our lives free of GreenCorps. It's been easy to pretend they don't exist, but the messenger today was a reminder of the outside world.

Hayden is a lazy ass and a jealous, petty person. Don't know how I didn't see it before. Guess I blamed the drugs, not him. He's been clean six weeks since the overdose in Salt Lake. Thought he'd be better by now, more helpful; which is why I'm giving him a chance to redeem himself, but he hasn't done his part. He needs to accept Elsa and that our lives have changed, but he's worse. Makes me want to shake some sense into him.

I don't trust him in the outside world because he's prone to relapse. I've seen it before. Despite his complaints and negative attitude, he's stayed. For now. But I'm afraid it's just a matter of time before he does something stupid. We watch him closely and I'm prepared to make him leave if he puts us in danger. That time is approaching.

We agreed to stay on the farm for our sakes, as well as Caitlyn's, but Hayden's been sneaking off at night. At least twice this week. Tatsuda came to me. Thought I should know. Hayden thinks I don't know about his late-night disappearances. Asked Tatsuda if he could follow next time without being seen. The kid looked at me with an expression that said it all. Next time Hayden disappears, he'll have a silent shadow. When we know what he's doing, we can determine if he'll bring trouble to the farm. That wouldn't be fair to Caitlyn. We already owe a debt to both Caitlyn and the rebels that we cannot repay.

CHAPTER 2: ELSA PLUS CAITLYN

The merciless yellow sun beat down on Elsa and Walker as they walked the extensive fence line, keeping a lookout. The other buildings were beyond the horizon, the flat land empty. Fat brown grasshoppers sprang from near Elsa's feet at every step through the thin golden grass as if they could escape. Her straw hat protected her face from the bright sun and the Uvee light. She breathed a sigh of relief that so far, all was quiet. They turned onto the third edge, closest to the mountains, where they had the least chance of being seen.

It also had a long narrow patch of shade running along the cliff face.

Her shoulders loosened, feeling the solid mass of the mountain close at her back, while the prickling possibility of being watched faded. On the plains, her head had been on a swivel all day.

"This looks like a good place for lunch." Elsa pushed her goggles up after stepping out of the sun's glare. Walker dropped his pack from his back, leaning it against the orange-colored stone face of the mountain. Soon the sun would clear the mountains and there'd be no refuge until the sun went down and the land cooled—it would be midnight or later.

Sweat trickled down Elsa's back but evaporated before it dampened her clothes. SoCal had never been this hot. Plus, most of her days had been underground in the scavenging tunnels, without the direct sunlight, so while she liked the fresh air, she hadn't gotten used to the open expanse.

A canyon mouth with tumbled broken stone, greenery, and a rushing creek ran east to west a few hundred yards beyond their position. The sound of the moving water was soothing. One of these days, Elsa wanted to explore the canyon, though she hadn't yet found the time. Helping on the farm kept her days busy. Today was as good as a vacation, despite their assigned rounds and their vigilant watch for unexpected visitors.

Elsa slung off her daypack, removing a folded blanket and the picnic lunch Caitlyn had provided. It was still hard for Elsa to believe the amount and quality of the food that she had access to now that she'd left home. On Caitlyn's farm, there were fresh greens and new vegetables from the garden, fresh berries, eggs, and milk. Her "wealth" was because of the proximity to the black market in Salt Lake City—the only place a limited selection of non-GreenCorps seeds existed.

Caitlyn had taught her to bake biscuits and bread, though their supply of flour was low. Elsa had grown up on processed protein bars, oatmeal, and a smattering of dried fruit. All food in SoCal had to be purchased through the GreenCorps stores. Eating had been necessary, but monotonous. Now every meal was a feast.

Having choices and fresh food was one thing that felt almost unreal, like living in a dream. Spreading the blanket, she kicked off her boots, slid off her socks, and wiggled her toes. She relished the feel of bare feet.

"Food first?" Walker sat on the blanket next to her. Emulating her, he tossed his hat aside and kicked off his boots.

Elsa's answer was to pull off her shirt, slide closer to him, and tug his head down to hers so she could kiss him the way she wanted. While they had a private bedroom at Caitlyn's, the walls were thin and their host was close by. It didn't stop them from having sex, but were aware of their surroundings and kept quiet. He responded by pressing her against the blanket, pinning her with his solid weight.

She gasped when his iron-like arms raised her arms over her head and held them with one hand. His intent look made her core tighten. He gazed at her, his gray eyes locked on her topaz ones, a crooked grin on his face. Reaching over his shoulder, he tugged his shirt over his head and threw it toward the packs.

"I like when you're eager." His mouth reclaimed hers.

When they were both breathless with tingling lips, they removed the rest of their clothes. Despite her eagerness, she didn't rush. Making love with Walker was worth being patient. He was a walking contradiction. He was fast and strong, but his caresses were as gentle as a kitten. His voice out in the world was loud, but his tender whispers were for her ears alone. Other words of love, she interpreted from his breath and his touch against her skin.

The crazier for him she became, the slower and more patient he became. Before long, they were tangled and naked, taking turns controlling the pace. He took her apart and wrecked her with desire before she turned it about and did the same for him. When at last she shuddered to her climax, he came too. There was nothing about Walker she didn't appreciate. To her, he was love.

It was dangerous to lie naked and unprotected in the harsh sun, but she enjoyed the feeling of bliss and the breeze on her bare skin for as long as she dared. Walker traced circles on her back and touched the bones of her spine—as though counting. When he finished, he pressed a kiss to the nape of her neck. She sighed, turned over, and covered herself before her skin burned.

While they dressed, they talked about the farm.

"It isn't my home, like the cabin, but it feels like a home. I can see why Caitlyn loves it there." Walker leaned on his pack and drank from his canteen, his muscles glistening.

"I think she really only loves the animals," said Elsa. "Her face changes when she's caring for them. It's too bad she doesn't have children." She blushed, recalling Caitlyn's frank assessment that Elsa and Walker needed to take precautions if they didn't want to start a family right now. Caitlyn had given her an injection that would act as birth control for at least a year. Though Elsa and Walker had left the cabin at Lake Tahoe behind, in her temporary stay it had felt like home, though she'd known it was temporary. Maybe someday they could go back. If they had children in the future, that would be the perfect place to raise them.

"Maybe someday," said Walker, his words echoing her thoughts. "She's still young enough. She's only about thirty. Think she married young. She mentioned the other day that her Mathew's been dead almost exactly a year."

Elsa's throat tightened. Losing Walker would be more than she could bear.

"She cashed out from the rebels and left them early last fall. Used her back pay and her husband's death fee to buy stock and winter supplies on the black market in Salt Lake. Got some garden seeds that would regrow. Said she'd lost her heart for fighting and just wanted to go home." Walker was good at finding things out without being intrusive.

If Elsa was alone, where would she go? She couldn't go back to SoCal, even if she wanted to. With Granny dead, the reason for returning had diminished. Her sister and her nieces were there, but with Jaxon running their lives, Elsa couldn't return. Walker was her home. Without him, she wouldn't belong anywhere.

Not wanting to dwell on depressing what if's, she shoved the thought away, rolled over and grabbed the remainder of the lunch. Wincing, she rotated her arm at a twinge as she hefted the pack closer. Her mouth watered as she unpacked ham sandwiches on homemade bread and baby carrots—ones she'd harvested yesterday. She dug deeper for the container of bright red tomato slices. It was still hard to get over the vibrant colors of food.

"How's your shoulder?" Walker sat up and kissed the top of it, smoothing her tousled hair from her face with a small smile.

"It still hurts sometimes," she said as he traced the puckered scar where Jace's knife had penetrated. "Not often. I try to be careful, but it must be almost better because I keep forgetting." She tried not to think about Jace McCoy or the fact that she'd killed him.

It had been self-defense, a kill-or-be-killed situation, and he'd been a despicable person, but she hadn't liked to do it. He'd been someone's brother, someone's son. There might be people out in the world who missed him, even if he'd been cruel and hard. She pushed the thoughts deep down again, not wanting the memories to taint the pleasant day. Jace was gone and he couldn't hurt her anymore.

* * *

August 9th, 2195
Dearest Mathew,

I haven't written to you since the group came to the farm to stay. Maybe I've been embarrassed to write to my dead husband in front of them, but tonight I don't care. It's been nice to have companionship and to share the workload. Elsa and Walker have made themselves indispensable, and while Tatsuda is quiet, he's one of the most likable people I've met. I can't help but laugh at his sly humor. He reminds me of your younger brother, the one who joined the Saints, not the rebels.

Most of my guests have been helpful with the garden and the animals. Hayden's another story. That kid is trouble with a capital T, more like your other brother John than is good for him. I'd like to believe the best of him, but I don't think he's been clean long enough to walk away from temptation. One chance to get high, and he'll take it.

While Elsa and Walker have become friends and Tatsuda's a good kid, they don't belong here and will move on. It might not be this summer, and I'd welcome them over the winter, but at some point they're leaving. It will go back to being too quiet here. I've been thinking about what to do after they go.

As much as I enjoy caring for the animals, I'm not meant for a solitary life. I'm also not ready to rejoin the rebels and watch idealistic young men and women take too many risks and get hurt, then expect me to patch them up. But I might consider what Grady has for me in Salt Lake City as part of his inner circle.

I can't take another winter here alone.

I miss you every day.

Your Caitlyn

CHAPTER 3: GINGER

Ginger found it hard to contain her upwelling of giddiness as she dressed. Tomorrow, she started her apprenticeship at GreenCorps publishing. She'd always been interested in books and reading, and now she'd have a chance to learn about publishing. It would also be a taste of freedom.

Twirling, she spun toward the enormous windows and the bright blue summer sky that surrounded her fourth-story corner room. There wasn't a cloud in sight. A perfect day for a walk by the lake. Her bubble of excitement popped, and she sighed. If only.

The sprawling estate below held extensive grounds with bountiful gardens and lush green lawns surrounded by walls to keep the peasants out. She'd explored every hidden nook on the grounds as a child, and a handful of times since, and there were never surprises. She'd smelled the flowers and tasted the fruit. Being supervised everywhere outside her rooms removed the flavor, and no matter how many times she sat on the velvety grass, the expansive walls always blocked her view of what lay beyond.

At least her room was high enough that she could see beyond the massive walls, and her gaze wandered to the more distant view. The rugged mountains that ringed Denver were craggy and tipped with snow, even now in August. They protected the city like a fortress—or like a prison. She sighed again. She'd been nowhere else. Even excursions into town or the lakeshore had been rare.

Footsteps on the stairs made her turn from the window. She tamped down her impatience, schooled her face into a pleasant mask, and sat. Being churlish was not the way out. She arranged her pale pink skirt and waited.

Though expected, the inevitable knock still made her jump.

"Come in." She faced the door. It wasn't exactly permission because even if she said nothing, they'd enter just the same.

The lock turned, and her father opened the door to her suite. His burly frame filled the door and sucked the oxygen in his direction, making it hard for her lungs to gather a full breath. His large personality didn't leave space for anyone else, least of all her, his inferior female offspring.

"I've got something for you." He strode into the room without making eye contact and dropped a stack of books onto the coffee table. Dark rings circled his haggard eyes as he snagged a cookie from her always-full cookie plate and popped a few green grapes into his mouth. He spoke between mouthfuls.

"Don't read them all at once. I'm going away soon and won't be here to replenish your supply." He paced across the hardwood floor, stopping once for more fruit. Why couldn't he just sit on the couch and relax? Maybe talk instead of giving orders.

"Maybe I could go to the library myself if I finish them?" Ginger's voice sounded tremulous, uncertain. She hated sounding that way. She wanted to be decisive, powerful and instead, she sounded like a little girl, despite her approaching eighteenth birthday. Her chest tightened as she pushed her agenda forward, even if it wouldn't be popular. "One of the guards could take me."

He shook his head. "After what happened this spring, I'd prefer you stay here."

"Father, I finished the school's high school program two months ago. You promised when I was done that, as an adult, I could find a safe place to spend my days off the grounds." Her voice trailed off as the hard, brittle look entered his eyes. Her freedom. It was slipping from her grasp.

"After what happened with your brother, I've changed my mind."

"I'm sorry about Jace, but that shouldn't affect my future." Her voice shook. She'd loved her oldest brother, even if he'd become sarcastic and mocking once he'd started working for GreenCorps. He hadn't always been that way. That was what the world had done to him.

"It affects everything." His mouth twisted in anger as his blazing dark eyes met her hazel ones. "Show some respect." His lips turned white and his nostrils flared.

Ginger blanched, flinching away from his fury. She should have known mentioning her brother would set him off. That had been a miscalculation. Her palms grew sweaty, but she jumped to her feet, standing her ground though she itched to step back.

"What happened to Jace was far away and couldn't happen here in Denver, the GreenCorps stronghold. I won't take risks like he did. I'd just be here in town." She tried to infuse confidence into her tone, at the same time being reasonable. Anger would get her nowhere.

"Jaxon says the criminals remain at large. They could be anywhere. I'm not risking your life for a few books." Her father narrowed his eyes. "That's not a good enough reason."

"Father, you're right. It isn't just the library books. You promised I could start my apprenticeship at the publishing company. I need to feel useful." She hated she ended with a whine, but she was desperate to make her point. Had he forgotten?

"No."

It was like arguing with a stone.

Tears filled her eyes and her lip trembled. She paused to catch her breath. "The branch of the company is here in Denver. What could be safer?" A few hot tears escaped.

"No," he repeated, the ominous rumble in his voice rolled through the room. "You're my daughter, and it isn't safe out there." He shook his head and clenched his fists at his sides, causing her to take a step backward, bumping into the couch.

He had that look in his eyes again, but her mouth wouldn't stop. She'd bottled her feelings up for too long for them to be contained.

"Father, I need more to do. You agreed that if I did well, I could get a job."

He cut her off with a sweep of his hand. "That's a very liberal interpretation of what I said. You don't know how lucky you are."

It was too late to stop now. "I don't feel lucky. I feel trapped. I haven't even been off the grounds in almost two years."

"I don't want to hear it." He spoke through clenched teeth and tugged at the back of his cropped iron-gray hair. Hair that was grayer than it had been before her brother's murder.

"Father, please," Ginger said, trying to reason with him. Futile or not, she had to try.

He took two steps toward the door, muttering, but the words were clear. "I bring you whatever you want, you ungrateful little bitch. You don't need to go anywhere. Just like your mother. Trying to leave when you have everything you could want. It's a familiar theme. Both spoiled."

Her heart twisted at the casual cruelty, and her tears overflowed. Her throat tightened, and she couldn't force herself to continue. She'd been trapped here forever, and he'd slammed shut the only door, her opportunity for something more than this room.

"Read the damn books and stop your complaining, or they'll be the last ones you see. I declined the apprenticeship months ago. Work isn't for my daughter, after all. Jaxon and I have figured out something different. Maybe marriage will give you something better to do than sit and whine."

"Marriage?" She couldn't help herself. Surprise drew more words, though. "To who? I've met no one outside the family, other than servants." Her father stared through her as she gulped for air. She might have crossed the line with the questions.

To her surprise, he answered. "An arrangement with someone in the Midwest could strengthen our alliance. Jace had ideas. Even Jaxon recommends following through. The cities out there might reconsider letting our trains through if they have the right incentive."

First canceling the apprenticeship, now this. He would send away her from everything familiar without being consulted, and it broke her heart that her opinion mattered so little. It brought her near her breaking point.

"Don't I have a say?" Ginger swiped at the tears on her burning cheeks.

"What in your life made you think that? You're here at my whim and pleasure. I didn't want you. You were your mother's idea, but I've raised you as she asked. I've done my duty. You sometimes forget that you're living a life of total luxury, with access to things most young women would kill to have." His words were no longer fire, but ice, and they stung.

He'd never said those heart-wrenching words before, but they weren't a surprise. He treated her like a disappointment. He'd probably wanted another son for his empire.

"Like what? What do I have that the others don't?" Her voice shook and her chest heaved. "I didn't ask for this life. I want to see something beyond the windows."

"You've got a safe, clean house filled with servants. Beautiful flowers, your own rooms, and you always have food. You never go without. Not to mention the god damn books." He shook a fist in her face and she waited for the blow. "I wish you'd never learned to read. Life was easier when you knew your place and sat there with your mouth shut."

"Others don't have food?" Ginger frowned, feeling her face tighten in confusion, stuck on his words about people going without. Food was a basic necessity. Like air or water.

Her father shook his head, his lip twisted in a sneer. "You're a naïve little fool. You know nothing."

A pang of guilt stabbed through her. Though this life of luxury wasn't her fault, she'd never missed a meal in her life. He wasn't wrong about that. She looked down at her rounded arms and comfortable shape.

Her father spun on his heels, heading for the door once more. "I've arranged visits for a potential suitor. A week from today. You're expected to come downstairs for dinner, look pretty, and speak only when spoken to. If you can't do that, I'll figure it out on my own."

"I won't marry someone just because you say so."

"That's where you're wrong," he said over his shoulder as he slammed the door, the windows rattling.

The lock clicked as the key turned. Stomping footsteps receded down the stairs and faded. He wouldn't be back for a few days, time enough to cool his temper.

Ginger collapsed to the floor in tears. Once more, alone in her cell.

ABOUT THE AUTHOR

Award-winning author, Lena Gibson is a storyteller as an elementary school teacher and keeper of the family lore. She holds a First Class Honors degree in Archaeology, with minors in History, Biology, Geography, and Environmental Education from Simon Fraser University.

A voracious reader from age eight onward, Lena seeks wonderful books in which to escape. Because of her passion for different genres, she combines elements of many in her writing. As an adult newly recognized with autism, she often creates characters that reflect this experience.

When Lena isn't writing, she reads, practices karate, and drinks a ton of tea. She resides in New Westminster, Canada with her family and their fuzzy overlord, Ash, the fluffiest of gray cats.

https://lenagibsonauthor.wpcomstaging.com/

OTHER TITLES BY LENA GIBSON

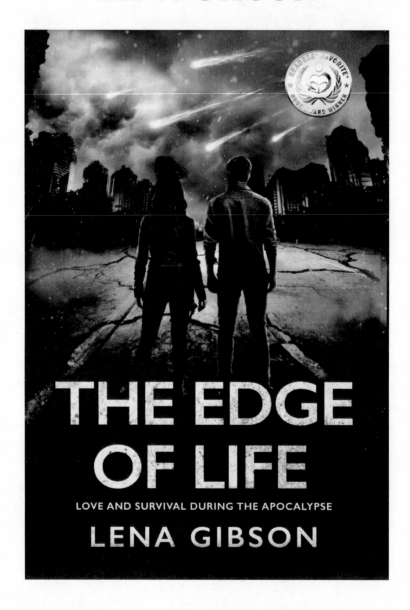

THE WISH

LENA GIBSON

Note from Lena Gibson

Word-of-mouth is crucial for any author to succeed. If you enjoyed *Switching Tracks*, please leave a review online—anywhere you are able. Even if it's just a sentence or two. It would make all the difference and would be very much appreciated.

Thanks!
Lena Gibson

We hope you enjoyed reading this title from:

www.blackrosewriting.com

Subscribe to our mailing list – *The Rosevine* – and receive **FREE** books, daily deals, and stay current with news about upcoming releases and our hottest authors.
Scan the QR code below to sign up.

Already a subscriber? Please accept a sincere thank you for being a fan of Black Rose Writing authors.

View other Black Rose Writing titles at
www.blackrosewriting.com/books and use promo code
PRINT to receive a **20% discount** when purchasing.

Made in United States
North Haven, CT
23 February 2024

49100179R00217